LAST BRIDE STANDING

LAST BRIDE STANDING

PATRICIA ANNE PHILLIPS

Kensington Publishing Corp.

DAFINA BOOKS are published by

Kensington Publishing Corp.
850 Third Avenue
New York, NY 10022

ISBN 0-7394-6437-X

Printed in the United States of America

Acknowledgments

To my daughter, Cassandra; my son-in-law, Chris; and my son, Darren; and Arabya, Javyn, and Aaren. I am so lucky to have all of you in my life.

To my sisters, Jacqueline, Diane, Janice, and Stacey, and my brothers, Charles and Stanley, my sister-in-law, Heather, and my brother-in-law, Michael. I love the laughter and good times we have when we are all together.

Thank you Rosie Milligan for being the agent for this book, and thank you Maxine Thompson for your editing.

And to all my fans, thank you for your support.

Chapter 1

Los Angeles, January 2001

"I can't believe you're really leaving me, Wanda," Steven said, as he sat on the edge of their king-sized bed, watching as his wife took up most of the bed packing her suitcases.

Her back was turned to him, but from the melancholy in his voice, she didn't have to look in his face to see his unhappiness with her decision.

Wanda gently closed the suitcase, walked around the foot of the bed and turned to face him. She took a backward step beyond the foot of the bed and leaned against the year old oak dresser which stretched almost the length of the wall. She folded her arms across her chest and stared into his drooping brown eyes, trying to gauge the depth of his distress.

"Besides," he continued. "I don't like the idea of your connecting flight being one of those small private jets. The *Tribute* should have paid for you to stay on British Airways." He got up, took her hand and pulled her down beside him. "I just don't understand why you had to accept this assignment."

She placed one hand under his stubborn set chin, kissed him on his cheek, and ran her fingers through his black, close-cut hair. He looked so sad; she was beginning to hate leaving him, even if it was only going to be for three weeks. But he should have known that one day this would happen. After all, it's what she had been striving so hard for over the last year—to expand her talents as a lead journalist for the LA *Tribute* to include taking trips to places like Africa. Wanda landed her position at the Los Angeles *Tribute* newspaper three and a half years ago. The *Tribute* paid her for her move to Los Angeles from Chicago.

"I'll be back in three weeks, honey. I'll make it up to you. This is my big break, Steven, don't make me feel guilty for accepting this assignment."

Wanda sat beside him. He held her tight in his arms as he looked down at her smooth, brown thighs. Her short black bathrobe had fallen open and stopped halfway up her thighs.

"I'm a journalist, Steven. This is what I do. I've worked hard for three years for a break like this one, doubly hard over the last year to get this trip to Africa. Honey, just three weeks and we'll be back together."

Wanda followed his eyes as he looked over their bed. She could see the thoughts flooding Steven's mind—of him sleeping alone in this large bed they shared. She could imagine how lonely he must be feeling. Since they were married, they had spent no more than a week apart.

Wanda knew Steven hated being alone. It was bad enough that he had been an only child, ten years old when his mother abandoned him, Steven had been devastated.

Steven had lived with his mother in their small

wood-frame house in South Central Los Angeles for as long as he could remember. After she left, he continued to stay in the house alone for a week hoping she would return. She didn't, but she had contacted her only sister and told her that Steven was alone in the house and asked her to look after him.

Steven stayed with his aunt until he graduated from high school, moved out of her house to room with a couple of friends that graduated with him.

Before Steven met Wanda, he drifted from woman to woman, trying to find a woman that he could settle down with and fill the void in his life left by his mother's untimely departure. In some ways, he was still a child at heart, and could never get enough attention to appease him.

Wanda knew he depended on her to be there for him, and now she was leaving him, for what he must think to be an eternity. As she sat there watching him she wondered what he would do with himself while she was away?

Wanda could tell by the defiant set of his shoulders that anger had filtered into his sadness over her leaving. She knew him well enough to detect that one obvious sign of him being angry, although he was trying desperately to conceal it. Looking at him, she felt almost as though she was abandoning him—as did his mother.

Steven reached for her, held her tighter, and then pulled away to get a good look at his wife's face.

"Why don't you finish packing while I take a shower. It's early and we still have the rest of tonight, you know," he said, breathing in the scent of her perfume.

Wanda stood up in front of him, tipped her full,

pouty lips up in an inviting smile at her husband's suggestion.

As Steven got up to go to the bathroom, the phone rang. Wanda brushed passed him and went to answer it. It was Karen, her older sister. Wanda was thirty-three and Karen was three years older.

"Are you finished packing, Wanda?"

"Yes. I just have a couple of things that I can pack tomorrow morning. She pulled her bathrobe tighter, tied the belt around her waist. "How is my nephew?"

"He's feeling better. Some of the other kids at school had the flu, too. I hope you've packed enough warm clothing for your trip. I hear that January is cold in Kenya but the rainy season is March and April."

"I've packed enough. Steven says it's enough to last me for two months."

"Is he still angry?"

"Yes. But he'll get over it. I can't refuse an opportunity like this one. Besides, having some time apart might be good for both of us." But Wanda wondered if it was true. She and Steven had a good marriage, but lately they both seemed to be going in separate directions. When she came home on time, he was late, and when he came home on time, she was late. There was always something to do.

"That man loves you, Wanda. Now, take care of yourself. And remember. You and Steven promised to come home this summer. I still can't believe you left Chicago to live in Los Angeles. It just doesn't seem the same since you left, and that was four years ago."

"I love you, Karen. Tell mom I'll call her when I get to Kenya so she won't worry about me. I'll call you as soon as I get back."

"I'll tell her when I go to see her tomorrow on my way to the office, and I'll talk to you in three weeks."

Wanda hung up and stepped out of her bathrobe, letting the belt drop to the floor.

The décor in their bedroom was done in neutral colors of sand pebble, with ivy and some prints, except for the organza cushions piled high on their king-size bed that were all bright colors. The wallpaper, in pale green moiré silk, was framed with sanded down woodwork to its natural oak. The drapes and carpets all through the apartment were also sand pebble.

Wanda ambled softly into the bathroom and climbed into the shower with her husband.

Steven smiled, invitingly, when he saw her climb in. The water was hot, as Steven washed her back she could feel her body relaxing. She would miss this, she thought.

After they finished their shower, Steven led her to bed and made love to her slowly, touching every part of her body. Three years and he still wanted only to fill himself with the taste of her. He kissed her over and over again. The melodious tone of Wanda's voice as she moaned and whispered his name, feeling her warm body tighten around his, made him want more.

Steven was always ravenous when making love to Wanda. She had that effect on him. The other women he slept with were "only a roll in the hay," or "a quick piece of ass," as Steven so often put it. But Wanda was more. They made love to each other, knew what each wanted and needed from the other.

After three years, she still felt the tingling of every nerve in her body when they made love. Even with their busy schedules, they somehow managed to make love countless times a week, either at night or in the mornings.

It was late in the day after Wanda and Steven lay breathing deeply and had talked for hours. Night had fallen by the time Steven fell asleep.

Wanda got out of bed and went into the kitchen to get a glass of water. Having so much on her mind she couldn't sleep. As soon as this assignment was over, she would talk to Steven about having a child; their child. She smiled in the darkness and the quiet around her.

Wanda got back in bed and snuggled close to her husband. They usually slept spooned together. Sleep was long in coming, but at dawn she was wide-awake again. She got up and went back downstairs into the kitchen to start a pot of coffee. Maybe she could get some sleep on the plane, she thought as she sat at the table and looked at the clock on the wall. It was only five o'clock and pleasantly quiet in the apartment.

Steven and Wanda lived in a three-bedroom townhouse in Woodland Hills. Wanda had bought it six months before she met Steven. She loved living in the valley, even though the oppressive heat during the summer months could border on unbearable. The townhouse was a two-story combination of East and West Coast architectures—red brick and stucco with wood trim. Its roomy interior provided enough space to accommodate her sister or mother when they came to visit.

Wanda went into the bathroom downstairs, and washed her face as the coffee was perking in the kitchen. She looked at the reflection of her face in the mirror, her round eyes were red from lack of sleep. She pushed her dark brown hair back, splashed warm water against her face. She stopped for a moment to take stock of her facial features, looking for any sign of aging. She had a delicate mouth, a straight nose, both to her liking. She wore very little make-up, her flawless skin was honey brown and buttery smooth. Wanda was petite with breasts that leaned toward large for her small build, and a pair of absolutely sensational legs that most women would kill for.

At 6 A.M. the phone rang. Wanda ran into the living room to answer before it woke Steven up.

"Did I wake you?" It was Marie Wilson, her closest friend, came from the same neighborhood in Chicago. She got married and moved to Los Angeles four years before Wanda. But her marriage had only lasted two years. Still, Marie and Wanda were as close as they had been when they were teenagers.

"Wake me? No, I couldn't sleep and got up to make some coffee. But Steven is still asleep."

"Are you all packed and ready to go?" Marie asked.

"Packed, but not so ready. Steven is giving me a hard time. I feel so guilty, Marie," she said, flopping down on the sofa. "I don't think he really thought that I would go."

"Look, Wanda. He'll get over it. It's only three weeks. And it's your job. This is something you've wanted for a long time. I used to do everything that ex-husband of mine wanted and look where it got me. So, I say, go on and do what pleases you. Besides, if it were Steven he wouldn't care about leaving you alone for three weeks."

Wanda frowned as she listened to the bitter tone in Marie's voice. "Gee, you sound so pessimistic, Marie."

"When it comes to men, honey, I am pessimistic. They're all selfish . . . want everything their way. Besides, how do you know what he'll be doing while you're away?"

"What's that suppose to mean?" Wanda asked with an edge to her voice. Marie was beginning to get on her nerves. She sighed, and rolled her eyes up in her head. Sometimes she felt sorry for Marie. She had turned bitter after her divorce, and lately, was getting difficult to get along with. But at least she'd stop drinking as much as she used to. Her consuming too much alcohol was beginning to be a problem and only brought out the worst in her. It made her moody, rude and disagreeable.

But, in spite of their differences, Wanda loved Marie.

"It means you're too trusting, Wanda. Anyway, Steven can take care of himself while you are away. After all, he did before you married him, didn't he?"

"I know, Marie. " Wanda looked at the clock again. "I better get off this phone and get ready. My plane leaves at ten and I still have a few things to do before I go."

"Okay, girl. And remember what I said. Steven can take care of himself."

"Oh, how can I forget what you said. You just take care of yourself." They hung up, and Wanda went back to the kitchen. Talking to Marie only made her feel worse. Steven had always told Wanda that Marie was too pessimistic about life. She was a leech, not a friend. Misery loves company, Steven always said. That was his description of Marie. One would think that he disliked her. But Marie was still and would always be Wanda's friend.

The later it got, the more depressed she felt about leaving Steven. As they dressed, lingering in the enormous marble bathroom they shared, having just made love again, she could barely speak, thinking of how hard it would be to say good-bye to Steven.

Steven saw the sadness in her eyes. "I'm sorry, Wanda . . ." He was beyond pressing the issue with her anymore. But, he was sad, too.

"I know this assignment means a lot to you, Wanda, and I feel so selfish." He held her in his arms. "I'll tell you what, baby. In three weeks we have a date. I'll be waiting at the airport with flowers in my hand. Date?" he asked, watching the frown in her face relax into a smile.

"Three weeks. You've got a date. It'll be wonderful, Steven."

Steven had finished putting the luggage in the back seat of his 1999 green Volvo. Wanda came downstairs, wearing jeans, a navy blazer, and boots. She wanted to dress comfortably for her long flight. She stood in the living room looking around and making sure she hadn't forgotten anything.

Suddenly she had a nagging feeling that she was leaving something behind that she needed, but she couldn't think of it.

"Well, I guess I'm ready, baby." She looked up at him and forced a smile.

"Let's go then," Steven said, pulling the keys from his pocket and locking the door behind them.

Once they arrived at the airport, Steven waited at the gate with her until it was time to board the plane.

"Take care of yourself, baby." He kissed her on the cheek. "Don't forget our date."

"Three weeks, love," she said.

As she walked away, she turned around and blew him a kiss. "I'll be back."

* * *

After the plane took off, Wanda did some work on her laptop computer, writing a list of things to do on her first day in Kenya. Finally, she finished and pulled a novel from her purse and read, then took a nap.

Wanda was happy to board her second flight in London because it meant half her journey was over. She read on the plane from Los Angeles, but now she was getting sleepy and no one was sitting beside her to keep her awake. The flight was small with two rows of seats on each side. It was half-filled compared to the plane coming from LA to London.

When the flight attendant asked Wanda if she wanted anything to drink, she ordered tea. After she finished, her empty cup was taken away, she adjusted her seat and lay her head back, closed her eyes and fell into a deep sleep.

Wanda vaulted into what she thought was a dream. First, it felt as though Steven was trying to awaken her and she couldn't wake up fast enough. Suddenly, managing to snap her eyes open, she realized it was only a dream and she remembered that she was in a plane, not at home in her bed. Heavy turbulence had awakened her, but being a seasoned traveler, Wanda gave little thought to the very bumpy flight and closed her eyes in an attempt to relax herself back to sleep.

A moment later, Wanda sat up with a lurch when the tall, blonde flight attendant touched her firmly on the shoulder and told her, just as firmly, "Miss, fasten your seat belt please." She hurriedly left Wanda to make the same request of the other passengers.

The worried expression on the flight attendant's

face convinced Wanda that the flight was even rougher than the flight attendant expected. She glanced at the window by her seat and saw raindrops beating intensely against the thick plastic pane.

Wanda's heart clutched, her stomach quaked. She looked around the cabin only to see all of the other passengers' faces frozen in quiet, terrified, pleading stares at the adept flight attendant moving quickly through the cabin.

The rain pelted harder against her window. She heard a child cry out from the row behind her and felt the plane begin to dip, as if preparing to land. The angle of the dip caused her to feel slightly nauseated. Wanda glanced behind her when she heard the old couple in the seats directly behind her, praying. The rougher the flight became, the louder they prayed.

"Help us, Lord! Keep us safe as only you can. We need you, Lord!"

"Yea, though I walk through the valley of the shadow, I shall fear no evil," another woman prayed.

"Pray for us sinners now and at the hour of our death," someone else intoned.

"Attendant, please help us!" a woman yelled to the flight attendant, but got no answer. The flight attendant had locked herself into her seat, her hands covering her face, trying to hide the fear already evident in her eyes.

A young British couple held hands, as tears welled in their eyes. "I love you," they said to each other, kissing, crying and softly whispering prayers to God.

Wanda felt hot tears spring from her own eyes and began a prayer of her own. The angle of the descent seemed to be even greater than only a moment before. The plane seemed to be turning to one side, spiraling. In her heart she knew the plane was out of control. She heard a loud cracking noise, clanging metal and screams all around her.

Suddenly she felt a hard wind blowing, then the rain hitting her face, blinding her, and her world had turned into a slow motion blur of confusing sights and sounds. She knew the end was coming soon, but she prayed for her safety in hopes that there was still a chance to land—to live.

Objects flew through the air, falling, bouncing noiselessly against the airplane bulkheads and onto the floor. Her heart pounded faster, harder against her chest, and the yelling and crying around her grew louder and more intense. The child cried out again. Wanda looked around to see who it was. The child's mother was holding her in her arms and praying to God to please spare her child.

Men and women screamed out their prayers, as the plane seemed to be falling lower. The interior lights disappeared into a wall of total blackness. The prayers and the screams around her increased as the plane slowly rolled onto its back in mid air.

Knowing she was about to die, Wanda quietly whispered, "Steven, I . . . love you . . ." She touched the gold necklace around her neck that Steven had given her on her last birthday.

There was scarcely a sound, just the fast downward plunge, the sharp, clean impact, the quick shifting of direction, more falling as the inverted plane came crashing down into the rain-soaked highlands of Mount Kenya.

Chapter 2

Los Angeles

Steven Gray was in the Valley End Bar in Burbank near the office of the accounting firm. Some of the employees from his office met there every Friday evening before going home. It was a way to start their weekend. The bar was large and vigorous, people drinking and releasing the stress of a long workweek.

It was Friday evening, and Steven didn't want to go home to a quiet and lonely apartment. His wife had left the day before. All Steven wanted to do was have a few drinks with his friend, Chuck, and two other guys that he worked with, get drunk, and go home so he could get some sleep.

He was getting a pretty good start when one of the guys told them to be quiet and listen to the news on the big screen television sitting high above the bar. The news rivaled the music blaring from the jukebox at the same time. The camera cut over to the footages of an airplane crash. Just watching the newscaster's face as she stopped and shook her head in disbelief, he knew it was bad news. But, before he paid really close attention he ordered another drink. He didn't want to hear any bad news about anything. He wasn't going to let anything spoil his evening.

"Hey, did she say Africa?" Steven heard the voice from the end of the bar. He absently placed his glass on the bar and focused his attention on the television. His ears perked up; his skin rained needles and his heart jerked fast inside his chest. He and Chuck looked at each other and back at the television.

The wide picture, obviously being recorded from a great distance, showed what appeared to be bodies strewn carelessly on the ground around the scattered remains of the destroyed plane.

"Turn that up," Steven yelled at, Joe, the bartender. "Where did they say the plane crashed? Did I hear someone say Africa?" he asked nervously.

"Kenya, Mount Kenya, flight number 32," Joe said.

Steven felt as if his heart had stopped. He shook his head as though he were trying to clear it. Had he heard right? "Did he say flight 32?" But, as he asked the question out loud, the men he worked with stopped talking and looked in his direction. He jumped away from the bar, knocking his drink to the floor. Chuck followed Steven to the phone booth that was in the corner, stood outside of it while Steven talked.

After a few moments Steven began yelling into the phone, trying to get answers about the plane that went down in Africa. He dropped the phone and held his face in his hands. Chuck opened the door and Steven fell into his arms.

"My wife was on that plane. I didn't want her to go."

Chuck led him back to his seat at the bar. Unable to stand any longer, Steven fell into it. "I've got to get home and call her mother and sister." He was frantic and talking fast. "God, what do I do? What do I do, now?" he asked as if someone there would answer, but everyone just stood and watched, shocked to hear the news. No one was talking in the bar, even the people that didn't know Steven felt sorry for him. They stopped talking, looking from Steven and back to the television, grasping all the information they could hear about the crash. An airplane had crashed in Kenya and the man's wife was in it.

"Come on, Steven. Let me drive you home," Chuck was saying. "You don't need to be behind the wheel of a car right now." Chuck had worked in the accounting firm with Steven for five years and had gone to his wedding when he had married Wanda. "She was such a sweet woman. We can come back for your car later or tomorrow, Steven."

"Chuck, I can't believe this," Steven said, wiping tears from his eyes. Chuck helped him into his blue mustang. Steven never stopped talking as Chuck drove him home.

"Maybe Wanda wasn't on that plane. You know, sometimes things happen, and they put you on a different plane."

But Chuck didn't answer. He felt so sorry for the poor guy. He was so out of it. Fighting to believe there was still hope for Wanda to be alive. But what could he say to his friend? Chuck continued to listen to Steven talking randomly, not realizing what he was saying, and he silently prayed that maybe there was hope, if only a little, that Wanda had not been on that doomed flight.

"If my wife was on the plane, maybe there were some survivors that haven't been found yet. Just because she was on the plane doesn't mean she's dead."

"Yes, that could be true, Steven. When we get to your place we can call the airlines and get some answers."

Once Chuck parked the car, Steven jumped out and ran to the door, unlocked it and ran inside with Chuck walking fast behind him. Steven turned on the television as soon as he stepped inside. He rushed to the phone and started to dial, instead he hung up and decided to listen to the messages on the answering machine. Maybe it was Wanda or the airlines.

"Wouldn't it be something if Wanda's voice came through and said, "Steven, I'm all right so don't worry about me." But the first voice was Karen's, Wanda's sister.

"Steven, where are you? Steven, by now I'm sure you've heard. There were no survivors on the plane. My sister is dead. . . ." She burst into tears and hung up. The next message was from Marie.

"Steven, oh Steven. Please call me as soon as you get this message." She wasn't crying but she was shouting so loud and talking so fast he could barely understand what she was saying. Steven cringed inwardly as he listened to Marie's voice. He wouldn't return her call, and he didn't want her to come over. All he wanted was his wife to be alive.

"Are you all right, man?" Chuck asked.

Steven had flopped down in the large chair in the living room. Chuck was sitting opposite him on the sofa. For a while they were silent.

"Are you all right, man?" Chuck asked. He wondered if he should leave Steven alone.

As though he was in a trance, Steven murmured something under his breath. He, then, started talking —mainly to himself.

"I guess you know it wasn't Wanda speaking on the

phone. I don't understand how a thing like this could have happened, man. She's here yesterday, gone today. I wonder if she was in any pain. God, I hope it was quick," he said, tears flowing down his cheeks.

He excused himself and went into the bathroom. Once he was in there he bent over the toilet and vomited. A few minutes later, he stepped out rubbing a wet cloth over his face. Chuck was pouring two glasses of brandy and handed one to Steven.

"I can't return any phone calls tonight, man. I can't even think straight, yet."

Chuck down his brandy and sat next to Steven. "I'm going to leave you alone, man. But you can call me if you need me to come back. Maybe it's better if I take you back to your car tomorrow."

"Thanks, man. Tomorrow is soon enough. Right now I need to be alone. I need to call the airlines and get some answers. I need . . . I need . . . my wife . . ." Unable to say another word, Steven burst into tears.

Two days later Steven waited outside American Airlines for Karen and Betty, Wanda's sister and mother. He felt as though he had just done the same thing with Wanda. Waiting and hating every minute of it. But this time the waiting was different. Waiting with Wanda meant she was going to return to him, but waiting for Karen and Betty was all so different, so sad. He was sure that he would wake up any moment from a bad dream. It was inconceivable that his sweet Wanda was dead, and what haunted him the most was the pain she may have suffered. Was she awake and knew that she was going to die, waiting for that final moment? He couldn't bear to think of it.

When Betty, Karen, and her son, Jeffrey, walked

through the gate, they saw Steven. He looked hung over, and needed to shave. Karen was sure that he'd lost weight, his face was gaunt and hardly recognizable until he called out Karen's name. He'd had it hard since he'd heard the bad news of her sister, Karen thought, as he got closer.

Steven held his mother-in-law by her arm and led her to a seat.

Betty watched Steven through tears forming in her eyes. Seeing him made Wanda's death so real. She remembered how she cried when she lost her husband, and when Wanda accepted the job as a journalist in LA. She didn't want her daughter to leave Chicago. Now, she's gone forever and will never return home again. Saying very little to each other, they rushed out of the airport.

As Steven pulled his car into an open space in front of the townhouse, he frowned in anger at seeing Marie standing by her car, parked across the street. Marie rushed to the group as they exited Steven's car and hugged Betty and Karen, but when she held her arms out to Steven, he turned his attention back to Betty. He had intended to return Marie's phone calls, but he just couldn't talk to her. It was just too soon, and she was so close to Wanda.

"Let's go inside and talk. I bought some food for lunch. I figured Jeffrey would be hungry," Steven said, smiling at the handsome boy that his wife loved so much. As he stared at the gangly young man, he wondered what would it have been like if he and Wanda had had a child together. They never really talked about it. He blamed that on their busy schedules. Steven regretted it now.

Everyone stepped inside. The first thing Karen did was open the blinds and windows. The place was dark and stuffy. Jeffrey took their luggage upstairs while the others took seats in the living room.

"Is there anything that I can do for you, Steven?" Marie asked. "I've been trying to contact you since I heard the news. Finally, Karen called to let me know they were flying in." Marie looked as if her feelings were hurt. She was Wanda's best friend and Steven didn't return any of her calls. She had no other friends that she was as close to.

"I know, and I'm sorry. I've been talking a lot with the airlines. They still haven't found all the bodies, but they are convinced that there were no survivors. They're calling off the search."

Betty jumped up from the sofa. "Can they do that? What if some are still alive? My child's body is one that is missing," she cried. "How can they be so sure she's not alive? How can they?" She placed her hands over her eyes, and lay her head back on the sofa. Was this really happening? Had she really lost her youngest daughter? she kept asking herself.

"If they are absolutely sure that no one could survive in the accident they can call it off, Mama," Karen said. "How many people live through a plane crash?"

"I was thinking of flying to Kenya," Steven said.

"For what, Steven?" Marie asked. "To put yourself through more grief? There's nothing you can do there. Wanda was like a sister to me, we all loved her, but nothing will bring her back, Steven," Marie said, sobbing.

Steven looked at Marie as though he was going to disagree when Karen interrupted.

"She's right, Steven. All we can do now is get things ready for her . . . you know . . . her funeral." Karen was unable to continue and turned her face away.

"I have to go and lay down. I can't take any more

of this kind of talk," Betty said and rushed upstairs. She stopped as she was passing the door to Wanda's bedroom. Unable to bring herself to step inside, she pressed her hands to her face and peered in through teary eyes.

She could still smell her daughter's perfume lingering in the air as though she was still there. Her white slippers were in the corner and her white bathrobe was hanging on the door. The bed looked as if it hadn't been slept in. Betty was sure that Steven had probably been sleeping on the sofa. She continued on to the other bedroom and closed the door. There was too much in the apartment reminding her of Wanda. She knew she had to go back to Chicago as soon as possible.

Downstairs Karen, Marie, and Steven discussed the arrangements to put Wanda to rest.

"This is all so strange to be sitting here talking like this. I just want it over with as soon as possible before my mother gets ill. It hurt her so much when Wanda left Chicago to live here. Steven, they haven't located anything that belongs to my sister?"

"Nothing. Most of the luggage had fallen out of the plane before it dropped. I didn't want to say it in front of Betty, but it's possible that wild animals could have eaten some parts of the missing bodies."

Marie made a choking sound and ran into the bathroom. Karen ran in behind her.

Three days later, Wanda's memorial was held at a small Catholic church in Encino, California. Since her body wasn't recovered, a picture of her in her wedding dress was placed at the center of a large floral display. A small group of people who had worked with Wanda and Steven came to the service. Afterward, only family, except for Marie, went back to the townhouse.

They all stayed inside that day. Karen was afraid for her mother's health and Steven wanted to be alone. The apartment was quiet and no one ate but Jeffrey. No one smiled—they all cried.

In her will, Wanda left her townhouse to Karen for Jeffrey, and half the money from her insurance for Jeffrey and her mother. She bequeathed her jewelry to her sister and mother and a necklace that she always admired for Marie. Her Lexus and the rest went to her husband.

Karen told Steven to stay in the townhouse as long as he wanted to. She would figure out what she would do with it in a year. A year should give him enough time to make other plans.

A week had passed and Steven was at the airport again. Wanda's family was leaving. Almost four years of his life was now only a fond memory. He watched as Wanda's family boarded their plane, certain that he would never see them again.

Chapter 3

Late the same night that Wanda's family left, Steven's doorbell rang. He was lying on the sofa staring up at the ceiling. He lazily made his way to the door. When he opened it, he stared in surprise.

"I thought they would never leave. I've missed you so, Steven. I've missed your touch." She kissed him hard on the mouth.

"I've had so much to do. It's hard to imagine she's gone. I can't stop thinking about her, wondering if she had been asleep or aware of what was happening," Steven said. He did not mention that he had even had a nightmare about wild animals eating Wanda's body and each time he woke up calling out her name. And when he woke up, he stayed awake the rest of the night.

Steven pulled away from her and returned to his spot on the sofa.

Marie plopped down beside him. "Why don't we go to bed? Now we can spend the entire night together."

He looked at her for a few moments before he thought to respond. But, before he could say anything

Marie got up, stood in front of him and stepped out of her dress. Steven looked up to see she wore nothing underneath. She started to walk into his bedroom and he rushed to stop her.

"No. Not this room. This was Wanda's room and mine. We'll go to the guest bedroom."

Marie stopped, looked at him strangely. "But now it's only your room, Steven."

"I said the guest room. If it's not good enough for you, we can just sit and talk," he hissed impatiently between gritted teeth and started to walk back into the living room.

"Okay. The guest bedroom," she said with disappointment written all over her face. At that very moment she knew that she had a lot of work ahead of her to help him realize that she was here, and Wanda wasn't.

This time there was no romance. No affection. No words. It was fast, just a need for the moment. It wasn't as intense as it had always been between them. Now that he could be with her whenever he wanted her, something had changed, but what? she wondered.

"I know it's a bit soon, Steven. But, I just couldn't wait. We've been stealing time together for a year, but today, I just couldn't wait." She lay on the bed, holding on to him, inhaling the sweet, masculine scent of his body. She didn't want him to get up, to send her home. Why shouldn't she stay the night with him? "She's gone, Steven. We both loved her, but now she's gone. We can have our own lives to live." She lay flat on her back and gazed at his face. "Have you heard anything I've said, Steven? We can be together now."

"Yes. I heard you." He got up, lit a cigarette, and sat

back on the edge of the bed with his back to her. How dare this bitch come here tonight, he thought . . . so soon after my wife—and her best friend—has died? And, what makes her think that we could have a life together, just because Wanda was gone? He blew a stream of smoke out in an angry puff.

He'd never made any promises to Marie, never even said that he loved her. He only wanted her because she was there, and she was easy and jealous of Wanda. He looked at her long, dark brown beautiful body, her long French braids resting on her shoulders. Her dark eyes were half-closed. And when he looked at her long legs again, they were slightly parted, inviting him back, and he went to her. As always, he went back to her. When he didn't, she would call and beg him to come back.

It all started a year earlier on a cold and rainy Saturday morning. Wanda had gone to her office to finish a report that was due on Monday.

Marie had dropped by the townhouse to see Wanda only to find Steven answering the door in his bathrobe. When Steven told her that Wanda wasn't home, she asked to use the phone. Marie made a quick whispery call and daintily returned the phone to its cradle. Steven remembered how she started for the door, and he was right behind her. When she came to a quick stop, she caused him to almost plow into her. She turned, her face only inches from his, their bodies softly touching.

His right hand found its way to one of her large breasts. She smiled and guided his free hand to her other breast and held it there.

Steven made love to her on the sofa. It was wild, hot and exciting. After that day, he would stop by her apartment on his way home when Wanda worked late. They would start at the door, against the wall, on the sofa, the floor, until they worked their way into her bedroom. And just as fast, he was gone.

Marie was back the following week. This time their lovemaking was good. She could feel him relax. She had given him the time she figured he needed after such a terrible week with his crying mother-in-law, the loss he had experienced, and the arrangements he had to make for Wanda.

"So, what are you going to do now, Steven?"

He was baffled by her question and couldn't see the expression on her face in the dark bedroom. "What do you mean, Marie?"

"I mean, what are you going to do with your life? You're a free man now, baby. You can do whatever you want."

"I don't know. Wanda just died, remember?" An edge of irritation cut through his voice.

"Honey, I know that. I was just trying to make conversation to get your mind off things. We have all the time in the world now, Steven. No more sneaking around, taking an hour here and an hour there. I don't think we ever spent more than an hour at a time together. We can go out for dinner, dancing. Have the life that we've been wanting." She whispered in the darkness, "Thank God."

Steven got up again and put his bathrobe back on. He went downstairs and made himself a drink and sat on the sofa. After an hour had passed he went upstairs to look in on Marie. She was asleep. He went back downstairs and fell asleep on the sofa where Marie found him the next morning. She made him a pot of fresh coffee and woke him. He opened his eyes and saw that she was still here, fully dressed.

"I thought you could use this." She put the cup on the coffee table in front of him.

He nodded and took a cautious sip. "You're right. I can use this. I've had a headache for a week now." He sighed and rubbed his eyes. "It's Saturday already. I guess I'll go back to work on Monday. Everything happened so suddenly that I haven't a clue what to do next."

She looked at him; he looked really sad, as though all the life had been beaten out of him. Maybe he did love Wanda. After all she was beautiful, smart and she was a good person. When they were in high school and college all the guys wanted her. She was always the prettiest one, the aggressive one, who always knew what she wanted. And furthermore, she got it.

Looking at him now, Marie was beginning to wonder what he really felt for her. Was she included in any of his plans for a new life? She had waited a year, which was long enough. Before Wanda died she had gotten to the point that she couldn't wait much longer for Steven to make his mind up. Wanda was gone. Too bad it had to happen this way, but it had and she was gone forever.

"You've got to get yourself together, Steven, and start living again. We have a life of our own now. You have me."

But he just looked at her as though she were a stranger. Someone that he didn't even recognize. Marie got up and placed the strap of her purse on her shoulder. She sighed deeply. Nothing she said seemed to arouse any real interest for Steven.

"Why don't you come over tonight? I can cook you a good meal and I'll buy a nice bottle of wine for you.

Your favorite." She kissed him on the cheek. "We can continue where we left off last night," she said, smiling down at him.

"Okay, I'll be there." But, by eight that night Steven had had too much to drink and was out cold on the sofa again.

Chapter 4

Two weeks had passed since Wanda's death. Steven had called the airlines more than once to inquire if the missing bodies had been found. But each time he called the answer was always the same. They're dead, and may not ever be found.

Steven couldn't sleep at night without a drink, and he had to drink until he passed out so he wouldn't dream of Wanda's death. The next day he'd go to work with a hangover, but his employer was sympathetic, knowing that, with a little time, he would be back to his old self again. All he needed was time.

He was beginning to get tired of going to work with a throbbing headache, tired of Marie calling him at his job, and at home at all hours of the night, checking up on him. She didn't trust him, but he understood why. If he cheated on Wanda with her best friend, then, how could he expect the best friend to trust him? But he didn't really care what Marie thought of him. He had told her constantly that he owed her no explanation of his whereabouts, which always resulted in an argument. She had even thrown in his face that he only made fifty-thousand dollars a year and Wanda's salary was one-hundred-twenty-five-thousand. Wanda had never cared. The money had never been an issue. It had made no difference to her or their marriage.

Steven knew that Marie was still angry that Wanda had left most of her valuables to her sister, including the townhouse. He didn't mind having to move out of the townhouse because there were too many memories in it. And after all, Karen did give him a year. He could drive Wanda's Lexus because he did sometimes when she was alive anyway. Hell, he thought as he sat on the sofa with a drink in his hand. A car is just a car. But maybe if he moved out, he could sleep better at night and start a new life. He looked around as though seeing the room for the last time.

A month had passed and it was Friday evening. The guys from the accounting firm convinced Steven to stop and have a few drinks at their Friday night bar before going home. As Steven walked inside the bar, his eyes adjusted to the darkness. The bar, carpets and tablecloths were dark red. The music and the chatter seem to boom off the walls with excitement. And all of a sudden he felt a boost of energy that he hadn't felt since the plane crash.

Steven was drinking his first glass of beer when he felt someone watching him. It was a young woman. A stunning young woman. She was standing at the bar waiting for her drink. She looked as though she was in her twenties, thin, nicely built with a butt that he would love to just sit and mold in his hand. Her hair was in a short cut style. But what Steven noticed most about her were her eyes. They seem to draw him to her. He couldn't see them well enough to distinguish if they were dark brown or black.

Returning to her table, she looked at Steven and smiled as she took a seat with two other women who seemed to be the same age as she. Steven stopped a waitress and ordered a drink for the lady. When he looked at her again she motioned for him to come over. He hopped off the barstool. "See you guys later," he said to one of the men he had been drinking with.

Chuck slapped him on his shoulder. "Hope you're lucky enough to get laid tonight, man." Maybe a change would do him good, he thought. He had been so lonely.

"My name is Steven Gray. I've been watching you for a while."

"Kimberly is my name, and this is Dalasha and Terri. We just got off work and thought we would make a stop before going home."

"Maybe I can have my other two friends come over," Steven said as he looked toward the bar where he had left them.

"I'm sorry. But I have to get home. I have a date tonight," Dalasha said, standing up, pressing down the wrinkles in her black leather skirt.

"And I have to pick up my baby from the babysitter. So I have to get out of here, too," Terri said.

"No. Don't tell me that you have to go, too," said Steven. "We haven't even gotten a chance to get to know each other."

Kim cocked her head to one side. "I can stay for a while. There's no one waiting for me. No husband, no kids. It's just me," she informed Steven with a dazzling smile.

Steven looked at her lap and could see her small

hips on the edge of the chair. He wanted to kiss this woman until she got weak in those long legs of hers. He eased into the chair next to her. "There's no one waiting for me either. Damn, I'm glad you're not married."

"No. But are you, Steven?"

"No. And I live alone, too."

"Looks like tonight is my lucky night," she said. "I was going straight home and my friends talked me into stopping for a beer. Now, I'm glad I did."

She smiled up at him flashing even white teeth.

"I'm glad you did, baby. You see, my wife died some time ago. So I've been alone. And need a nice woman to keep me company. And, who knows? I'm a good guy. Maybe you're the woman I've been hoping would come my way."

She giggled. "Where do you live, Steven?"

"In Woodland Hills. And you?"

"Northridge. We don't live too far from each other," she giggled again. How lucky she was to meet a nice guy and so handsome, too. He was of medium height with dark skin and beautiful, smiling eyes. And she loved his thick, black mustache, so neatly trimmed. He was well dressed in a gray suit and tie. When he put his glass on the table she noticed his manicured fingernails and a gold ring on his finger. Yes, Kim, how very lucky you are, she thought.

"Why don't we have a quiet dinner someplace so we can talk and get to know each other? This place is getting too noisy and it's too early to go home," Steven suggested.

"Sounds like a plan to me."

Steven knew of a small restaurant in Van Nuys and Kim followed him in her car. Once they were inside,

Steven requested a corner booth. One that was quiet and apart from the other tables.

They ate pasta and salad and talked. And when it was time to leave, neither of them wanted the night to end.

"What are you going to do tomorrow evening?" Steven asked.

"I haven't any plans," she answered with her fingers crossed, hoping that he would ask to see her again.

"Is it all right if I call you? I would like to get together with you again."

"Yes, sure," she answered anxiously. "I would like that, too."

He walked her to the parking lot. Steven kissed her long and hard, hating to let her go. She felt so good in his arms and her body was warm against his. While kissing her, he forgot about his own problems, forgot Wanda's death. He had gotten caught up into the moment with Kim's lips against his.

Once he got home, as soon as he turned the answering machine off, the phone rang. Steven hoped that it was Kim, but it was Marie's voice on the other end.

"Steven, where were you? I've been worried sick about you. You've been acting so strangely lately. What's gotten into you, Steven?"

"Don't worry about me, baby. I just stopped off and had a couple of beers and dinner with a couple of the guys from my job."

"Steven, baby. I miss you. Why don't you come over and spend the night with me? Come on, Steven. It's been over a week since I've seen you. We were together more when Wanda was alive."

He sat up straight when she mentioned Wanda's

name. For a few hours, he had almost forgotten the terrible plane crash. "Okay, but you'll have to come over here. I've been drinking and I don't want to be stopped by the cops."

"Sure, Steven. I'll be right over."

When Marie arrived Steven opened the door in a pair of navy blue briefs. She looked at his flat stomach, as she looked lower she saw that he was ready for her. She smiled and rubbed her body against his. "I'm here for you, Steven," she whispered in his ear, feeling her legs weakening.

He led her to the bedroom that he had shared with Wanda. After all, it was his room, now. And tonight was the beginning of a new life for him. He was so turned on by thinking of Kim that he made love to Marie as though he couldn't get enough of her. When he started to get off her she held him close.

"I knew you needed me tonight, Steven. You were so wonderful and made me so happy, baby."

He had even taken a step forward by taking her to Wanda's bed. Tonight was the beginning of a new life for them, she thought, and smiled with complacency. Every muscle in her body relaxed. God, how she loved that man.

"Yes. You were good, too, baby," Steven whispered in the dark. He opened his eyes, flipped the lamp on next to him.

The lamp was on and she looked at his body and admired it as she always does. He was such a good-looking man and she was deeply in love with him. He just had to get over Wanda. Tonight, she smiled, he seems to have made a good start. She knew that it would take time. And time was one thing she could give him. She would give him anything. It wouldn't be long before they could be married and living a happy life of their own. Marie could tell by the hot, passionate love he'd made to her. It was better than it had ever been.

Steven had fallen asleep and Marie turned the lamp off and curled under him to keep warm.

In the middle of the night he was dreaming of making love to Kim. Her beautiful face close to his, her peaceful smile as he took her into his arms and kissed her tenderly, and the excitement he felt as he watched her lay down in the middle of his bed, waiting for him, inviting him to touch her.

Marie heard Steven moan and felt him hard against her. She touched him in all the places that pleased him. He rolled on top of her and again, her body welcomed him, holding him, kissing him. He wanted her even more than he had earlier that night.

Marie knew that she had him, there was no turning back now. The year she waited was like a lifetime, a year of waiting for the phone to ring, a year of sneaking around and making every minute count and a year of listening to Wanda brag about her loving husband, the vacations they took together as Marie waited for his return. Marie already knew how loving he could be. Now Steven was hers. Wanda was gone, forever.

Chapter 5

Thika, January 2001

Thika, a small town between Mount Kenya and Nairobi, is just a tiny dot on a map of East Africa, at the spot where two rivers join. In 1913, that was how Thika was started—a favorite camp for big game hunters. Beyond this point, only bush and plain rambled for miles and miles. The dusty roads ran through a mixture of bush and native shambas, where shaven-headed women in beads and leather aprons weeded, dug, and drew water from the swampy streams.

That particular day in January 2001, the temperature was cold at the Bakari Safari Ranch set in the middle of Thika. The main road to the ranch stretched for a mile after the sign that read Bakari Safari Ranch with a handsomely carved B, which they also used as their brand. Bakari (meaning promising) was the name of the family's great-grandmother and no one had the heart to change it. After all, she had always promised them a better life than she had.

You could see the mountains rising high behind

the ranch, stretching out to meet a blue sky that flowed from horizon to horizon.

Bakari Safari hunting over the years had slowed considerably. There were still wild animals roaming the thick, grassy, brush surrounding the ranch, lions, zebras and elephants, but only a fraction of what had been a wild game hunter's paradise.

Young children playing, yelling from one small ranch house to another gave the small ranch a warm, family environment. Most of the children had been born on the ranch and now worked there helping their parents raising cattle, planting the fields, hunting, building or cleaning the stable.

The grass was green for miles and at night the stars were so brilliant that they seemed low enough to be almost within reach.

The ranch consisted of a large main house—large by Thika standards—and a row of small houses that were made like huts, for the employees. The main house looked like an oversized brown wooden cabin surrounded by flame trees. The house was on a ground level with six bedrooms; a dining room with a long table and ten antique chairs made of wood carved by Gyasi's hands; a well-stocked library; a large kitchen and three baths.

The ranch itself was old, all the buildings made of hand-carved wood from local trees in the rich floral area around Thika. The ranch is still as bright and beautiful as when it was built by members of the Kikuyu tribe, two generations earlier.

Thirty-three-year-old Ahmed ran the ranch. He was the older son and took over when his father died. Coffie, his younger brother, twenty-eight years old, helped him raise cattle, plant coffee beans, tobacco, and corn. Ahmed mostly took care of buying and selling cattle and took charge of the business side of running the ranch.

When Ahmed first took over, the ranch was losing money. It had become neglected over the years because of the declining health of his father, Gyasi.

Gyasi was from the Kikuyuian tribe and Nyela, his wife, was Arab. She was of Swahili culture, born in a coastal town on a small island called Lamu. Her family came to Africa many years ago as traders. When Nyela was fourteen, she ran away and married Ahmed's father. For a long time the other tribes didn't accept them as being married, as two different tribes. They never reconciled with the in-laws. But, he loved her and he loved the two sons and the life they shared together.

Ahmed and Coffie never knew their mother's family. There were no pictures and no one to ask.

Ahmed was away in college when Gyasi suffered a fatal heart attack. Shortly after his father's death, his mother, Nyela, became ill and died of grief over her husband's death.

Ahmed had no choice but to leave college and return home to take over the ranch. He wasn't his father and had no idea how he would run a ranch that was losing money, or what he could do to earn enough money to save it.

Busara, his sixty-eight year old aunt, also lived on the ranch. She told him stories of how her father and brothers used to run the ranch and make a profit. Ahmed listened to her stories but the ranch had depreciated too much and her stories were of little help.

He often got very little sleep at night, staying awake for hours reading books on farming, planting, and how to raise and sell cattle for profits. He didn't want to sell the ranch. Besides, Bakari Safari Ranch was in such deep debt, he wouldn't have made much of a profit.

Moreover, he felt responsible for his ranch hands and their families. Where would they go, how would they feed their families? Many of them were uneducated and depended on him for food and shelter. But they were loyal, all hard workers and were all like family. And it was the only home that Ahmed, Coffie, or most of the ranch hands had ever known. It was where his parents married and died. It was where he and Coffie were born.

Ahmed's younger brother, Coffie, couldn't imagine living in the city or going away from his home to attend college. He was willing to work hard and help Ahmed save the ranch. So Ahmed and Coffie worked, shoulder to shoulder with the ranch hands. They worked the fields, bought, raised and sold cattle, worked the crops.

At a point when the ranch reached its lowest ebb, Ahmed even sold some of the antique furniture that had been in their family for three generations— carved by his father's and grandfather's hands using a handmade knife and their own strength and sweat. But he had to pay the workers who remained on the ranch and were willing to work long hours by his side.

Only after two years of hard work, paying the men, and holding on to the ranch, did Ahmed first see a small profit. He began making repairs on the ranch, buying more and more cattle, working longer days and into the night. And today, the Bakari Safari Ranch was one of the largest and richest ranches in Thika for miles around.

Ahmed was a serious, no-nonsense man. He was honorable, well respected and known by some as being a dangerous man. Anyone who knew him, knew never to cross him and those who didn't know him had heard.

Later, he met a wonderful girl, Ezma, who was Kikuyu, and married her. She worked by his side. They had planned to have a family the following year but Ezma was struck by a passing bus on a dirt road near the ranch. It had been three years since Ezma's death; Ahmed never got serious about another woman. He only worked harder and made more money each year than he'd made the year before.

Ahmed had been away on business for three days and would return home tomorrow.

Coffie was in the stable feeding his horse as the episodes of the day kept going through his mind. He wondered what he would tell Ahmed about the woman that was found at the end of the ranch. He closed his eyes, but could still see her laying unconscious, looking as though she had been beaten, maybe even raped, and he was concerned that she may not live through the night.

Earlier, gusty winds and cold blasts accompanied the rain when Coffie and Dume had decided to quit for the day. Coffie was riding his horse ahead of Dume when Dume stopped and yelled for Coffie to come back.

"Something has spooked my horse," Dume yelled. His horse had reared back on its two hind legs. Not sure if he should get off his horse, Dume looked ahead but saw nothing.

"Man, it's cold out here. Come on. It's probably some dead animal. We can take care of it in the morning," Coffie yelled back at him, and shivered in his saddle from the cold rain and winds penetrating to his bones.

Dume had to find out why his horse reacted so wildly out of control. "Just give me a minute." He grabbed his rifle from his saddle and rode to the tall bushes that were blowing in front of him. He looked back at Coffie about twenty-five feet behind him.

"Hurry it up," Coffee yelled impatiently. I'm tired and the rain is coming down harder."

But Dume felt leery with a bad feeling in his gut: his horse never reacts for no reason at all. What if a dangerous animal jumped him? He couldn't see anything in the rain and it was pitch dark. He cocked his gun; with one foot he pushed a tall bush aside and jumped back. "What the hell . . . ?" he said out loud. "Coffie, I see something that looks like a body." Dume pointed to the area where he saw a woman's leg sticking out from a bush.

"So who is it, man?" Coffie yelled, still not moving from his horse. "Who would be out in this weather, Dume? Have you lost your senses, man?"

"No. Come and see. Come now, Coffie, I tell you."

"Is it really someone? It's cold and I'm hungry. So stop playing games and come on, Dume." Coffie and Dume had been playing jokes on each other since they were young boys. But, the rain was coming down harder and Coffie was getting edgy and impatient with Dume. This wasn't the time for jokes.

"Coffie, it's really a body." Dume pointed at the woman again, his eyes round and wide in the darkness of the night. The full moon over his dark face gave just enough light to see the shocked expression in his eyes.

"All right. You better not be joking with me, man." But when he rode beside Dume's horse, he too, saw a woman's small foot with a black shoe on it that was soaked with mud. Dume stood staring at her.

"Damn, who is it?" Coffie asked, jumping from his horse to get a closer look at her.

The small woman was lying on her side wrapped in a dirty and wet brown blanket. "Goddamn, what happened to her, and who did this?" he asked out loud.

Dume pushed the wet hair from her face to get a better look at her. "Gee, God Almighty. Do you see this, Coffie? Somebody tried to kill her. I wonder where she's from?"

When Coffie pulled the blanket they saw her clothes torn to rags and soaked with bloodstains, mud and dirt. She looked barely alive.

Coffie touched her slender hand and felt her pulse. "She's still alive, Dume."

"What do we do with her, Coffie? Her tribe is probably looking for her right this minute. If we move her it could mean trouble."

Coffie looked at the reflection of Dume's dark, round face. It was wet and shiny. "She's on our ranch, so how can it mean trouble? Are you suggesting that we leave her here to die? Are you crazy, Dume?" he asked, looking down at the young woman's thin face.

"So, what do we do with her, Coffie?"

"We take her home. Auntie Busara will know what to do. She'll die for sure if we leave her out here."

"How will we get her to the ranch?" Dume asked.

Coffie sighed and looked at him. Dume was handsome and amiable but not particularly clever. "Man, sometimes I don't know where your head is, Dume. I'm going to climb back on my horse and you will lift her up to me."

"That could hurt her, Coffie, Old Dead Josi said you don't move a person with broken bones. What if we hurt her?"

"That's why Old Dead Josi is dead. He talked too

much about things he didn't know. Now, shut up man. She's already hurt. How much more hurt can she be? There's no time to go back to the ranch and get the jeep. Now, give her to me," Coffie said, climbing on his horse. The rain was coming down hard and the wind was blowing the rain against his face. "Cover her face, Dume," he yelled, his voice bellowing between the rain and wind.

Dume covered her face first, picked her up as gently as he would a newborn baby and lifted her up to Coffie.

Coffie sat her on the saddle in front of him, holding her limp body close against his, her head in the middle of his chest. He tried to keep her warm. Her poor little body didn't need to get any wetter or colder. They rode slowly; the ride home took less than ten minutes.

Coffie doubted if she would last being taken to the hospital, and he wasn't going to send anyone to be blinded by the rain and have a deadly accident on the dark roads. He wondered if she was dumped near the road where he found her or if she had been living near the ranch with another tribe. He had never seen the young woman before. Although some of the tribes had gotten sophisticated through the years, there was something distinctively different about her.

She looked like a young, small girl, maybe a teenager, or a very young woman. But he was certain that she couldn't be any older then he was. Maybe she had been attacked by a wild animal and was too hurt to get back where she'd come from. But Aunt Busara will know what to do about her.

Well, too late to worry about what Ahmed would say. The girl was hurt, and she needed a warm bed to sleep in. Ahmed would have done the same. But, the girl definitely needed to be in the hospital, he thought, walking out of the stall where the horses were kept.

"It's too cold to be out in the rain, Coffie. The horses will be all right. You're the one that will take sick outside," Aunt Busara said. She was standing near the door waiting for him to come inside the house. "Ahmed should be home early tomorrow. That's what he told me when he telephoned an hour ago."

Coffie followed her inside. "He telephoned? Why didn't you call me, Aunt Busara?"

"Are you crazy, boy? Why would I go out in the cold? He will be home tomorrow anyway. Tell him what you want then." She walked away from the door and stood in front of the fireplace to warm her hands.

Busara's white hair was plaited in braids, pinned on top her head. She had dark skin, small dark eyes, high cheekbones and a nose too long for her slender face. Because of the horrible scar on her right leg that she had gotten in a riot as a child, she wore only long dresses that stopped above her ankles. And when the weather was cold, she had a limp that was barely noticeable.

Busara walked gracefully, held her head high as though she were an African queen. She took full charge of the house and prepared all their meals. She had lived on the ranch when her father, Ahmed and Coffie's grandfather, owned it. Her cousin came in to clean for her once a week, but the rest was her responsibility. Everyone that lived on the ranch knew Busara and respected her. She was a wise woman who never gave up on what she wanted, never took no for an answer, and wasn't afraid of anything. And what she wanted and lived for was to see that her two nephews were happy, protected, strong and healthy since she had no children of her own. She wanted to live to see their sons and daughters playing and working on the ranch, see them working by their parents' sides, loving the ranch as much as they did. And since her nephews seemed to be taking their time at finding women to marry and start a family, like everything else, she decided to take a hand in that, too. After all, it was to help her family.

In a quiet way, Busara was just as strong-willed and controlling as Ahmed was. She had seen lots of death in her lifetime, hunger and sorrow.

Busara was married when she was fourteen. Shot down in front of her own eyes, Busara's husband had died in her arms a year and a half later. She was four months pregnant at the time of his death and lost their child two weeks after. She never remarried and had never been touched by a man since her husband's death. Her father was weak and too ill to force a young woman as stubborn as she to marry anyone else.

A midwife, Busara delivered babies and made her own herb mixtures to heal anything that anyone would complain about.

Busara had cousins that were paid to work on the ranch. They occupied two of the smaller houses. A family that was employed there occupied the third house.

"How is the girl, Aunt Busara?" Coffie asked, standing in the door of the small bedroom. He watched the girl closely. Her breathing still seemed shallow. "Has she opened her eyes even once?"

"No, but at least she moved into a different position. We'll have to get her to the hospital tomorrow. The rain seems to be getting lighter."

"But what if she doesn't regain consciousness to say where she lives? We'll never get word to her family."

"She'll stay in the hospital until she does regain consciousness and be well enough to leave. She'll be there for a while anyway," Busara answered. "Then she'll be able to tell where she lives or what happened to her. We've done a good deed for her. The rest is not our business, Coffie. No business of ours." And she wasn't their business but instantly, for some incomprehensible reason, Busara felt an affinity between her and the girl.

"She's so small and broken. I feel so sorry for her. How can one hurt a girl so small?" Coffie asked. But he knew there were men capable of such brutal beatings. The men on the ranch told their wives what they could or couldn't do, but he never saw any of them purposely hurt a woman except for old drunk Benya. Ahmed threw him off the ranch. His kids were born on the ranch and Ahmed let the wife and kids stay and work, but mean and lazy Benya had to go.

"Coffie, you don't know what happened to her. Maybe no one harmed her. Or maybe someone from one of the villages brought her here to be helped," Busara said without changing her expression. "And if someone did harm her, well, I've seen worse in my day." And she had seen worse. Busara had seen tribes go to war, kill each other, mothers die during childbirth, people burn to death, hang, be beaten or starve to death. Indeed, she had seen worse.

"I'll sit here so I can see her during the night. I can be close if she wakes up or gets any worse."

"Okay, Aunt Busara. But, call me if you need any help with her."

"You go to bed, boy. You have to get up too early to be standing around worrying about women's work."

Coffie went to the end of the long hall to his room. He grimaced every time he pictured the girl's face.

In the small bedroom, Busara sat in a chair and watched the girl. She looked at her thin face. At least she was clean now. Busara and her cousin, Ifama, washed her body and hair gently without hurting her. She was filthy; her hair stuck to her face with mud, and dried blood was under her nose. She had so much hair that it was hard to wash the mud out of it.

The girl lay in bed with her head hanging over the edge. Ifama held a bucket of warm water against her head while Busara washed her hair with lemon soap. Busara made her own conditioner with lemon, coconut and mineral oil. She didn't believe in all the mixed shampoos, conditioners, and medications that were sold in the stores and made by white people. What did they know about our hair, or needs, she always said.

After they stripped her naked, Busara threw her pieces of clothing in the trash and replaced them with a pink flannel nightgown. It had long sleeves and would keep her warm.

Busara and Ifama noticed that she had a perfectly shaped body with curves that no man could miss. Underneath the bruises in her face, one could see that she was beautiful. Her eyes were closed, but shaped like large almonds. Her skin was the color of wet sand, and her mouth was bow-shaped. Busara watched her, wondering what color her eyes were and how tall was she. The injured woman didn't seem to be over five-foot-three. But it was the color of her hair that fascinated Busara. It felt soft and silky as she towel-dried it, it fell into ringlets of curls. She had come from a lighter tribe.

As Busara sat in the chair near the bed she fell asleep.

"So, what do we have here?"

A loud male voice boomed at the doorway. Busara jumped with a start as she heard Ahmed's voice.

"I had fallen asleep." She looked at the small clock on the wall. She had been asleep for two hours. Busara stood up, stretched and looked at the young woman, who looked as though she hadn't moved.

"Well, who is she?" Ahmed asked, still staring at the bed. He had never seen this woman before.

"She was hurt, Ahmed. Coffie and Dume found her when they were out today. Two of the men had gone hunting and Coffie and Dume were coming back to the ranch when they saw her poor body." Busara's words were tumbling out so fast, she had to stop and catch her breath. Wearily, she watched Ahmed's eyes shifting from her and back at the girl in disbelief.

She continued. "It was too cold, too late to take her to the hospital, or call the doctor. But, she will have to go to a hospital tomorrow. And you are early. Why are you here? I was expecting you tomorrow."

"First of all . . ." Ahmed's voice sounded angry, "I'm here because I live here. I was able to get a plane late tonight. You mean no one knows who she is?" He touched the growing beard on his face and decided that he would shave first thing in the morning.

Busara tried to explain. "No, I tell you. She hasn't opened her eyes. She doesn't move. Can't you see, man?" she said, motioning for him to take a closer look at the girl.

"Yes. I can see, Auntie. But what if she dies in the

night? Do you really think it was prudent to move her? Doesn't anyone think while I'm away?"

"Say words that I can understand, Ahmed. What do you mean 'prudent'? I didn't go to school and no college, you fool," she said, sitting up straight in the chair with an edge of frustration in her voice. She turned and looked at him again, mumbling some-thing unintelligible under her breath. What did he know anyway, she thought.

"Sorry. Did you think it was wise to move the girl, Auntie?" he said slowly so she could comprehend what he meant. She still didn't understand every word that was clearly said in English.

"Yes I did." She pointed one finger to her head. "Now you think, think, Ahmed. The girl was found on our ranch, the weather was too cold to leave her, and still is, and raining too hard, the wind blows too hard. Coffie and Dume had no choice but to move her and bring her here for help. Do you under-stand me?"

"Okay, okay. I guess you are right. But we have to get her to a hospital as soon as possible. I don't want a dying woman in this house," he said, stepping closer to the bed to get a better look at her face. "Bad weather or not, she has to go to the hospital in the morning. She looks half dead. Is she a woman or a girl? She looks so small."

"She's a young woman, man."

"How do you know that, Auntie Busara?"

"Because I am an old woman and because I un-dressed her. At least I took off the small amount of clothing that was left on her."

He just stared at her. "I can't even see what her face looks like. She took a bad beating. I wonder what really happened to her? And I wonder how she got to this ranch. By the looks of her, someone had to have left her here."

"That is what we've all been wondering. But someone may have left her here for help. I wonder what tribe she belongs to?" Busara said, looking up at her nephew. His eyes looked tired and red.

He walked back to the door. "I'm tired. I had a rough trip but I made a good profit. I'm going to bed. Have her dressed early so I can send her to the hospital. But now, I need some sleep."

"Are you hungry, Ahmed?"

"Yes. But I'm too tired to eat." He turned to walk out again.

"Ahmed?" she called out.

"Yes, what is it now, Auntie?" His voice was deep, tired with an edge of frustration. He sighed as he stood against the door waiting for Busara's response.

"I'm going to the hospital with her tomorrow."

He looked down at her. She was a tall woman, but Ahmed was very tall, too, being six-foot-four, and well over two hundred pounds. His jet-black hair was soft like his Arab mother's, almost touched his shoulders. His eyes were black, he had a straight nose, a thick, black mustache, and a square, stubborn chin with a visible scar where he had fallen on a piece of glass as a boy. The mixture of Arab and Kikuyu blood made his complexion a golden-walnut brown.

"Why would you want to go to the hospital with her? She won't know you're there."

"Because she has no one else. Because, I've been nursing her, and it's what I want to do," she snapped, making it as clear to him as she possibly could. She didn't like being questioned, and he knew it, but he did anyway.

"I'm too tired to argue with you tonight, Busara.

Just be ready early in the morning." Taking long strides, he ambled off to his room.

Busara could hear his heavy footsteps as he walked and murmured something about the girl. But what did he know, she thought.

At six-thirty the next morning, Ahmed was up, showered and dressed. He walked into the kitchen and found Busara already dressed with breakfast on the table waiting for him and Coffie. His coffee mug filled to the brim, tall enough for two cups.

Busara looked at him. A big man with a big appetite, she thought.

"Where is Coffie?" Ahmed asked.

"He's in the stable. Sit and eat your breakfast before it gets cold," Busara said, drying her hands with the white apron tied around her waist.

"Is the woman still unconscious?" he asked, as he sipped his coffee.

"Yes, and she's still breathing. She has a fever, too. The rain has stopped so we can take her as soon as you finish eating."

Ahmed nodded in answer. He had so much work to do and it still looked like rain. But, no, he had to take the time to take a sick stranger to the hospital. If only the rain would hold until their return, he thought.

Coffie walked in, grabbed a bottle of milk from the sink and took his seat at the table. "Did you see the poor woman, Ahmed? We found her near the road at the end of the ranch. She was just lying there, lifeless. At first I thought she was dead."

"Yes, I saw her last night," Ahmed answered dryly.

"We had no choice but to pick her up and bring

her home. Dume was scared out of his wits. Besides, you would have done the same. How was your trip?"

"Long, cold, and rainy. It's not a good time to travel, but at least I made a good profit. I want to buy more cattle, too. Next month, I'll go again to look over a couple of race horses."

"Race horses?" Busara asked and took a seat at the table. "You're going to buy race horses? There's no end to what you may do, Ahmed. You need to get married again and have a family. A wife and child. No, a wife and lots of children to keep you home."

Ahmed looked at her, astonished at what she just said. It was the first time she spoke of marriage to him since he had lost his wife. He hadn't brought any girl home since her death. And he had no answer for Busara's comment.

They had finished breakfast when Ifama walked in. "Do you need help with the girl, Busara?"

"Yes. I need you to help me get her into my warm coat and wrap her in a blanket. She needs to be warm. I don't want her to take a death of cold out there."

Ahmed went to his room to get his coat and hat while the women prepared the injured woman for travel.

"We're ready, Ahmed. You can put her in the car now," Busara yelled from the long hall. Ahmed's room was next to the library and the injured girl was in the room next to Busara's.

"Coffie, drive the car in front of the house so I can put her in."

"Sure thing," Coffie said, and rushed out the house to start the car and warm it before they put the injured girl in it.

Ahmed went into the bedroom and picked her up as though she were a baby.

"She's as light as a feather. I don't think she weighs a hundred pounds." He tried to visualize what she would look like without the bruises and cuts and gently pushed her hair from her face. Her hair was long, fell past her shoulders, with ringlets of soft curls falling into her face.

Coffie stuck his head in the door and called for Ahmed to bring her out. "Wrap her well, Ahmed. It's windy out here."

Coffie opened the back door, the car was already warm inside. Busara had gotten in first. Ahmed lay the young woman on the back seat so her head lay in Busara's lap.

"I wonder what the poor child's name is?" Busara asked.

"You'll probably never know, Auntie," Ahmed answered and drove off.

Chapter 6

Los Angeles, February

"Steven, everyone knows by now that Wanda is dead. I know it's hard for you. But, it's hard for me, too. Why can't we make plans for our lives together? It will do you some good if you move forward," Marie pleaded.

They were sitting in Steven's living room while Steven sipped a cup of coffee with brandy in it. He threw his hands up in the air and walked over to the barstool in front of the kitchen counter, added more brandy to his coffee and took a seat facing Marie. She followed him and stood against the sink holding a cup of coffee in her hand, but there was no brandy in it.

"You're pressuring me, Marie. I need time to sort my life out."

"I don't talk to you unless I call you, Steven. You never call anymore. I sit at home every night waiting for you to be your old self again." She looked at him. He didn't seem sad or depressed. Surprisingly, he looked quite happy. Why was he changing so drastically toward her, she wondered? All she'd ever done was what he wanted, and now, he treats her coldly as if he didn't care if he saw her or not.

"You're making too much of this. I have a job, a life to get used to. Everything is different for me now and everything happened so suddenly." The phone rang and he got up to answer it. Steven was holding the phone and pacing backward and forward as he talked. The telephone conversation only lasted for five minutes. Out of the corner of his eye, he could see Marie watching him, listening to every word that he was saying. He turned his back to her, looked out the window as darkness approached.

Steven hung the phone up and sat back at the kitchen counter. Impatiently, he looked at his watch.

Marie watched every move he'd made, she even saw him look at his watch. Anger started to build, but she kept it inside. The conversation was very delicate, like walking on eggshells. She had to think and find the right words; she had to make him understand what he was doing to her.

"But you have me, Steven. Why are you doing this alone? You don't have to be alone at a time like this. We could be good for each other, we need each other, Steven."

Marie sounded as though she was on the verge of tears. She had been in his apartment for almost an hour trying to convince him to go ahead with his life, their lives.

Was she really gullible enough to think I've been alone? Steven wondered to himself. He watched her sitting on the edge of the barstool facing him; her brown thighs were slightly parted. She pulled one of the thin straps of her tight-fitting sweater off her shoulder. Before he could say another word, Marie sat on his lap and placed her arms around his neck. She kissed him on his neck, his cheeks and finally his mouth, placing her free hand inside the zipper of his jeans.

Steven closed his eyes. This was how she always got him, but he would be strong this time. She had to know. He needed space and he needed Kim. He sighed and started to pull her hand away when he felt his fly open and Marie's hand touching his bare skin. He had forgotten how fast and smooth she was. He sucked in his breath, surrendering to the throbbing as her hot tongue found its way to the weakest part of his body. And as she took more, he felt his body tremble uncontrollably. When Steven thought he could no longer control the trembling of his body, he led Marie to his bedroom and to his bed, where they made love blissfully. After it was over he turned his back to her and went into a deep slumber.

Walking to the bathroom, he looked over his shoulder at her but she was still asleep. Marie had spent the night with him.

Without opening her eyes, Marie reached over for Steven but he wasn't there. Her eyes flew open; she heard water running from the bathroom.

Disappointed, Marie stayed in bed waiting for him, and ten minutes later, Steven walked out wearing a pair of navy jogging pants and a light-blue T-shirt.

Puzzled, she sat up in bed when she saw him fully dressed. It was the weekend, why was he up and dressed so early? She had intended to spend the entire day with him, maybe even the weekend.

"Honey, come back to bed. We have some unfinished business to take care of."

"I'm going to the gym and you'd better get dressed. I have a hundred things to do today," he replied without looking at her.

"But honey, it's Saturday. We can stay in bed late today and I can cook you breakfast." She looked up at him with a sleepy smile. "I've always wanted to sleep late on the weekends with you, Steven. We have so much to catch up on. So many thing we're free to do now that you have no one but me."

Steven sat on the bed next to her. "Look, Marie. Like I said last night. You are pressuring me. I need a little freedom now. I'm no longer a married man . . ."

"What are you saying, Steven?" Marie jumped out of bed naked, both hands on her hips. "What do you mean, you need your freedom? Freedom to do what, Steven?" Marie had forgot that she was naked until she felt a chill, and grabbed Steven's white bathrobe to cover herself.

He stood up and faced her. There was no easy way to tell her but to come out and say it and get it over with. After all, it was his life and like she said he is a free man.

"Marie, sex alone is not a sufficient basis for a lifetime together. I need more. I've met someone else, and I want to spend some time with her. Have I ever made any promises to you? No, I don't think so. I don't want to start lying to you now." He looked down at her as she perched on the edge of the bed.

Steven folded his arms in front of him. He felt sick inside watching the tears slowly falling from her eyes; her shocked expression changing from hurt to perplexity. This wasn't the way he had planned his weekend.

Marie shuddered at the thought of losing him to another woman. Her eyes became stoney as she remembered his words. "You slept with me last night, Steven. We made love to each other last night. And you say this to me the first thing the next morning? How could you?" She used the tail of his shirt to wipe the tears that were rolling down her cheeks. Makeup had smeared on it but she didn't care.

Steven looked at the large dresser, remembering how different it looked when Wanda's cosmetics were there with his. All of a sudden he felt as though he was suffocating in the room that he and Wanda had shared. He had to go to another room in the apartment. He went into the kitchen, leaving Marie to get dressed.

He stood in the kitchen looking around at more memories of Wanda. He wondered what was wrong with him this morning. Every room reminded him of Wanda. The large ashtray on the table that was handmade by one of her co-workers, the painting on the wall of a Black church with small children playing in front of it that he and Wanda had selected together. He heard Marie clear her throat and turned around to face her.

"How could you do this to me, Steven?" She glazed at him, her hands hanging by her sides clenched into two tight fists.

"I didn't invite you over here, Marie. You came on your own," he said in a cold tone of voice. "You took too much for granted, baby. Obviously, I didn't feel the same and I never pretended to."

Feeling as though she was losing control of her life, Marie shut her eyes tight trying to control the sick feeling in her stomach. She opened her eyes again, but nothing had changed, it was all so real. If only she could close her eyes again and open them to find their lives hadn't changed and they were still in love. He had to have loved me once, just once.

"Are you in love with her?" she asked, hearing her own voice tremble.

"I want to be with her, Marie. You can come around when I have time. But, right now, in this stage of my life, I need no pressures. I'm not in love with anyone. I'm sorry, baby, but it's the way it is."

She held her hand up to slap him, but he was too fast. He grabbed her arm and pushed her away from him.

"Don't try that again." He picked up her skirt and threw it hard into her face. "Get dressed," he snapped, turning his back to her.

"You jerk, you two-timing jerk. You are a user and a loser. You had nothing before Wanda picked you up. But what can one expect from someone like you? I loved you, Steven. I would do anything for you. All I wanted was for you to belong to me," she said, holding one hand across her stomach. She looked as though she were ill.

Marie's skirt had fallen to the floor. She began getting hysterical, flailing her arms, crying and pushing at him. But Steven didn't move. He just stared at her and knew that he had made a terrible mistake by getting involved with her in the first place, one he may regret later.

"Please, you don't need her, Steven. She doesn't know what you need. Does she please you as much as I do?" she pleaded, waiting for him to answer.

Finally he spoke, "Don't put yourself through this, Marie." He felt sorry for her. She looked so pathetic, so sad. "Just go and forget about me." He reached out to try and comfort her, but she pushed at him again.

"You'll pay for this, Steven. When she leaves your ass, don't come back crawling to me. Do you hear me, Steven, do you hear me?" Marie ran to the door with her clothes in her hand. She took one step forward attempting to plead with him one last time, she had to get through to him, make him understand, but looking at him, it became alarmingly clear that he didn't want her. Her eyes squinted in rage and she curled her lips into a snarl. "You son-of-a-bitch. I hate you. I hate you, Steven Gray." She ran out the door.

Steven closed the door and locked it behind her. He went back to the bedroom, sat on the bed and dialed the telephone. "Kim, baby. I'm picking you up for breakfast in thirty minutes." He hung up.

Screw the gym today, he thought. He wanted to be with Kim, and walked out the door.

Back at her apartment, Marie poured herself a tall glass of Jack Daniel's and held the glass in her hands a few seconds before she put it to her mouth. She stood at the kitchen sink and started to pour the Jack Daniel's into the sink. Her hands were trembling so; Marie couldn't help herself. Finally, she sighed, held the glass tightly and swallowed long and hard. She closed her eyes feeling the liquor smoothly penetrating through her system like silk sliding down a naked body. God, how she needed this drink. She could now see her life moving into a different perspective.

Marie looked at her clothes, anyone who had seen her come inside the building must have known she had gotten dressed in her car. She stepped out carrying her shoes in her hand, her skirt was unzipped and her hair wasn't combed. She had gotten rid of her braids and was wearing a short, cute cut that now looked like wild feathers sticking out all over her head. She threw herself across her bed and sobbed and sobbed until there were no more tears left. Finally, she undressed and made herself a cup of coffee. But instead of drinking the coffee, she put the cup aside and poured herself another drink. With her second drink in her hand, Marie sat at her table in the small kitchen to try to think of what she could do to get him back. She wouldn't give up so easily. She had waited, and planned too long to lose Steven now, and to another woman. Oh no, that's just not going to happen. Right now, he's just confused, maybe even a little guilty because he was cheating on Wanda. But he would understand that no one could love him as much as she does. He was weak, and Wanda was always there for him. "He would need me again," she whispered.

The first night she set her eyes on Steven she wanted him. It seemed as though it was only yesterday when she and Wanda met on a Friday evening after work. The bar was lively, people laughing, drinking, and telling jokes. Steven was sitting at the bar staring at her. Every time she looked at him their eyes met and held for seconds.

"You see that man sitting alone over there?" Marie asked Wanda.

"Yes. He's good looking, too, girl. Every time I look in his direction he's watching me," Wanda said and smiled.

"What do you mean, watching you? That man is looking at me, Wanda."

"Sorry. My mistake. Besides, I see a better looking one that my eyes are on." She laughed and looked at

Marie. "My mistake again. That one just walked off with someone else."

"Well, if this one ever stops looking so hard and comes over, we'll know who he's looking at. The best woman wins," Marie said. "We've had nights like this before."

When Steven got up and walked to their table, Marie thought her heart would leap from her chest. She could almost feel his hands moving slowly over her body, his full lips against hers.

"I've been watching you for a while. My name is Steven." He held his hand out to Wanda and she gently took it.

"I'm Wanda and this is Marie. We just came in to have a couple of drinks before going home." Wanda gave him a dazzling smile, her ringlets of curls unruly all over her head.

Marie smiled, but it was killing her inside. For a moment, she felt as though she couldn't breathe. She wanted this man, and looking at him close she wanted him even more than before. How could this be when he was watching me? Why did he change his mind? Dammit, she wanted him.

There was no way she could sit through this. "I have some work in my car to take home, so I'll just say good-night and it's nice to meet you, Steven."

"Oh, Marie. Don't go so soon. We've only been here for an hour," Wanda said.

"No. I really need to leave. Since you have someone who can stay with you, I'll get home early enough to complete the work that's in my car."

She had no work but she had to leave. And as for Wanda, she had done it again. She always got the boys when they were in school. And now she gets the men, the best jobs, was always the happiest as though she had no problems at all. It was always Wanda. Marie still didn't understand how it happened. Steven was looking at me, she thought.

Six months later, Wanda and Steven were married and Marie was included as a bridesmaid. Four months later, Marie was married to a man that cheated and lied the whole time they were married. The divorce was a bitter one and two years later, Marie was sleeping with Steven. She had gotten tired of men coming in and going out of her life. It wasn't long before she was deeply in love with him. The only reason she hadn't told Wanda was because she would have lost Steven. Now, she's lost him to a stranger, but not for long, not after all she had gone through. She would be waiting and watching. She would be there when the time came. No matter what she had to do to get him. Already feeling deflated, she would not take this sitting down. But when she looked at the empty glass sitting in front of her, all she felt for the moment was a need for another drink.

Chapter 7

Thika, East Africa

She was dressed in all white—a long, white dress that you could see through. Her hair had blown back from her face as the mild winds whistled against her ears. Like the sweetest angel, she spread her wings; white feathers flapped through the air. She could hear the angels singing, she smiled, inhaled the mild, calm air and watched the clouds dancing around her.

As she flew near her destination, her right wing fell away, floating slowly through the clouds before she could catch it. Her heart jerked inside her chest. She looked around for other angels for help, but she was alone, floating, falling . . . she was all alone.

Again, she jerked, closed her eyes tightly, then opened them slowly. First, there was the dim light. Chattering that got louder, nearer. She tried to adjust her eyes to the light and touched each arm. There were no wings, no feathers. She had been dreaming.

She turned her head from side to side but felt pain penetrate from one temple to the other, which caused her to cry out.

"You're awake?" the woman's voice boomed against her head and caused her to jerk with excruciating pain that burned through her entire body.

The young nurse rang a bell over her bed and two more nurses rushed into her room. Finally, she realized that she was in some strange hospital. But where? One nurse was tall and white, the other one was black, very dark, her hair was loose and natural. She spoke with an accent, a strange accent that she had never heard before. God, what had happened to her, why was she in such insufferable pain? Where was she? she thought with apprehension. She tried to raise her body, but the pain that shot through her back forced her to gently lay her head back on the pillow. The fast, excited beat from her heart was alarming. She yelled out loud, "Where am I?"

The doctor rushed in behind the two nurses while the first nurse took her pulse.

She started to speak again . . . but stopped as she watched the doctor examining her, moving slowly and thoroughly, careful not to cause more pain. His hair was white as snow, he had blue piercing eyes and spoke with a slight accent.

"You're alive, thank God, and completely conscious this time," the doctor said. "The nurses thought you would never see the light of day again. Well, I always knew you would make it all along," he said to her. "I'm Doctor Fields. You've been here for a while." He sat on the edge of the bed and held two fingers in front of her face. "Look at my hand."

She did as she was told and looked from side to side following the doctor's fingers.

Doctor Fields pulled the blanket from her legs; she was bandaged from her thighs all the way down to her ankles. What had happened to her?

She took a deep breath and screamed out loud, holding each side of the bed.

"You have two broken ribs. It's going to hurt if you move too much." Doctor Fields gave her a shot for the pain. He looked at her face again and wondered what tribe had done this.

Doctor Fields was from London and had only been practicing in Africa for three years. He still wasn't accustomed to the African ways. And looking at this young woman's battered body, he doubted if he would ever get used to their cold unusual ways. But he had saved lives sometimes operating on one for hours. And he wanted to save this young woman's life as well.

"Now, young lady, what is your name, and who in God's name did this to you?"

The three nurses stopped talking and waited for her response. They all wanted to know.

"I . . . I . . ." Tears formed in her eyes as she looked from one face to the other. She tried so hard to remember, but all she could remember was the dream of the beautiful angel that lost her wing. She held her hands over her mouth and cried out. All of a sudden, she was feeling the medication relieving the pain, making her drowsy. Who was she? "Oh, God. Who am I?" She looked in all their faces as they waited. "Where am I? Who? Where!?" she yelled at the top of her voice.

"Calm down," the doctor said. "It's okay, darling, just calm down." He held her hand and in seconds she was fast asleep.

The doctor looked at the African nurse. "What do you think happened to her, Adia?"

"I'm sure I don't know," she answered, knowing that he was really asking if another tribe could have done something so terrible. "Anyone could have done this, even a white man," the nurse snapped and walked out.

The next day Adia walked into the young woman's room and took her temperature, changed her bandages, and tried to make her comfortable. "You still don't remember who you are, do you?"

The young woman just shook her head in answer. "I don't know who I am, or where I live. What will happen to me when I'm released?" She was so frightened, so alone.

"You might remember by then. Don't try too hard. It will happen. I'm here from seven to four. My name is Adia. I'll help you in any way that I can."

The young woman was so overwhelmed with tears that she couldn't speak. She felt the nurse squeeze her hand.

"I'll be back and see you in a little while."

"Auntie Busara, why do you feel the need to go to the hospital every other day to see that woman? You owe her nothing," Ahmed said, sitting at the kitchen table wolfing down his breakfast.

Every morning at six-thirty, Busara had breakfast on the table for Ahmed and Coffie so they could start their day. She couldn't drive, and when she had her shopping to do, either Coffie or one of the men on the ranch would drive her. Today, she needed a ride to the hospital again.

"Because she has no one else. She's talking now, Ahmed, and like I said before, the poor child doesn't even remember who she is."

"She doesn't remember anything?" Coffie asked with interest, his round eyes wide.

"No, nothing. And she has broken ribs, a broken leg. Thank God she's still alive. Oh, and scars all over her body, too. I just wonder where she's from? So much happens and so many people are hurt then die," Busara said.

"You mean she doesn't remember even who she is?" Coffie asked, and placed his fork on his plate. "She must be scared out of her wits."

"She is. The nurse says it does her good for me to visit her. Anybody want more ugali?"

"No, I've had quite enough, Busara. I'll have Atu drive you this morning. But what will happen when her doctor releases her? Where will she go?" Ahmed asked. "I'll go tell Atu to be in front around noon." He grabbed his jacket from the back of his chair and stalked out.

"Yeah, Auntie Busara. What will happen when the doctor releases her?" Coffie asked and pushed one of his braids aside from his face.

Busara just shook her head. "I don't know, Coffie. I have to figure something out."

Coffie didn't like the sound of that and as usual, his round eyes got bigger. All his emotions were in his eyes. If Busara wanted to know if he was happy or sad, she only had to look into his eyes.

"I didn't hear you say that, Auntie Busara." He leaned over where she was sitting, kissed her on top of her head and went out the back door.

"Has she had any visitors today?" Busara asked the nurse. Busara wiggled her nose, snuffing the smell of medicine. The hospital was small with only two floors and three beds to each room.

"No, no one. And she doesn't remember one

thing. Remember, the doctor says it could possibly be a long time before she remembers or it could be very soon. In the meantime, we'll just have to wait and help her in any way we can," Adia said. She was tall, not very attractive, but nice, with large round eyes. She was there the day that Busara and Ahmed checked the young woman into the hospital. Although she had been scraped and bruised, one could see that she had been well kept. Her teeth were in good condition and her skin was as smooth as butter.

Adia walked off. The young lady was lucky to have someone who was concerned for her. But where would she go once she's released from the hospital?

Busara went into her room but the woman was asleep. She took a seat in the chair next to her bed and watched her as she had when she stayed overnight at the ranch. Busara looked around the room, sniffed again, and frowned at the scent of medicine floating in the air. She hated hospitals, had lost people she loved in this hospital. Her brother, Ahmed's and Coffie's father, and Ahmed's wife died here, too. It brought back so many sad memories.

Busara sat up straight when she heard the girl murmur something in her sleep. She was speaking perfect English, Busara noticed.

The young woman jumped and looked at Busara's face.

"I didn't hear you come in. Have you been here very long, Miss Busara?"

"No, not long at all. How do you feel today, much pain?"

"Only when I try to move and sometimes during the night when my body gets cold and stiff, my chest feels like it's been caved in from the broken ribs."

Busara looked at her puffy, red eyes. She looked as though she had been crying. And as she turned her head, she had started to cry again. A tear rolled down the side of her face.

Busara moved the chair closer to the bed. "What is it my child? Are you remembering something that upsets you?"

"No. What will I do if I never remember who I am, or where I came from? Is there some sort of a rehabilitation center around here that I can go to recover fully?" she asked, more afraid than ever before.

She looked small and dejected. There were some of the African nurses that didn't like her and never answered when she needed help. But Adia was always there for her, and now Miss Busara.

"If you don't remember by the time the doctor says you can be released, then, you'll just have to go home with me. I won't leave you here alone."

The woman was shocked. Why would a complete stranger be so nice to her and how could she ever repay her? "I can't let you do that, Miss Busara. You are already doing so much by coming to see me." But she was so overwhelmed by Busara's generosity that she began crying again. "I'll work, clean your house, do whatever it takes to pay you back, Miss Busara." She was trembling and sobbed openly. The thought of being alone frightened her. Everyone and everything was so foreign.

"Now calm down, girl. Don't make yourself any sicker by getting upset." Busara stood up over her and patted her hand to calm her down. "God works in mysterious ways. There must be a reason why you were left at the ranch. Now, the first thing we have to do is give you a name. Think of a name that you've always wanted."

But how could she, she didn't remember anything she always wanted.

Busara squeezed her hand and gave her a smile that warmed her heart.

She closed her eyes for a few seconds but came up with nothing. "I can't think of any names and I don't remember any that I've always wanted."

"Okay. I have the perfect name for you. How about Orchid? That's my favorite flower. It suits you well, girl."

"Orchid? Okay," she beamed with a smile. "It sounds great. Orchid, huh?"

Now, all Busara had to do was explain the situation to Ahmed. But she was sure that once he meets her, he'll feel differently.

Orchid looked at Busara. She was such a nice woman, how could she ever repay her? No one else would take a stranger into her home but Busara.

"Please tell me more about the ranch, Miss Busara."

"You'll love it. It's one of the biggest ranches in Thika. Three of us live in the large house with six bedrooms, three baths and a library that is also used for Ahmed's office. I have a lovely garden with orchids blooming and other flowers. My cousin comes in one day a week to help me clean. She's a good, strong woman, works hard, but she repeats everything twice. One has to get used to the way she speaks. At six-thirty every morning the two men eat breakfast and go off to start the day. So we will be left alone most of the day."

"I'll make sure that I stay out of the way, Miss Busara. When I'm strong, I can help with the housework, the cooking, or whatever you need me to do."

"Yes. When you are strong enough. Don't worry,

child. Everything will be all right." Busara looked at the round clock on the wall. "I better be getting back. I'm sure Ahmed or Coffie have something else for Atu to do when he gets back to the ranch." Busara squeezed Orchid's hand. "Rest well." She walked out with her head held high as Orchid looked after her.

The next week Busara found Ahmed and Coffie in the library going over some legal documents for the ranch. When they looked up, Busara was standing in the door waiting patiently for their attention. She hated disturbing them when they were discussing business but she had to speak with both of them right away.

"Can I help you with something, Auntie?" Coffie asked.

"No. I just need to discuss something with you and Ahmed," she said with a serious look in her eyes. Busara sat in the chair next to Coffie facing the tall, ceiling-to-floor oak bookcase.

Ahmed looked at her with concern and placed a stack of bills down on the desk.

Busara cleared her throat. "I made a decision and a promise. I told Orchid that when she's released from the hospital she might stay with us for a while. The girl has no place to go." She stopped when she heard Ahmed sigh. He and Coffie looked at her as if she had lost all her senses.

"The doctor doesn't know when she'll remember her past. He said amnesia could be short or long term. The nurse says it's a temporary loss of consciousness caused by shock, pain or a head injury. No one knows what happened to the girl or what caused her amnesia."

Ahmed and Coffie looked completely baffled. "Who is this Orchid?" Ahmed asked.

"She's the hurt girl that stayed with us, Ahmed. Who do you think she is?" Busara asked. She was getting angry but this wasn't the right moment, so she looked sad, humble and held her head down as she continued to explain.

"Why do you think the girl needs to stay here?" said Ahmed. "She's a complete stranger. How do we know what type of person she is, or her family? We don't even know what tribe she belongs to. And I can't believe you asked her to stay in our home without this discussion. Obviously you've made up your mind already."

Busara looked at her oldest nephew. He was as stubborn as his father, and just as big and pigheaded. At this very moment she wanted to take off her shoe and beat him over his head. But at that moment she had to appear docile to get what she wanted. Later, if he brings it up again, she would take her shoe to him.

"How soon will she be here, Auntie Busara?" Coffie asked, not at all surprised with Busara's decision to bring the girl home.

Busara held her head high. "Tomorrow."

"Tomorrow! You say tomorrow?" Ahmed yelled. "What has gotten into you, Auntie? You know nothing of this woman and you tell us of your intentions the night before!"

"I know she needs someone, Ahmed. Isn't that enough reason to help her? We are blessed with so much," she said, looking around the room. Why not share with someone in need? The girl is in need, you know. "

"Maybe she could stay for a while, Ahmed," Coffie

interjected. "When she's better, she can help around here."

"She won't be around that long, Coffie. As soon as William, my lawyer, finds out who she is, she will be leaving."

"But in the meantime, that's what she offered to do. Stay and help. She says she'll earn her keep. I can't let her be put out on the streets until she's well enough to take care of herself. So she can stay and help," Busara said.

"What if she never remembers?" Coffie asked.

"What do we do if she doesn't remember, make her an abiding member of our family? You keep her out of our way, Auntie," Ahmed warned.

"I will, Ahmed. I'm sure after she meets you she won't want to stay too long. We have this big house with only the three of us living here. Unfortunately, everyone is not as lucky as we are," Busara said. "Don't be selfish, boy."

"Luck has nothing to do with what we have. We've worked day and night to get it. It has nothing to do with being selfish, Busara. But, she is a stranger."

"Ahmed, Auntie Busara has already given the girl her word. We have to honor it." Coffie looked at Busara. "Tomorrow I'll take you to the hospital to get the girl. After she's here for a while, we can decide what to do with her. Okay, Ahmed?"

"We'll send her on her way," Ahmed answered, and threw his hands up in the air. "I guess you are right, since the decision was made without discussing it with us first."

"No one uses the room she was in before. I'll take care of her. You'll hardly know she is here," Busara said and walked out slowly. Once she was in her room and closed the door, she smiled. Once again, she had gotten her way. Ahmed was bullheaded, but once she'd given her word, looked sad, and stood her ground, she knew that he would come around. And as for Coffie, he wouldn't say no to her about anything. Besides, a new face, and a pretty one at that, was needed in this house, she thought, wondering just how would Ahmed handle it. And at that very moment, Busara imagined Ahmed and Orchid as husband and wife. She laughed out loud wondering how Ahmed would handle that, too.

Busara began to make plans for her new friend.

The next morning they were quiet at breakfast. Busara filled their cups with coffee and took her usual seat at the table.

"Is her room ready?" Coffie asked.

"Yes. There wasn't anything to do to it except get another blanket to put on the bed. And I'll have to make her eat. She didn't eat much in the hospital and doesn't seem to have much of an appetite. Poor thing is almost skin and bones. How nice to have a young woman around the house for a change," she said looking at Ahmed.

"There are enough young women around the ranch, Auntie Busara. Why do we need one whining woman in here?" Ahmed answered.

"And why do you persist on making this out to be such a big deal, Ahmed?" Busara asked. "We're only giving someone in need a helping hand."

Ahmed sighed and turned his attention to Coffie. "Have Atu drive Auntie today. We have too much work to be galloping back and forth to the hospital." He placed his cup back on the table and catapulted out the kitchen. Busara and Coffie heard the door shut behind him.

A frown flashed across Busara's face. She stood up with her hand on her hip. "I won't let your brother ruin my day. He's just like your father and my father. Stubborn. Pigheaded," she mumbled.

"He'll be all right once he gets to know her. Who knows, they may become good friends? What you're doing is a good thing, Auntie."

"Thank you, Coffie. Now, tell Atu to be in front of the house by noon." She walked off mumbling to herself, "Pigheaded fool, just plain pigheaded."

Coffie went outside and saw Ahmed standing in front of the stable. "What are you staring at, Ahmed?"

"Nothing really." He leaned against the door. "I was just thinking of the plane crash that wasn't too far from here."

"And? Have you heard anything new about it?" Coffie asked, looking at Ahmed curiously.

"No, and I'm not sure how far away it was. But it can wait until she gets here and we can have a talk with her."

"You forget, man. She can't remember anything."

"We'll find out once she gets here. We don't know anything about this woman, Coffie. It's best we know who she is and send her off packing to her family. Now, you better get Atu before Auntie comes out yelling like a tomcat."

Chapter 8

Thika, East Africa

The ride home was quiet. It was the last day in February, and the weather was windy. Orchid stared out the window as Busara pointed out a tribe of ten men and six women that were walking in a straight line along a narrow path. As Atu drove closer Orchid got a closer look at the women. They were all tall, thin and leggy with very dark skin. Long beads hung around their necks in bright colors, baskets on their clean-cut heads that shone as though they were waxed. One woman with a wide, flat nose looked their way and smiled with missing front teeth.

The land looked wild, strange, intoxicating to Orchid. And at the same time it gave her a feeling that it could be dangerous, demanding. A place that rules their lives against their will, but only if they didn't love the land. She wondered what it felt like to kick her shoes off and run free through the wilderness.

Orchid felt tired and leaned back in the seat and closed her eyes, letting the cool, crisp air hit her face. Busara was sitting in the front seat with Atu.

Not wanting to miss anything, again, Orchid sat up straight as they were approaching the ranch. The grass was green; rolling fields of corn, coffee beans, and tobacco were planted. She watched as workers were pulling up corn from the ground. They were singing a song that was unfamiliar to her ears. Their bodies moved to the rhythm of their singing. It was like being born into another part of the world.

Finally, Atu parked the car in front of the large flat house. Busara helped Orchid get out. She stood in one place looking at the smaller houses, three of them in a straight line, built close together. The women stopped what they were doing and glared at her as though she was an intruder in their world. None of them smiled or spoke. One had a large tin tub filled with water and was washing clothes using a wooden washboard.

"Don't mind them. They're just curious and you are a stranger," Busara said, and held her hand out to Orchid. "Karibu."

There was a glimmer in Orchid's eyes, but she only looked at Busara.

"I said, welcome, child."

"Oh, thank you, Miss Busara. Thank you for having me."

Orchid smiled at Busara, but just as quickly she screamed and jumped in back of Atu, almost falling to the ground. Atu grabbed her arm. She was still in no condition to stand well on her own without help.

"What is it, girl?" Busara asked, with a frown deepening across her forehead.

Orchid's mouth was open but she couldn't speak. She pointed toward the right and Busara saw an elephant standing close to a tall tree looking in their direction.

"Will he hurt us?" Orchid asked, still hiding in back of Atu. Her eyes were wide as she looked around to see if there were more. She had jumped too suddenly and now it seemed that every bone in her body was hurting.

"Come, Orchid," Busara said. "While you are here, you will see more than elephants coming even closer than that one. Don't be afraid, girl. You'll get used to it."

Busara led her into the house, down the long hall into the guest bedroom that she would be occupying during her stay.

Orchid was glad when she got to her room. Atu helped her to the bed, but it was hard to keep from moaning with pain. She held her breath, gritted her teeth. All she wanted to do was sleep so she couldn't feel the pain in her legs, her ribs, and head.

Night had fallen before Orchid stirred in bed. The ride from the hospital, and the stress of settling into her new home had exhausted her. She was still weak from fatigue. The chill in the air had wakened her. She opened her eyes slowly feeling the presence of someone near by.

Orchid heard him clear his throat. She looked at the open door and saw his black and dusty knee boots pulled over tight fitting jeans. He stood straight with his long, thick-muscled legs apart. There was an athletic hardness about his body, and he was tall and trimly built around the waist. His arms were folded across his wide chest. The muscles in each arm looked as though they would burst the upper sleeves of his black T-shirt. He was so tall she had to strain her neck to see his face.

Orchid looked into his eyes; they were dark, dangerous, and slightly slanted. But they also were wise and intelligent in a face that was amazingly beautiful for a man. Outrageously beautiful, so perfect in every detail, the eyes, nose, his whole face.

Orchid sat up in bed, holding the blanket tightly against her body. The cold air made her teeth knock together and her body still ached.

Ahmed saw her tremble. "Are you not warm enough, girl? Why haven't you asked for another blanket?"

Without realizing it, she jumped to the sound of his deep voice. His accent was the same as Busara's. But she could understand him better. She heard footsteps and felt safe when she heard Busara's voice behind him.

"You're awake, Orchid. Are you hungry?"

"The girl is cold, Auntie. She needs another blanket," Ahmed said, and stood aside to let Busara pass. "Can she not speak?"

"Yes, of course she can speak. Don't frighten the girl, Ahmed."

Orchid just stared, unable to speak and didn't appreciate Ahmed speaking of her as if she wasn't there. She managed to clear her throat. "Yes, I can speak." But she sounded so weak, and her body couldn't stop trembling. To keep him from seeing her tremble uncontrollably, she lay her head back on the pillow and closed her eyes. He was so big and intimidating.

"So, she's awake?" Coffie asked, stepping inside the small room.

"Yes, and she speaks," Ahmed said, as though she was a mute. "I'll get more wood for the fire. She can't seem to stay warm." Ahmed walked out.

Busara covered her with another blanket and placed pillows behind her head. "Now, is that better?" She turned the lamp on beside the bed, closed the red and yellow curtains that were hanging at the window.

Ahmed walked in again with an armful of firewood. "This should help."

"I'll get you a hot cup of tea, Orchid, a bowl of soup and fresh-baked bread," Busara said.

"Thank you," she answered. She looked at the small fireplace as Ahmed rearranged the wood in it.

Once he finished, he stood close to the bed and got a good look at Orchid's thin face. The bruises were still there, but her coloring was coming back. Her hair was in disarray, lying like a halo, spreading on the pillow; her hands were folded, resting on top of her stomach. But the texture and red highlights in her hair fascinated Ahmed.

He watched her hands as she slowly moved them, feeling the soft, thick quilt that Busara had made in all different colors.

"What is your name, girl?" Ahmed asked.

"I don't know my name. Your aunt calls me Orchid."

He smiled, then frowned. Like one of her flowers in her garden, he supposed.

"What kind of name is that?"

Orchid didn't see what was so amusing to him. Was this giant of a man plain arrogant and rude, or was he just stupid? Didn't he see that she was sick and had lost her memory?

"I think Orchid is a nice name. Miss Busara named me after her favorite flower."

"I see," was all he said. Without another word he leaned down and touched her hair, looked in her eyes, turned on his heel and walked out, leaving her speechless.

Orchid took a deep breath and exhaled. She was relieved to see him leave her room.

When Busara returned, she looked around the room. "Ahmed gone so soon?"

Not soon enough as far as Orchid was concerned. "Yes, Miss Busara. He just left. It was nice of him to make me a fire," she said dryly.

"You just relax and eat your soup. Tomorrow, you can eat the same foods as we do. I've got to fatten you up, girl."

An hour had passed and Coffie came in to check on Orchid. He tiptoed into her room but her eyes were closed. As he softly closed the door, he heard her voice.

"I'm not asleep," she said.

"Are you all right, Orchid?"

"Yes. Thank you. I forgot your name," she said, and sat up in bed so she could see his face clearly.

Coffie was tall and thin, but not as tall as his brother, with warm maple syrup-colored eyes. His skin tone was dark, and his hair was kinky and in braids, not as straight as Ahmed's hair. When he smiled his cheekbones were high and his chin pointed. He spoke softly and affectionately, also with an accent. Orchid was at ease with Coffie because he made her feel welcome in their home. Not at all like his bullheaded, rude brother, she thought.

"I know you must be afraid in a strange place with all strangers, but you will get used to us soon. Welcome to the Bakari Safari Ranch, Orchid."

Busara decided that she liked the girl. She was soft-spoken, pretty, and in time she would make her one of the strongest women on the ranch. Yes, she would teach her everything, make her shine in Ahmed's eyes.

Busara saw the way Ahmed looked at the girl as though she was a precious stone that had to be touched gently. He touched her beautiful hair as though something had driven him against his will. And then Busara saw him step back and look at the girl again as though he had seen her for the first time. Busara wanted this stranger to stay long enough until they got to know her better. Who knows what could come of it? Ahmed hadn't dated anyone since he lost his wife. It was time that he re-married and had a son of his own. He needed someone to carry on after him. As for Coffie, he could still wait. In so many ways he was still a boy.

As Busara walked past the library, she overheard Ahmed speaking to William on the phone.

"Yes, William, that's exactly what I said. I want you to investigate as soon as possible. Who knows who this woman is. I have no idea how long it will take her to remember. And I have a feeling she could have been in the plane crash."

Busara didn't want him to know she was standing in the hall listening to his conversation. She moved closer against the wall so he wouldn't see her, but she stayed within hearing distance.

"Look, William. You're beginning to sound like Coffie. Man, I know a half-dead woman can't walk from the accident to my house, but she is not African, I tell you. Just find out who she is, William." He hung up and sat behind the desk.

Busara went on to the kitchen. She had to think of something fast. She smiled to herself and placed the dishes in the wooden cabinet. She knew what she had to do. William owes her a favor and it is time he pays it. First thing tomorrow morning, she would call him.

The muscles in his cheeks tightened when he heard Busara's voice tumbling through the receiver and hitting him in his chest like a sharp knife. He knew from the desiccated tone in her voice that it was time he returned the favor for her keeping her mouth shut, but at what cost, William wondered. What did the old woman want? He placed his gold pen on his desk in front of him, loosened the brown tie around his neck.

William hadn't seen Busara frequently during the years because it brought back all the painful memories from the past. And when they did see each other she was always discreet, but always reminded him of that cold winter night she had visited her cousin Sada.

William was born into a well-to-do family and his father, Gater, had sent him away to be educated and get his degree in law. He had just returned home to begin his career as a lawyer.

Busara and Sada had walked outside to see if Coffie had arrived to take Busara home. There was a movement in the bush and Sada called out to see who it was. She was carrying her youngest son on her hip. She called out to her middle son and the movement in the bush stopped. The night was eerie, quiet, and Busara was ready to go home.

"Go inside, Sada, it's too cold out here for the baby. I'll find your boy and take him inside." Sada agreed and went into the house.

Busara called the boy's name, but no answer. She stepped closer and pulled the tall bush apart and saw two men standing over a young white man. He was dead, his left eye was open wide and the right eye hanging out of its socket, a stream of blood coming from the back of his head had soaked into the dry grass.

Busara's eyes blinked, she opened her mouth to scream but stopped when she recognized William and Gater. William had a large rock in his hand with blood on it. He looked wild, deranged, one hinge short of a madman.

"What have you two fools done?" she questioned, keeping her voice low, waving both hands in the air. "Are you crazy man? What if you get caught?"

"Please, Busara. He's the white man who killed my youngest son. No court would convict him. I've waited for this moment, dreamed of it. When we saw him in town we followed until we ran him off the road. No one saw us with him, except you. We had to get justice the only way we knew how. For years they've come over and taken our land, killed our people. No one has to know about this." His face was distorted with pain. And he held his hands to his face and screamed, then looked up at the sky. "Victory at last, my son," he shouted, held both hands in the air, tears rolling down his face.

Busara looked at the blood on William's hands. She looked around to see if anyone was coming.

William dropped the rock, knelt and wiped the blood off his hands with the tail of the dead man's shirt. "I went to school for my law degree to help my people, Miss Busara. I've never hurt anyone in my life, except him." He looked at the blood left on his hands, his mouth puckering as though it had a sour taste in it.

"I beg you not to say anything, Busara. My second

son's blood will be on your hands," said Gater. "Can you live with that?" He sat on the ground, his face in his hands as he rocked back and forward.

Busara bent down closer to him. "Don't you try and put that guilt on me, Gater. You lost one son and have taught the second one to kill, not me. But since you lost one son I won't be the reason that you lose the only son you have left. If I ever need a favor, you will be beholden to me. And I won't forget it. Now get this man far away from my cousin's house. Her children shouldn't have to see this." She turned and walked away. Busara took five steps and stopped again. "Don't you forget this when I need a favor, Gater, and you, too, William." She rushed back inside the house.

William and Gater looked after her with admiration. She didn't cry or get hysterical like some women would have. But the older people had seen so much, suffered and lost so much.

"How can I help you, Miss Busara?" William finally asked.

"Ahmed called you last night. I know because I overheard every word he said. I don't want you to investigate the girl in my house."

William waited. Maybe he hadn't heard her correctly. "Why wouldn't you want me to? You know nothing about the woman, do you?"

"No, William. I don't know the woman but I will if you do as I say. Stall Ahmed. I don't care what you tell him, or what excuses you find. But hold off until I tell you to. Do you understand what I'm saying, William?" she said, her voice low and calm.

"But Miss Busara, I'm Ahmed's lawyer and advisor.

How can I lie?" What was the old woman up to, he wondered?

"I'm Ahmed's aunt and I'm the old woman that kept your secret for so many years. I've never asked you for anything before. And the woman is no danger to anyone. I want her to stay here and marry Ahmed. I tell you, William. Hold off until I say what to do. When Ahmed calls again, tell him you are trying, but haven't come up with anything. You're the lawyer, the advisor. I don't need to tell you what to say. In a few months I'll call you again."

"But, Miss . . ."

William heard the phone click. She had hung up. He sat back and stared at the phone. He would call Ahmed in a week or two and tell him that he is doing all he could to find out who the girl is and about the five missing people that were in the plane crash. All five were from different states. It could take time to investigate all five of them. For some moronic, ridiculous reason the old woman wanted Ahmed to marry a woman that may remember who she is any moment. Ahmed, marry? William didn't think so. In the old days parents told their sons who to marry, but the old days were over. It's best the old woman realize it and stop this foolishness, he thought. But William knew he had no choice but to do as she tells him. No choice at all.

Chapter 9

Los Angeles

It was Friday night and Marie hadn't heard from Steven in weeks. Weeks of jumping every time her phone rang at home and at work. Weeks of waiting, with stress and tears. Why couldn't he understand what he was doing to her? She knew him better than anyone else, even better than Wanda had. But she had never expected this, for him to find himself another woman. Their lives together hadn't even started. She had no doubt of getting him back. But how, if he was in love with another woman?

Marie finished her drink and decided to get dressed and go to see Steven. Maybe if he saw her he would feel differently, or even have her stay overnight. Just one more night and she would convince him that she was the woman for him; the one who really loved him.

First, she took a long shower, dressed in a tight-fitting red dress and pumps. She looked in the drawer for a pair of black panty hose and changed her mind. No, Steven would get all bare skin. No panty hose for him tonight. Marie wanted this night to be special. After she had finished dressing she took one last look in the mirror. Any man would want to get next to this, she thought, smiling and smoothing her dress over her hips, and waltzed out the door.

As Marie walked to the front entrance of Steven's townhouse, she heard his voice and ducked behind a tall tree. He walked out of his apartment with his arm around a young brown-skinned woman.

They stopped and kissed before they got to his car. The woman was all over him and it seemed as though Steven couldn't keep his hands off her. As he kissed her, he held her butt, bringing her firmly against him. The woman responded to him as though she was a woman in love. But what mystified Marie was the way Steven looked at the woman as their lips parted and he kissed her deeply. Was he in love with her as well? How could that be? They'd only just met, but she had loved him from the first day she met Steven. Deep inside, Marie felt sick, used as one would use a trash bag and toss it away and pick up a new one. The way he looked at that woman made her heart sink. He never looked at her that way.

Marie closed her eyes feeling the life draining from her body and leaned against the tree. Her legs were too weak to hold her up. And when she opened her eyes again, Steven was driving off with the woman sitting close to him, in Wanda's Lexus.

Marie stood there for another five minutes before she could find the strength to walk back to her car.

Once inside her car, she sobbed and sobbed. Her life was falling apart, her heart broken.

She got home, undressed, and made herself a drink. As she walked into the living room, she flung her shoes against the wall and flopped down on the sofa.

Marie curled her legs under her, sipped on her Jack Daniel's, lay her head back on the sofa and closed her eyes. But every time she closed them the picture of Steven and the woman flashed in front of her. She became more inebriated as the night wore on. She heard a noise outside and walked to the window. Raindrops had began to pelt the windows, trickle down the glass in quickening runnels, drawing Marie's thoughts back to her current problem. Marie went back to the sofa and refilled her glass. She couldn't sit still any longer and started to pace the floor, went back to her bedroom and hurriedly pulled her dress back on again. She went back into the living room, slipped on her shoes, grabbed her purse and rushed out of her apartment. She couldn't stay inside any longer, even if the rain had began to come down harder.

Marie drove down Pacific Coast Highway and stopped at a store to purchase a half pint of gin. She had had a drinking problem before, but stopped drinking. Now, with the problem she was facing of losing Steven, she had started to abuse alcohol to desensitize the pain she felt. But this time it was different. She had the drinking in control. "Totally in control," she whispered to herself. She could stop if she wanted to.

Once she got back inside the car, she popped the bottle open and started to drink out of it. Without putting the top back on it, she sipped on the bottle as she drove.

After cursing for a while, trying to see where she was going while sipping from the bottle, she wasn't aware that she had started driving too fast and heard a siren behind her. "Damn! Damn! Damn!" she said, pounding both fists on the steering wheel. "What do the cops want with me?" she yelled out loud, looking in the rear view mirror.

There were two officers. Marie saw one go to each side of her car and she placed the bottle on the floor between the two front seats to hide it.

The minute Marie was asked to get out of her car, the officers didn't have to ask if she had been drinking or not. She almost fell in the middle of the street and cursed out loud, turning to face the officer and stumbling against him.

"Okay, Miss. Let's try it again and don't turn around this time unless we ask you to," the black officer said.

"Sure, sure," Marie mumbled. She placed both hands in front of her and stumbled as she made her second step. She laughed out loud, and laughed more when she saw them looking at each other. She wanted to stop laughing but couldn't, and after a few moments, she felt the tears burning her eyes, fighting their way through, and rolling down her tear-streaked face. The laughing disappeared, replaced with sadness, realizing what she had done.

"Stop right there," the tall white officer instructed. "We're taking you in." His voice was so deep, she jumped at the sound of it.

Marie looked at the black officer as he pulled the handcuffs out. The clicking sound and the sickness that she felt inside her stomach made her cry softly.

"Why aren't you guys out chasing killers and rapists? Why in the hell are you picking on someone who has never broken the law?" she said, looking from one officer to the other one. She was angry, frightened and cold.

The black one handcuffed her and led her to their

car. "We're arresting you for breaking the law, Miss. You could have killed someone or yourself."

"Bull shit. I wouldn't have. I'm minding my own damn business," she snapped.

"You're drunk. You're going to jail. Maybe tomorrow you'll understand," the white officer said. They led her to their car and took her in.

She sat alone in the back seat of the black and white car. Marie had never felt so lonely and abandoned in her life. She wanted to die, prayed that she would before she was locked up in a cell. And as she thought of being locked up with other criminals, her body was racked with fear.

The next morning Marie was completely sick and humiliated. Of all the people in the world, she had to call Steven to get her out of jail. But she had no one else.

She was quiet as he drove her to her car. After seeing her reflection in the mirror she kept her head turned, looking out as though she was looking at the view. She looked horrible, she knew. Her eyes were red, her hair wasn't combed and she needed to brush her teeth, shower, have a pair of sunglasses to prevent the sun from hurting her eyes and a steaming cup of black coffee to help her think clearly.

"No use looking the other way, Marie. You smell like a goddamn gin bottle. What were you thinking? Drinking and driving, I can't believe you could be so stupid," he was saying to her. "It's bad enough that you are drinking again, but driving? How stupid can you get?" he said roughly, and turned the corner.

Why couldn't he just drive and shut his mouth. She was dying inside, her pride was about two inches long. One more reason that he wouldn't want her, she thought with disgust.

"Look, I've been under the weather lately. Why haven't you called me, Steven? How could you just turn me off so abruptly without a second thought?" She turned her back to him and looked out the window again. Her right temple throbbed as though she had a drum beating inside her head.

"Please don't start that again. That's no excuse. Now you have a drunk driving record on your hands. What are you going to do now, drink all your problems away?" he asked with an angry snort. "Drinking won't help anything."

She had tried to hold it in, all the humiliation, the anger and jealousy. But it was too much. All she wanted to do was get out of his car, out of his sight, hide, and run as far as she could.

Finally, she spotted her car and told him to stop. "I'll pay your money back on Monday." Before he could answer, she was out of the car and running to her own car.

After Marie arrived home, the first thing she did was stand in a hot shower to wash the filth off her body. She felt dirty all over her face and hair and stood there for half an hour while hot water ran over her body. She washed her hair, brushed her teeth and made the cup of coffee she was craving for.

Marie went back to her bedroom, carrying her cup of coffee in her hand. She sat on the double-sized bed and sighed, still visualizing the image of Steven's face when he saw her today, the disgust that he didn't bother to conceal from her. She had failed terribly, she knew. Fatigue from the hard bunk and lack of sleep, she was too debilitated to stay up any longer. It took only minutes for her to fall into a deep sleep.

* * *

Two months later, Steven and Kim were still dating and seeing more and more of each other.

"Steven, I could have cooked dinner at your apartment tonight. You're spending too much money on me," Kim said, sitting across the table from him. "You've been taking me out to dinner, movies, and concerts." She looked around as people were still coming into the restaurant for dinner.

"Baby, I'm so proud to have a woman like you. I'll spend every dollar I have on you, Kim, you know that, baby."

She giggled. "You say the sweetest things."

"Why don't we get out of here and go to my apartment? I need to touch you, baby. I can't keep my hands off you." He motioned for the waiter to bring the bill.

The drive from Burbank to Woodland Hills was not far. As soon as they entered Steven's townhouse, he undressed her before they could get to the bedroom. As they entered the bedroom, he undressed. Kim was lying in the middle of the bed watching him. He climbed in bed beside her, kissing her lips as he told her how much he wanted her. He had waited until he was sure that she was ready. But tonight, they wanted each other.

Steven was on top of her, and she circled her arms around his neck. They were caught up in a world where it was just the two of them, kissing, touching, and holding each other.

After they made love, Steven held Kim in his arms. Was he falling in love with this woman? "Baby, why don't we get married? I'm tired of all this backward and forward from my place to yours." Before she could answer he kissed her long and hard.

She opened her eyes wide and looked at his face. "But, we've only known each other for three months. It's such a short time, Steven. We don't know anything about each other yet."

Not agreeing with her, Steven nodded his head. "I know all I need to know about you, Kim. What is it you need to know about me? Come on, ask me anything." He held himself up on his elbow and gently ran his fingers through her hair. He remembered doing the same with Wanda and quickly snatched his hand away.

She looked scared and confused. "Will we live here?"

"No, I'll buy you a new place. We can move right away." He talked fast trying to convince her that there were other townhouses nearby that were just as nice.

Kim sat up in bed. "Why would we move? This is such a beautiful place, lovely view and large enough if we wanted to start a family later on. We have all we need right here, Steven. "

He looked at the serious expression on her face, but he had no intention of telling her that this was Wanda's townhouse and that he only had a few months to move out. With the money he had gotten from Wanda's insurance, he could afford a new place for them to live in.

"I want us to start off fresh, baby. We can have a whole new life together. Just you and me, baby," he said and tightly held her small hand in his. "We can pick a new house out together."

Her face crumpled in disappointment. She loved this place and had always wanted a place like this of her own. This apartment was where they first made love, where he asked her to marry him.

"I want to live here, Steven," she pouted. "I don't want to live anyplace else but here."

Now, she was beginning to annoy him and he had to put a stop to it, now. "This is not your place, Kim. It's mine, and I say we move to another one," he said without smiling. He was getting impatient with her and his voice had taken on a frosty edge. And he only wanted to start fresh. This wasn't the place to do it. There were too many memories here that he wanted to leave behind, both of Wanda and Marie. The only way he could start a new life was to move out of Wanda's townhouse.

She poked out her bottom lip and lay on her back again. "I know it's not my place, Steven. It's just stupid to move out of a beautiful place and buy another one. It's money we could use for something else that is really needed, that's all."

Steven had done everything that Wanda wanted because Wanda had made the most money, and Wanda was too smart to settle for less than what she wanted. But Kim only made twenty-four thousand dollars a year. And she was younger. He would train her exactly the way he wanted her to be. *And whatever he says to her, it's best she learns to deal with it*, he thought as he lay on his back looking up at the ceiling.

"This is all I need, Steven. Just to lay here with you, looking at the beautiful view and knowing that we will spend the rest of our lives together is all I need," she said, trying to read the expression on his face. The weekend had been so beautiful and she didn't want it to end in an argument.

He gave her a lazy smile and looked at her. She was so sincere and so in love, he knew. He pulled her on top of him and made love to her again and again until they both were out of breath, and lying on their backs, not moving.

"This is the way I always want it, Steven," she whispered. But when she heard his soft breathing she looked at his face and he was fast asleep.

For a few seconds, Kim felt a chill and shivered. Somewhere in back of her mind she wondered if Steven loved her as deeply as she loved him.

Chapter 10

Thika, March 2001

"This is my favorite spot, my garden where I can look over my beautiful flowers," Busara said. "Fofois means flowers. That's the way it's said in my language."

Orchid walked slowly around the garden. It was well manicured with no dry sedge. The African marigold plant had yellow flowers growing in the middle of the garden and the African violets were pink. The smell of all the flowers combined in a sweet scent floating in the air.

"Can you smell it?" Busara asked, as she sniffed the air. "Here, in my garden, everything is sweet and peaceful, separate from the ranch, the fears, bad weather and the wilderness. It's just me and my fofois."

Orchid kneeled down and inhaled the scent of a long-stemmed lily. "Yes. It smells so sweet, Miss Busara. I could sit out here all day, too," she said, and looked up at the sun, feeling the warmth against her face and bare arms.

"I can work out here all day if no one ever reminds

me that it's time to stop and cook dinner. I've loved flowers since I was a child," Busara explained. "When the grass is dry and needs to be pulled from the ground, everyone knows not to touch my garden. Everyone doesn't have the hands for gardening, you know." She was on her knees, wearing an old straw hat, plastic gloves, and a long shirt that was big and long enough to belong to Coffie or even Ahmed, and a pair of old brown boots.

"The weather is so beautiful today," Orchid said with a deep sigh. The sky was light blue and she was enjoying Busara's company and wisdom and the wise tales she always told her about Africa. She took two steps toward Busara and jumped behind her. "God, a rhinoceros? Gee, it's so big." She still hadn't gotten used to seeing wild animals running on the grounds so close to the house and the sound of wolves howling in the middle of the night, the crow of a rooster or an eagle's cry near her bedroom window.

"Busara, do animals come any closer to the ranch?" Her eyes were wide and frightened. She stayed in back of Busara, peering out from behind her.

"Yes they do. You will see more than just rhinoceros here. Just stay away from the wild hungry dogs."

Orchid had to listen closely to Busara. Her broken accent was hard to understand the first time Orchid met her. But she was beginning to understand her more clearly as she heard the same accent from everyone on the ranch.

At times, the ranch seemed so peaceful and other times it was busy, wild and exciting, the smaller children ducking around the tall flame trees, laughing and playing games. But the women didn't seem very friendly toward Orchid. They looked at her as though she wasn't a part of them, as though she

didn't belong there. Some would pass not even acknowledging her and would ask Busara a question in
their language. Orchid never knew what they asked,
or what Busara answered.

"I'm so glad I can walk around without someone
holding me up. I feel so much stronger than before,"
she said, bending down to inhale the scent of a red
rose. Busara picked one and gave it to her.

"Yes, but you can't overdo it and stop bending so
much," Busara scolded. Your cheeks are filling out
and your complexion is getting clearer now. Keep
using the herbs I mixed for you."

Busara smiled as she remembered the expression
on Ahmed's face that morning when he walked into
the kitchen and saw Orchid sitting at the table to
have breakfast with them. Coffie chattered through
breakfast, but Ahmed just stared at the young
woman. Busara was certain that he hadn't realized
just how pretty the girl was. Yes, as Coffie said before,
a young female face was needed in this house for a
change. All one had to do was plant the seed and
watch it grow. Busara had planted the seed and
would enjoy watching the love grow between Orchid
and Ahmed.

"Hey there, Auntie Busara." She turned around
and saw Chiku standing in the doorway behind her.

"So you are up and around now, lady. Are you feeling better?" Chiku asked Orchid. "Everyone's been
talking about you."

Orchid could understand Chiku's English better
than some of the others. "Yes, thank you. I am feeling better, stronger, too. What's your name?"

"My name is Chiku. I'm a cousin that lives on this

ranch. I have an older brother and four other sisters and brothers. And I'm sixteen years old."

Orchid studied Chiku. She was very pretty but looked younger than her sixteen years. Her hair was black with long braids all over her head, her round eyes were happy and alert in a thin face as dark as black coffee and as smooth as butter. She was tall and skinny, wearing a pair of blue shorts. Orchid looked at Chiku's legs, which were long and thin, and as she looked down at her feet, Orchid was sure she wore a size twelve shoe.

"You two can talk while I go inside and start my Senegalese beef stew cooking." Busara got up and walked inside, leaving Orchid and Chiku sitting near the garden.

When Chiku turned to the side, Orchid saw a small scar on her face that she hadn't noticed. "How did you get the scar on your face?"

Self-consciously, Chiku's hand brushed against her face. "It happened when I was only nine years old, but now it's smaller than it used to be."

She sat on the ground next to Orchid. "My mama was cooking dinner and I was supposed to stay close to the house because there were wild dogs barking nearby. But I wasn't afraid and decided to take a walk." She swallowed hard and continued to talk. "Two boys, ages fourteen and seventeen, attacked me . . ."

"Oh no, Chiku," Orchid murmured, feeling her insides cringe. "You don't have to talk about it."

"I can talk about it now. Anyway, the youngest was hitting me in the face because I was fighting to prevent them from raping me. I fought and fought, but he only hit me harder." She frowned, folded her arms in front of her as if she could still feel the pain of him hitting her.

"The other boy grabbed my hands and I felt something sharp against my face. I was lying on my back and blood ran down my face and into my ear. It felt so warm and strange. But I was lucky."

"Lucky, how?" Orchid asked with tears streaming down her face.

"My father and brother had just gone out searching for me and heard me scream. They found us before the rape could take place. They chased the boys away. But late that night, they went out again. A few days later it was said around the ranch that the oldest boy had lost one of his hands."

Orchid sucked in her breath and frowned. "Oh Lord," was all she could say.

"The boys never came around here again, but one day, months later, I saw him and his hand really was missing. I think my brother chopped it off. Bastards," she spat out as though she'd eaten something distasteful. "I wish my brother had killed him," she said angrily. But, all of a sudden she looked at Orchid and smiled. "It's over now. Why are you crying, Lady? Do you always cry so easily?"

"I don't really know. It had to be a frightening experience for you. For anyone. I can't imagine having two boys holding me down." But it was more than that. Orchid was feeling sorry for herself that day. She had no one, no home. She knew she spoke English, so as Busara said, she must be American, but that's all she knew about her past.

"Have you seen either of the boys recently?" Orchid asked.

"No. I only saw the one with his hand missing. It was said the other one was sent away by his parents. They weren't sure if we would have brought charges against them, or simply just kill him. Prison time here is harsh, especially for an African," Chiku said bitterly. "Well, I better go home and help Mama cook dinner. Sometimes I just watch the babies while she cooks." Chiku started to walk off and turned around to face Orchid. "Hey, Lady, don't cry so easily. There will be enough for you to cry about before you leave here." She turned on her heels and ran off to her small house.

"Fire! Fire!"
She thought she heard a voice in her dream. Orchid turned over in bed. A nightmare, she thought. She'd had all sorts of crazy, unexplainable nightmares since she'd been staying at the ranch.
"Fire!"
This time her eyes flew open; she wasn't asleep or dreaming. Footsteps were rushing down the long hallways and doors were slamming. Orchid looked at the window in her bedroom and saw the flames coming closer and closer. She could smell the smoke and scrambled out of bed, slipped into a yellow housedress that Busara had given her. The dress was long, but it didn't matter, she held up the sides with each hand and ran out of her room.
Once Orchid ran out of the house, the smoke hit her in the face and she started coughing, her eyes were watering. Finally, through the smoke, she saw Ahmed, Coffie, and Busara were already out there. The ranch hands were running with long water hoses. Water was everywhere. The wind blew, rippling the water in the cold, brisk air.
Busara was with the women, filling the buckets with water. Orchid stood beside Busara, passing

bucket after bucket of water from woman to woman until they reached the men who had no water hoses.

The wind was so strong that it made the fire spread faster, and they were struggling to control it. Then, it looked as though the clouds had opened up as the lightning lit up the ranch and thunder rumbled. Seeing through the smoke, the skies went from blue to almost black as the rain began. The animals were frightened, running wild into the woods, dogs barking.

They all welcomed the rain, but they had to race against the strong winds.

The cold water was whipping at Orchid's face so hard it almost blinded her. Her hair was wet and her dress had gotten dirty and wet, too. Her face and eyes were burning from a mixture of smoke and water, the hard winds were cold and the lightning again lit up the sky.

The men and women were working unceasingly. It was so cold, and the buckets were so heavy that it was almost impossible to flex your fingers.

Busara sent Orchid to get more empty buckets and Orchid ran as fast as she could. Once she got into the stable, Orchid scrambled around, looking from corner to corner to find more buckets. She ran to the back of the stable, frantic, when she saw three buckets filled with water and sponges that were used earlier to wash down the horses. Orchid emptied all three buckets and ran back outside with them.

In another flash of lightning, Orchid noticed the larger branches of trees beyond the small house swirling chaotically in the forceful winds that were sweeping about Busara's head. Orchid had never seen such lightning. It lit up the ranch like it would swallow it.

She dropped the buckets and started running as fast as she could toward Busara, screaming out her name, at the top of her voice. But every time she opened her mouth the smoke choked her and she began coughing.

She took a deep breath and called out Busara's name again. But her voice seemed to get lost in the gusty winds, the crackle of the fire and the yelling from the men for more water, and the thunder.

Oh God, the larger branch was going to fall on Busara's head. It would knock her to the ground, Orchid thought. "Busara! Coffie! Ahmed!" she yelled at the top of her voice, but it was too late. No one heard her screams.

Busara finally heard Orchid's screams as she heard wood cracking over her head, but before she could move, the branch fell and Busara went down. Orchid yelled for Coffie again and this time, he heard her.

When Orchid and Coffee reached Busara, she was half-conscious, murmuring something in her Swahili tongue. She closed her eyes and Coffie picked her up in his arms, running inside the house, Orchid beside him. By then, fire trucks had surrounded the fire.

Inside, Coffie lay Busara on the sofa and Ifama started examining her.

"What is your name?"

"Busara," she answered.

"How many fingers do you see in front of you?"

"Two, you fool." She tried to get up but Coffie made her lay still.

"Auntie, please do as you are told. Ifama knows what she is doing."

Ahmed ran to her side. "Well, is she all right?" he asked, looking down at his aunt.

That was the first time Orchid had ever seen any reaction from the man. His face had softened as he knelt in front of his aunt. And Orchid looked at Busara closely and felt frightened. The only person in the world that cared anything about her was Busara, and now she was hurt.

"She needs to see a doctor, but it can wait until tomorrow, yes it can," Ifama said.

"Are you sure she doesn't need to go to the hospital tonight?" Ahmed asked with concern and impatience.

"No," Busara yelled. "You heard the woman. It can wait until tomorrow morning. Is the fire out?" Busara looked around and they were all standing around the couch watching her. "Is there work to be done outside?"

"Yes. Don't worry about the fire, Auntie Busara," Coffie said.

Ahmed and Coffie walked Ifama out of the room and Orchid sat on the edge of the sofa with Busara.

"It's my turn to take care of you now, Miss Busara. Let me help you to your room."

Orchid managed to get Busara to her room and undressed her for bed. "You lay still and I'll get you a cup of warm milk."

"Wait, Orchid. There's a small white box in my bathroom. Bring it to me."

"Are they herbs?" Orchid asked.

"Yes. I have something for the pain in my shoulder."

As Orchid entered the room again with the milk in her hand, she stopped when she saw Ahmed sitting on the edge of Busara's bed. She hadn't heard him walk back inside the house.

"Excuse me," Orchid said. "This milk is for Miss Busara."

"I see that you are feeling better now, girl," Ahmed said to her.

"Yes, thank you I am," she said, adjusting the pillows under Busara's head.

"Good. Then you can help around here while my aunt is recovering."

"I had every intentions of doing just that," she replied, with her back still turned to him. She didn't appreciate that arrogant tone of his. But since it was the only way he spoke to her, she should be used to it by now, but she wasn't and she was no longer afraid of him.

"Are you warm enough, Miss Busara? I can get you an extra blanket." Orchid saw her rub the back of her head.

"This is fine. I'm just tired and my head hurting. The herbs will stop it some." Busara placed a small amount of white powder on her tongue and washed it down with the warm milk that Orchid had given her.

Busara drank the full glass of milk and closed her eyes. She was asleep in just a matter of minutes.

After Busara fell asleep, Ahmed, Coffie, and Orchid walked outside. Everyone was inside their homes except some of the men. They were looking around the ranch to see what all had to be repaired, or rebuilt, as did Ahmed and Coffie.

The three walked back inside and sat in the living room.

"Do you think that you are up to taking over for Auntie Busara, Orchid?" Coffie asked. They were sitting on the sofa and Ahmed was sitting in the chair opposite them. The living room was big and cozy with brown paneling on the walls, Nigerian sculptures in the corner, and over the fireplace was a large painting of Nelson Mandela in a handmade gold picture frame. The hardwood floors were shining and a large round green and red rug of African prints sat in the middle of the floor.

"Yes, Coffie. I can take over things while Miss Busara is recovering. That's the least I can do." She said, and smiled as she looked at him.

"Well, I guess we got that settled. We eat breakfast every morning at six-thirty. After breakfast, Coffie and I will take Auntie to the doctor," Ahmed said, looked at her for a few seconds longer and walked out of the room. Coffie walked out behind him.

Orchid was left alone.

They were all up early the next morning except for Busara. "What the devil is that smell, girl?" Ahmed asked, looking around the kitchen. He was standing in the middle of the floor, his arms folded across his chest. "And where's my coffee?" He gave her his coffee cup that was on the table next to his plate.

She couldn't believe that someone had to fill his coffee cup. Why couldn't he fill it himself? Busara had spoiled both of them. And now she had to do what they should have been doing for themselves all along.

Coffie walked in and frowned as he sniffed the burnt ugali in the air. Ugali was made with white cornmeal, but since it wasn't as creamy as cream of wheat, Orchid didn't care for it.

First, Orchid filled their bowls with ugali. Gave them each two slices of toast that were too dark. Orchid remembered to chop the cabbage and onions in fine pieces, and scrambled the eggs in it, but she forgot the chopped tomatoes. She had fried the bacon just right.

She did not sit at the table with them. Ahmed looked awfully angry so she faced the sink with her back turned to him and washed the dishes that she had used.

"This coffee is too weak. You didn't say that you couldn't cook, girl," Ahmed grumbled and sat his cup down hard on the table.

Orchid turned around to face him. "I don't remember cooking this type of food before. I'll try and do better tomorrow." She tried to keep her voice placid.

"What type of food did you cook?" Ahmed asked.

"As I said, I don't remember. I don't even remember what foods I like or dislike."

"That's just fine. Auntie is sick and you can't cook."

"Maybe tomorrow will be better," Coffie interjected. "Today is only your first day and you were up late with Auntie Busara last night. Every day will get better," Coffie assured her, and looked at Ahmed. "Right, man?"

"I do hope so."

Coffie forced down as much food as he could to keep from hurting her feelings. She looked so sad and Ahmed could be so callous. He would speak to him later and tell him to give the poor girl a break. Coffie swallowed the weak coffee, forcing himself not to scowl in front of Orchid.

"Well, I have lots of work to do before Auntie is ready," Coffie said. He got up and walked out the door. Ahmed followed.

After Coffie and Ahmed had worked side by side for an hour, Coffie pulled his horse to a halt and Ahmed stopped beside him.

"What is it, man?" Ahmed asked.

"I think you were too hard on her, Ahmed."

"Too hard on who? What in hell are you talking about, Coffie?"

"About Orchid. Why do you insult her every chance you get? She's trying to adjust in our lives, and she's willing to help while Auntie Busara is recovering."

Ahmed ran his fingers through his hair and wiped the sweat from his forehead with the back of his hand. He wasn't quite sure why he insulted her so much. She was like a thorn in his side, an intruder in their house. And that damn William wasn't working fast enough. Which reminded him that he had to call him again today.

"I need a damn hair cut. Now, what do you expect from me, Coffie? The girl can't cook. Can she even take care of Auntie Busara? Is she good for anything? I should never have let Auntie talk me into agreeing to let Orchid stay with us. Or whatever her name is. Orchid is a stupid name. Nonsense is what it is." He pushed his fingers through his hair again. It had grown past his neck almost to his shoulders.

Coffie turned in his saddle and looked at Ahmed's face. "You don't mean that. You're just upset because Auntie was hit and you couldn't stop it. I know you like a book, man. You don't fool me at all."

"Maybe I am being a little too hard. But damn her, she better learn to cook and learn fast. Right now, I'm hungry as hell, and she's the one who is cooking our dinner today."

Coffie laughed out loud. "So am I. But, give her time. The worst that can happen is we may have to get Ifama to do the cooking and Orchid to clean the house and look after Auntie Busara. Right now, we better get her to the doctor to see if she's really all right."

"You're right, Coffie."

* * *

"Does your hip hurt, too, Miss Busara?" Orchid asked.

"Yes. It wasn't hurting when I first woke up this morning but it does now. What is this called, some kind of delayed reaction?"

"Could be. Here, sit on the bed so I can take a look at it." Orchid helped Busara ease down on the bed and when she pulled up her pink-flowered gown there was a large, round black and blue bruise on her hip. Orchid gently touched it and felt a knot.

"Oh, that's painful. Don't tell Ahmed or Coffie."

"Don't tell Ahmed or Coffie what?" Ahmed asked. They were standing at the door.

Orchid jumped. "Ahmed, I didn't hear you come in."

His eyes shifted from Orchid and back to Busara again. "Let me see what you were looking at?" he said, as he stood close to her bed.

"No. You won't see under my clothes, you two fools," she snorted.

"Yes, we will," Coffie answered. "It could be serious, Auntie."

They managed to pulled her gown up and saw the nasty bruise. Coffie and Ahmed looked at each other.

"We're getting you to the doctor's office right now," Ahmed said. "Coffie, get Ifama here to help get her dressed," Ahmed said over his shoulder, walking to the door.

"No need. I can help her dress, thank you," Orchid snapped with such an irritated edge to her voice that they all stopped and looked at her.

"Okay. Okay," Ahmed said, with both hands in the

air. "But make it fast, please." He and Coffie rushed out and Busara laughed.

Busara looked at Orchid and smiled to herself. This was going to be very amusing, she thought. And I love it. My dear Ahmed has found his match, at last. Orchid seems to be feeling better and getting stronger.

At the doctor's office, Ahmed and Coffie had discovered that Busara was in more pain than she had revealed. She complained about her head throbbing and the pain in her hip made it hard for her to move or sit in a comfortable position in the car, and she was unable to move her left arm where the branch had landed. But she still complained about going to a doctor when her herbs could help her just as well.

The doctor gave her strict orders to stay in bed until he saw her again, which would be in three weeks.

By the time they got Busara home, she had fallen asleep. When Orchid ran to the car to greet her, she looked tired.

"Oh God, is she all right?" Orchid asked looking at Coffie, and trying to avoid Ahmed.

"No. She's not all right. The doctor gave her a muscle relaxer but it's going to be difficult to convince her to take medicine that a doctor prescribed. She'll only take her herbs. She did take one of the pills in the doctor's office only because Ahmed and me were standing over her. It made her drowsy," Coffie said. Coffie and Ahmed carried her to her room. Orchid helped her out of her clothes and put her to bed.

"I'm so glad you're here, Orchid."

"I'm glad too, Miss Busara. But, if I weren't, Ifama

would be here to take care of you. But, I am glad that I can be some help. You are the only friend I have right now." She sat on the bed beside Busara. "You're like family to me." She held her head down. "When I go outside, the other women won't even speak to me. They just stare and pass right by me as though I don't exist," she said sadly.

"It just takes time, dear, and after a while they'll change. Everything will change for you. Just wait and see. Now, I can hardly keep my eyes open." Busara raised one hand in the air. "Oh, and Orchid, don't let Ahmed bother you none. He's just used to having things his way, that's all."

"He won't bother me, Miss Busara." But Orchid wasn't at all comfortable around the man. She looked at Busara again and she was fast asleep.

After lunch, Orchid washed dishes and Ahmed walked inside the kitchen. She had thought that he had gone out but he was in his library. Orchid looked around and saw Ifama walk past the kitchen door.

"Girl!"

"My name is Orchid. Please do not continue to call me girl." She was placing the last dirty dish into the sink to be washed.

"All right then, Orchid," Ahmed said and sighed. I've decided to have Ifama come in and do the cooking. Coffie and I thought it would be best if you just took care of our aunt."

She stopped and turned to face him. He was so big, and so intimidating. And it seemed as though his black eyes were piercing straight through her. She never looked directly at him unless he was at a distance and didn't see her, or if he made her angry, like now.

Ahmed was leaning against the doorframe with his

long legs spread apart, his arms folded over his chest. And Orchid was trying to keep her eyes on his and not on his long legs or his tight-fitting jeans or his wavy hair, his sexy mouth.

"Orchid?"

She jumped and cleared her throat. "You were saying?"

"Are you listening to me, girl?" he asked impatiently.

"Of course I'm listening. Orchid. My name is Orchid," she answered in the same impatient voice as he, only a level louder.

"Auntie Busara isn't telling us how badly she is really hurt. I need you to give her your full attention. You can run the house, as she orders you, of course."

"Of course," Orchid answered, waiting for him to say more.

"Ifama can do the cooking or anything else Auntie wants her to do."

"So you don't want me to cook anything at all, is that it? That's what you're saying, right?"

"Yes, that's it. That's exactly what I'm saying. At least not until you learn, if that is possible."

She sighed and placed one hand on her hip. "Was it really so bad? Did it kill you to eat it and give me a chance to learn?"

"No. It starved me to eat it because I couldn't get through a full meal." He turned on his heel and stormed out of the kitchen. A minute later he went into the library, but he heard her footsteps close behind him. Now, what does she want, he wondered?

She stood in the door, both hands on her hips. "Tell me, Ahmed. What is it that you don't like about me? Is it that I'm not pretty enough, smart enough or maybe too smart? Or is it because I'm not African enough? Oh, maybe it's that I don't obey your every command? Just what is it you don't like about me?" she asked, standing straight, pushing her hair from her face. But she didn't take her eyes off his. She stood and stared him down, waiting.

He was shocked at her abrupt brazenness, but she looked so cute when she was angry. He did all he could to keep a smile from playing across his lips. For a few moments he leaned back in his chair and only looked at her.

"None of that. Just learn to cook. As for how smart you are, you haven't showed me that you are yet. Now, I think my aunt is in need of your help." He picked up a sheet of paper from his desk, started to read as though he had already dismissed her.

She cringed inwardly, balled both fists and held her temper in check. If he weren't so big she would sock him right square in the jaw. She would not let his thoughtless insults get to her as they had this morning and every morning since she arrived. Orchid spun around and walked out.

She took Busara a tray with hot tea, toast, and a small bowl of ugali. Orchid hadn't yet acquired a taste for the porridge. But Busara loved it. She ate a bowl every morning.

"Was that Ahmed's voice I heard?"

"Yes. He was laying down the law of the land. Never stops giving orders, you know. But I didn't let his insults get next to me this morning. Here, let me fix your pillows so you can sit up more comfortably, Miss Busara."

"Ahmed is hard to understand, Orchid, but once you get to know him, you'll be crazy about him. He'll give you the shirt off his back. And he does so much for others and asks for so little in return."

Orchid listened to what Busara was saying about Ahmed. She seemed so serious.

"Will you teach me to cook, Busara? Maybe until you are well enough, you can give Ifama instructions to let me help her in the kitchen."

"I will. I can also sit in the kitchen and teach you, too. You'll learn, the men will love it." Busara just shook her head and looked at the poor girl. She was trying so hard to be accepted in their world.

The door opened and it was Chiku. "Are you all right, Auntie? We were all worried about you."

"I feel better, girl. Now, why don't you take Orchid to my garden and water my flowers? Not too much water. Remember not to pour too much water," Busara yelled behind them.

Orchid and Chiku went outside and looked over the garden. Chiku got one of the buckets that were used the night before and filled it with water. As they walked back to the garden, Orchid saw a young girl walking by. She looked straight ahead, as though she wasn't aware they had passed her. Her hair was nappy, disheveled, and stood up all over her head. It looked as though it hadn't been combed for days and as Orchid looked closer, she was dirty. Her long dress was a faded, dirty gray. She was too thin and bowlegged, wore no shoes, her toenails were gray, curling over her toes. Orchid was sure she wore at least a size eleven shoe. As Orchid continued to look at her she saw no life in the girl at all. She walked softly and slowly, only looking ahead of her. Orchid just stood and watched her until she was out of hearing.

"Who is she, Chiku? Does she live around here?"

"That is Naja, she's Somalian, and lives with her aunt and uncle. They are ignorant people. None of them can read or write and Naja doesn't go to school."

"But, what's wrong with the girl?" Orchid asked, still looking after her. She wondered how far she would walk before she got back. "Is she allowed to go alone?"

"No one in her family cares, or even misses her when she leaves. She is fifteen years old. Been like this for two years since her circumcision ceremony."

"Her what?" Orchid asked in horror. "What do you mean, circumcision ceremony? What does that have to do with a girl?"

Chiku looked at Orchid's face and could see that she really didn't know what she meant. "The Somalia have their young girls' clitorises clipped to prevent them from having any sexual desire. They sewed her private parts closed, if you know what I mean. It was done by an old woman that didn't know what she was doing. She almost bled to death."

Orchid looked after the girl as though she could envision her suffering and feel her pain, tears forming in her eyes. Orchid imagined the pain she suffered. The girl was slowly, almost imperceptibly fading from a world that had been cruel to her.

"Naja got very ill with an infection. Two years later she was brutally raped. After the rape she tried to kill herself by jumping into a swamp, but one of the men in her village saved her. Now, she just exists from day to day with no life left in her. Her soul is even dead," Chiku said, shaking her head.

"I can't imagine such a cruel treatment of such a young girl," Orchid said, disgust written all over her face. "What kind of place was this?" she whispered.

"Once I'm eighteen, I'm leaving Africa. The ways of the people here are outdated. The men tell their women what to do, how many children to have. I won't spend the rest of my life here. In California, women make their own choices."

"Not only California. There's other places not quite so far away as California, you know." They were watering the flowers and sat on the steps still holding the buckets in their hands. The sound of hammering was heard all over the ranch, the men working on what was burnt or damaged the night before. The smell of burnt wood and ashes were in the air.

"I want to go to California and live in Hollywood. My father is going to try and convince me to stay, but I won't. I want to live my own life and I want it to be a modern life, where women have their independence, with beautiful clothes and a beautiful apartment." Her eyes were sparkling. She could visualize it all so clearly.

"And what will your mother say about all of this?"

"She'll cry and beg me to stay home. But she has too many children as it is. She does whatever my father tells her to. Aunt Busara isn't like that and I see the way you look at Ahmed when he tries to order you around. I will not stay," she said firmly. "I want to live my own life."

Orchid sighed and watched the determination in Chiku's eyes. Chiku had made up her mind and it would be hard to change it.

"I don't know if I've always lived here but I see Africa is a hard place to live. I can't imagine what it was like a hundred years ago. I guess you have to love it, its wildness, the dark and quiet at night along with the peacefulness and excitement. But it never seems to be at peace for very long," Orchid said.

"Well, I should go and give Mama a hand with my

sisters and brothers." She went into the house and through the back door.

After Chiku left Orchid peeked in on Busara.

"I'm awake. Come in so we can talk." Busara sat up in bed.

As Orchid walked in and sat down in the chair near Busara's bed, Busara scanned her face. "Why are you so sad, child?"

Orchid fumbled with her hands. "About a dozen reasons. I have no home, no family, I don't even know who I am, Miss Busara. I appreciate your graciousness, but this isn't my home. How long can I stay when it's not my home or family?" she asked sadly.

"As long as it takes. Now, stop the fretting. You're welcome here, child." Busara reached over and touched her hand.

That night Orchid lay in bed and tossed and turned, but she couldn't sleep. The house was quiet and there were not even the sounds of animals outside her window. She got up and peeked out the window at the darkness and lay back down again. After tossing and turning for another hour, Orchid decided to go into the library and find a book to read. Reading would make her sleepy and as she thought that, she wondered how she knew when she couldn't remember anything about herself.

She stood in the middle of the library and visualized Ahmed sitting behind the polished mahogany desk, his long legs stretched out in front of him. Whenever she passed the door he always had his head down going over papers or discussing business with Coffie about plans for the ranch or on the phone giving orders. She looked at the bookcase that was wall to wall with books. She wondered how many he had read.

Orchid selected *A Grain of Wheat,* written by Ngugi, and read the back of the book cover. On a small table next to the large desk, she spotted the *Daily Nation* newspaper and read the headlines.

"So I see you couldn't sleep either," Ahmed said, as he stood in the doorway looking at Orchid's legs under her short, purple nightshirt that stopped above her knees.

She jumped, dropped the paper to the floor. "I was . . . was just looking for a book. I'm sorry if I woke you."

"You didn't wake me, Orchid. I had too much on my mind to sleep." He noticed that she wasn't wearing shoes either. She looked younger, but sexy, her red-brown hair was curled and framing her face. He could stand there and look at her all night, but made no attempts to get any closer to her.

"I guess I should go back to bed now." She started to walk out and Ahmed touched her arm.

"Aren't you forgetting your book?"

"Yes. Silly me. I had forgot just that fast." She sounded nervous, even to herself. He was just so big and overpowering, and so good-looking that he frightened her.

Two weeks had passed and Busara was getting stronger, but not strong enough to cook and run the house.

"Today, we will cook together," Ifama said, as they cleaned the kitchen together. "Soon, you won't need me here to cook at all, Orchid. Now, I'll cook the beef steaks and kidneys and you can mix the Tanzanian pineapple nut salad."

"What's that?" Orchid asked and frowned.

Ifama pulled a large bowl from the cabinet, for the coconut, cashews, bananas, cream and honey. "All you do is mix it together. You'll love it. Tomorrow, you'll cook some kima."

"And what's kima?" Orchid asked.

"It's chopped beef chili fry. Every day we will cook together until you learn."

Two weeks had passed and they were seated at the table for dinner. Orchid brought out a large bowl of curry beef Cameroon and rice and corn bread. The smell of curry floated in the air all through the house.

"Ifama did a swell job with the Cameroon," Coffie said, reaching for the bowl to refill his plate again.

"It wasn't Ifama who cooked today. It was Orchid," Busara said, looking at the shocked expressions on Coffie's and Ahmed's faces. She almost laughed out loud.

"You cooked this? When did you learn?" Coffie asked in amazement.

"Ifama's been teaching me every day. I can cook dinner from now on without her help. I learned fast," she said with pride.

"Indeed you have," Ahmed replied. "I didn't think you ever would."

"Thanks for your vote of confidence in me, Ahmed," she snapped back with an icy edge in her voice. She looked down at her plate as though she had lost her appetite. Was there anything she could do to please the man?

Ahmed was sorry as soon as he blurted the words out. She had been trying so hard to please everyone and to be accepted. She had earned her keep and all he could do was insult her. Moving his chair back from the table, he couldn't even look at her as he walked away.

"Guess I'll have to try harder," Orchid said.

Busara and Coffie looked at each other and shook their heads.

"You did good, Orchid. The dinner was perfect," Coffie said, and refilled his plate for a third time. "This beef is tender with just enough curry."

"How about the corn bread, Miss Busara?" Orchid asked.

"It is as good as my sweet cakes."

The next day Orchid was depressed. Busara was asleep and there was enough curry beef left from the night before. She didn't have to cook today. She had baked teacakes earlier and Busara said they were very good.

As she strolled around the ranch, she could hear the children playing and the men working. The hard rains had stopped and the men were chopping wood and rebuilding one of the smaller houses that had burned. Orchid could still smell the burnt wood.

The weather was getting warmer and Orchid wore the long, orange dress that Busara gave her. It had short sleeves and was ankle length.

She walked in no particular direction, looking at the mountains and wondering where the ranch ended. As she walked further, looking at a tall tree with hanging branches, Orchid decided to stop and sit under it.

It was so quiet here, peaceful, and no one seemed to be passing in this direction and no one could see her.

* * *

Losing track of time, she lay her head back against the tree and fell into a deep sleep.

It was past four and Busara was beginning to worry. "Ahmed, I had fallen asleep and when I woke up, Orchid was gone. God, I hope the poor child isn't lost and wandered off too far."

But Ahmed was even more worried than Busara. He could see it happening all over again. His wife lying on the side of a dirt road where the truck had hit her. The impact was so hard that she died as soon as they got her to the hospital. He shook his head to clear the vision from his mind. The girl should have stayed on the ranch. If she were lost, where would she go, he wondered? At this very minute if he saw her, he would shake some sense into that hard head of hers. "I'm going out to find her."

Before Busara could say another word, Ahmed had walked out the door.

Riding his horse, he tried to follow her tracks, feeling the anger building inside him. He thought he had lost her trail when he saw her footprints going the opposite direction. She had walked near the high bushes. Good thing she wasn't trying to hide from someone since she wasn't clever enough to hide her tracks. A blind bat could find the girl. He almost laughed but he was too angry with her for not having the sense enough to be afraid to wander off.

Orchid jumped with a start when she felt someone watching her. She opened her eyes wide and started to scream when he grabbed her shoulders. He began to shake her, squeezing her shoulders so tight she was sure he would leave the mark of his large hands on her.

"Are you crazy? Do you know what can happen to a young woman out here, alone? You are asking for trouble, but I knew you would the day I laid eyes on you," Ahmed yelled at her. He looked in her large round eyes and pulled her up.

As he held her he pulled her closer to him and his lips brushed against her neck. He was so glad to see that she wasn't hurt but was half out of his mind with rage. Sensing his concern for her, and to assure him that she was all right, Orchid held his arms and laid her head against his chest.

Ahmed's eyes dropped to her lips and stayed there for a heart-stopping moment. He pulled her closer and their lips met, and they kissed. Her lips were hot and sweet as he felt explosions in his head and in his blood.

Orchid put her arms around his neck, pressing her breast against his chest, moaning to his every touch as she felt his tongue in her mouth.

Ahmed shook his head as though he was coming out of a hypnotic state, pulled her arms from around his neck, and sighed deeply.

He stood up and looked at her with a frown. "Come now, it's getting late. Busara was worried about you." He lifted her onto his horse, then got on in front of her.

Orchid placed her arms around his waist and laid her head against his back.

On the way home they said very little. Worrying about her today made Ahmed realize that all the anger he felt for her was love. He had tried to hold it back so many times. She was the first woman that he was actually attracted to since his wife's death. In some ways, she reminded him of his dead wife. Her independence could not be denied, even though she was in a strange home, in a strange land. And he loved the way her curly, unruly hair bounced all over her head, falling into her face.

When they got home, Busara was waiting in the living room. "Where were you, child? I was afraid you had gotten lost."

"I'm so sorry, Miss Busara. I went walking and lost track of time. It was such a warm and lovely day." She looked embarrassed. "I fell asleep under a tree. When I awakened, Ahmed was standing there." She could still feel the excitement inside just from the thought of him holding her so close to him. Lord, what had happened between them and how many times had she said that she hated him? Now, she wasn't at all sure if it was hate she felt or not.

"I'm really sorry that I worried you, Miss Busara."

The next morning Orchid came into the kitchen to cook breakfast. At six-thirty Coffie sat at the table and waited patiently for his breakfast.

Orchid waited for Ahmed. "Where is Ahmed this morning?" she asked, still peering through the door, expecting him to walk in any minute and take a seat at the table.

"Oh, you didn't know? He left for Nairobi at five this morning."

Her heart crumpled in disappointment. He had left, and hadn't even said good-bye.

Chapter 11

Los Angeles, April 2001

They were standing outside on the balcony in Kim's favorite spot of the townhouse. From where they were, there was a view of the valley. And Kim could see the lights in the Sherman Oaks Mall. Steven was standing behind her with his arms circled around her waist.

"The weekend in Palm Springs was beautiful, Steven. You're just too good to me," Kim said, snuggling against him. "We've been together every weekend since we've met."

"Baby, that's what love is all about, 'togetherness,' spending time with each other."

It was warm that night and Steven wore a pair of brown short pants and a white sleeveless T-shirt. His hairy legs looked strong and had gotten darker from the hot sun in Palm Springs.

"I'm going to miss this place," Kim said. "I fell in love with it the first time you brought me here. It was almost as if it's where I belong. Did I tell you that when this complex was being built, I used to pass it in the car and wished I could have bought one of the units? And to think that I've fallen in love with someone that has been here all the time. "

"I'll buy you another townhouse like this one. Why don't I get us a glass of wine and we'll just chill out?" Steven said, and kissed her on the back of her neck. "You make yourself comfortable," he said, hoping it would stop her from whining about the apartment again. The day had started off so well, and they had been getting along so well. He just didn't want anything to spoil it tonight.

Kim went into Steven's bedroom to get her short satin robe out of his closet. In the corner, she noticed a shoebox with the picture of a woman's shoe on it and, curious, opened the box to see what was inside. There were wedding pictures of Steven and his dead wife. She was wearing a beautiful white suit and Steven was dressed in a black suit. She was so beautiful that Kim felt a thrill of jealousy and wondered why he was holding on to the pictures and the memories of their life together. The second picture was of Steven and his wife, kissing. Did it mean so much to him? Had he really gotten over her? She placed the pictures face down and picked up a medicine bottle that was prescribed for Wanda Gray, Steven's wife. As she read what the medication was she noticed the date, her eyes blinked wide and her heart sunk. Oh, why had she opened the box, letting curiosity get the best of her? Looking at the date again, she couldn't believe her eyes. It was dated only seven months ago. Steven had mentioned more than once that his wife had died two years ago. What reason did he possibly have to lie, she wondered?

Kim hung her robe in the closet and went back into the living room. She was glad that Steven was in the bathroom. After putting the medicine bottle next to his wineglass, she strode brusquely out the door. Let him figure out why she had left. She was too angry to try to explain it to him. And she was afraid he would only tell more lies to cover up that one.

"Baby, what are you doing in there so long?" Steven yelled from the living room. No answer. Don't tell me she's asleep, he thought. He smiled, picked up his glass and sipped his wine. As he placed the glass back on the table, he saw the bottle, read the label and rushed into the bedroom. He called Kim's name twice, but he knew she was gone. And he knew why.

She wouldn't get to her apartment for at least fifteen minutes. What would he say to her?

Steven called twice, but Kim didn't answer the phone.

"Pick up the phone, Kim. Baby, please let me explain." But, again, she didn't answer and she didn't return any of his phone calls.

The next morning at eight, Steven was ringing Kim's doorbell. She answered the door, rolled her eyes up at the ceiling, and walked off leaving him standing holding his arms out to her. He knew that she was still angry with him.

Steven hung his head down, he had practiced his plea while driving to her apartment.

"Baby, I can explain. I know you have a reason to be pissed off at me."

"You just don't know how pissed off I am, Steven. Two years? You liar," she scolded, and turned her back to him. She was so upset she had to move, turned away from him, and walked around her apartment without looking back. He followed her into her bedroom.

Kim sat on the bed and crossed one leg across her knee. Her apartment was small and she had felt she couldn't wait until she and Steven got a larger place together. Now she wondered if they would. The bedroom had a small dresser, a bed and two nightstands, with ten pillows of all colors arranged on her bed. But it was so small that Kim always felt trapped inside of it.

"Look, Kim. I told you that Wanda had died two years ago, because I didn't want you to be comparing our relationship with my marriage."

She turned to face him and shook her head, confused. "How can I compare when I didn't even know her, Steven? I don't even know you as well as I thought I did," she said, and turned her back to him, her yellow T-shirt above her knees.

"Some women will compare even if they knew the woman or not. Like, if I buy you a pair of earrings, you may wonder if I would have paid more for my wife's. Women do things like that." He looked sincere and hurt. But most of all, he was afraid to lose her. She was his new life, and he needed a new start so badly.

"Maybe I was wrong for lying, I admit. But, baby, I don't want anything to come between us. Please, Kim. Baby, I couldn't sleep all night. If you leave me, I have nothing, no one. You see, you made the pain go away, you gave me a reason to go forward."

She looked at him and his eyes were red and filled with tears. Maybe he was telling her the truth. And after all, she didn't want anything to come between them either. She was totally in love with Steven. No man had ever taken her to so many nice places as Steven did.

Kim lay her head on his shoulder, her eyes misty with tears. "No more secrets?"

"No more. I promise, baby."

He held her close in his arms and kissed her slender hand.

"Want a cup of coffee?" Kim asked.

"Yes. I could use one, and some sleep, too." But when she got up he pulled her back down on the bed.

"Kim, baby?" He looked so serious.

"Yes, Steven? What is it, honey?"

"Will you marry me?" he asked, holding her hand in his.

Tears rolled down her face. Her hands trembled, but this was the happiest day of her life. No more of the dating games that men played, the cheating and heartbreak. She was going to be married, and be happy for the rest of her life.

"Oh yes, Steven. I'll marry you," she cried with disbelief.

After breakfast they went back to his apartment. When they got out of the car, walking to his door, Steven had his arms around Kim's waist and stopped to kiss her.

Marie sat in her car and watched. She hadn't talked to Steven since the morning he got her out of jail. And her blood boiled as she saw him kiss that little slip of a bitch that was hanging on to him. She had to make a plan, and stop this affair before it got too serious. She had waited too long to lose him to someone that he had just met. It was she who waited for him when he was married to Wanda.

Damn him. She would most certainly put a stop to this, soon.

Chapter 12

Thika, East Africa

Two days had passed and Ahmed hadn't returned. Orchid missed him terribly, missed his deep authoritative voice. She even missed his complaining at six-thirty every morning. The ranch wasn't the same without him.

Busara's hip had begun to bother her again. Coffie stood over her while she lay in bed. "You've been up and down on your feet too much since Ahmed went away. Auntie Busara, you're not as young as you were before and it takes longer to heal. You must take it easy."

Busara held her hand up in a fist. "I'm not too old to take my fist to you, boy," she said, and sat straight up in bed.

Coffie ignored her sharp tongue. "When Ahmed comes home he won't like this a bit. You do not listen to us."

"I'll see that she stays in bed today, Coffie. Don't worry too much and Ahmed won't have to know,"

Orchid said. "I'll see to it that she doesn't get up for anything at all today."

Orchid left the room and walked back in with two magazines in her hand and placed them on the small table next to Busara's bed.

"Okay. I'm going back to work, but I'll be keeping an eye on you, Auntie," said Coffie. He walked out hoping that she would do as he said, but he knew her better.

The blinds were opened wide so the sunlight could warm her room. Orchid loved Busara's room because the colors were all so bright and lively. The comforter that Busara had made herself was red, green and yellow, as was the large round rug in the center of the floor which had the same pattern. Busara had made the heavy quilt on Orchid's bed, too, using some of the same colors.

"What would you like for lunch today, Miss Busara?" Orchid asked.

Busara didn't say anything for a few seconds. "I don't know yet. Lying around all day is driving me out of my mind and you've been quiet today, Orchid. Are you feeling all right? Or do your muscles still ache?" Busara looked at Orchid with a sharp eye; she had been sulky since Coffie had told her that Ahmed had left. Things seem to be going in the direction she wanted.

"Not as much as before. I've just been doing a lot of thinking this morning. It's hard to imagine living from day to day and not knowing who I am, where I came from or if I have a family? I'm all alone, Miss Busara. Sometimes I forget about it and other times it's all I can think of."

Busara held her arms open. "Come here, girl." Orchid sat next to her and lay her head on the older

woman's shoulder. Busara was so kind and understanding. What would she do without her? Where
would she go? Just thinking of it caused a lump in
her throat.

"You are not all alone. You have us and you can stay
as long as it takes for you to regain your memory."
Busara hadn't said anything to Orchid about wanting
her to stay with them and marry Ahmed. She would
make him the perfect wife. Together they could
make some fine-looking children, and children were
needed in this house. Ahmed worked too hard, and
it was time that he got serious about someone. He deserved to be loved and have a family of his own.
Busara was still young enough to know that when he
went to Nairobi, now and then, he had a woman
there, but that wasn't the same as having a family and
a woman that he really loved. It was just having what
he needed as a man. At least Coffie did talk about
marriage and a family. He just hadn't found the right
woman yet.

"Auntie Busara!" Orchid and Busara heard the ur-
gency in Chiku's voice and both looked at each other
as the girl ran into the bedroom. She was breathing
hard and Busara knew instantly that something was
wrong.

"Mama's in labor. I think it's too soon and she's in
lots of pain. I need help," Chiku said, gulping deep
breaths.

Busara tried to get up and frowned, feeling the
pain in her hip.

"Please, Auntie Busara, we need help now."
Chiku's dark eyes were wide, looking to Busara and
back to Orchid.

"Okay, help me up," Busara said to Orchid.
Orchid pulled the blanket back to help Busara out

of bed. "Are you sure that you can make it? You can hardly move, Miss Busara."

"I have no choice. Have you ever delivered a baby?"

"Me? You mean me? I don't know, I don't remember . . . I don't think so . . ."

"You will today."

Orchid gasped when she saw the frown on Busara's face. She opened her mouth to protest . . .

"I'm all right. I'll be there to tell you what to do. It's something you need to know anyway," Busara said. She grabbed her shoes from the floor and Orchid gave her a sweater to slip on.

"Chiku, go and start heating as much water as you can get on the stove. Orchid and I will be there. Now, scoop, girl, go on."

Chiku ran out. Busara heard the door close hard behind her.

Just minutes later, Orchid and Busara were entering Eno's house. They heard her screams before they entered the room. But Orchid wasn't prepared for what she saw.

Eno was tossing and turning in bed. Her gown was open in front, revealing her naked, round stomach. Her face was sweaty and her hair was wet. The other small children were sitting on the sofa, scared silent by their mother's loud screams.

"Hurry Chiku, and Orchid, come on, child! You can't help deliver a baby standing there with your hands in your pockets looking as though you're going to faint," Busara ordered.

Another loud scream and Orchid jumped, grabbed Eno's hand and held it.

Whenever Eno felt a pain, she spoke loudly in their language. Orchid let her hand go, ran back into the kitchen, and returned with a bowl of cool water and a small towel for Eno's forehead.

Busara pulled the blanket down and examined her again. She looked worried this time. As she worked with Eno, she had almost forgotten the pain in her hip, but was sure she would feel it tomorrow.

Orchid held Eno's hand in hers and had her squeeze every time the pain hit.

"Eno, Eno, are you listening to me?" Busara asked, her hand still moving on Eno's belly. "I think the baby feet's are going to come out first. That could be dangerous, you know, and quite painful, too. We had better get you to a hospital."

Eno grabbed Busara's hand. "Please don't send me away. When my sister went to the hospital to have her baby, she died there," she whispered between pains, and began breathing hard through her mouth, her face twisting in such pain that her words were barely audible as she spoke.

"But you could die here," Busara answered.

"If I die, I want to be home," she pleaded. "Try and turn the baby around."

"I can't, but I'll try everything I can to keep it from being so painful," Busara said with dread, sweat dripping from her forehead. From her pocket, she took out a small package containing white powder and opened it. "Here, take this. It should help deaden the pain."

Orchid gave Eno a small glass of water to wash it down. This would be a long day, she thought.

Orchid was so scared that she was having difficulty keeping her breakfast down. She held Eno's hand, washed her face, gave her cold water to sip and prayed that she and her baby would live.

An hour had passed and the screams got louder.

Chiku stayed in the small living room taking care of the younger children and trying to keep them out of their mother's room.

Finally, Eno's husband, Din, and his son, Dume, came home. Din rushed to his wife's side and held her hand. His pleading eyes looked at Busara, depending on her to save his wife and child.

Eno screamed again, this time louder as she twisted her body from side to side. Orchid cried as she talked to her; prayed for her. There wasn't anything else they could do, but wait, and wait.

Eno could feel the baby moving lower, tearing at her womb as though it was screaming, fighting to come out into the world. And at times, she felt that the baby was so big, and her small, fragile body had no room to hold it inside any longer. And every time the pain began, she felt it coming from her back, settling in the middle of her stomach as blood gushed from her womb.

All Eno could do was scream for God Almighty to help her though this labor. The sheets were wet, pulled down to her feet.

Suddenly, the baby was coming out and the only thing that Busara could do was use her hands to help Eno as her cervix began to open.

Orchid brought in more hot water, sheets and towels. The blood rushed from under Eno's gown, streaming like an ocean from her womb, sinking into the sheets that were under her.

Orchid's hands trembled, she almost passed out. But she knew Busara needed her, Eno needed her, and she would not let them down. All she wanted was that the mother and child live. And with a rush of energy, she rushed to Eno's bedside and held her legs wide open as Busara yelled for her to push.

Orchid looked at Eno's face, their eyes met and held as she held her legs wide apart with a tighter grip to assure her that she was by her side and it would be over soon, and she was there for her.

The pain got worse, and Eno felt as though the baby was stuck in one place, tearing her insides. She couldn't breathe, and yelled and yelled for God to help her, but this was a task she had to do alone, giving birth to her child.

She took another deep breath and listened to Busara's instructions.

"Breathe in and out, woman. Eno, push, push, harder, now harder," Busara instructed.

Eno pushed harder and longer with an inner strength she didn't know existed inside of her, a breath of fresh air went down her lungs, caught up with a loud, anguished cry. She was sure that she would pass out and held on to both sides of the narrow bed while Orchid held her legs spread apart as wide as she could spread them. She tossed and turned, screamed and cried, pushed and breathed. She held her breath and pushed harder.

Orchid looked at Busara's face; she was shining with sweat rolling down her face onto her neck. The top of her dress soaked with sweat and Eno's blood.

Eno pushed again and the baby cried out. At the sound of the baby's voice her husband ran back inside the room with tears streaming down his dark, thin face. His eyes were round, red, tired from a long day's work and a tortured evening waiting for his wife to deliver their sixth child.

"Thank you, Busara. Thank you, Orchid, and thank you, my God." He held the baby up in the air, closed his eyes and shouted. "Thank you my Lord for another son."

Eno was so tired that she lay limp in her bed, not moving, just smiling up at her husband and baby. This pregnancy had been harder on her and she had lost more blood giving birth to the baby. But she never complained to her husband how tired she always was during her pregnancy and prayed that the baby would be as normal as their other children. She was a strong woman and had five other children, all with the help of Busara at her side.

As Orchid stood close by Eno's side, she grabbed Orchid's hand. "Thank you. You were brave, Orchid. You did well."

For a few moments Orchid was unable to say anything, Orchid shook her head and kissed Eno on her forehead. "You have a beautiful baby, and you too, were brave, very brave."

Orchid asked Dume to see to Busara getting home all right as she helped Chiku clean the room, change the sheets on the bed, and help put the younger children to bed. When she left everything was clean and put back in place. She felt good. She had helped someone when they needed her.

And in her heart, she was a part of Africa.

After Orchid went back to the house, she stood outside in the garden for a while. She needed fresh air and she needed to be alone. The experience was overwhelming, and she had been a part of it.

It was dark, quiet, the stars seem so low it felt as though she could reach out and touch them. She could hear the sounds of animals but she had gotten used to it and wasn't afraid. The fragrance from the flowers floated in the air around her. The garden had become her favorite place just as it was Busara's.

For Orchid, it was her quiet place that she went to often to try and remember her past and make some sense of the life she was now living. Where did she come from, and where would she end up?

Orchid pulled her sweater closer around her and lay her head back against the bench. Wearied, she closed her eyes and relaxed.

"Auntie Busara is so proud of you, Orchid," said Ahmed.

She jumped up and turned around to face him. Hair had grown on his face and his shirt was open and pulled out of his jeans. She could see the black hair on his chest. "You're back," was all she could say. Her heart was racing at a pace that clouded her thinking.

"I'm proud of you, too. Everyone on the ranch will be talking tomorrow." He stepped beside her and she looked up at him. His hair had grown down his neck and she ached to touch it, to run her fingers through it and bring his face down close to hers. But she didn't. He had left without even saying good-bye to her. Would it always be this way between them, like two passing ships? Does the man get close to anyone?

"I'm tired. Will you be coming inside soon?" he asked.

She wondered why he wanted to know? What did he really care if she came inside or not? It was obvious to her that he hadn't felt that way before he left—without saying good-bye.

"In a little while," she answered, turning her head away from him. "It's so peaceful out here. Finally, I can come out alone at night without being frightened at every sound I hear."

"But I'd feel better knowing you are safely inside. You can't be too careful, Orchid. Keep that in mind."

"I've been out here at night while you were away," she replied.

"But, now I'm here. As I said, I'd feel better knowing you are safely inside."

She looked him straight in his eyes. The warning was clear, he wanted her to do as he said. But she was still angry with him, and he wouldn't get his way with her. She would stand her ground. "I'll be in when I'm ready," she snorted.

Ahmed was taken aback at her sudden bluntness. And why was she being so cantankerous?

Before Orchid could protest again, he had circled his arms around her waist, picked her up, stepped inside, closed the door and locked it. Ahmed brushed his lips against hers and sat her on the sofa. "Good night, Orchid. Don't stay up too late." He walked away without looking back.

She sat there, not believing what he had just done. "Big fool," she hissed under her breath. But being so close to him took her breath away.

She was falling from the top of the mountain, but it took forever to reach the bottom just as it had the last few times she'd had this nightmare. She floated in the air, as the rain hit hard. Her hair blew, wet, and every bone in her body ached. She knew that once she hit the bottom she would die; parts of her body were falling in broken pieces. She flipped over like a falling bird struggling to flap its wings, losing control in the air, almost at the bottom, but she still hadn't hit the ground. And now, the rain was hitting harder against her, knocking the breath out of her, blinding her. She shook with fear as the wind blew her small body to the right, to the left, and eventually she was so close to the bottom she could feel her own death. Then, feeling lighter, she began flying in the opposite direction, but the wind pulled at her, carrying her to the bottom. And, suddenly she dropped. Plummeting toward the ground, she reached out, grabbing at something to hold on to, but nothing was there, just the cold, angry winds, the hard rain, as she fought to stay alive.

Orchid was fighting to save her life. If she hit the bottom, it would be all over for her. If only the rain would stop, if only it wasn't so cold. She fought, hitting, flailing, screaming, both hands in the air.

Ahmed went straight to his room, but once he got there, he wasn't sure if he would get any sleep. When he picked Orchid up in his arms, her lips were so close to his he could feel her breathing, her hair smelt like the flowers in Busara's garden. After tossing and turning for an hour, he fell into a deep sleep.

Hearing her screams, Ahmed's body jerked. He jumped out of bed and ran into her room. "Orchid! Wake up! Orchid, it's only a nightmare," Ahmed said calmly, not wanting to frighten her any more than she already was. He gathered her into his arms, kissing her forehead as though she were a child.

"Orchid, stop it. Stop it. It's only a nightmare." He reached over her and lit a candle on the small table next to her bed. Ahmed held her close against his chest, hoping that she wouldn't waken Busara or Coffie.

She opened her eyes slowly and looked in Ahmed's face. "Oh, my God," Orchid sobbed, holding her fist to her mouth, trying to muffle her cries. "It was terrible this time. This one was the worst."

"You've had this same nightmare before?" he asked.

"Yes, several times. But I've never been this close to dying, and I don't know what the dreams mean. Maybe I'm going to die, Ahmed," she said. Looking at him, his hair shone in the dark and his voice sounded deep and sexy. She looked at him and he was in his underwear, blue, light blue, she would remember them. He must have jumped out of bed and ran to her room.

He could feel her body trembling under the blanket. "No, I won't let that happen." He held her closer to him, feeling her body beginning to relax in his arms.

He got up and pulled the blanket to her shoulders.

"Please, Ahmed, don't leave now. I need to stay awake a while longer. If I fall asleep right now, I may have the same nightmare," she pleaded, sitting straight up in bed.

"Okay. He sat back on the bed and held her again. Her head was against his chest and the blanket had crept down her brown thighs.

She couldn't take her eyes off him. For a man, he was as beautiful as a painting. Orchid didn't know what had come over her, but she ran her fingers through his hair as she had wanted to do so many times before. Just being so close to him made her heart race out of control.

Ahmed's eyes dropped to her lips and stayed there for a heart-stopping moment before he held her face close to his, and kissed her ever so gently. And as he realized what he had done, he tried to pull away but couldn't stop himself. He had wanted her far too long, and it had gone too far to stop now. He kissed the voluptuous swell of her breasts, cupped one in his hand and kissed it over and over until he was out of his mind with desire, his hot blood running through his veins.

Orchid felt the same desire deep inside the pit of her stomach and nuzzled closer against him, kissing him with just as much excitement, his passion taking her higher with a need she had never felt before, or remembered, or wanted to remember.

Ahmed stopped suddenly, realizing his actions were wrong. He got off the bed and looked down at her. This wasn't the time and place for pleasures to explode. He had to think with his brain instead of the hard throbbing that had developed for her. First, Orchid had to remember who she was. What if she was married or had children of her own? God Almighty, what was he thinking of?

Her eyes opened wide as she fought to breathe. Orchid moved out of Ahmed's arms making more space between them. Feeling a chill in the air, she shivered, held the sheet against her chest with one hand, running her fingers through her hair with her free hand. What had stopped him, why did he stop, she wondered, embarrassed?

"It's all right, Ahmed. Thank you for coming to see if I was okay." That was all she could manage to say at the moment.

"Orchid," he said, taking a step forward. "I didn't mean for . . ."

Orchid held her hand up to stop him. "Please don't say you didn't mean to touch me, don't say you don't want me, and I promise this will never happen again." She covered herself and turned her back to him.

* * *

At five the next morning, Ahmed got out of bed, but he was tired. He smiled as he inhaled the aroma floating in the air from the kitchen. But he frowned when he thought of Orchid. The hurt in her eyes, the abrupt dismissal she gave him. And he had deserved it, he knew. Coffee, black coffee was what he needed, he thought as he went into his bathroom to take a shower.

Orchid got up and started breakfast just as she had done while Ahmed was away. She hummed a song she had heard Eno's children singing as they played on the grass just beyond the kitchen window. But when she heard his footsteps, she stopped. It was Ahmed. She knew the sound of his footsteps, heavy with long strides.

Damn him.

Chapter 13

Los Angeles

Marie decided to take matters into her own hands. After all, this was her life, her happiness. No one was responsible for it but her. She still hadn't heard from Steven, and she had given him enough time to come to his senses, but to no avail. Wanda had been dead for three months and she was alone, with no one. She had been true to Steven, even waited patiently for him to divorce Wanda, although he had never said he would. But Marie was certain that one day Wanda would find out about Steven's perfidy and throw him out. Then, he would come running to her. And she would be there for him.

Marie watched Kim leave Steven's apartment and drive off in a late model red Ford Mustang.

Marie had already followed Kim to her office and today she would see where Kim would lead her. If only she could get her alone, so they could talk. Maybe today would be her lucky day.

Kim drove into the parking lot of the Pizza Hut on Ventura Boulevard, in Encino. She parked and went inside. Marie waited for ten minutes and went inside to see if she was alone or there to meet someone.

It was noon, and the restaurant was getting busy for lunch with two and three people walking in and out at the same time. In the playroom, children were running around, riding in small cars and playing with the slot machines. There were so many children, so much noise it looked like a nursery school.

Marie stood inside and saw Kim sitting alone at a table. She went straight to the line, picked up a tray, selected what she wanted for lunch which was a salad, a slice of pizza and a tall Coke and paid the cashier. She walked straight over to Kim's table.

"Miss, are you saving a seat for someone?" Marie asked with a warm smile.

"No. Please sit down. I hate eating alone."

"So do I. My name is Terri," Marie said, carefully not giving her real name. All she needed was Kim to mention it to Steven. She would lose him for good.

"Kim Richards. Glad to meet you, Terri. Do you eat here often?" Kim wiped her hands with her napkin, folded it neatly and placed it back on her lap.

"No. I had some business nearby and thought I would eat before going back to my office. I live in the valley, but work in LA. The drive back and forth is a bomber."

"The 405 Freeway? I hear you, girl. It is a bomber," Kim answered.

They were quiet for a few moments as Marie was trying to build up enough nerve to get what she had been waiting for. Now that she had the opportunity, she was nervous as hell.

"You look so familiar to me, but I can't remember where I saw you," Marie said.

Kim laughed. "Guess I have that kind of face. Everyone says I look like someone they know."

Marie looked as though she was trying to remember. "Oh, now I do remember where I saw you. I went to Steven Gray's house one morning and as I was getting out of my car, Steven was saying good-bye to you. You two were standing outside of his apartment unit. He said that you two worked together and you had dropped by his apartment to give him some work he had forgotten." Marie could see Kim's expression change from happy to deep concern. "Steven was married to my best friend." Marie held her head down as if it was difficult to continue. "She was such a good-hearted person. Steven took her death pretty hard and he still talks about her as though she just died yesterday. He was just saying a week ago that he could never love another woman as much as he loved Wanda."

Kim's interest perked and it looked as though all the blood had disappeared from her face.

"You know Steven?" she asked with concern. "And he said that we only work together? Steven was married to your best friend? What a small world, isn't it? And we've never met." Kim moved nervously in her chair.

She was rambling on so fast that Marie could hardly understand what she was saying.

"I miss Wanda so much," Marie continued. "They were married for three and a half years before she died. Shame. He'll have to move out of her townhouse in about six months. She left it to her sister, you know." Marie looked around to make sure no one could hear. "But she left her Lexus and money from her insurance to Steven. She was so young, so beautiful." Marie looked at Kim; it seemed as though she was in shock.

"Kim, are you all right?"

"I'm sorry. I was just thinking of Steven's loss." Kim couldn't believe what she was hearing. She turned her head to hide the hurt in her face and placed her fork on her plate, unable to eat another bite. How could this be happening to her? She was supposed to be getting married soon. But she needed to know more about Steven's life before she marries him. She had to know more, no matter how bad it hurts. Kim had to play along with this woman to find out all she needed to know about Steven.

"I heard about Steven's wife's death. But I wonder why she didn't leave the townhouse to him? Don't you find that a bit strange? Did she ever mention it to you?"

"Well, it was hers before she met Steven. The Lexus, the townhouse. Steven had nothing before he met Wanda. She bought it all." Marie leaned forward as though she didn't want anyone to hear and lowered her voice. "Steven would kill me if he knew that I've told you so much. Please don't reveal a word of this to anyone else at your job. He's a man that I have no respect for. She left him once. I tried to tell her not to go back to him." Marie took a sip of her Coke and cleared her throat. As she studied Kim's face she wanted to laugh, but she wouldn't. She had to act out this little charade as convincingly as possible. And she had to convince Kim that Steven wasn't the man for her. This was her only chance. If she failed to convince Kim to leave him, she may never get another chance again.

"Why?" Kim sat straight up in her chair waiting

to hear more. She pushed her plate to one side of the table.

"He cheated on her. Would you believe that it was with one of our best friends, too. That did it for me. I have no respect for him anymore. One would think he would have cheated with a woman that Wanda didn't know. But her best friend? I'm telling you, if he's seeing someone, she better know that he can't be trusted. Marie sipped at her Coke again and looked into Kim's eyes. They were beautiful, light brown but now they were sad and watery, filled with misery.

"The woman that he cheated on Wanda with said he lied to her. Told her that he and Wanda were discussing a divorce. He lies about everything. He tries to pretend that he has more than he really does. That's how he got Wanda in the first place, with lies. A lying ass," she mumbled. "I really shouldn't be telling you all of this, but I'm just so hurt over Wanda's death. Sometimes talking to someone that you don't know is easier than talking to someone you do know," Marie said, as she dabbed at her eyes with her napkin. She acted as if grief was taking over and took a deep breath. "It just breaks my heart when I speak of Wanda. We were friends for so long."

Kim's heart was broken, but no matter how much it hurt her, she had to listen. She wanted to know the man that she was going to marry, or had planned to marry.

"Please never tell Steven that I told you so much about him. But I was so hurt when I found out that he is still seeing the woman he cheated on with poor Wanda, I could kill him."

Kim looked as though she would choke with pain

and disappointment. All of a sudden she felt like her
entire relationship with Steven was a fiasco.

"Why do you think he's still seeing the woman?"
How could that be, she wondered, when they were
always together? But after what she had just heard,
who knows what Steven would do?

"She told me so herself, and I saw them together
with my own eyes. It was about a month ago on a
Sunday morning." The same Sunday he got me out
of jail, Marie thought, and smiled to herself. She
knew for certain that he wasn't with Kim that Sunday
morning. "My sister saw them together for lunch
about a week ago. And guess what?"

"What?" Kim asked, bracing herself for the answer,
for more hurt and disappointment.

"She had a black eye. He has a very bad temper so
I know he did it to her. Well, enough about Steven.
Now, tell me about yourself. Are you married or seriously involved with anyone?" Marie asked with a
smirk slowly playing across her lips with the pleasure
of seeing the hurt on Kim's face. Looking at Kim, she
was sure that she might burst into tears any second.
She hadn't touched her lunch, Marie noticed.

Kim sighed. Terri was right. Steven does have a
temper that she had experienced as well. And more
than once.

"No, I'm not seriously involved with anyone, not
any more. I was engaged to be married. But, now,
that's over with, too. You see, I was in love with a
man I hardly knew; I trusted and believed everything he told me." She couldn't say any more and
grabbed her purse, took a drink of her water. She
was so choked up; she walked out fast without saying
good-bye.

Marie sat and watched Kim as she rushed out the

door; watched her as she got into her car and drove off fast. She had done the right thing. Kim would never be woman enough to keep Steven. She smirked, and decided to finish her lunch. Once she finished, she would take the rest of the day off, go home, mix herself a nice, strong drink. She deserved it. No, she shook her head. She wouldn't make herself a drink. It was time to clean up her act and wait for Steven. He had called her a drunk, but no more. After Steven tries to win Kim back, and fails, he'll call her. And she would be sober, and their lives can finally begin.

Marie left a tip on the table and walked out. What a nice day it turned out to be. She smiled all the way to her car.

Two weeks had passed and Steven tried to convince Kim that he was her man, that he loved her. But, no matter how hard he tried, she wouldn't take him back. Their last conversation about the townhouse blew up in a heated argument, and he completely lost his temper. Now he was sorry. He had tried to make it up by sending her flowers, asking her to go on a weekend trip, but nothing he said would convince her to take him back. He left her several messages begging her to come out for a quiet dinner so they could talk, but she had very little to say and none of it made any sense to Steven. He still believed it was the argument about moving into another townhouse. Steven tried to remember everything he had said to Kim that day. Maybe if he could remember, he could correct it. What had happened to make her turn against him? He just couldn't figure it out. It just didn't make sense.

Kim had telephoned Steven the same day she had

lunch with Marie. She decided to talk to Steven, to try one more time to discuss the townhouse hoping he would tell her the truth once and for all. After all, how could she marry a man that lied to her? What kind of life could they have together if she couldn't believe anything he said to her? And he promised her the last time he got angry with her that he wouldn't lose his temper, but he had.

"This is my townhouse, if I want to sell it, it's my business."

"But it doesn't make sense," Kim said. "To sell a place that is large enough and one that is so beautiful to buy something as small as the one you took me to see." But she was even more relentless about it, hoping he would get angry enough to tell her the truth, that it didn't belong to him. And once again, she was hurt and disappointed in him. He still didn't tell her the truth and he still pretended the townhouse belonged to him. He had lost all credibility with her.

They were standing in the living room and Kim had picked up her purse to leave but with a last ditch effort, she tried again. "We need to talk about this further, Steven . . ."

"No, we don't have anything to talk about. This conversation is over so just get used to it. I'm the man around here, not you," he yelled at her. "You have nothing, a lousy-paying job, a three-room apartment. I treat you better than any man has ever treated you. And this place is the best you've been in. But it's not yours. What gives you the right to tell me what I should do, where I should live?"

He looked so angry, so ugly that Kim hardly knew the man she was talking to. What had happened to the man she was in love with? But she knew the answer, the real Steven was standing in front of her. She just didn't know him before now.

As she stood there, purse in hand, ready to walk out his door forever. Steven pointed his finger so close in her face that it touched her nose. "Live where I put you. It's my money that will pay for it. What the hell do you want from me anyway?"

Kim stared at him in disbelief. For the first time she was afraid of him. If she had any doubts about what the woman had told her at lunch, Steven had just confirmed it. She backed away out of reaching distance and ran out the door.

Kim heard Steven calling after her, heard him say that he was sorry. But, it was too late for them. She would never see him again. No matter how much he called, or how much he pleaded, it was over.

Chapter 14

Thika, April 2001

"What did you tell William to look for? We don't know her name, age or where she lived before we found her?" Coffie asked. "What's taking the man so long?"

"I don't know. I called him just this morning. He says he's waiting on a call from New York and one from Los Angeles on the last missing body. Apparently it's not too easy because all five missing people lived in different states. But, I told him to call again tomorrow if he hears nothing today. I have a feeling that one of them is Orchid."

"But why would you think that, Ahmed? We may not know for a long time to come."

If only that could be true, Ahmed thought. "No, Coffie. I can feel it in my gut. One of the two missing people is Orchid."

Ahmed rubbed the back of his neck. "I've looked in the newspapers to see if anyone of her description was reported as a missing person, but nothing comes up. It's time we find out who this woman is in our house, and in our lives," Ahmed answered. And in my heart, he thought to himself. For weeks she had very little to say to him and his feelings for her grew deep and hot. He still remembered so vividly the way she felt that night, her soft lips against his. He had to know who she was.

"And if we never find out?" Coffie asked.

"Busara will be happy. Orchid is like the daughter she never had. She's getting too attached to her," Ahmed said. But, he was getting too attached to her in more ways than one. Every time he walked in the door, the first face he looked for was Orchid's. Even thinking of her now he could feel the need to be near her and keep her safe and happy. That's what a man is supposed to do with the woman he loves, keep her safe and happy, he thought. He had just realized that she was the woman he loved and it frightened him.

"When are you leaving?" Coffie asked.

"In about two days. I have to look at more cattle while I'm in Nairobi, too. Make sure that Auntie Busara doesn't do too much while I'm away, Coffie. I'll speak to Orchid about her long walks before I go. I want her to stay close to the ranch while I'm away."

"I don't think she'll do that too soon," Coffie replied.

They started discussing business as Orchid approached the library.

She stopped short when she got to the door. "I just wanted to replace this book," she said, and turned around to walk back out again.

"Come in, Orchid," Coffie said. She replaced the book and quietly walked out.

Ahmed and Coffie continued to discuss business and plans for the ranch.

"Another thing, while I'm in Nairobi, I want to transfer money into an account for Chiku. Din says she wants to leave Africa as soon as she is eighteen. If she's leaving and going to a place where she knows no one, I want her to be well educated. Maybe when she finishes college she may even change her mind and stay in Africa where she belongs. But if she doesn't, I want her to be self-efficient, educated so no one can take advantage of her."

"Why would she want to leave home? Is the girl crazy? All her family is here," Coffie asked, as the frown deepened on his forehead.

"She's just too damn independent and hard-headed. And she has too many sisters and brothers to take care of. I think she wants to be able to get out more, meet other girls her age. Besides, television and books about other places make her want to see them. Every time you see the girl a book is in her hand."

"If money is put away for her now, it should pay for her education," Coffie agreed.

"I'll tell Din tomorrow so he won't have to worry. He has enough mouths to feed."

Ahmed looked at the large, round clock on the wall above the leather chair and was surprised that it was already past ten-thirty. "I'm tired. I think I'll go to bed."

"So am I. I was up at four this morning and worked straight through lunch. And now you're talking about buying more cattle. Man, you are going to work us to death," Coffie said, and stood up.

"Yes, its hard work, but its called security, brother." Ahmed slapped Coffie on the shoulder. He didn't want the ranch to deteriorate and lose money like it had when his father was ill. Coming back to run the ranch had robbed him of his youth. But that was the way of life in Africa. Once he and Coffie got married and had children, he wanted all their futures to be secured.

Coffie walked out and Ahmed sat back in his chair. He had never considered remarrying or having children again. Had never thought that he would ever love enough again, but now he wasn't so sure.

The next day Orchid went to see Eno and the newborn baby. Chiku opened the door to let her in.

"I'm glad you came over to visit us, Orchid. Mama hasn't had time to go over and thank you and Auntie Busara." She led Orchid to the sofa. The kids were running all through the house. The two smaller boys, five and six, turned flips as they ran around the small living room.

"Hey, you boys stop the roughhousing. Sit down and read your books," Chiku told them. They stopped and looked at Orchid, just getting used to seeing her come into their house. Their wide eyes and wide smiles made them look so innocent.

"Every year, Ahmed buys them stacks of books so they could read by the time they start school. My mother or father didn't go to school and my mother can't read at all. My father can only sign his name."

"The children are lucky they have you to teach them," Orchid said. She looked around the small living room. There wasn't much in it, just a sofa, chair and small table. The dining room consisted only of a long, wooden table with five handmade chairs lined up on each side. There were long strings of beads of all colors hanging to divide each room.

Chiku heard her mother's voice. "I'll tell her you are here."

When Chiku came back into the living room, she yelled at the children again, threatening to make them take a nap.

"Orchid, Mama says to come in."

Orchid smiled and went into the small bedroom. It was quiet, not at all like two nights before when everyone was running into each other. Orchid peeked at the baby, but he was curled up in bed and sound asleep.

"That's all they do when they're newborns," Eno said. "But I guess you wouldn't know that. Thank you for all you did to help me. It was a very painful and hard delivery. The doctor came the next day, and said this would be the last child I will be able to give birth to. I know women with ten children. I had six and can't have any more," she said sadly.

Orchid was amazed that she actually looked sad about it. After that last birth one would think she would never want to get pregnant again.

"I didn't think both me and the baby would live."

"I wasn't too sure either, Eno. I don't know anything about giving birth, or I don't remember." That night, Orchid had wondered if she had any children of her own, and if so, how long would she be away from them before she remembers. Still, having kids was something she couldn't imagine. Something inside made her feel certain that she didn't have any. She had no motherly instincts. No, she was sure that she had no children of her own.

"I told all the women how brave you were, Orchid," Eno said, her nappy hair falling down her dark, gaunt face.

She was lying across the bed, but she still looked

weak and tired to Orchid. And Orchid was sure that having another baby would kill her.

"I only did what Miss Busara told me to. But, I'm just glad you are all right. Please send for me if I can be of any help," Orchid said with concern. She had so much to do with her children still being young. Orchid was afraid that it would take Eno longer to recover after such a hard delivery.

The baby started to wail and Orchid touched his small face. "Oh please, can I hold him?"

"Yes. Just hold one hand in back of his head," Eno said, and sat up in bed.

Orchid picked the baby up gently and kissed him on his forehead. He was so small and so innocent, she thought. But when the baby started opening his mouth and turned to place it on her breast, she quickly gave him back to his mother. "I think he's hungry."

Eno laughed out loud and popped out one of her large, dark breasts without any embarrassment. The baby began sucking greedily, and Orchid knew he would be fine.

"Well, I guess I better get back. It's about time I start dinner." Orchid took one last look at the baby and left.

Back at the house, Orchid cooked dinner, read a book, and went to Busara's room to keep her company. She went back to the library early before Ahmed and Coffie went there to conclude some business before Ahmed leaves tomorrow. Maybe after he gets back they could talk and the tension between them could come to an end. She now realized that he didn't want her. But she wanted things as they were before he came to her that night.

It was late and Orchid had fallen asleep with the

book lying open on her chest. She didn't hear the soft knock on the door.

Ahmed quietly stepped into Orchid's room, closing the door behind him. He didn't want to awaken Coffie or Busara. He sat on the edge of the bed watching her sleeping. The lamp by her bed was still on. Ahmed just sat there and watched her. This would be a moment he would never forget. Her hair was curly, framing her face. She was wearing a pink flowered nightgown that he had bought for Busara a year ago. Orchid's lips were turned up in both corners as though she was smiling.

Orchid's thick lashes fluttered and her eyes opened, startled at first. "Ahmed, what are you doing here?" she whispered and looked at the door to see if he was alone.

"I had to speak to you. I'll be leaving early in the morning."

"And?" she asked.

"And I'm sorry if I hurt . . ." He cleared his throat. "If I hurt your feelings, Orchid." He was so close to her and felt stupid for stumbling over his words like a lovesick fool. But it was hard being in her room, just the two of them, alone, together.

"It's all right, Ahmed. What happened that night wasn't all your doing. I had a hand in it, too." She looked at his mouth, his eyes and nose. How could a man be so good-looking? The light against his hair made it look blacker, if that was possible. He made her blood run hot and her brain go into every direction except the right way. She sat up in bed with her knees bent and her elbows resting on each knee.

Orchid didn't know what had come over her, but as she talked she ran her fingers slowly through his hair letting it fall slowly through her fingers like she had wanted to do so many times before.

Ahmed's eyes dropped to her lips and stayed there for a moment. He wanted to get up and leave her room, but he couldn't. "Oh hell, I can't do this," he whispered.

A man had to be strong, stay in control and know right from wrong, but a man had urges, too. And if he loved a woman he wanted her. And Ahmed had tasted Orchid's lips, had touched her body and it wasn't enough, but just enough to drive him crazy when he was this close to her. He loved and wanted Orchid. "I can't do this," he repeated again, in his head and to her.

He held her face close to his, kissed her ever so gently, and as he realized what he had done, this time he couldn't stop, didn't want to stop. He wanted this woman and kissed her hungrily, her eyes, lips and down her neck. Her brown breast looked like a beautiful rosebud, ripe, ready to be touched and he couldn't stop kissing it. Ahmed stood up and Orchid jumped, looking hurt again. But he only stood up long enough to remove his jeans, his shirt and in the next moment he was in bed beside her.

Desire went through her body like electricity. The warmth and excitement she felt in the pit of her stomach made her moan and she nuzzled closer against him, feeling his warm, muscled nakedness against her own. His passion was taking her higher with a need she had never felt before, or remembered. Her body screamed for more of him. He held the middle of her back. Feeling his hand, she realized that the gown had been removed, but didn't remember when he removed it.

"Oh, Ahmed," she whispered close to his ear,

molding her body to his. Her heartbeat became rapid as she watched his eyes drift down her body, feeling his hands slide down her thighs. She moaned and jerked until she was under him, feeling the weight of his body on top of her.

As he entered her, her body felt like a beautiful flower floating in a warm summer breeze. Her legs were wrapped around him, bringing him deeper, deeper inside her. And she knew that she belonged to him.

Ahmed had wanted her too long and as he entered her, feeling her warm, moist body wrapped around his he knew his life would never be the same without her. He kissed her, bit her bottom lip, his body stiffened, then jerked but he stayed inside and felt her tighten around him to keep him there until all the energy had drained from him.

She lay in his arms and slept. At four in the morning, he kissed her again and left her room.

Ahmed was up early and ready to leave. This time it was different. He kissed Busara on her forehead. Orchid was in the library because she didn't want to see him leave. Ahmed stepped inside the library and kissed her lightly on her lips. "Take care of yourself while I'm away," he whispered into her ear. Their eyes locked and she wanted to cry before he turned and walked out.

Unable to speak, all she could do was nod her head.

Orchid hated to see him leave and couldn't wait for his return. Every time she thought of him, she inadvertently touched her lips where he had kissed her.

Later that day, she walked outside to the patio where Busara was sitting down looking at a magazine.

Busara looked up at Orchid, closed the magazine

and placed it in her lap. Things were taking place as she wished. The night before she got out of bed to get a glass of water and heard Ahmed in Orchid's room. The sound of their lovemaking was so intense that Busara smiled all the way to the kitchen. They were in love and Orchid would one day be his wife. But the phone call from William worried her. It appears that Orchid already has a husband. But after Busara told William to get a private detective to follow Steven around she was convinced that their marriage was over. In time, she would tell William to tell Ahmed that he'd finally found out who Orchid really was. By then, their feelings for each other would be so deep and strong they would only want each other. The God Almighty had a way of working things out for the best. It's best that Orchid and Ahmed be married and done with it.

"Why the sad face, my sweet child?"

"Oh nothing, Miss Busara. I was just thinking of Eno and the baby," Orchid answered.

"But, why are you worrying about them? They are all right. Eno has had enough babies. Three she lost at birth."

Orchid looked surprised. "You mean she would have had more?"

"Yes. That's the way life is here for some of the women, Orchid. Now don't worry about Eno and her baby. They're both all right."

"I guess you are right, Miss Busara. I was just wondering would I ever experience such happiness with anyone. What if I can't have any children at all?"

"It's foolish to worry about 'what ifs.' What if you could have ten children? You don't know yet, so don't worry about it, girl. You will make yourself sick."

Orchid took a seat next to Busara. "You're so wise and so much like family to me, to everyone on this ranch." She heard a small child cry, the little girl's mother picked her up and carried her inside. Such a beautiful child, she thought. Lately, she had began to think of having children.

"They are all like family to me, too. In some ways I feel responsible for them. I've delivered their babies, mixed my herbs to heal them when they were ill, taught them to plant vegetables, and helped prepare the dead for burial. When you are here longer, you will feel the same," Busara was saying. She got up and pulled up a dead plant from her garden.

But Orchid couldn't get too attached. She didn't want to feel too close to the people that she might not ever see again after she left. All of a sudden she felt downhearted knowing that one day she would have to leave. Lord, don't take me away from Ahmed, the man I love and adore. Orchid looked up at the blue sky and closed her eyes.

Her gown was wet, clinging to her body as she sat up and screeched in the corner of her bed. The dreams had become more frequent and violent, and this time Ahmed wasn't there to comfort her, hold her in his arms, and assure her that she was safe.

What did the dreams mean? This time she was only inches from the ground before she awakened. Orchid pushed her hair from her face and got out of bed and walked to the window. In the first dream, she had slipped off a high mountain and began to fall, but awakened just as she started to hit the ground. In every dream she had fallen closer to the ground before she awakened. But tonight, she was almost there, only an inch from the bottom. She was so close to the ground that she could actually touch it with her hand.

Orchid closed her eyes, trying to remember more. It was raining and she was completely wet from head to toe. The thunder was so loud, she thought the ground would open up and she would fall in.

Orchid walked around her room, afraid that she would fall back to sleep too soon.

From a distance, she heard a dog bark, a hawk scream overhead, and the sounds of wild animals. Orchid was warm and changed into a thinner gown, sat in the middle of her bed with her knees up and her elbows resting on her knees. She was so lonely, Lord, so very lonely and afraid.

An hour had passed, so she decided to lay down and slide back under the covers. When she woke up again, it was morning. But, she had to wait another night before Ahmed got home.

The next day after lunch, Orchid was still depressed over the horrible dreams she'd been having lately and last night was the worst. She was convinced there was a meaning to the dreams. Maybe she was going to die. There had to be a reason why she was continuously having dreams that she was so close to death.

She decided to go out for a while and get some fresh air. Ahmed was on his way home by now.

"Orchid, where are you going? Wait for me," Chiku yelled. "My sisters and brothers are down for a nap. I can come for a while before Mama needs me again."

"I'm glad to see you today, Chiku." She knew that Chiku would change the melancholy mood she was in. "Come on. I was just taking a short walk." She noticed that Chiku had gotten taller and thinner since she first met her.

"It looks like a rainstorm may sweep this way by night."

Orchid whipped around fast looking up at the sky. She was looking for a sign and saw no change. "How do you know a storm may come?" she asked Chiku.

"Look over there. The clouds are darker, and I can feel it in the air, and by the way the animals are reacting to it. It could hold over until late tonight or tomorrow morning, but one is on the way.

Orchid looked up again and this time she thought she felt a chill in the air.

Last night was warm, the sky was lucid, and today a storm was threatening to erupt. They stopped for a while. To Orchid, for some reason that she couldn't explain, the clouds began to look scary, angry. She couldn't understand why she felt so cold and shaken all of a sudden as if she knew something bad would happen.

She rubbed the back of her neck. Just jumpy she supposed because of that terrible dream, she told herself. As she walked and talked with Chiku, she looked at the view ahead of her. Africa was beautiful, wild, exotic, and sometimes dangerously exciting.

"We shouldn't go too far. The last time I went walking alone, I sat under a tree and fell asleep. Ahmed was furious with me," she said, remembering the way he held her close and stared deep into her eyes. Orchid folded her arms, feeling a light breeze blow across her face.

"Do you believe in love, Orchid?"

Looking at Chiku, Orchid laughed out loud. "Are you in love with someone? Come on, tell me, Chiku." Orchid stopped and looked up at Chiku. Chiku was taller than she was.

Chiku picked a flower and started to pull the petals apart, leaving a trail as they walked. "It's this one boy in my class that's kind of cute, if you know what I mean. But I'm going to college. I don't want some boy playing with my head, not to mention my body," she laughed.

"You have a good head on you. Keep thinking like that. Now, I can see the clouds are getting darker and it does look like a storm is coming soon."

"Yes, it does. Anyway, next year Ahmed is sending me away to college. He says since I want to leave home he wants me to go to school. No more babysitting, no more being bossed around. I'm so happy, Orchid. And we better get back."

On their way back, Chiku pointed out the different birds that were flying over their heads. At a distance, she saw a lion and pointed it out to Orchid.

"Oh God, will he eat us?" Orchid asked. She started to walk faster and stopped, looked around. "I'm lost," she said, with a worried look as she looked at Chiku for help.

"Don't worry. I know the way back. I guess we should take the short cut home."

They started to walk home, fast.

"Wait! Be quiet." They stopped in their tracks. "Do you hear something?" Chiku asked. She grabbed Orchid's hand to stop her from walking.

Orchid stopped, listening and instinctively moved closer to Chiku. They could hear voices that weren't familiar.

"Don't shoot any animals unless I say so. I don't

wanna hit anyone out here. And I don't want anyone to know we're out here," the strange male voice yelled out.

"But, what if we're caught?" a different male voice answered. But his voice wasn't as deep. And he sounded afraid, worried.

"If we're caught, then, we'll have to shoot. But only if we have to. We're only here to hunt, and this ranch belongs to Ahmed. I hear he can be dangerous. Crazy African sum-bitch. We don't want anyone telling him we're on his land. But, I don't want to have to shoot anyone, either."

The voices were as loud as if they were getting closer, and Orchid or Chiku didn't recognize any of them. It sounded like there were two or three different voices. What if they're seen, would the men kill them, or rape them, Chiku thought. But she knew the answer. Chiku and Orchid heard two men speak, but how many men were actually out there, two or more, and could they outrun them?

Orchid was trembling and Chiku firmly held her hand.

"Quiet, Orchid," she whispered. "They don't know we're here. There's a cave right up above us. We have to get there. Follow me, but keep quiet." Chiku took her hand.

"But what if they know where the cave is?" Orchid whispered, trying to get the words out of her mouth. Lord, why hadn't she stayed inside today?

"They don't know where it is and they won't find us once we're in there." Chiku heard footsteps and placed one finger against her mouth, signaling Orchid to keep quiet. "Come," she whispered. "We have to get out of here, fast, real fast."

They climbed up a small path with lots of tall grass.

As the path got narrow and wound around tall bushes, it led them down and around a hill. They spotted a lion and Chiku stopped, with a signal for Orchid not to cry out.

"He doesn't see us," Chiku whispered. "We have to keep going."

Orchid couldn't see where she was running and hit her foot hard against a sharp rock, falling to the ground, dust flew up in her face and blood ran down into her shoes. She almost yelled out loud when Chiku placed her hand over her mouth.

"Quiet! Quiet! I know it hurts, but do you want them to hear us?" Chiku hissed through closed teeth, and stood up to see if she saw anyone coming.

"Can you walk? We're almost there."

"I think so, but you'll have to help me up." Tears were rolling down Orchid's face. She felt something crawling down her leg and thought it was a bug. But when she looked down she saw that it was blood from her knee. She hadn't even realized that she had also cut her knee.

Chiku pulled her to her feet but it was too painful for Orchid to put all her weight on her leg. But to save her life, she knew she had to.

"What the hell was that?" one of the men asked. "Didn't you hear something?"

As Orchid and Chiku listened, they realized the voices were closer than before. Orchid closed her eyes tightly, holding her breath, her heart frozen. The pain in her foot was throbbing unbearably and she was afraid her leg would give in.

"I was sure that I heard something," the man repeated.

"That's your imagination running away," his friend answered. His voice sounded angry and impatient.

"Now, come on before anyone comes out here and sees us."

Orchid was sure they would be shot if the two men saw them. She tried to move as fast and as quietly as she could. Breathing hard to keep air in her lungs, she stopped, but only for a few seconds.

"We have to keep going, Orchid."

"I know, I know," she managed.

"George should be meeting us with the truck by now."

Orchid and Chiku looked at each other. Oh God, there's more, Orchid thought. She felt sweat rolling down her back and her legs were going weak under her. Orchid held Chiku's hand tighter.

As though Chiku could read Orchid's mind, she pulled Orchid's arm and began running faster, leading her down the rest of the path. They ducked lower into the bushes so they wouldn't be seen. Chiku picked up a fallen tree branch, swept it over the ground where there was dirt to cover their footsteps. She did not want the men to see their tracks and follow them. They had to believe that they were out there, alone.

"There, over there," Chiku pointed.

"I'm in so much pain, Chiku," Orchid said falling to the ground, taking deep breaths, her heart pounding hard against her chest. She looked at Chiku and the girl didn't even look like she'd been running, she didn't seem to be nervous or afraid, just brave and determined.

"I know, but if we want to live, we have no choice. We have to move faster, Orchid." They ran a few feet and Chiku pulled more tall bushes apart so no one could see the cave ahead of them. "There, crawl in there," she said, pointing to a small pile of dry bushes.

As Orchid got down on her knees the pain was unbearable. She crawled into a tight hole. Her hair was falling in her face. Her dress was dirty, bloody, and had torn in the front. The pain in her foot was beginning to penetrate up her leg.

It had gotten cold, damp, and dark inside the cave, but after Chiku crawled in behind her and covered the hole so no one could see, she felt as though she could breathe again.

They crawled another two feet and listened for voices. Orchid held her breath when they heard footsteps and voices right outside the cave.

"We got here in the nick of time. They won't find us here. I covered the hole and made sure we didn't leave a trail," Chiku said, motioning for Orchid to follow her deeper into the cave. Orchid looked around with a deep frown on her forehead, her face twisted with pain. "How much farther will we have to go? I don't think that I can go any farther," she said feeling waves of nausea. She tried to see deeper into the cave that was carved out of the rock-filled earth. But it was too dark.

"We're here now, Orchid. This is the cave and we are safe now." They were sitting against the wall. After coming in from the light their eyes still hadn't adjusted to the darkness.

"But, it's so cold in here, so damp and dark," Orchid said, pulling her lightweight sweater tighter against her body. "Lord, the pain in my foot is excruciating. I can hardly move it." She wanted to cry so badly. But she couldn't in front of Chiku. If there was one thing she had learned the last few months, was that the African women were very strong. Even delivering the baby, Eno never cried.

"I know it's dark and cold. But I can't let any light in here until I'm sure we are safe. And even then we have to keep it covered so no wild animal can see it. As for being cold, all we can do for now is sit close together. At least we're alive, Orchid."

"Yes we are. That's something we have to be thankful for. But, do you really think they won't find us? Are we really safe in this godforsaken place?" Orchid asked, rocking backwards and forwards in the corner.

"Yes, and that's the good news. The bad news is if the storm comes, or if it gets too cold and dark outside, it will be hard for anyone to find us. I did a pretty good job with covering our tracks and no one knows about this place except my brother. It's been ages since he and I have been up here in this old cave."

Orchid sunk against the dirt wall and closed her eyes. No light, no food and no warmth. And the pain in her foot was getting worse. She tried to move it but couldn't. If only she could stretch her legs, but she couldn't move them. Her back felt as though it was broken, her knee was bleeding and her foot had swollen too much to keep her foot in her shoe. And now, she thought, Chiku says we may be in here till morning, Orchid wiped a falling tear from her eye. She sighed. Ahmed would be home soon.

She wished she was there to welcome him.

"Auntie Busara, has Chiku been here today?" Coffie yelled, walking from the living room into the kitchen.

"No, I haven't seen her. That child can't come out

as much as she used to since Eno had the baby." Busara was walking down the long hall and into the kitchen when Coffie stopped her.

"But, one of the ranch hands says she and Orchid were seen walking together today. Where is Orchid anyway?" He grabbed an apple off the table and took a huge bite out of it.

"She's not in her room," Ahmed answered, walking into the kitchen where Coffie and Busara were standing. "I bought her some clothes and put them on her bed, but she doesn't seem to be anywhere around. I told her before I left not to go far from the house."

"Sometimes she goes for a short walk during this time of day. Since the last time you had to go and look for her, she doesn't stay out this long," Busara said, wearing a worried look. She filled her cup with hot water, dropped a teabag in it and sat it on the table.

"She is always here before it gets this late to start dinner. This doesn't sound too good to me, Ahmed. And she and Chiku were together today. I saw them walking from my bedroom window," Busara said.

"Eno can't find Chiku either and she's getting worried. I'm going to round the men up," Ahmed said, as he was leaving the kitchen. He had a bad feeling in his stomach about the two women missing together. If Orchid was alone, he would think that she was lost, but that wouldn't be the case when Chiku was with her. Chiku could find her way home in the dark around the ranch. If they're together, something is very wrong, Ahmed thought.

"Wait a minute, Ahmed. Give them another half-hour. It's really not that late, you know," Coffie suggested. "They could be here any minute. Let's not get too excited about this. You're such an inveterate worrier, man."

But as Ahmed looked at Coffie's face, he looked just as concerned.

"Okay, a half-hour, no more." Ahmed strolled into the library, but once he got there, he paced the floor looking at his watch every minute.

Ahmed's trip to Nairobi was remunerative, but there was no news as to who Orchid was or where she came from. He sat at his desk and tried to read the newspaper, but he couldn't concentrate. It wasn't supposed to be this way. She was supposed to run and jump into his arms, see her new clothes, kiss him and later that night he would look forward to seeing her walking out of her room, her long, curling hair falling into her face and looking beautiful, dressed in her new clothes as she walked in front of him for his approval. He smiled to himself as he imagined her pushing her hair from her face.

Busara was worried, but as she peeked into the library and looked at Ahmed she knew that he was just as worried as she was. She knew that they were in love. She had seen the passion in Ahmed eyes when he sat at the dinner table across from Orchid, and Orchid's face would glow with excitement. Funny, she thought. She knew they were in love before they did. I may be old, she thought, but I know the look of desire in young eyes. And she knew that sometimes help was needed to help them make a decision.

Ahmed went out the door and came back inside. "It's getting cold and late. Get the men, Coffie. Din agrees. He's also worried about Chiku,"

Orchid frowned in pain as the rocks that were scattered across the floor of the cave pressed against her back. "Oh God, it hurts. I can't stand this awful pain."

She tried to find a comfortable position to settle her leg, but couldn't. Chiku had made her take off her sweater so she could fold it to elevate her leg, but the colder it got, the pain worsened.

The ground was cold. After Chiku looked outside and saw that the men were nowhere in sight, she pushed some of the bushes aside, just enough to let some light in but the cold weather was seeking inside the cave as well.

Orchid jumped and screamed. "What was that? Did you hear it?" She grabbed Chiku's hand, holding on to it tightly. The move caused the pain to shoot from her ankle to her knee. She shivered, lost her balance and fell over Chiku's lap.

"Calm down, Orchid. It's only the wind or a wild animal running around. No one knows we're here."

"What time do you think it is?" Orchid murmured. "Are they looking for us, now? They have to know something is wrong by now." God, she wanted to cry and she was so tired. It felt as though the cold air was making her bones ache. She had skipped lunch and hadn't eaten anything since breakfast.

"Yes, I'm sure they're looking for us by now. I think it's safe enough for me to go out. I can get help." Chiku started to get up but Orchid grabbed her arm.

"No. No. Don't leave me alone, Chiku. No matter how much it hurts me, you are not going out there alone. It's too late and too cold. What if you run into those terrible men and get caught? And some animals can see in the dark, too." She sound nervous, her voice started to quaver as she talked.

"I won't run into them. Besides, they're off the ranch by now. Don't be afraid, Orchid," she said softly, holding Orchid's hand.

"No. We stay here together. It's just too cold and

dark out there. A storm could start up before you get help. Tomorrow morning, we can go together," Orchid said and groaned out loud between words. Just the thought of staying overnight frightened her. She tried to rub her foot but it was too tender to be touched.

"You can't make it, Orchid. Tomorrow I'll have to go and get help."

"I won't let you go alone." She stopped in midsentence. The pain in her foot had ricocheted up her leg, causing her to double over on her side. She couldn't seem to get into a comfortable position to sit or lay down. And it was so cold inside; the draft was causing her to quiver while worry ate at her nerves.

Chiku got up and peeked out the cave to see if the storm seemed any closer or if it had passed.

"Chiku, where are you going?" She was panicky and screamed out loud. Chiku ran back to her.

"Try and calm down, Orchid." Chiku got down on her knees beside Orchid. "What can I do to help you? Here, lay your head in my lap so you can get comfortable." She knew Orchid was in pain and she wasn't accustoming to their way of living. She was small, fragile and wasn't used to living out in nature.

Chiku held her tight to keep her warm. Orchid's forehead felt warm and Chiku could feel her body squirming every time she felt the pain. But there was nothing either one of them could do, but try to get some sleep, wait, and pray.

"Spread out, but not too far apart," Ahmed ordered. Ahmed, Coffie, Din, and Dume were on horseback running down a dark, dirt road with flashlights in their hands. They were wearing their heavy coats in anticipation of bad weather—clouds were darkening and threatening to burst into rain, the storm was getting closer. Ahmed was in the lead riding ahead of them.

Coffie had two of the men come in the jeep, so the women could ride back. No one knew what condition they would be in once they were found. Five men were on foot looking for tracks, but none were found.

As Ahmed's horse broke into a fast gallop, sand kicking up in the air behind him, the others followed. He rode hard and fast into the high bushes, almost like a forest, oblivious to the scraping both he and his horse suffered from low hanging branches. Having reached the top of a small rise, he reined his now snorting animal to a halt. He was alert, listening, looking for clues, a trail, a footprint, anything that would lead him to the women. His eyes were sharp, and had gotten used to the darkness.

Frustrated, Ahmed zigzagged through paths as he began lashing out to cut tall branches that blocked his view. If he never saw Orchid again and never got the chance to tell her how he felt about her—no, he wouldn't think that way. But if anyone harms her, he will kill them with his bare hands. His thoughts went back to poor Chiku; he wanted her to go away to college. She's so young, so inexperienced and needs to be educated before she goes out into the world. He wanted that for her.

With his rifle by his side, he rode furiously against the wind. His wind-blown hair, his angry eyes and his blue shirt opened revealing his wide, hairy chest made him look like a knight riding into battle.

Trying to imagine where his daughter was, Din grew more anxious as the hours passed. Din loved all his children, but Chiku was his heart, his first daughter. She could hunt, shoot, and run as fast as any boy her age. He had taught her when she was a small girl. So, why couldn't he find his own daughter? Din kept asking himself.

Dume tried to remember all the places that he and Chiku had gone when they were children. They had run up and down this same path so many times together, the road that led them here, but so much had changed, a new trail here and there. He just couldn't remember every trail anymore. And if they went home without her, his mother would surely die. As children, Dume had always protected his sister. God, he prayed, that he would get that chance again.

"Stop!" Ahmed squared his hands around his mouth and yelled so every man could hear. "Everyone come back here," he said as he jumped from his horse with his rifle in his hand.

"We'll go back to that small river, half way back to the ranch and start over. Maybe we've missed something."

"No," Din yelled in response. "That's a waste of time, man. We can't afford to waste any more time. Look up at the sky above you. It looks like a bad storm is coming our way." His voice was loud, overcome with fear. And it had gotten darker and colder. The clouds were moving in fast, lurking dangerously over their head.

"No, Papa. Ahmed is right," Dume suggested. "We're riding in circles and haven't found anything yet. I think we should go back. It's not that far. We rode off so fast, maybe we missed a trail or a clue that could lead us to them. We may find something the second time around."

Din looked at his son. He was now a man, tall, dark

as the middle of the night, quiet, but always knew what he was talking about. And Din knew Dume wanted to find his sister just as much as he wanted to find his daughter.

"Agreed?" Ahmed asked.

"Yes," the men answered. And Din nodded in agreement.

"We go back," Ahmed bellowed as he jumped on his horse, taking off fast without waiting for any other responses.

It was well past midnight when Orchid finally fell asleep. Chiku had found some dry grass and used it as a cushion under her head, and wrapped Orchid's sweater around her foot for warmth. She did all she could to help make Orchid comfortable.

Chiku sat in the corner, her head lying back against the dirt wall as she watched Orchid. Even as she slept, her face was twisted with pain. Dirt was on one side of Orchid's face, her yellow dress was dirty, and Chiku had torn the bottom off it for bandages. There wasn't anything else they could do tonight but try to sleep. If they were lucky, they wouldn't awaken before daylight.

And it had gotten so cold that Chiku's bones had started to ache and she was hungry. What she hadn't told Orchid, was that the only hope of being found was for Dume to remember the cave. It had been years since they had played here together. The trees and tall grass kept the cave out of sight and Chiku was worried because so much had changed. She was afraid he might have forgotten. But, she knew her brother would never stop looking until he found her. Besides, Ahmed, would never stop looking until he

found Orchid. Chiku closed her eyes falling into a
deep sleep.

As Ahmed rode in front, he stopped and turned
around in his saddle, holding his hand up for the
others to stop. He patted his horse on the back of the
neck. Something had spooked him. "Did you hear
that, Coffie?"

"No. Hear what, man?" he asked.

Ahmed jumped off his horse. Using his flashlight
he looked around to see if there was anything there.
It was the same lion that Chiku and Orchid had seen
earlier. As he leapt at Ahmed, Ahmed shot him right
between his eyes. The lion slowly crumpled to the
ground as he gave Ahmed one last look. Ahmed
picked up his flashlight and jumped back on his
horse.

"That was close," Coffie said. "I think it's the same
one I saw near the ranch. I should have shot him
when I saw him walking around the ranch yesterday."

Ahmed signaled for the men to continue looking
for Orchid and Chiku. He thought he heard a noise
and stopped, sat in his saddle and looked up as he
heard the hoot of an owl, a branch moving, and a
large black cat with eyes sparkling like green marbles
shot out of their way. Ahmed turned back in his
saddle and signalled for the men to continue.

They had gone a few feet when Dume stopped
and looked around as though he'd heard something, too.

"Wait, Ahmed," Din said, looking at his son as he
stopped his horse, sitting still in his saddle.

Ahmed and Coffie stopped. "What is it, man, do
you hear something?"

"No," Dume said. "But, when Chiku and I were growing up, we used to play in a cave along this path, but now it looks so different. If she and Orchid would have had to hide for safety, Chiku would have gone into the cave." He looked at his father. "No one knows about it but us."

"Are you telling me you can't remember?" Ahmed asked, feeling more frustration. He had some hope building inside, now the fool says he can't remember? "What's wrong with you, man? Think hard, damn you! Think hard."

"Wait, Ahmed, give him time," Coffie protested and held one hand up to silence his brother and spotted the torn sleeve on his shirt. He figured he must have torn it on one of the trees they had passed. "We're all upset right now."

Ahmed threw his hands up in the air and sighed. "Now Dume, try to remember where the damn cave was, man! One of them could be hurt, we have no time to lose."

Din jumped off his horse. "Leave the boy alone. He has a good head. He'll remember." He looked at his son with hope.

Dume looked east, then west. He turned his back to them.

"Over there. Wait! Everything changed since the last time we were here." Dume walked another four feet and saw a flame tree that they used to pass on the way to the cave. "That's it," he said. "That's the same tree. I'm sure of it," he beamed.

"Tree? Tree?" Ahmed rushed by his side. "What does a tree have to do with anything? Where's the cave? Dume?" Ahmed shook his head impatiently and waited for Dume to answer.

"We used to pass that tree going to the cave."

Dume threw his hands up in the air and whooped out loud. "I remember now. It's down the hill and up again. When the path gets narrower, we'll find the cave at the end." He started to run up the path and everyone followed, rushing, hoping he was right.

Coming out of a deep sleep, Orchid opened her eyes. She had almost forgotten where she was until she tried to move her right leg and the pain from her ankle pricked her memories. It took all the strength she had just to sit up straight without awakening Chiku. She looked around, but saw nothing. She knew it was her imagination but she had a feeling that someone was watching them. As she lay her head back against the dirt wall, she blinked, her eyes opened wide. Was something moving toward her? She could barely see it at first. Oh, God, she thought, whatever it was, it was long, ugly and moving fast.

A long, thin tongue flickered in rapid motions in and out of its mouth, slowly turning up at the tip, its eyes were shining, small, mean, and were looking at her. Orchid managed to keep her entire body from shaking or moving suddenly. She tried to think fast, but couldn't seem to get her brain to adjust to what she was seeing. With fear paralyzing her, she was so shocked and afraid, she felt dizzy enough to pass out. The anticipation of what would happen next caused a wave of nausea to swim inside her stomach, and she held her breath to keep from retching.

The snake came closer, slithering fast on its stomach, its long green and black spotted body shining in the dark as though it was wet. As its flat eyes switched from Orchid to Chiku, it kept coming in Orchid's direction.

The perspiration was rolling down her forehead and into her eyes, blinding her. The underarms of her dress were moist and warm. Orchid could feel the sweat rolling down her sides and back, but she didn't move. She couldn't speak, and got dizzier from the fast motion of the snake. She couldn't call Chiku's name because the snake might change its course and turn to Chiku. But once he finished with her, he might harm Chiku anyway. There was no way she could save Chiku if she couldn't wake her up. Oh God, what should she do? Should she scream, cry out? What? What should she do, she wondered as the snake came closer, so close she couldn't breathe.

Finally, Orchid opened her mouth, but no words emerged. She looked at Chiku's face as she slowly stirred and opened her eyes.

Chiku looked up at Orchid. Her back was straight, up against the wall like a stiff piece of board. She was crying so softly that Chiku could barely hear her.

Orchid's eyes were glistering with tears, her mouth dry, and her hands were flat on the ground on either side of her, holding her for support. Chiku was mystified; the expression on her face had changed from confusion to fear. She wondered what had happened while she was asleep. Moving closer to Orchid, Chiku followed her eyes down to the ground and saw the snake moving close, fast in Orchid's direction.

"Nyoka," she whispered to herself and moved aside slowly, her hands over her mouth. She looked around with wide eyes. There wasn't anything to kill it with and no one that could help save Orchid's life.

The snake was so close Orchid could smell it and without a doubt, she knew she would die. Her vision began to blur as the cave started to spin. She was certain she would faint, and held her breath praying she wouldn't vomit. The cramps in her stomach were hitting hard and for a moment she thought her heart had stopped, but she still didn't move or cry out. Her body was frozen and paralyzed with fear.

Chiku could no longer sit still. She had to do som thing, anything. Suddenly she screamed, not recognizing her own voice. The snake changed its direction. Its head went up and it seemed as though the head turned around in a circle, the small eyes shifting, its body seemed to get longer and thicker as it got closer.

The mouth opened, releasing a hollow noise that caused Chiku to jump and yell out. She knew she wouldn't live much longer.

Chiku and Orchid's eyes met and held as though they were seeing each other for the last time and silently saying their "good-byes."

The snake's head moved so fast Chiku didn't realize it was on her until she felt the cold body moving over hers, prickling every nerve in her body. As the snake opened its mouth again, its top lip skimmed over and up, two long, sharp teeth on each side snapped deeply into her arm causing her to crumble flat on the ground. A hot pain moved through her body, she felt the heat rising from her toes to her head, causing her to shiver into a ball with her knees curled up under her.

Orchid saw shadows moving in slow motion as the snake's body was snatched off Chiku's body. Another shadow was pulling her up from the ground, yelling out her name, but the voices seemed so far away she wasn't at all sure that what she saw and heard was really happening.

Orchid screamed out loud as she heard the explosion from the gun ricocheting off the cave wall, making the ground shake in a cloud of dust flying in the air. There was another shot, and a third one. The snake's body jumped off the ground, pieces flew up and fell separately on the ground, and the head rolled in the dirt between Orchid and Chiku. The eyes were still open, the tongue had fallen out.

No one was prepared for what they saw when they entered the cave. Orchid was crawling around in a circle as though she didn't know where she was. Her screams sounded as though they were coming from a wounded animal.

When Ahmed grabbed her, she didn't recognize him. She was fighting, flinging her arms wildly, screaming, and kicking. Dirt was in her hair, her face, and her clothes were dirty, torn and spotted with blood, and she was wearing only one shoe.

Finally, Ahmed had to slap her across her face before she stopped yelling and opened her eyes to focus on what was going on around her. She looked wild, as frightened as a child. Ahmed wasn't sure if she recognized any of them. Every time she looked at the snake, she screamed and shook her head back and forward, placing her hands hard against her ears to close out the echo of the loud gun shots that she had heard only minutes ago. Her ears still ached and the ringing was loud and stinging. The scheme played in her head over and over again, the snake shot up into the air, the tongue falling out, pieces of snake near her on the ground. She cried and cringed against Ahmed, calling out Chiku's name. She buried her head into Ahmed's chest and tried to blink the horrible experience out of her head. But so clearly it was still there, in front of her, around her, buried in her memories.

Dume and Din worked vigorously and fast on Chiku's snakebite. "Cut her arm while I hold her down, Papa. Here, tie the string tight where the blood is sinking through. Tight so it doesn't flow through her body," Dume ordered loudly, wiping the moisture off his forehead with the back of his hand. They were working furiously and fast. Chiku was lying on her back; her eyes rolled up in her head leaving only the whites to be seen. Her fists were balled up by her sides; her legs shook hard as though she had no control over them. The chills caused her to tremble uncontrollably and she emptied her stomach in Dume's lap as he held her while his father tied her arm with a piece of cloth from Orchid's dress. She started to vomit more and Dume turned her face with his free hand.

"You men bring the jeep as close as possible. We have to rush her to the hospital." Coffie ordered the four men that stood and watched, praying that Chiku would live.

Ahmed had calmed Orchid down and kept her in the corner of the cave watching the men as they carried Chiku to the jeep.

Orchid looked down at her leg as though she couldn't move; the pain in her foot felt as though it had made its way all through her body. She held her hands out to Ahmed to help her up off the cold damp ground.

The small hole of the cave was no longer covered and the sun was shining through, giving enough light so they could see what they were doing.

When Ahmed picked her up from the ground to carry her outside to the jeep, she twisted and turned to get her ankle in a comfortable position. He sat her in the back seat of the jeep and placed her leg across it.

As one of the men started to drive the jeep, Orchid

looked back at the cave. She and Chiku had been in there for hours, in the dark, the cold. She would never go near another cave again.

But the cave had kept them alive.

Chapter 15

Los Angeles

As she drove to Steven's apartment, Marie felt her hands shake. She was flustered, and felt her stomach knotting. She hadn't seen Steven for much too long as far as she was concerned. She stopped for a red light and looked in the mirror one last time. The red lipstick looked sexy and smooth over her full lips. Looking into the mirror, her skin was glowing and she felt better since she had stopped drinking and taken charge of her life again. This time, she would continue to attend her AA meetings. She just felt better about herself these days.

As she got closer to his apartment she wondered if he had even thought of her since they had last seen each other. God, he took his own time in calling her. She was certain after the last time she saw him that he would have called her sooner but he hadn't called her at all.

Marie tried to remember word for word of their conversation when she called him. He was surprised to hear from her, she knew, but he sounded happy.

Marie got out of her car, smoothed her dress down while ringing the bell so he could let her in.

When she got to his apartment the door was opened and she stepped inside. All of a sudden she didn't know what to say and seeing him wasn't as easy as she anticipated. Looking into his deep brown eyes, she had to clear her throat before she could speak.

He led her to the sofa. Marie placed her small black purse on her lap. "You bailed me out of jail, Steven, here's your money." Marie placed the five one hundred-dollar bills on the coffee table where she and Steven were sitting. She almost felt sorry for him. He looked tired, his face looked thinner. The coffee table and the dining room had newspapers and dirty ashtrays strewn all over them.

Marie stood up, Steven stood so close to her she could smell the alcohol and cigarettes on his breath. "Are you smoking again, Steven? You haven't had a cigarette in three years."

He had a cigarette in his hand and placed it back on the table. "Wanda didn't want any smoking in the house, so I stopped for her. And yes, I'm smoking again," he said dryly, looking like a child that had just been caught stealing a candy bar.

She saw his eyes drop to her breast and licked his bottom lip in a suggestive manner. She could see the hunger in his eyes, had seen it so many times and so many times she satisfied it. Without saying a word, she always knew when he desired her.

Marie had to force herself not to smile or give in to him. She purposely wore a tight-fitting dress just low enough to reveal the tops of her full breasts and short enough to rise high on her thighs.

But, she had no intentions of sleeping with him tonight. She wouldn't be as easy or weak as he was used to. He had to want her, bad, and enough to make a commitment. And from his present appearance, it shouldn't be too long. When the time came, she would be ready. It was only a matter of time. No Wanda. No Kim. It would just be her. She could wait until Steven came running back to *her*.

Marie started to the door and was delighted to see the disappointment in Steven's face, but not enough to keep her there with him, at least, not the way he wanted to. He was so used to having his way with her. Now, seeing him needing her made her happy and in control for once. He would have to wait just as she had to.

"Why don't you stay a while, baby? We can go out to dinner later and, perhaps you may want to spend the night with me. You know, for old times' sakes."

"No, Steven, I only came to repay you. Like I said, I've tried to call you more than once, but you never returned any of my phone calls."

"I know. I've been pretty busy. It wasn't that I didn't want to talk to you. I've thought of you a thousand times, Marie. It's just that we parted angrily. You were in such a huff the last time we saw each other, you know." He nervously lit another cigarette and closing his eyes, he took a long drag on it.

As Marie watched him she almost reached for his hand but the thought disappeared just as he turned around to face her.

They were still standing close but she kept him at a distance. If she got too close she would fall over into his arms. And if she weakened, she would have to see him on his terms again. To prevent any further anger between them, Marie opened the door, he followed her. Marie gave him a quick kiss on his cheek. "See you later, and take it easy, honey." Determined she would not weaken, she walked out before he could touch her.

Once Marie got outside of his apartment, clutching her purse tight in her hands, she leaned against the wall, closed her eyes feeling the air going down her lungs.

Visiting Steven was much harder than she had anticipated. She wanted so badly to stay with him, love him, and touch him. God, she needed him so badly. Her life was insignificant without him. There were times when she felt as though she had run into a cement wall and was only existing from day to day, waiting for him to come back to her.

Steven wanted her. He really wanted her. She had recognized the spark in his eyes, the way he ran his tongue across his bottom lip. She had seen it so many times. She smiled and happily nodded her head. "You go, girl," she said feeling a gust of triumph and drove off.

As Marie drove, her phone rang. She pulled it out of her purse and answered. When she recognized the voice she frowned with frustration, sighed and rolled her eyes up at the sky.

"Marie, it's Danny. What's going on?"

Marie didn't answer for a couple of seconds. Just holding the phone to her ear, she was trying to decide if she should hang up in the bastard's face or wait to hear what lie he had to tell her.

"Look, I need to talk with you. Can you come over?"

"What is it this time, Danny?" It was her sorry-ass, back-stabbing cousin. When they were young they were very close. But after she was married, Danny and her ex-husband, another sorry-ass man, became friends. Later, Marie caught him and another woman in Danny's house, and in Danny's bed. The closeness in their relationship diminished. He had betrayed her and she and Danny hadn't talked in two-and-a-half years. Now, out of nowhere he's calling. Why now, she wondered?

"I said what do you want, Danny?" she yelled into the receiver.

"Don't be so mean, Marie. I'm leaving Los Angeles. I just wanted to see you before I left."

She held the receiver at her ear and shrugged. What could it hurt to say good bye and good riddance in person? "Okay," she sighed. "I'm not that faraway. I'll see you in twenty minutes."

Twenty minutes later, Marie was walking into Danny's apartment. She looked around; most of his furniture was gone.

"So, you didn't pay your furniture bill, or what? Where is everything?" she asked, walking around in his living room. There was never much of anything to look at in his apartment, but now his living room was half-empty. There wasn't even a sofa to sit on.

"I sold almost everything I have. No use taking old shit to make a new start." He walked over to the kitchen counter and dropped his cigarette in an ashtray filled with cigarette butts.

Marie followed. They sat on the black barstools in the dining room. When they stood again, they could look at each other eye to eye since Marie was just as tall as he.

Danny was wearing a red baseball cap turned backward on his shaved head. He was medium height, brown skinned, and thin.

"Does Aunt Mae know you're going back home?" Marie asked him.

"Yeah. She's happy, too. But, that's not what I wanted to talk to you about."

Marie cocked her head to one side and looked at him. What does he want now, money?

"All right, what is it you really want from me, Danny? I don't have time to be listening to all your small talk." She sat impatiently, waiting for his response. "All right, what is it?" she asked curiously.

Danny held up both hands. "All right, chill, I'm getting to that. You don't go home anymore since your mother died, and I don't have any reason to come back here. I just wanted to say that I'm sorry about the way things happened between us. I was wrong, 'cause you are family."

All of a sudden she felt sad. Danny was the only family she had here and she hated him. Wanda was like family, but falling in love with Steven changed the affinity they once had between them. Maybe not for Wanda but it had for Marie. But seeing Steven, she had to maintain her friendship with Wanda.

"I'm sorry, too, Danny. I just never understood how you could have done that to me, to family. You betrayed me. John wasn't worth it."

"I know. I don't even hear from him anymore. I'm asking for your forgiveness, Marie. I mean, we are bloods, you know. I should have called you after I heard about Wanda's death, but I didn't think you would talk to me. I know you must have taken it hard. Would you please forgive me for everything I've done?" He took a long drink from the bottle of Coors beer he was drinking and waited for her response.

"Maybe one day. But right now, my life hasn't gone in the direction that I had expected," she said, and placed her hands on top of the counter. "Sometimes,

I don't know if I'm coming or going." She sighed, looking around the half empty room. "It's time my life changed into something that can make me happy."

"Is there something I can do?"

"No, Danny. In time it will fall into place. I'm doing all I can to change things."

But as he looked at her face, he wasn't so sure. Marie hadn't been happy since her divorce and that was four years ago. "Hey, look around and see if there's something you can use. Like I said, I'm not taking all of this crap with me."

"Sure. There must be something in here that I can use." She walked from the kitchen, through the living room and wandered into the bedroom. Marie stood in front of the dresser.

"Danny, come in here," she yelled.

Danny stopped at the doorway of his bedroom. "Okay, girl. What have you found?"

"You've been promising me for years that you would take me to buy a gun. What about one of those?" she pointed to the guns on the dresser. "After all, I'm a woman that lives alone. I need some kind of protection. What if someone tries to break in on me?"

"Here, take the .22. It's small and easier to handle. I call it a ladies' gun." He opened the drawer and pulled out a box of bullets.

"Now, don't use it unless you have to, and know what you're doing when you do use it."

"I won't use it unless I have to. And it's only for protection you know. I don't really like having a gun around, but since you are giving it to me, I'll take it."

"That's what I've been telling you for years. Want a

drink?" He got up to get himself another beer out of the refrigerator.

"No thanks, Danny. I'm trying to go easy on the alcohol." And she had tried. She hadn't been drinking since Steven had to bail her out for drunk driving. That was the most humiliating day of her life. And she was trying to clean it up. Maybe one day Steven would forget that day.

Steven stood in front of the mirror to straighten his tie. He had no desire to go to Chuck's birthday party. But he had promised Chuck that he would stop sitting around the apartment alone and would go to his party. After all, Chuck had stood by him after Wanda's death.

Steven took a deep breath, inhaled deeply as he thought of Wanda. Thinking of her still left a lump in his throat. It seemed that nothing had gone right for him since her death.

Chuck's wife had been giving him birthday parties for the last five years, ever since his thirty-fifth birthday. Wanda had gone with him to Chuck's last party.

At the last minute, Steven picked up the phone to call Kim. The conversation they'd last had came to mind, and he hung up. She'd made it clear that she didn't want him. All his hopes and dreams of starting a new life had gone up in smoke. He had wanted Kim so badly and cared enough for her to want to settle down with her into the married life again. He was a man who couldn't live alone. Steven had to have someone to go home to at night, to be there waiting for him with open arms. His life would be entirely different from the one he'd had with Wanda. She was the one who made the most money, had the big car, but she was generous and passionate. With Kim, it was just the opposite. He made more money, and had Wanda's big Lexus. Now, he has to move forward. But as he made an assessment of his life, could it be that maybe he had met Kim too soon after Wanda's death? As he thought of Kim, he realized he was never really in love with her. She was just the ticket to a new life, and with time he could have fallen in love with her. After all, he did like her enough. Since Wanda's death, life had been so unsettled and turned upside down for him. He shook his head, trying to ward off the ache he felt inside, and looked in the mirror one last time, turned out the light and left.

"Steven, we haven't seen you in months. So glad you could come. Chuck had to make a quick run to the store. He'll be glad to see you," Brenda said with a wide smile, leading him inside. "Go to the bar and get yourself a drink."

Steven hugged her, but she had to leave him to see to one of her other guests. He looked at her as she walked away, wearing a long blue dress that hugged every curve on her body. Nice, he thought.

Steven got a glass of wine from the bar. He spoke to some of the guests and scanned the room to see if there was anyone he knew. He spoke to a woman that had passed him going to the bar to get another drink. As she walked away he saw her looking back at him, giving him a warm smile, as though she was saying, "I want to get to know you better."

In the corner was a couple that walked out into the middle of the room and danced to a slow song by Smoky Robinson, but Steven couldn't remember the name of the song. Everyone was dressed nicely, men in suits and the women looking sexy in their long or short dresses. Steven decided to walk around until Chuck got back.

As he walked past the patio with the glass doors, he saw her standing with her back turned to him. Steven couldn't see her face, but he saw her legs, and he knew they belonged to Marie. His first impulse was to turn around, and go home. But, looking at her with her black tight-fitting dress, well above her knees, and her black hose, her hair swept up off her neck, she looked so good to him. She held her head up with so much confidence that he almost thought he had mistaken her for someone else, until he looked at her legs.

Steven saw her holding a glass in her hand. Then she walked to the corner of the patio as if she wanted to be alone. He stepped lightly in back of her, circling his arms around her waist, his hot lips against her neck.

"Guess who's here, baby?" he whispered close to her ear.

"I know it's you, Steven," Marie whispered. He was there alone, which meant he was still alone, with no woman in his life. She felt his hand on her stomach and gently pulled away, trying to fight the excitement that was building deep inside her. But he only got closer. She moaned out loud when his hand roamed passionately against her thigh.

"Steven, someone might see us. It's too soon after Wanda's death for us to be seen like this."

Again, he had to ward off the effect of the mention of Wanda's name. "No one can see us unless they walk out, I will hear anyone walking toward us."

"Now, baby, come home with me. There's nothing going on here, but a dead party. We can have a party at my place, just me and you, Marie."

"No. I thought I had made it clear to you. I'm no one-night stand, Steven. Not for you, not for anyone."

"I know you're not. It's not just for one night, Marie. Baby, we go way back, you know that." It was almost as though he had met her for the first time. Marie had changed and he wasn't sure how to handle her. But, he liked the new Marie. She looked so good to him tonight.

She turned to face him. "Yes, I know we go way back. I knew that when you said that you didn't want me. What's so different now, Steven?" She knew what was so different. He had lost Kim, but she wanted to hear what explanation he would give her.

"I've come to my senses. After Wanda died I didn't know what I wanted. My life was turned upside down. But I don't want to be alone, Marie. I need you to be with me. Maybe I can make it up to you for hurting you the way I did. Come home with me."

He stood behind her again, his hands inside her low cut dress, cupping each breast.

Marie closed her eyes, feeling the touch of his hands. Her body had betrayed her, and the need for him had taken over, again. She needed him so much.

As Brenda walked past the glass door she felt a chill and stopped to close it. Someone had left it open. As she was sliding the door closed, she heard voices outside and saw two shadows. Brenda quietly stepped outside. No one heard her, her mouth opened in shock. It was Steven and Marie. When did that happen, or was it going on when Wanda was alive? Brenda wondered. She had never liked Steven, had never thought he was good enough for Wanda. After tonight, she would tell her husband that she didn't ever want Steven in their house again. And that slut, Marie, was supposed to be Wanda's friend. She was no longer welcome in her house either.

Marie followed Steven in her car to his place. Once they were inside, he kissed her until she was weak and could barely stand on her feet. They went into the bedroom, pulling at each other's clothing. They made love, long and hot, and then made love again, tenderly.

After they made love, for the first time Steven didn't just turn over and fall asleep. They sat up and talked most of the night. She told him that she had been attending her AA meetings, and about her promotion on her job as an editor. She had been trying to get some perspective into her life. They didn't get out of bed until nine the next morning.

Steven went to the bathroom, when he came back into the bedroom, Marie was awake and had started to get dressed.

"Where are you going? It's Sunday, you don't have to work today."

"I don't want to wear my welcome out," she said dryly, already holding her purse in her hand.

He walked in front of her and pulled her dress down from her shoulders, threw her bra and purse on the bed. He kneeled down in front of her, pulling her black bikini panties to her feet and motioned for her to step out of them.

She was quiet as he undressed her with an expertise that she had never experienced before, he was so swift and smooth.

Steven stood up in front of her and looked down

at her body. "Now, where are you going, baby?" he whispered. "You're staying here today, you'll be back tomorrow, the next day, and the day after. Now, come on, let's take a shower together."

Chapter 16

Thika, East Africa, April 2001

Orchid was in the hospital overnight suffering from a broken bone in her foot. Chiku had been lucky, with the knowledge the men had with snakebites; they managed to get her to the hospital before the poison had spread all through her body. Busara had told her that the gods favored her and seemed to be with her. But she had been ill; the vomiting, the headaches, and body pains were insufferable. In the beginning, they weren't sure if she'd live or not.

Orchid was sorry that Chiku had to be left in the hospital. And every time she thought of the cave, the snake, and saw the picture in her head, she had to fight back the panic that she felt all over again.

Busara walked out of Orchid's room and went into the kitchen where Ahmed and Coffie were having lunch. The aroma from the curried chicken floated through the house. Orchid loved the smell of curry that tickled at your nose and mixed with the sweet bread that Busara was baking. But she just wasn't hungry.

A week had passed and Busara, Coffie, and Ahmed were in the dining room having dinner. "She still doesn't eat enough. She's getting too thin, doesn't talk to me as we used to. I don't know what to do about the girl anymore," Busara said, taking a seat at the table opposite Ahmed and Coffie. "Her eyes are red as though she cries all the time."

Puzzled, Ahmed put his fork down and listened to Busara. "It seems as if she had gotten used to our way of life here. I don't understand how getting lost in a cave would affect her so. It's not as though she's a weak woman or was bitten by the snake. She can do anything the other women do, or anything she wants to."

"Maybe she's suffering from depression. If she goes too far, she may not come back," Coffie said, and looked at Busara. To him, Orchid looked worried and tired.

It was dark in her room and that was the way she wanted it. She had gone through so much, had experienced so much pain. Just when she was happy, she found herself sadder than she had ever remembered. And now she has remembered Steven, her family, Marie, everything. The loud gunshots from the rifles were so shocking and frightening that her ears rang. At first, she went deaf and shook her head to clear it, to stop the ringing in her ears and the memories that came floating back, especially the husband that was left behind. She felt an excruciating pain in both temples and pressed her hands hard against her head. When she started to hear again, she thought she heard a crash, flashes of the plane crash started coming back in bits and pieces. First, she saw the faces of people crying, screaming, and praying for help. She even heard their voices over and over again. Then, all of a sudden she was so cold, she felt ill. Chills shook her body.

Orchid shut her eyes tight and cried out loud, remembering how the plane started to go down, falling out of the sky like a bursting cloud. She didn't want to remember any of it and nodded her head as though something were weighing her down, forcing her to remember a life she no longer wanted, but would be forced to go back to.

She was alive as Orchid, but her life as Wanda was dead. She wanted this new life, not the life she had lived. Funny, she didn't even like the name anymore. "Wanda," she whispered. It wasn't her. Africa was home to her now.

How could she tell Ahmed the truth? Why did she have to remember now? "Oh, why, why?" she whispered. Turning over in her bed, she cried and cried until she felt sick.

Orchid got up and dressed. She took the crutches from beside her bed and put them back again. She could walk without them now, and went out to the garden. Air, she needed to feel some fresh air against her face.

"It's good to see you dressed and out of bed. I went to see you late last night, but the pain pills had knocked you out," Ahmed said, standing in back of her.

Orchid jumped with a start. He had frightened her. She didn't hear him walk behind her. She felt his hands on her shoulders and closed her eyes.

Orchid couldn't tell him, but she wasn't asleep.

What could she say to him now, how could she tell him that she has to leave?

Orchid turned to face him and opened her mouth as though she wanted to say something, but instead, she fell into his arms. "I missed you so much, Ahmed. I don't want to ever leave you."

He pulled her arms from around his neck so he could see her face. "You don't ever have to, my love. This is your home now; I am your man. Now, tonight, if you are not in pain, don't take your pill. I just want to lay beside you and hold you in my arms. I want to make you feel safe again, Orchid."

"Oh, Ahmed, I was sure that I would never see you again. I was so worried," she cried.

He kissed her tears away. "Never think that, Orchid. I will always be here for you." He cupped her face in his hands and kissed her tenderly.

The next day, Orchid went to visit Chiku and the young children were happy to see her. They were outside playing and followed Orchid into the house. They had gotten used to seeing her on the ranch. One of the other women had stopped to say hello to her.

Orchid took the small boy by his hand. "How old are you, Kino?" she asked.

He held up five fingers. "Tano."

"So you're five, huh?" She smiled and knocked on the door.

Eno greeted her. Orchid was now one of them. She helped deliver Eno's baby, and she could now run the house just as well as Busara could. Eno and the other women no longer whispered when they saw her outside or ignored her when she tried to talk to them. Everyone knew that Busara was fond of her. All the women followed Busara's footsteps.

"You and my daughter were lucky," Eno said. "God

watched over you and I prayed to Him to save you and my Chiku. I prayed that He return her to me, and you as well, Orchid. You two could have been killed." Eno raised her hands to the sky. "Thank you, my God."

"If I were alone, I would have been killed. Chiku is smart and brave. She was never afraid."

Eno led the way to Chiku's bed. The room was small and Orchid strained her eyes to adjust them to the darkness in Chiku's room.

The small room had three beds in it and one window and a chair. Chiku opened her eyes when she felt Orchid sitting on the edge of her bed. They hugged and cried together.

"You were so brave, Chiku. I'm so proud of you. Now, tell me, how do you feel?"

"After not keeping food down for two days, I'm still a little weak. But I do feel better now that I'm home. I hated the food at the hospital. Are you still in much pain, Orchid?"

"Sometimes. But, I can live with it. It's nothing like the pain I was in when Coffie and Dume found me and I came here from the hospital. It took months for me to recover and stop feeling pain."

"You're much stronger now, Orchid, and are in better shape than you were then."

"I know. But it's all been so stressful. I'll be all right, I'm sure of it." But she knew that she would only get worse. And the pain she felt in her heart when Ahmed kissed her made her want to die. It was much worse than the pain in her foot or the pain from the plane crash, because she knew she would recover. But she would never recover without Ahmed's love. How could she live without him?

"You need to regain your strength and get some rest, Chiku. I'll come back tomorrow."

"You promise?"

"Tell you what. I'll come every day even if it's only for ten minutes. If you are asleep, I'll sit by your bed until you wake up. Besides, Coffie is waiting outside to help me back and Miss Busara will worry if I stay away too long." She kissed Chiku on the forehead and limped out of the room.

That night, Ahmed did come to Orchid. She held onto him as if it was their last night together. He held her in his arms and ran his fingers through her hair, rubbed her back and legs where she complained she ached. For a while she had forgotten who she was and that she was a married woman. But she had to tell him; she just couldn't do it right now. This was something that had to be thought out and told at the right time. First, she had to be strong enough to stand up to him, take the pain of looking into his eyes and seeing the hurt and disappointment. Right now, she couldn't take it; she wasn't strong enough to see him hurt, to hear him say she wasn't his. In her heart she was only his.

The rest of the week was better. Orchid had started to eat more and visited Chiku every day, just as she promised. Orchid and Busara sat in the garden and had their long talks about the family, the other tribes, and the history of Africa. Orchid loved hearing the stories about what Ahmed and Coffie had done as children. She wanted to know everything about the man she loved.

She and Ahmed had made love the night before, and it had been weeks for both of them and it was like they couldn't get enough of each other. Still, she couldn't bring herself to tell him that she remembered, and she couldn't bring herself to want to go back to Steven. After Ahmed, how could she want any man? But, she knew that time was running out for her.

Everyone in the house had noticed the change in Orchid. She stayed close to the house, but spent more time in her room or peacefully sitting alone in the garden.

Busara thought it was because her leg was still healing, but the healing of her leg didn't explained why she had became so remote and looked so dejected.

The evening before, they were having dinner and Busara smiled to herself when she noticed the long pensive stares between Orchid and Ahmed, even though they both were trying to keep their love a secret. And she was certain that was only because Orchid hadn't regained her memory and they had no future until she did, that is if they had one at all. Still, it didn't keep the two apart at night, and they stole every moment they could together.

Orchid was peering through the living room window at nothing in particular.

"Orchid!"

She jumped and turned around. "What is it, Coffie?" she answered, and smiled. He was always so kind and gentle.

"You haven't been out lately. I have to take some supplies to Auntie Busara's distant cousin. Would you like to join me?" he asked, hoping she would accept his offer. Lately, she seldom smiled and looked so sad. Coffie felt sorry for her.

At first Orchid looked skeptical and wondered how far it was from the ranch. But she would be safe with Coffie. Maybe getting away for a while would take her mind off her current problem. And what was there to worry about, after all, she would be with Coffie.

"Yes. I think I would like that, Coffie. Just let me get my jacket," she said anxiously.

"Okay, good. I'll get the jeep and meet you out front." He walked out taking long strides, happy that she had accepted his offer.

Orchid brushed her hair and looked at the long dress that she was wearing. It was one of the dresses that Ahmed bought from Nairobi. He had carried her to her room in his arms when she came home from the hospital and the large box was on her bed waiting for her to open it. She kissed Ahmed and cried when he sat the box in her lap and she opened it.

Orchid rushed to the dining room where Busara was spreading a multi-colored tablecloth on the table. The tablecloth had some of the same bright geometric patterns as the rug on the hardwood floors. Busara looked up and smiled at the excitement in Orchid's eyes. She sounded unusually jovial today, Busara thought.

"Miss Busara, I'm going with Coffie to deliver food to your cousin."

"Good, you need to get out of this house for a while and meet new people." Busara smiled again. Her cousin would be very different to Orchid. But, going out would do her some good.

Orchid rushed out the door and Coffie was waiting for her.

They chatted during the ride. It was April, and although spring had arrived, the weather was still a little chilly. But only chilly enough to wear a sweater.

"What's in the back seat?" Orchid asked, looking in the back of the jeep at the large white cloth bags.

"Flour, sugar, corn meal, rice, and coffee. Aunt Busara sends it to her cousin once a month. She has a small house filled with children and a lazy husband who doesn't do well at supporting his family."

He pointed toward another path. "This is a part of Africa that you haven't seen before. Or at least you don't remember yet. I mean, if you're from here."

When Coffie corrected himself about her remembering, Orchid blinked her eyes and held back the tears, swallowing the lump of memories in her throat. She turned her head away from him so he couldn't see her expression and start asking questions that she wasn't prepared to answer.

"Africa is full of surprises. There's peace, but there's never a dull moment here," Orchid said, looking at the beautiful view of tall mountains and green grass, the clear blue sky. She loved the way the stars glowed so bright at night as though they were watching over her.

"In another year, you'll appreciate the peace. It never lasts too long," Coffie was saying. "There's always something to interrupt the peace."

Coffie drove through a narrow path and back to a dirt road with thorn trees, and tortured-branched erythrinas, with flowers the color of red sealing wax. The dusty road ran through a mixture of bush and native shambas. Along the road ten people were walking in a straight line. The women walked with baskets on their shaved heads that shone like large black marbles. They wore colorful beads and long earrings that appeared to be too heavy. Their children ran and played along the road behind them.

Coffie parked the jeep in front of a small row of

shanties where small children created dust clouds running across barren soil and through scattered sun-parched brush that had grown too tall in front of their homes. One of the children ran inside the shanty farthest from the jeep and came out with a tall, barefoot woman holding his hand in hers.

"Well, here we are. That's Auntie's cousin coming toward us," Coffie said to Orchid as he jumped out of the jeep and started to unload it.

"Hey man! What you got there for me today?" the woman asked, walking toward the jeep.

"Sada, this is Orchid," Coffie said.

Sada was wearing a long brown dress, her wiry hair was unkempt and natural, and when she smiled, Orchid saw that at least three of her front teeth were missing. Her years battling with harsh dry seasons and the bitter monsoons of the long wet seasons aged her beyond her years—only thirty-eight. Life had taken a severe toll on her from raising eight children and dealing with a lazy and abusive husband and living in such abject poverty.

Sada looked strangely at Orchid, and walked around her to look her up and down. "Are you sticking this woman, Coffie?" she said, still looking at Orchid.

Coffie looked at Orchid's face and laughed. Her mouth had fallen open, she looked at Sada as though the woman had clearly lost her mind.

"I say man, are you sticking this woman?" Sada asked again, standing tall with her long legs apart.

"No Sada, I'm not. She is a guest in our home."

"Oh, she is, is she? So who's sticking her, man?" Sada laughed out loud, her tongue flopping between the open gap in her full mouth. "I know, Ahmed is sticking her. He gets it every night, ha, girl?" She patted Orchid on the back. "Is he good, girl? I've always wondered."

Orchid cleared her throat and groped for the right words. She was having a difficult time trying to respond to the woman's crude question.

"How dare you speak so carelessly about me having sex with someone? Ahmed is not *sticking* me, I mean, having sex with me," she corrected herself. This woman wasn't entitled to know her personal business anyway, Orchid thought to herself. Whatever happens between her and Ahmed was their business, their business alone. What kind of person is she? Orchid wondered, staring at Sada.

Orchid's spirits had been lifted when Coffie first invited her to join him on this outing, but Sada's outburst had dampened them to a certain degree.

"I don't believe you, woman. Sticking is good, ha? My man sticks me every chance he gets. The children plays in the yard is mine, and all because my husband sticks me good. But if Ahmed is sticking you, it's not my business. You can't tell me a man so big doesn't have a large appetite for sticking. My man has it all the time. And I bet Ahmed feels the hunger all the time. Come on inside, Coffie. You too, girl."

The kids grabbed the bags and took them inside. Coffie and Orchid followed. Once they were inside, Orchid was surprised. The house was small, with old wooden furniture that looked as though it was poorly handmade, but was very neat and clean. Coffie and Orchid sat on a long bench that was in a room that needed more light.

"How's Cousin Busara? Is she feeling better these days?"

"Yes, much better, Sada. She's getting around and is her old self again."

"Good, good. She never forgets us. The woman has a heart of gold," Sada said, still looking strangely at Orchid. "Where did you come from, girl? Your hair looks like the tribe far away on the other side of the rivers."

Orchid moved uncomfortably on the hard bench and flipped her tongue over her teeth. "I don't remember. I lost my memory months ago. I was hurt and Miss Busara took me in."

"Well, kiss my ass and call me Joe," Sada said and laughed out loud. "Ain't that just like Busara to take in a lost bird. Now, I understood why you got so upset with me when we were outside."

Sada turned to Coffie and declared, "The girl is simple. She doesn't even know where she's from. She looks pitiful, and too weak. She'll never last. The men will stick her and send her away." She then clucked her tongue in distaste and pity. Did Busara send me some tobacco, Coffie? I got a yen for some.

"Yes of course, Sada. It's in the smaller bag."

"Well, kiss my ass and call me, Joe," she said again and whooped into loud laughter. She saw Orchid staring at her as though she was out of her head.

"You know there's a story about Joe. Many years ago he had a gang of his own. They lived in the woods. People in his gang used to fight, kill, and rob for him. Every time they caught a woman prisoner and took her back to Joe, he would always say, "Kiss my ass and call me Joe, and maybe I'll let you go." She clapped her hands and laughed out loud. But Orchid only stared at her.

"You don't get the joke, do you girl? Forget it. I need my tobacco to chew on. I chewed the last piece two days ago." Sada looked over at one of her boys. "Go outside and find me a spit can for my chewing tobacco."

Orchid looked at Sada in disbelief. Was the woman completely ignorant? Spit can?

Looking at Orchid, Coffie stood up. "It's time we go, Sada. I've still got work to do at the ranch." Orchid stood up beside him. She was ready to leave. She looked down at Sada's bare feet. The toenails had grown so long they were brown and had curled over her toes. The little boy gave her a small pack of chewing tobacco. She tore off the paper and bit a piece out of it, closing her eyes as though she could feel it soothingly satisfying the craving she had.

Sada walked them outside and they said good-bye, until next mouth.

"Don't pay any attention to what Sada says. She's uneducated, never gone any further than the woods. She and her husband have never gone to school. She means no harm, she just doesn't know how to use the right words."

"How old is she, Coffie?"

"She's in her mid-thirties. But the life she lives isn't an easy one. Too many mouths to feed and too little food."

"But what does her husband do for a living?" Orchid asked with interest.

"Apparently not enough. I offered the lazy dog a job on the ranch. He wasn't reliable enough to come to work every day. And when he did, he was caught sleeping on the job and stealing whatever he got his hands on that he could sell. The man would steal food out of a baby's mouth if he thought he could get away with it. Now, he just accepts odd jobs that barely feed his family.

Orchid asked questions about Sada's family as they were riding back to the ranch.

* * *

The phone rang and Ahmed answered. It was a call from his lawyer, William. But he had no news to tell Ahmed about Orchid.

Ahmed took the phone to the library and took a seat behind his desk.

"In my own opinion, and from what you have told me about the woman, she was probably visiting here and was lost, or left behind," said William. "And if that were the case, you would think her family would have filed a missing person report. Maybe she was left behind purposely. After all, she was hurt when Coffie and Dume found her. It just doesn't add up, Ahmed. But that's just one theory. The other one is she's the missing woman in the plane crash. My man is working on the last one from California. It's probably the woman," William said.

Ahmed tapped a pencil against the desk. Will he ever find out who Orchid really is? William is unusually slow with this job. He was always so fast in taking care of business for Ahmed. But Ahmed knew that if it took William this long, it had to be hard to find out where Orchid was from. After all, William was the best man for the job.

"So far, I can't come up with any missing person that compares with the picture you have showed me," William was saying. "But I've narrowed it down to the last person."

William thought of the phone call he had gotten from Busara that morning. She still wanted him to hold out another month. He wondered just what the old woman was up to? Ahmed was a smart man. William told Busara that he had to tell Ahmed before he called him again.

Before William called, Ahmed had mused over some vouchers and went over accounts that had to be paid. He placed them down on the desk and listened to William.

Ahmed had taken a picture of Orchid when he caught her outside alone and she didn't see him. He mailed the picture to William to compare against all missing person reports.

"Why don't you just marry the woman and forget it?" William asked, amused.

"And if her memory returns and she's already married?" Ahmed asked, not amused at all with William's prankish suggestion.

"Deal with it after she remembers."

Ahmed rolled his eyes up at the ceiling. "I don't need any of your expedient suggestions right now, William. Just keep investigating and keep in touch," Ahmed said, not in any mood for jokes. "It seems to be taking a long time, William."

As Ahmed replaced the receiver back in its cradle, Coffie and Orchid walked inside the house. Orchid told Ahmed about the day she and Coffie had together. She was smiling for a change.

Ahmed came to her room that night. Each time they made love it was always better than the time before. When he first walked into her room, she was so still, he thought she was asleep. As soon as he sat on the edge of her bed she welcomed him with open arms. And when he climbed in bed beside her, it was like their first time again. The more he had her, the more he wanted and needed from her. He heard her whisper against his ear, felt her legs circling around his waist, he couldn't hold back with Orchid. She whispered his name over and over with such passion, he went wild with desire.

Her body tingled from his touch as she felt a tremor course through her, not ever wanting this moment between them to end. Orchid held on to him as his body stiffened and relaxed. She closed her eyes and wondered how could she ever go back to Steven. She felt as though she was deeply in love with Ahmed.

They talked for hours getting to know each other better. He wanted a child and so did she. They were so perfect together. So perfect for each other.

The next day Orchid and Busara talked. Orchid wanted to tell her, but couldn't. It was so much to carry inside and it was beginning to weigh her down. Busara and Orchid had started out the back door when they heard a knock at the front door.

Busara stopped and looked at Orchid. "Did you hear that, was it a knock at the door?" Busara asked.

"Yes, I'll get it." Orchid ran through the house and to the front door.

"Is Ahmed here?" the man asked.

"He's working outside on the ranch." She stepped out the door and pointed in the direction where Ahmed could be found. The man stared at her, making her uncomfortable. But it was no different from the way everyone else on the ranch used to stare at her. She had gotten used to it.

"Thank you, Miss." He looked as though he wanted to say something, but turned and walked away. He stopped, looked back at her again, but she had closed the door.

There was something familiar about the man's voice, the cold blue eyes and blond hair that was almost white. What was it, she thought? The only people she knew were here on the ranch. And it kept nagging at her during the day.

Instead of going outside, she went into the library to read the newspaper. As she took a seat on the leather sofa she thought of her mother and sister. It had been since January, and now it was the end of May. What would she say to them when she calls to explain what had happened to her? No, she couldn't call with news that would shock her mother so profoundly. The best thing would be to fly to Chicago and see her face to face. And Steven, what would she do about him, and what has he done with his life since the plane crash? Who knew? Maybe he didn't even love her any longer; maybe he has someone else? Orchid lay the newspaper in her lap and looked as though she was staring into space.

Even if Steven didn't want her any longer, she owed it to him to go home. After all, he was her husband and she knew her alleged death had to have been hard on him. And Marie, her best friend, she would be so happy when she returns. They had been like sisters for so long. Marie and Steven were the only family Orchid had in California.

Orchid got up and placed the newspaper back on the desk. She touched her face and felt the tears as they began to flow. She hadn't realized she had been crying.

As Busara stood in the door, she could see Orchid's shoulders heaving, and knew that she was crying. She rushed to her side. "What is so bad, Orchid? Why are you so unhappy lately? Talk to me, girl." Taking Orchid by the shoulders, Busara turned the younger woman around to face her.

Orchid dropped her eyes. How could she tell Busara how miserable she really was, and that she was married and had to go home to a husband she was no longer in love with, and leave a man that she wanted more than life? How could she?

"I'm just so lonely, Miss Busara. So frightened by the realization of my life." She cried out loud from deep within her soul.

"Oh, Orchid, for now, we are your family, this is your home. Everyone on the ranch loves you. Maybe if you stop worrying and thinking about it, you might remember. Sometimes trying too hard is harmful."

She stopped crying. But she didn't feel any better. If only Busara knew why she hurt so badly. If only she had died in the plane crash. Life for her would be so much easier, and less painful. If only. . . .

Chapter 17

Thika, East Africa

"Ahmed, I have a woman that I want you and Auntie Busara to meet. I think I'm falling in love with her."

"Coffie, you've never mentioned this woman to me before," Ahmed said, and slapped his brother on his back. "Who is she?" They were in the stable placing saddles on their horses. It was a warm morning and they had lots of work to do. Ahmed decided if they got started earlier, they could be back before the heat baked into their skin. The later it got the heat got hotter. "Who is this woman?" Ahmed asked again.

"It's Nordia. You've seen her. She lives near Sada. She's only a couple of years older than I, but she's so pretty and sweet. I can't get her out of my mind, man. It must be love."

Ahmed studied Coffie's face, his eyes were gleaming and he looked happier than Ahmed would have liked. Nordia slept with any man that wore expensive clothing, or had a good paying job. She had flirted with Ahmed more than once, not to mention the one night they slept together, and before he could roll off her, she was asking for money.

"Are you sure it's love, Coffie? Maybe you should take your time and really get to know her first. Or maybe you're confusing love with passion."

"I know all that I need to know, man. I want her." Coffie seemed to sense the disappointment in Ahmed's face. "I know what you're thinking. But she was younger. Now she's older and has settled down. Have you seen her out lately?" he asked, trying to defend the woman he wanted to marry.

"No, as a matter of fact, I haven't seen her for at least a year. I just want you to make the right decision, Coffie. I don't want to see you hurt," Ahmed explained. But although he hadn't seen her, he knew her too well to believe she had changed. And maybe she had for a while, maybe the men she's been with have grown tired of her. And now she's on the prowl for a new one, with money.

"Okay, Coffie. Bring her home so she can get to know the family. If she's changed, I hope she'll make you a happy man." But he hoped that in time Coffie would wake up. As if he had no problems of his own with a woman that has no idea who she is, or where she came from. Now he has a problem with Coffie's woman as well. Maybe Auntie Busara could tell him what to do, he thought.

Ahmed finished his work for that day and was home before Coffie. He walked inside the living room and yelled out Busara's name. "Auntie, I need to talk to you."

"I'm in the kitchen, Ahmed," she yelled back to him.

Ahmed hurried into the kitchen. He had to speak with Busara before Coffie came inside.

Busara was cooking dinner. "What is it, Ahmed? You look so serious. Is there something wrong? Is Coffie all right?"

"I am serious, and yes, there is something wrong. Very wrong, if you ask me. Coffie is in love with Nordia. He wants to bring her here for dinner. He's never brought a woman home before. And of all the women, he picks someone with way too much experience with men, and specially young men like Coffie. Besides, he's used to seeing younger women. The woman is a gold digger and a whore. She's no good for my brother." He was quite serious and determined to dissolve this relationship before it went any farther.

Busara shook her head in disbelief and sat next to Ahmed at the table. "Oh, this is serious. When does he want to invite her?" She leaned backward, grabbed the dishcloth from the sink and dusted the crumbs off the table.

"I don't know. I'm sure he'll speak with you first. She's no good for him, Auntie, and she's no good for this family. That woman will have every man on this ranch hemmed in some corner with her. We've got to stop her. Coffie doesn't know the woman."

"Oh, he knows her all right. He knows what's under her dress. And that's why he's out of his mind. She'll run the boy crazy. But, we'll find a way. Have him invite her. I need to talk with her to see where her head is. She can't fool me, the whore she is."

"But, Auntie, we know where her head is. She wants to marry money," Ahmed said, as he grew even more determined to put a stop to it. "Coffie doesn't know what he's getting into." He grabbed a piece of bread that was freshly baked and still warm.

"I know that. But I need to talk to her anyway. Then, we can decide what to do. Remember Ahmed, you can lead a horse to the water, but you can't make him drink it. We have to show Coffie that she's no more than a whore without him knowing we had anything to do with it. We can't force him to give her up. She has to do it, we just have to help her."

The next week, Busara and Orchid buzzed around the house preparing dinner. The evening arrived when Nordia would be joining them, and they wanted everything to be prefect.

Orchid measured the nuts for her Tanzanian pineapple nut salad.

"You're becoming a good cook, Orchid."

"Thanks to you and Ifama," she said. She mixed the ingredients with two large wooden spoons.

"What does she look like, Busara?"

"Nordia is a pretty woman, but a little too mature for my Coffie. She's had more men than he has had women. Nordia has been around the block a time or two, if you know what I mean." Busara was standing in front of the stove peeling the last potato and dropped it in the pot of stew.

"But, what are we going to do if Coffie loves this woman? He's such a sweet man. I don't want to see him hurt," Orchid said.

Busara sighed. "After we see her tonight, we can decide how to handle things. I have to know what's on her mind, and what she's planning. Together, we can figure something out. I intend to run her off this ranch and out of Coffie's life. When we finish with her, he won't want her any more." She squeezed Orchid's hand.

For that moment, Orchid felt as though she was a part of their family. Busara had even included her in finding a way to get Nordia out of Coffie's life. She felt better today than she had for a month.

At six that evening, Coffie and Nordia strode hand in hand into the living room.

"Orchid, they're here," Busara said sticking her head inside of Orchid's room.

Orchid looked into the mirror to check her hair and followed Busara into the living room.

Coffie was dressed in a pair of black slacks and shirt. He looked handsome, even taller, and he was already six-foot-three and lanky.

Nordia was tall for a woman, but it seemed to Orchid that most of the women here were taller than she was. Nordia had dark, smooth skin, a long nose, French braids, and too much makeup. She was wearing long, colorful earrings. Her gaudy green dress was short and tight-fitting against her slender hips, well above her knees, revealing long thin legs. She turned her face to look at Coffie and Orchid noticed a long scar on one side of her neck. Orchid wondered if it was a scarification as part of her tribe ritual.

As Orchid was introduced to Nordia, Orchid noticed the woman hardly looked at her and was cold toward her, but very warm toward Ahmed.

"It's so good to meet Coffie's family. Ahmed, it's good to see you again," she said, giving him a warm, lingering smile. "And Miss Busara, Coffie always speaks of you." She looked at Orchid. "Oh, and you must be the cook or the housekeeper?" she asked with a smirk.

"No. She is a guest that is living with us," Busara interjected.

Through the corner of her eye, Nordia saw Ahmed give Orchid an admiring smile. "I'm sorry. I didn't know," she said, looking from Orchid to Ahmed. It didn't take much to see that he wanted the woman, or already had her.

"It's quite all right. How would you know," Orchid answered. But it was obvious that Nordia didn't like her. Was it because she wanted Ahmed? What was she really up to, Orchid wondered? Did she want Coffie or Ahmed?

They all talked for a while and went into the dining room for dinner. Coffie asked Nordia to sit next to him, and Ahmed sat at the head of the table, Orchid and Busara sat opposite Coffie and Nordia.

"This ranch is beautiful and so large, too. Did you decorate the inside, Miss Busara?"

"Yes. When Ahmed came home from college, he changed a lot inside and outside of this house. Cut down trees to get African mahogany wood for paneling the walls and rebuilt the roof, ceiling and the floors. Little by little, you could see it was becoming a new house. I decorated the inside, at least most of it. We kept most of the furniture that was made by my father. Coffie and Ahmed worked hard. If their parents could see them now, they would be proud. "

Nordia looked at Coffie and smiled. "When we are married, I would love to live the rest of my life here with you, Coffie."

"Yes, on the ranch. But I intend to build my own house. There's a place on the west side of the ranch I would like to build on."

Ahmed was quiet, but the disappointment on Nordia's face didn't go unnoticed. Everyone was quiet for a few moments. It was too soon to be speaking of marriage.

"Are the people on the ranch friendly?" Nordia asked Orchid.

Orchid knew she only asked to break the tension. "They are all very nice people."

After the birth of Eno's baby, Orchid was overwhelmed with their acceptance of her. Now, the women treat her as though she was one of them.

"I imagined at first the women probably made the same mistake as I did by thinking you were hired here to help," she said with the same smirk across her face.

Orchid's eyes flared at her insults. Easy girl, she thought to herself. "I don't think so. But the people here are so intelligent, they would never say so even if they did think it." Not only were her eyes glinting with an icy stare as she looked at Nordia, but Orchid knew for certain that she didn't like this woman. And by the expressions on everyone's faces as she spoke to Orchid, her acrid remarks did not go unnoticed. Orchid looked at Coffie. He looked like a lovesick boy and doubted if he had heard anything Nordia had just said to her.

The dinner went smoothly after the small milestone between Orchid and Nordia. After dinner, they all went into the living room and talked about their families, which again, left Orchid out of the conversation.

"I haven't seen you in over a year, Nordia. What's been going on in your life? I was sure that you were married by now," Ahmed asked with interest.

"No. I hadn't found a sweet man until Coffie came along. I still live in the same place, but I've been working and keeping busy. There is nothing exciting going on in my life, except now," she looked at Coffie again, touched his hand and smiled.

"I've found the man of my dreams. So, let's talk about yours," she asked and looked at Orchid.

Nordia had noticed more than once how Ahmed's face softened when his eyes met Orchid's. And the little red-headed, pitiful woman couldn't keep her eyes off him.

Nordia was angry, Ahmed was the brother she really wanted. Had wanted him for years. They slept together once, but she had never gotten over him. Every time she saw him, he never had much to say to her. But getting Coffie meant getting closer to Ahmed, and in time, she would get her chance. Even if she and Coffie got married and moved into this house, she still had a chance to get Ahmed. Coffie was young and would get over her. Now, this stranger was in her way.

Busara watched Nordia closely and listened to her every word. Coffie would be hurt once this relationship was over, but letting it lead into marriage would be worse. Busara looked at Ahmed and repugnance was clearly written across his face.

"I have some work to do in the library. Will you all excuse me," Ahmed said, standing up as though he couldn't take any more of this woman. He would leave the matter with Busara.

Nordia stood up and reached her hand out to Ahmed. "It was good to see you, Ahmed. We'll be seeing a lot of each other." She flashed her widest smile, and again, their handshake lingered.

After holding his hand longer than necessary, Ahmed pulled his hand away. "I'm sure we will. As a matter of fact, I'm looking forward to it."

"Well, Nordia," Coffie said. "Why don't we go for a ride around the ranch? And as always, Auntie Busara, the dinner was perfect. Thanks to you and Orchid."

Nordia hugged Busara and said, "Good night."

"Good night to you, too, Nordia," Orchid said. And good riddance, she thought.

"Oh, did I miss you, Orchid? I guess I'll just have to get used to seeing you around," she said, her voice smothered with sarcasm. They walked out, but Nordia hadn't anticipated the evening to end so soon.

Once in the jeep, Nordia gave Coffie a long tender kiss. He drove her around the ranch showing her all the land they owned. He parked the jeep near a small pond. "It's so beautiful here, Coffie. And there's so much land." And lots of land, means lots of money, Nordia thought.

"This is where I will build our house. Our bedroom will face the pond, and we can lay in bed and watch the stars miles around us."

"I just don't see any reason to rush to build a house, Coffie. I just want to be your wife. We can live in the big house forever for all I care. I can't wait to be your wife." She lifted her right leg and laid it across his lap.

"Honey, it won't be long. I was thinking of three bedrooms, and three baths, and you know the rest. When we have our children it will be enough space. I would love to have a son and daughter. This is a nice spot to build a home of my own for just my family to live and lots of space for my children to run and play in."

She felt disgusted. He had made plans without consulting her. What if she didn't want children? After all, she wasn't as young as he was. Sure, she'd told him that he was only two years younger than she, but the truth was, she was eight years older and had been married once before, even though it only lasted for five months before her husband beat her and walked out without ever coming back.

"Don't you understand? I want my wife and children in their own home. If anything ever happens to me, you'll have a home of your own," he said, trying to make her smile again. He wanted so much to please her and make her happy.

Nordia sat close to Coffie and lay her head on his shoulder. "I know, baby, but just think about it. It may take too long to build. I don't want to wait that long to marry you. I love you so much, Coffie." She wanted to live in the same house as Ahmed, and she wanted Orchid out.

He felt her hot breath against his ear and kissed her long and tenderly. "I love you, too, Nordia. But it won't take long. Just trust in me and you'll have a happy life." He couldn't wait to get her home so they made passionate love in the back seat of his jeep with a beautiful view of the clear, blue sky and the shining stars above.

"Miss Busara! What's this I hear about Coffie wanting to marry Nordia? All the men on the ranch are talking," Ifama asked as she dusted the furniture in the living room. "I had heard the news from one of the ranch hands and was sure that it was just a rumor. Yes, I was sure it was. Just a misunderstanding, I said."

"You probably heard right. He does intend to marry her."

"Well, he's a fool and a blind one, too, yes he is. If he really wants to marry someone, what about that pretty little Orchid? Why go after someone with two kids, sleeps with any man that gives her money, and can't keep a job, no she can't. Besides, she too old for my sweet Coffie," Ifama mused. She shook her head, disgusted at the thought of Coffie marrying that no good, sorry gold digger, yes she was, just disgusted.

Busara didn't say anything about Orchid and Coffie. She wanted Orchid for Ahmed, she wanted him to marry her.

"Two kids? Did you say she has two kids?" Busara asked.

"Yes. You mean you didn't know that? Her Papa got her pregnant when she was thirteen, and later she met a man that was just visiting here and got pregnant for him, too, yes she did. Now everyone knows it's not her fault that her Papa got her pregnant. He probably raped her. But she's bad medicine, Busara. She'll only use that boy and leave him high and dry," Ifama said, placing her hand in her apron pocket, pulling out a stick of gum, folded it in half and stuck it in her mouth.

"Hi, Ifama," Orchid said, walking into the dinning room where they were talking. "What are you two up to?"

"It seems that Miss Nordia has two children," Busara answered in disgust.

"Really. Who told you that?" Orchid asked.

"I did," Ifama answered. "And I know what I'm talking about. Nordia's aunt and I have been friends for years. She tells me all about that family. They are bad medicine with bad ways about them, yes they are, bad medicine. She's only their aunt through marriage and she hates them all. Now that she's no longer married to Nordia's uncle, she stays away from the entire family, yes she does, stays away all the time."

Orchid took a seat and listened. She wondered why

everything Ifama said, she had to repeat it again at the end of each sentence? Orchid looked at her hair braided all over her head with multi-colored beads running through each braid. She was almost as old as Busara. Her dark face shone, and she talked all the time and knew everything that went on around the ranch.

"I tell you, Busara. That girl is bad medicine." Ifama was standing with a dust cloth in her hand, a scarf tied on her head with her braids hanging from underneath the scarf and wearing an old gray dress that came down to her ankles to do her housework in.

"This situation is worse than I thought it was," Busara said, and plopped down in a chair. "What are we going to do? She shook her head. "We better do some fast thinking. Come on, I need a cup of hot tea after this news." Orchid and Ifama followed her into the kitchen.

The three women sat at the table with tea and sweet cakes.Busara got up again to slice a lemon and get some honey to sweeten her tea.

"I have to figure out a way to make my Coffie see Nordia for what she really is. I don't even know where to start. Two children, ha? Coffie doesn't know about that," Busara said. He's already making plans to have a family with her."

"You know, Busara. She dated a young man that used to work on this ranch, yes she did. He was angry enough to kill her before he left. She spent almost all his money and called the whole thing off. When she tried to get him back, he didn't want no part of her."

"Who was he?" Busara asked, trying to remember.

"It was Hasani. He's a good guy like Coffie. He just

fell in love with the money-taking whore, yes he did. And yes, she was a whore then, too."

"Where is he now?" Orchid asked.

"He works on that white man's ranch over yonder across the river. He left Africa and returned in three months. I think he was just too embarrassed to come back here. All the ranch hands knew how Nordia used him. He'll do anything to make some of the money she took from him, and I bet he'll do anything to get even with Nordia. Yes, I just bet he would."

Busara and Orchid's interest was piqued, as they listened to Ifama. Each one had ideas running through their minds.

"Busara, what if Coffie caught Hasani and Nordia together? What do you think he would think of her then?" Orchid asked.

"And how would we arrange such a thing?" Busara asked.

Orchid rolled her eyes up at the ceiling and looked at Ifama. "He'll do anything for money, right? And he'll do anything to get even with Nordia and get some of his money back at the same time. All we have to do is pay the man. Arrange for him and Nordia to meet and make sure that Coffie walks in on them. We just have to time it just right," Orchid said.

Busara and Ifama looked at each other. "What better way to stop her?" Ifama mused. "This sounds so good my insides tickle, yes they do, honey."

"No better way," Busara answered. She looked at Orchid and smiled. She knew the girl had wisdom and she was right for wanting her to marry Ahmed. "How can we arrange to have him meet us, and where?" Busara asked.

"Now you leave that up to me. I can have him

meet us someplace on the ranch where the men won't see us. In no time, we can forget Nordia," Ifama said, laughing out loud. "Send her off packing, yes we can."

Orchid listened to the two women and the idea was beginning to sound better and better as they made plans.

"How soon can you get me a phone number for Hasani, Ifama?" Busara asked, her eyes sparkling with mischief. She felt a little wicked, but it was fun, exciting and something different for her. Besides, she would do anything for her two nephews, the ranch, and what they worked hard for.

"I can get in touch with him by tomorrow. What do you want me to tell him, Busara?"

"Don't give him this number because Ahmed or Coffie may answer. But get a time and place so the three of us can meet him and make plans. It's time for us to go to work," Busara said.

"I agree, Miss Busara. The sooner, the better. With the talk of marriage, we don't have very much time," Orchid said. "Nordia may even suggest they go away and get married and tell us about it when they get back. We have to work fast. The woman seems a little pushy to me."

That evening, before Coffie came home, Ahmed, Orchid, and Busara discussed what Ifama had told them about Nordia and Hasani, and their plan to prove to Coffie that she is not the right girl for him. No one in the family would be responsible for their breakup, at least as far as Coffie would know.

"Do you think it will work?" Ahmed asked.

"Oh, yes. It will work all right. We have no choice but to make it work," Busara assured him.

"And it will take place this week. Ifama will speak to Hasani tomorrow. From what she tells me, the man wants to get even with Nordia," Orchid interjected.

"I remember when Hasani and Nordia had their affair. Some of the men and I tried to tell him what he was getting into, but he wouldn't listen." Ahmed didn't mention that he had slept with Nordia. It was not love, just a hot night of passion. After that night, it was over. He had no further use for her. Nordia was always so quick to get by everyone, especially if you had money. Her family was so poor that money was all that mattered to her now and she knew what to do to get it.

That night at dinner, Coffie was so happy, he continued to chatter away about Nordia. He wanted three or four children after he marries her. And he had already taken her the night before to see where he wanted to build their home.

"There's only one problem, Auntie Busara," Coffie said.

"What problem, Coffie?" Busara asked.

"I don't think she's sure if I can build a house fast enough before we get married. She wants to live here. She says it's big enough, so why would I want to build? I don't understand why she wouldn't want a home of her own, a home that she can run as she pleases. Most women would but for some reason she is fascinated with living here with you and Ahmed, and Orchid of course."

Orchid knew Coffie only named her, because he was such a nice man. But Nordia wouldn't want to live here if she stayed around, because of Ahmed. The way she looked at Ahmed didn't go unnoticed.

No one answered. But everyone knew. The big house represented money.

"It will all work out, Coffie. Just give her time," Orchid said.

"I know. Once we're married it won't make a difference as long as we are together."

Two days later, Busara and Orchid went walking outside.

"Where are you two going?" Ahmed asked as he rode by on horseback.

"We need the exercise," Orchid answered.

Coffie rode alongside them. "Just exercise? You should do it earlier in the day. Later on it will be too hot."

"You just go about your business, Coffie. We won't be out too long. After twenty minutes, I'll be ready to go back inside."

Coffie laughed, he and Ahmed rode off.

"Good. Now, we don't need him riding around to see where we are going." Busara pointed down the small trail. He can't see us over there. Look, Orchid. There is Hasani, waiting for us."

Hasani was standing behind a bush with a cigarette in his hand. He was medium height with a boyish, innocent face. He looked to be no older than twenty-eight or thirty years old.

Busara introduced Hasani to Orchid. Even as Busara talked to him he couldn't keep his eyes from glowing with desire for Orchid.

Hasani listened to their problem. "I could sleep with her again if I wanted to. We ran into each other a week ago and she invited me to her house, but I didn't take her up on it. I had no idea she was seeing Coffie. Never even mentioned his name. That woman actually had the nerve to come up to me and start a conversation," he said, his eyes roaming over Orchid's body.

Busara cleared her throat to bring his attention back to her again. "We need a way to make Coffie hate her as much as you do."

"I know a way," Hasani interfered. "I've been thinking ever since I spoke with Miss Ifama. I would love to see the hurt in her face."

Orchid looked into his dark eyes. "Coffie mentioned that Thursday evening he's going to her house for dinner. I noticed that every time they make plans to see each other, Nordia calls to confirm. If you want to see her on the same night she'll call and cancel her date with Coffie, right?" she looked from Hasani to Busara.

"Yes, that sounds about right," Busara answered. "She'll have to so Coffie won't walk in on her."

"Well, Thursday morning Hasani can ask to see her the same evening at the same time that Coffie is invited for dinner." She looked at Hasani, his eyes had dropped back to her breast.

"Are you listening, Hasani?" Orchid asked.

"Yes, babe, I'm listening. And I'm good enough in bed to make her cancel a date with Coffie," he said with confidence.

Arrogant little bastard, Busara thought to herself.

"Take her to bed just in time for Coffie to walk in on it," Orchid was saying.

"How can that happen, Orchid?" Busara asked.

"Easily. When she calls to ask one of us to tell Coffie that she has to cancel, we'll just forget to tell Coffie.

And of course she'll make it an urgent excuse not to see him. So as far as she's concerned, no way will he show up at her house."

"Orchid, you are the devil, but I like that. You got something there," Busara said. They were standing under a tree with lots of high bushes to hide them in case anyone rode by.

"I can convince her, I'm certain of that," Hasani assured them. "She only wants Coffie to support her. Like I said before, she loves no one. And she loves living on the edge, taking chances. Seeing me again will be exciting to her. It makes her feel she's still wanted. It's a challenge for her, wild and daring. She'll love the idea and she'll love the sex . . ."

"Okay, okay, I get the message. How much?" Busara asked. "And put out that cigarette before somebody smells the smoke."

"I need two thousand dollars. If I didn't need it I wouldn't ask. Just seeing the look on her face would be payment enough for me. I'll call you to let you know that it's all set."

"Good," Busara said. Now we better get back, Orchid, before anyone sees us. And I'll look forward to your call, Hasani." Busara started to walk off and turned around calling his name. "If you ever need a job, come to the ranch. You were a good worker."

"Thanks, Miss Busara." He walked off and disappeared into the tall bushes.

"He's certainly sure of himself. He must really know her," Orchid said.

"I don't care as long as he gets her out of our lives. We don't want Ahmed to have to handle her. It's better this way, Orchid. Coffie and Ahmed are all I have. They're like my own sons to me. Their father and me were close and protected each other. I plan to do the same for his sons."

"They know you love them, Miss Busara. Come on, let's get back."

Late that night as Orchid lay in Ahmed's arms, she told him about their plans. "I'm worried about Coffie. How will he get through this?" Orchid asked, thinking of her own problem and feeling her own pain.

"It's going to hurt him deeply, but better now than later. If Hasani is so convinced that he can rekindle old feelings between him and Nordia so easily, Coffie doesn't need her. He's better off. It may not be as hard for him after he walks in on her. Now, enough talk of Coffie. Have I told you lately that I love you?" he whispered.

Her heart pounded so hard she was sure he could hear it. How can she leave him? Once the problem was over with Coffie, she had to concentrate on her own situation. And she had to call Steven.

The two days wait was nerve racking. Busara and Orchid jumped every time the phone rang. Finally, at three o'clock it rang again and Busara answered. It was Nordia.

"Hello, Miss Busara. This is Nordia."

"Yes, I know."

"Would you give Coffie a message for me, please?"

"Of course, what is it?" Busara asked, waiting to hear what excuse she would use.

"My sister is very ill. She needs me to come over

and help her with her small children. I just couldn't
turn her down, you know."

"Yes, Nordia, indeed I do know."

"I'm so disappointed. I can't see my Coffie tonight.
God, I'll be so glad once we're married and can be
together every day."

Busara rolled her eyes up. She wanted to scream at
the lies she was listening to. All she really wanted was
this night to be over and done with.

"Please tell him that I love him and to make plans
for tomorrow night. My sister has no telephone so I
can't call him back."

"I'll tell him, Nordia. Don't you worry about
Coffie. He'll be disappointed but he'll get over it."

"Oh thank you so much, Miss Busara."

"Thank you so much for calling." Busara hung up
and looked at Orchid who was standing so eager to
hear what Nordia had said. When she hung up, she
went back into the kitchen.

"You know we're not really doing this to Coffie.
She's doing a good job herself. We only put it in
motion. It is Nordia who is hanging herself."

"I agree, Miss Busara. One phone call from Hasani
and she goes to bed with him," Orchid said with disgust. What we're doing is for the best.

They went back into the kitchen. Busara stirred
the mixture of meats, spices and tomatoes in the old
cast-iron skillet and waited for Coffee and Ahmed to
come inside from their long day's work. Coffie
would get dressed for his date and Ahmed would
stay home for dinner. After dinner, they would all sit
around and wait for Coffie's return. What if he
wanted to fight with Hasani, Busara thought? But
there was no reason to fight. After all, Hasani didn't
really want Nordia. Still, Busara was worried and as

she looked at Orchid walking into the kitchen, she looked just as worried. One night of hurt, deception and disappointment was better than a lifetime of betrayal. Nordia would divorce Coffie for another man and try and take everything they had worked so hard for. No, Busara would not let her destroy her family. And she knew that Orchid felt the same.

Coffie bounced into the kitchen where Busara and Orchid were cooking. "I'll be eating out tonight, ladies. My woman is cooking a dinner for me. Now is the time to find out if she can cook as good as she says she can."

"Okay, it's enough for lunch tomorrow," Busara answered. He looked so happy it almost brought tears to her eyes.

Coffie looked at her as though he was waiting for her to say something. "Are you all right, Auntie?"

"Yes. Why wouldn't I be all right? You go and enjoy yourself. Tell Nordia I said hello."

He kissed his aunt on the cheek. And looked at Orchid. "Looks like she has you cooking everyday now, Orchid. And you are doing well at it."

"I'm still learning. But I can finally make a meal without your brother frowning," she said and laughed. "At least he eats it now and doesn't wait to see that you taste it first."

"You're so perceptive, Orchid. How did you know that?" Coffie asked.

"I know. I used to watch him at the dinner table. Bet you didn't know that I have such a sharp eye."

He didn't answer her, just smiled and walked out.

Coffie jumped into the jeep with a dozen roses in his hand. He couldn't wait to see his woman's face.

She sure was pretty, too, with her nice shaped hips and short dresses that drove him wild out of his mind. And the night was just right, beautiful and clear. Once he got there he would build her a fire and tell her all the plans he had been making for their lives.

Coffie saw a truck parked in front of her small house but dismissed it. Since it was a row of houses, maybe the truck belonged to someone else.

He got out of the jeep, but as he got closer, he could see the door was slightly ajar. He took another step and stopped in his tracks. In the window was a shadow of a man and woman, they were getting undressed, and as he pulled her dress down from her shoulders he kissed her on her neck, his other hand was cupping her breast.

Without realizing it, the roses fell to the ground. Coffie shook his head hard. Was this a bad dream?

The man lay the woman on the bed and got on top of her. Her legs were spread open so there was no mistake about what they were doing. But no, it had to be a mistake. Maybe Nordia was letting someone use her house and she was waiting inside for him.

Coffie pushed the door open and slowly walked inside the house. Nordia wasn't in the small living room waiting for him, she wasn't in the kitchen. His heartbeat had accelerated, his fists balled by his sides, and he felt a nagging feeling deep inside that made him nervous. Had he walked into the wrong house? No, he had been here too many times before. He could find Nordia's house with his eyes closed.

Coffie went to her bedroom and stopped at the door. A suffocating sensation tightened his throat. Nordia was moaning with such pleasure Coffie had never heard from any woman before, at least not with him, and she pulled at Hasani, kissing him, whispering for more. Their clothes were on the floor and a small lamp was on the nightstand, it was dim, but it was clear enough to see everything, and her face.

Coffie's first instinct was to pick up the lamp and hit Hasani over the head. But what would it change? He wasn't raping Nordia. She wanted it, all of it. He wanted to turn and walk out, but his feet wouldn't move, his hands were trembling, he couldn't control them, or the anger rising in him.

As though she felt someone watching her, Nordia's head jerked up first. She pushed at Hasani. "Get up, you fool! Get out. See what you've done," she yelled, trying desperately to get from under him.

Hasani got up and looked at Coffie's face. "Sorry man, she didn't say she was expecting you. We go way back, don't we, Nordia? Tell him how you begged me to be with you tonight." Hasani grabbed his pants.

"No, no! Don't listen to him. Coffie, I can explain. Please, please, Coffie," she pleaded, picking up her dress and panties. Her eyes widened, she looked at Hasani's smirk in the corner of his mouth as he continued to dress.

Coffie started to walk out of the house and Nordia was running behind him, crying, pleading with him to let her explain. She grabbed the back of his shirt but he pushed her away.

He had to get out of there, he needed the fresh air to help him breathe, he needed to get drunk, but most of all, he had to get away, out of her sight before he went into a blind rage. At that moment he could have killed her with his bare hands.

He was trying to get into the jeep when Nordia slung her fist that connected to his jaw. He held her hands and pushed her again, but she was still fighting.

All Coffie wanted to do was get in his jeep and drive off, be alone, and get drunk. He turned his back on her. But she came after him again. This time he pushed her harder.

"Get out of my face, Nordia." She fell to the ground and just as fast a boy came running toward him. Coffie had no idea if the boy was in the house, or where he came from.

The boy swung his fist at Coffie. "Leave my mama alone, get out of here."

Coffie's eyes widened in shock. "Mama! Did you say 'Mama'?" He looked at Nordia, lying on the ground as if seeing her for the first time. She had lied about everything. He knew nothing about her having a child.

Hasani got into his truck and drove off, leaving Coffie looking as though he was in a state of shock. He felt sorry for the poor guy because he deserved so much more. The feeling of triumph as he looked at Nordia brought a wide smile across his lips. Hasani patted his pocket where he had put the $2,000. He had no plans to ever see Nordia again.

Nothing else went as planned that night. The boy was almost as tall as Coffie and looked to be at least fifteen years old. He was like an untamed animal, swinging his fist, yelling.

About the time he got the boy off him and restrained his hands without harming him, a police car raced into the yard and handcuffed Coffie.

"That man was hurting my mother," the boy yelled to the officer.

One of the officers grabbed Coffie, but Coffie held both hands in the air. Before Coffie could defend himself, he was pushed inside the car. He looked at

Nordia, but she said nothing to defend him. She
looked wild, her hair in disarray and her dress dusty
from the dirt she had fallen into.

"What's going on here, man?" the officer asked the
young boy.

"Can't you see? My mama was knocked to the
ground by this tall ox," the boy answered, pointing
into the car at Coffie.

Both officers were white. One stood near the car
and watched Coffie as the other officer took a report
from the boy.

Nordia just sat and cried, not speaking or looking
up at anyone. She just cried, and then she cursed at
Hasani for what she had lost with Coffie. And then
she cursed again because she would never get close
enough to get Ahmed.

Either of the officers asked Coffie anything, and
Coffie knew better than to speak.

Coffie was taken to jail.

They were all quiet that night. Ahmed looked at
the clock on the wall, it was past midnight. What
could have happened?

Busara and Orchid had gone to their rooms, but
neither one of them could sleep. If Coffee came in
and saw them all in the living room he might suspect
something. They were always in bed by ten, sometimes earlier for Busara.

Ahmed went to the library and took a seat behind
the desk. He sat with his elbows on the desk, his face
resting in his hands. After a while he started rustling
through papers that he had sat aside earlier, unable
to concentrate, but as he tried to read, again he set
the papers aside. He still couldn't concentrate on

anything until his brother was safely home with his family. Damn, what is keeping Coffie so long?

He started to go to the closet and get his jacket. It was time to go and find out if Coffie was all right. What if he had gotten drunk, or hurt? He pulled his brown jacket out of the closet when the phone rang.

Orchid and Busara ran to the library to see if it was Coffie on the phone. No one else called at this time of night.

Ahmed held the phone in one hand, and motioned for Busara and Orchid to be quiet with his free hand.

"Are you hurt, Coffie?"

"No man, just mad as hell. Just come and get me out of this squalid hellhole. It's been a long damn night and I'm dog tired."

"Okay, okay. I'll be right there." Ahmed placed the receiver back in its cradle.

"What is it, Ahmed? Is Coffee hurt, where is he?" Busara questioned with worry. Orchid was standing anxiously behind her. Both were afraid of what they may hear.

Ahmed looked at Busara's face, she looked tired, worried and older. This night had taken a toll on her, and she was just recovering from the fall she had during the fire.

Orchid was standing in the room wearing a long, pink cotton nightgown that Busara had given her. She held her hands over her mouth, listening closely for information about Coffie.

"He's not hurt, Auntie Busara. But he's in jail. I'm going to bring him home." Taking long strides, Ahmed stormed brusquely across the room. "If that witch calls this house again for Coffie, give the call to me." He walked out, livid with rage.

On the way to Thika Police Department, Ahmed wasn't only worried about Coffie being put in jail, but he was also worried and hoping that no cops had laid a hand on his brother. If they had, all hell would break lose.

He parked in the small parking lot, jumped out of his car and dashed inside. After he paced the floor for another hour, downed two cans of root beer soda, Coffie came out of the thick iron door. He looked tired, and his clothes were torn and dirty. But he had no bruises.

"Are you all right, man?" Ahmed asked, feeling his brother's arms, ribs, or anyplace he could be hurt. He wiggled his nose in distaste. "Damn, you stink."

"I was in a stinky, dirty cell. Luckily, I was only in there for a couple of hours. Some of the men had been in there much longer. Stinks like hell and the walls and floor were dirty, too." He sniffed and frowned with repugnance, visualizing the cell that he had been in and shivered.

"I'm pissed enough to break someone's jaw."

"Is this about Nordia?"

"Yes, and I tell you, she's no good. She certainly had me duped. She's a cockeyed, dirty liar."

"Leave it alone, Coffie. There will be other women, good, decent women. Forget about her. Come on, let's go home, brother," Ahmed said, and placed his hand on Coffie's shoulder.

Coffie followed him to the car. "I got to get my jeep."

"Is it at Nordia's house?" Ahmed asked as if he didn't know.

"Yes, it's still there. I don't want to leave it there any longer. By daybreak, it may be stolen or destroyed by that brat son of hers. And that damn boy has got a pretty good left hook, too," he said rubbing his jaw.

"Okay, Coffie. I'll take you there and follow you home. But that's all. Please don't knock on her door. I don't want to go to jail tonight, too."

"You can follow me, Ahmed. But I have no intentions of going anyplace but straight home. I don't ever want to see that woman again. I wonder how old she really is. That boy of hers looked to be at least fourteen, tall and lanky, with a dirty mouth."

"Don't forget the left hook," Ahmed said.

Coffie shook his head. "Oh, I won't. Believe me I won't."

The ride back to Nordia's house only took about twenty minutes, which gave Coffie enough time to tell Ahmed what had happened.

"Can you believe she asked me over for dinner and didn't have the decency to see Hasani another night? Can you believe that shit, man? They were going at it right on the bed, the door wide open. I wonder if I had arrived after Hasani, would she have slept with me, too?"

"Nordia has always been the kind of woman a man doesn't marry, Coffie."

Although it was summer, the weather felt damp. And there had been a full moon out.

"Thanks for giving me this information about her after I've made a complete fool of myself, Ahmed," Coffie snorted.

"Would you have listened if I told you last week or the week before?"

"No, guess not. Turn right here."

Ahmed stopped so Coffie could get out and get his jeep.

There was a light on in Nordia's house. When she

heard the engine start, she ran out the door wearing a red, thin see-through gown as though she was waiting for him.

"Coffie, baby. You didn't give me a chance to explain," she yelled, waving for Coffie to stop.

But Coffie didn't even look at her. He shook his head in disgust, sped off without looking back at her. It was the end for him and Nordia.

Breakfast was ready at six-thirty, the same time every morning, but Coffie slept later. It was hard to fall into a sound sleep after he got home, showered and settled into bed.

"Leave him be, Aunt Busara. He's tired. I heard him up at least two hours after we got home last night," said Ahmed.

"Good morning, everyone," said Coffie.

Everyone looked at him. His eyes were bleary, and despite his effort to look well, he looked tired and unhappy.

Ahmed looked around, surprised that Coffie was already up.

Coffie took a seat at the table and Orchid filled his cup with coffee.

"I guess everyone knows what a complete fool I've been," he said, as he looked at all their faces. "Now I have to live it down. Everyone on the ranch knows we were going to be married. I could abide anything, except the lying and unfaithfulness."

"No man would, Coffie. And you were no fool, you were just in love," Orchid said. She looked at Ahmed and wanted to cry for the love she would soon lose.

"Why didn't you sleep later, Coffie?" Ahmed asked. "It was morning when you got to sleep."

"I couldn't sleep. I just want to go out, work and forget what has happened." He sipped the strong, black coffee, feeling the warmth soothe his throat.

"Then we won't speak of it again. It's all over," Ahmed said.

They all nodded in agreement.

Chapter 18

Steven slammed the phone down. Three months she was giving him to find another place. Why had Wanda left her townhouse to Karen and not him? he had wondered so many times since her death. Karen had said he could stay a year, it's only June. While talking to Karen, he could hear Betty, his ex-mother-in-law in the background.

"Remind him that it belongs to you now, Karen. It's time he moves out."

He never liked the woman and had always tolerated her because of Wanda. Well, he still had three months to move out. And he would stay until the last day of it. As soon as he hung up the doorbell rang. He sighed and went to answer it.

Marie walked in with a bottle of apple cider. As she brushed past Steven, she kissed him on his cheek and stepped out of her shoes.

"You won't be kicking your shoes off in here much longer," Steven said, and took the bottle to the kitchen to open it.

Marie frowned. "Are you tired of me already? I thought we were doing well together." She was frowning and looked as though she would cry at a drop of a hat. Her eyes were beginning to water. She was so different from Wanda, and so insecure, he noted. Steven kissed her on the cheek and handed her a glass.

"Karen called me today to remind me that I only have three months to move out. Her son won't be going to college for two years. I wonder why she wants me to move so soon?" He sat on the sofa beside her and propped his feet on the coffee table.

"She'll rent it and make some extra money. She probably needs it to help pay for her son's education." She could breathe and felt relieved again. "My place is small, but we can get a place together, Steven. Maybe it's good she wants you out." But as she looked at him, he didn't seem amused with her suggestion.

"What I mean is, don't you think it's time we plan for some type of a life for ourselves? Everything in here reminds me of Wanda and I know it must remind you of her, too. You need a fresh start, in a new place. We've been getting along so well lately."

"What's the rush?" he asked.

"It's no rush, Steven. We were together almost two years before she died. Don't you think it's time? Are we always going to be running from your house to mine?" she asked desperately, hoping that he wouldn't get angry. This was a conversation that he had avoided.

Marie placed her glass on the table in front of her. This was the time to try to convince him that they should be living in one place, together.

"Steven? We can find a large place of our own. You said that you don't want anyone else and I know I don't." She held his hand. "So what's to stop us now? Baby, I promise I can make you happy, if you'll just give me the chance." She was trying hard, really hard to convince him.

He turned, facing her. Maybe it was time to settle down again. There was certainly no one else in the streets that he wanted, and he could forget about Kim. Sure, he wasn't madly in love with Marie, but she was a good woman, terrific in bed and she was in love with him, he could depend on her. All she wanted was his love in return. After Wanda died he was so confused. There wasn't even a chance to say good-bye to her, or to see her dead body. There was no closure, just a fast, unforeseen ending that left him angry and hanging on to nothing with no plans for his life. Maybe it was time to live and feel again. He knew that he was tired of existing from day to day, wondering what tomorrow would bring.

"I would like to stay in the valley, Marie. Is that all right with you?"

Her eyes lit up and she screamed, jumped in his lap and kissed him on the neck, his eyes and mouth. "Do you really mean it, baby? We are really going to move together?"

"Yes, but the only thing that frightens me, is next you will expect me to marry you," he said teasingly.

"What's wrong with that, Steven? Why must we live together forever and not marry? Why can't we get married?" she asked, with a sad look in her eyes. God, she had never loved a man the way she loved Steven. He was her world, her dream, her reason for living.

"Do you really want to get married again?" he asked, turning to face her.

"Steven, yes. Marrying you is all I think of."

He wanted to marry again, too. But he wanted to

be in love when he got married. He was in love when he married Wanda and he wanted it again. But maybe he could love Marie, too. In any case, he didn't want to start all over again with someone new. He had gotten tired of the dating game. It didn't seem to agree with him. There were too many let-downs, disappointments and lies. He had lost Kim and didn't want to start over again.

"Okay, three months?" he heard himself ask. He couldn't believe what he had said. The words just seem to tumble out before he could stop them.

"Three months you'll marry me, or three months we'll live together?" she beamed, and held her breath waiting for his answer.

"Three months for both."

She started to cry and laid her head on his shoulder, wiping her eyes. "Thank you, God," she whispered. All she'd done to get him, all the time she'd waited. But now he was hers.

"Now, let's celebrate." He took her hand and led her to the closet.

"Why are you getting your jacket?" Marie asked.

"Let's go out and see a movie, or do something. I don't feel like staying inside tonight." He had to get out, to get some air.

Marie really wanted to do something more roman-tic, but she would settle for a movie, or something. "Good," she chuckled all the way out the door.

Chapter 19

Orchid was in the garden pulling up weeds that had grown around the African violets. The flowers were blooming beautifully and she loved their mixture of colors. She wiped her forehead with the back of her hand. Looking up, Orchid smiled as Chiku strolled over to see her.

"Does your Mama feel better?" Orchid asked.

"Sometimes, but she tires easily these days. I asked her if I could go to college a year later than scheduled. She says by then she'll be well again," Chiku said, and took a deep breath. She looked around to see if Busara was watching and broke off an orchid and placed it under her nose. "Smells sweet."

"You better not let Miss Busara see you."

"Don't worry, I won't."

"Anyway, I'm sure Eno will be stronger by the time you're ready to go off to school." But Orchid wasn't so sure that Eno would get better. From what Ahmed and Busara says, her heart was very weak. And she had lost over fifteen pounds in one month. She was already a thin woman, but now she looked like skin and bones. The birth of her last baby was just too strenuous on her heart. The baby was two months old and Eno hadn't regained her strength. The other children were young, too. And Chiku's life was babysitting and helping around the house. She didn't have a life like a young girl of her age. But, that was common among the Africans.

"My dad's sister will be here in a week. She's older than my mama, but she has no family left in West Africa. Her sister died a month ago. Now she only has my dad. Ifama comes over to help every day, too. That's how I was able to get out for a while today."

Orchid looked at the barn and saw Coffie going inside. He had been quiet since his breakup with Nordia, but no one spoke of her in his presence.

"There's Coffie. He's not the same anymore. He used to tease me but now he looks straight through me as if I'm not there. My mama says the woman was a slut. Was she pretty, Orchid?"

"On the outside, but not pretty on the inside. She didn't like me very much. Coffie will be all right. He just needs time to heal, that's all."

"What are you two up to?" Busara said, as she walked out in her garden.

"I was pulling up weeds when Chiku came over. Are you going to stay out here with us for a while, Miss Busara?" Orchid asked.

Still holding the orchid, Chiku quickly put her hand behind her so Busara couldn't see the flower in her hand.

Before Busara answered, all three looked around at the same time.

First there was a loud scream, and then Ifama

came running out of the house. "Busara, Busara, come quickly, you too, Chiku. Come, come quickly."

Chiku took off running with a cloud of dirt behind her. Busara and Orchid were right behind her.

"Come!" Ifama screamed again. She was standing in front of the house and Dume and Coffie dropped what they were doing and ran toward the house.

When Busara got to the house, Ifama was panting out of breath, trying to talk, crying, and pointing at Eno's house.

"She's dead, Busara. Eno is dead. I went into her room and she's not moving or breathing. Her eyes are wide open, and all I could see was the whites in them, yes, that's all I could see. Only the whites."

Chiku ran right past them, Dume and Coffie still in back of her. Once Chiku entered the room, Orchid heard a scream so agonizing that it tore at her heart. She knew too, that Eno was gone. Six children, four to be raised without a mother. Orchid broke down and cried just as everyone had done. She had never remembered being as sad as she was today.

So much happens in such a short time. Two months ago she was helping with the delivery of a new life just to lose another life now. And when she looked at Dume on his knees in front of the bed where his mother lay, it was all she could bear. Orchid almost crumpled to the floor when Ahmed grabbed her and held her in his arms. She hadn't even realized that he was in the house.

"You've got to be strong, love. Chiku needs you. She needs your courage and your help. Be strong, my love," he whispered. Orchid nodded and stood up against him. When she entered the small bedroom, Chiku was standing near the door. Orchid grabbed her and Chiku lay her head on her shoulder. Instantly she felt the tears from Chiku's eyes through her dress.

Chiku cried and wrestled with her, trying to go to her mother's bed.

Orchid held her close. "Cry all you want, Chiku. I'm here, so cry all you want." She had her arms around Chiku, feeling her back and shoulders tremble as she leaned on Orchid for support. Chiku and Orchid went back to the living room. "Ifama, take the children to my house. They shouldn't be here," Busara ordered.

"I want to stay with Mama," Chiku said. "I need to stay with my mama."

"You can stay. But the small children should go," Orchid whispered.

"Will you go back into the bedroom with me, Orchid? I want to see my mama."

"Yes, I'll go with you. I'll hold you and be there for you," Orchid said, crying softly. Everyone on the ranch had heard and all the other women that lived on the ranch huddled inside the small house.

Busara kneeled down in front of Eno and rubbed her hands against Eno's face, closing her eyes. She pushed everyone out of the room except Orchid and Chiku.

Busara uncovered Eno and dressed her in a white nightgown, brushed her hair and pulled the bedspread up to her waist. "She doesn't even look dead. One would think she's only sleeping, resting after a hard day's work," Busara said, as she stood by the bed.

Orchid wanted to scream, run, and do anything that would give her some relief. She looked toward the window; the weather was cloudy, as dark as the lachrymose mood around the ranch. And the black cloud that lingered over Eno's house seemed to get darker, spreading wider.

Busara pulled the shades down in Eno's room. She lit a candle and prayed in her Swahili tongue while the others came back into the room, all holding hands circling the bed and joined in.

Din had heard the news and rushed inside the house. He was breathing hard, his eyes quickly shifting to everyone praying, crying and asking for their god's help. As he walked inside he knew what had happened.

Din ran into the bedroom and saw Dume standing in the corner. His wife's eyes were closed, now her face looked peaceful, not tired, or in pain, she even looked younger. He knelt beside her and took her hand in his, tears rolling down his face. He held his hands up in the air and screamed so loud that everyone looked at each other.

"Why, My God Almighty? Oh, why?" he yelled. "Why my Eno?"

Dume led everyone back into the small living room so his father could have that time alone to grieve for his wife and everyone followed. He was so shaken that all he could do was pace the floor while everyone held their heads down in prayer.

Din got up off his knees and sat on the edge of their bed, still holding his wife's hand and whispering her name. After the crying had stopped, he just sat there and stared at her face. Every minute of their marriage he had loved her. How could he go on without her? What good would his life be grieving from day to day now that his Eno was gone? How would he get up every morning and face the day without her?

Dume went back inside the room and lay his hand on his father's shoulder. "Papa, are you sure you want to be alone in here? I can stay with you and we can grieve together." Although Eno wasn't his mother, he loved her, too.

Eno and Din were married when Dume was seven years old, six months after his own mother had died.

"No, Dume. You go. I'll stay with my wife, my Eno. I want you to send Chiku to Ahmed's house with the rest of the children."

"Chiku will not leave you, Papa."

"Yes she will. You must make her leave." He stared at Dume for a few seconds before he could compose himself to speak again. "I'm so lucky to have you, my son." He wrapped his arms around Dume's neck, hugging him tightly. "Now, I must be alone with my wife. Go, send Chiku."

Chiku didn't want to leave, but she knew that the children needed her. The newborn and three of her sisters were still too young to understand what had happened. She did as her father requested, to see after the children.

After five minutes of silence, a loud scream came from the bedroom. Dume, Coffie, Ahmed and one of the other men ran toward the bedroom, but before Ahmed's hand touched the doorknob, they heard the loud roar of a gunshot that resonated through the door, causing the small house to shake as though a tornado had run through it.

Ahmed, Coffie, and Dume stopped and looked at each other. Everyone knew what they would find on the other side of the door, and everyone held their heads in their hands and cried out loud.

Busara and the other women fell to their knees and prayed. The other women cried, but as usual,

Busara was the strong one. She only prayed. Then someone started to hum a song and the others joined in, humming, crying and praying for their loss. The smell of gunpowder floated from the other side of the door and lingered in the air like a bad omen.

When the door was opened to the bedroom, they found Din had changed into all white clothes, one arm lay over Eno's waist, and his other hand lay beside him, still holding the gun, his finger still wrapped around the trigger. The blood was spilling from the hole in his chest onto the bed, and slowly soaking onto Eno's white nightgown that Busara had changed her into.

He couldn't live without his wife.

"Baba! Oh no," Dume screamed. "I should have known. He wanted to be alone with Eno, but he wasn't speaking rationally." Dume cried out as he knelt down in front of Din and Eno's blood-soaked bed.

"Oh Baba, I'm so sorry, I'm so sorry," he repeated over and over again, as he sunk to the floor, his balled fist pounding hard against the thin mattress.

And then there was quiet, not a sound, no one spoke.

Orchid couldn't move, she couldn't breathe. Feeling as if her back was against the wall, and no place to run, she felt as though she would never breathe again, then the flood burst and the tears spilled over.

All of a sudden she needed air, she needed to feel free to run, hide, scream, and quickly ran out the door. She ran as fast as her legs could carry her. The wind had started to blow hard against her face. She was out of breath when someone grabbed her from behind.

Ahmed picked her up as though she were a baby and carried her back to the house, sat her down on the porch.

She was breathing hard, trying to take long draughts down into her lungs.

"Why is this happening, Ahmed?" she panted, and held her hands over her eyes, crying. When she looked up again, she saw the dark, gray cloud that lingered over Din and Eno's house. She closed her eyes tight and held her hands over her face.

"It's the way of life here, Orchid." He looked at her and for the first time, he was certain that she had not lived here before she was found.

"What about the children? What about Chiku going to college? Damn," she cried. "What about the babies, Ahmed? What will happen to them?"

He held her in his arms and felt the tears forming in his eyes as well. "Din couldn't live without his wife so he took his life. It's sad, but it has happened."

"Sad! It's more than sad. The children have no mother or father. Oh God, what just happened here?" she cried, and looked up at the sky as though she was waiting for an answer, but there wasn't any, no words, no explanation to this madness, just the grief, the loss that the children will suffer. And then she looked up at Ahmed's face, her eyes wide. It occurred to her that Chiku didn't know.

"Chiku doesn't know about her father yet. How can we tell her, what can we say?" she asked with dread. "How do you tell someone so young that her mother and father are both dead?"

Ahmed sighed and looked up at the sky. The clouds were moving to the west and the darkness was disappearing into the sky. "In a day or two, Din's sister will be here to take care of the children. We have to hear what Dume will decide. He will have to help us make the decision about his family. Now, you have to find a way to tell Chiku about her father's death."

"Why me? I don't know if I can do it, Ahmed."

"Yes you can. She listens to you. I will be with you, and so will Auntie Busara. She has to know now, Orchid. Busara will help you."

She nodded her head in agreement and held his hand. "It's best she knows all the bad news tonight," she thought. But Orchid wondered how much more could a sixteen-year-old teenager take in one day? To lose a mother and father in an hour, she couldn't imagine it. And she thought of her own mother and how she must have felt when she got the news of the plane crash and began crying softly.

A half hour had passed before Ahmed, Busara, and Orchid took Chiku to the patio of their house. Orchid sat close beside her, placing her arm around Chiku's shoulder and held her breath as Busara started first.

"Chiku, we have some more bad news to tell you, child . . ."

"There's no news as bad as my mother's death, Miss Busara," she yelled. "What could be worse?"

"Yes there is something worse, Chiku. There is more," Busara said with dread, and took Chiku's hand in hers.

Chiku sat up straight on the bench. She looked at Orchid's face, but Orchid held her head down. She couldn't look the girl in her eyes and was glad that Busara had taken over.

"You know how much your father loved your mother. Her death was too much for him and . . .

well . . ." Busara swallowed hard and cleared the lump from her throat.

In a low voice, Orchid stepped in to help Busara explain. "Your father just couldn't bear to see another day without Eno. It's hard for some people to live with the death of a loved one . . ."

"What is it, Miss Busara, Orchid?" She looked in both their faces. Her large, round eyes wide and frightened. "Where is my father, where is Dume?" She tried to stand but Orchid held her close. Chiku started to yell. "Papa! Papa! Where is he . . . ?"

"Shhhhhh, Chiku," Orchid said. Feeling the girl's body stiffen, Orchid held Chiku's head against her chest.

"Your father took his own life. He shot himself, Chiku, he is dead."

Busara tried to be as gentle as she could. But there was no gentle way to tell a child that their parent is dead.

She had said it and now she was waiting for Chiku's reaction, as they stared straight ahead. Busara was beginning to wonder if she had understood what she had just been told.

For a few seconds, it seemed as though Chiku went deaf. While Busara's lips were moving her brain seemed to shut down, nothing was getting through to her. Now she could no longer hear the horrible words that seem to rush from Busara's mouth. She didn't want to feel the pain that might kill her. She closed her eyes tightly and saw her mother's body, everyone crying around her in their small house. The kids still playing as if nothing had changed, the screams, crying, and now even though she couldn't hear, she knew, she knew her father was gone, too, and that her life had changed forever. She didn't cry, she didn't speak, and she couldn't move.

Chiku still hadn't spoken as Orchid undressed her and put her to bed. The tears had formed in her eyes and slowly rolled down her face. She felt empty with no life left in her.

Busara poured one of her herb teas down her throat to put her into a deep, deep sleep. It was getting late and Busara and Orchid went to bed for the night.

The next day after Ahmed and Coffie had breakfast and went out to work; Busara went to the library and closed the door behind her. She dialed the phone and waited for William to answer.

"Hello," William answered. He wondered who was calling him at seven-thirty before he could get to his office.

"William, this is Busara," she said clearly into the phone.

"William sighed when he heard Busara's voice over the phone. What did the old woman want this time, he wondered?

"William," Busara repeated. "Do you hear me?"

"Yes, Miss Busara. What can I do for you so early in the day?" He didn't dare upset her.

"The girl is unhappy. Something about her has changed . . ."

"I knew it. I knew I should have told Ahmed. I told you she was in the plane crash, but no, you wouldn't let me tell Ahmed the truth when I found out. Now, how has she changed?"

"Listen to me, William, and stop running off at the

mouth. I have a feeling she remembers and is afraid to tell Ahmed."

"She is a smart woman, Miss Busara. Well-to-do with a good job. Why would she be afraid to tell who she is?" Was the old women losing her mind?

"Because she's in love with Ahmed and doesn't want to lose him, that's why. Now, they are both in love. It's time. Once he knows, it will hurt, but one way or another, they will be together, William. He will marry Orchid. Besides, I put a love herb in their breakfast this morning. They will marry, I know what I'm talking about."

William shook his head in disbelief. Love herb? The old woman is losing all her senses. "Okay, Miss Busara. I'll call Ahmed today and tell him to come as soon as possible." He hung up, happy to get the news to Ahmed and off his chest.

Two days later, they walked in two straight lines, carrying the bodies to be buried side by side, singing a song in Swahili. They were all dressed in white—the same color that Din and Eno died in and were wearing for their burial.

The weather was warmer, but the spirits were low. The dark clouds that had rested over the ranch two days ago seem to have vanished and were replaced by a bright, and warm day.

Everyone walked slowly with sorrow and grief heavy in their hearts. Ahmed and Coffie had picked out the mahogany wood caskets trimmed in gold. The caskets were already hand-carved and stored on the ranch.

The small children stayed behind with Ifama. Chiku walked beside Dume and Orchid walked with

Busara. Ahmed and Coffie walked along with the rest of the men that were pallbearers.

In front of the caskets, Orchid stood next to Chiku and held her hand. As the men lowered the caskets into the newest scar in the earth, Chiku covered the caskets with petals of roses and white orchids. And as she stepped back she could feel Orchid's hand again tightened around hers.

The men held their rifles high and shot twice up to the sky; one shot for each body.

Dume stepped forward and placed a picture of his mother, father, and the children on top of the casket. Unable to watch the dirt placed on top of their caskets, he turned and walked away.

After the service, they all walked back in the two lines, singing, some still crying, unable to believe what had happened.

Chiku and Orchid spent the day together with the children. They were sitting around the garden as the children played.

"I don't know what I'm going to do now, Orchid. I can't go to school and leave my sisters and brothers with a stranger. I haven't seen my aunt for three years. The younger children won't remember her at all," she said, her voice was only a level above a whisper.

Ifama called them inside for lunch. Chiku and Orchid went back into the library alone with two sandwiches and two tall glasses of milk in front of them.

"By the time you go to college your aunt won't be a stranger to the children. You need the education now more than ever for you and the children. And by the way, eat your sandwich before you get sick," Orchid said in a demanding tone of voice. "You need to be strong and healthy for the children and for yourself."

Chiku took a bite out of her sandwich and placed it back on the plate. "Dume hasn't said anything to me today. Even as we walked so close together to the grave, he didn't speak one word. What if he leaves us?"

"He won't. Your brother loves you, Chiku. He doesn't understand what happened either." Orchid wiped a tear off her cheek. Everything around her was making her nervous or making her cry. Eno's and Din's deaths changed lives for others, and she had her own personal problem that was waiting to be dealt with. It would change the rest of her life as well.

"Why did he do it, Orchid? He knew we would need him after mama died. How could he leave us this way? Damn, damn him." She stomped the floor twice. "He took the easy way out and left his children to suffer." She cried and Orchid held her in her arms and cried with her.

In a way, Orchid had to agree with Chiku. Din did take the easy way out.

Two days later, Adhiambo, Din's sister arrived. Even though she was sad over her brother's death, she was still jolly around the children. Adhiambo was a large-framed woman, with large, round eyes, dark-brown skin, short hair, a wide nose, and a full mouth. When she laughed, her entire body trembled.

When Busara and Orchid walked into the house, Adhiambo was standing in the middle of the small living room with both hands on her hips.

"We need some light in this place and Auntie Adhiambo is going to cook you children a nice pot of stew and bake some sweet bread. We need some laughter in this house, too," she said to the baby as she picked him up and watched him chuckle.

Chiku stood in the door watching her aunt, not saying anything.

Her aunt turned around when she heard Chiku's movement. "This is not Chiku is it? Honey, you grew to be a fine-looking young girl. Looks just like Eno when she was a young girl."

"Auntie Adhiambo, this is Busara and Orchid. They live in the big house on the ranch."

Adhiambo stepped closer to Busara. "Thank you for having Ifama look after the children for me. They're a nice looking bunch of children, too. Sit down so we can get to know each other better."

"I remember when you were here before," Busara said. "As you can see, your brother's family grew." Busara looked at the children. They were all sitting on the floor looking from Busara and back at Adhiambo.

"Yes, three of the children weren't even born yet. I remember you, too. But I don't remember you, girl," she pointed at Orchid.

"I wasn't living on the ranch then," Orchid answered.

"Did one of the nephews get married?" Adhiambo asked.

"No. Orchid is a friend of the family," Busara said, not wanting to go into any more details. This wasn't the right time.

"The loss of my brother and sister-in-law was a shock to me. I had no idea that Eno had been down with a sickness," she said, dabbing at her eyes. "Din was my last brother. Now I have no family except the children. I want to do right by them. They're my blood."

"Are you going to live here with us?" Chiku finally asked. It had been bothering her since her aunt's arrival.

"No, Chiku. I have a larger house. You can have a bedroom to yourself. It's too small here for all of us."

"But, this is the only house we ever lived in," Chiku protested. "I don't want to leave the ranch." She looked from Orchid to Busara as though she needed their help.

"Chiku, you'll love it there. Dume mentioned that you wanted to go away to college, you still can. When you come back, the room will still be yours. It's time for a change, honey." She felt sorry for the girl, but she knew no one here and the ranch wasn't her home. What else could she do?

Chiku's mouth turned down in the corners; she held her head down. She wrung her hands as if she didn't know what to do with them. Everything was changing too fast and her life had taken a turn for the worse.

"We can talk some more about this. But for now, we need to talk and get to know each other. Where is Dume?"

"I don't know. He doesn't tell me anything," Chiku said, looking down at her hands.

The younger children finally got up and started to run and play without a care in the world. "Where is mama?" a little voice yelled out.

Chiku ran to him and held him close. The other three women wiped tears from their eyes.

"Adhiambo, we're going home so you can get settled in. You've only just arrived today. We'll be back later," Busara said standing up. "If there is anything you need, just give me a holler."

Orchid stood up, too, and looked at Chiku. "You

get to know your aunt. She'll need your help to show her around."

Chiku nodded her head and watched Busara and Orchid walk out the door.

"What do you think will happen to the children?" Orchid asked as they walked back to the house.

"She'll take them away. Chiku will stay there until she goes to college. Dume will keep the house on the ranch as long as he works here. Who knows, he may even find himself a wife and she can move in with him and have his child. Maybe even more than one."

"It's so sad, Miss Busara. Every time I think of Eno and Din, and now the children, I cry for all of them."

"So do I, child. But now it's out of our hands. Poor Din just couldn't go on."

"It's cruel what he's done to his children. Now they have no one. They needed him."

Busara held up one hand. "Don't judge, Orchid. It's very possible he wouldn't have been in any condition to help his children after Eno's death. Some people grow sick in the head after losing a loved one. They may be better off with Din's sister. At least they won't be separated. They can grow up together. What if they had no one at all?" Busara asked.

"You are right. I hadn't thought of it that way. In a way, they are lucky."

They walked inside and started dinner. The day before no one cooked and no one ate.

Five days later, Adhiambo had made arrangements to take the children home. Everyone on the ranch was quiet and sad that day. It was as though family members were leaving and would never be seen again.

Dume and Chiku had started to talk again. And the saddest thing was that Chiku didn't want to leave her brother behind. She had gone to Orchid and discussed how miserable she felt.

"Chiku, he's twenty years old. He is a man and can take care of himself," Orchid explained. "Remember, he has friends here."

"I know. But I hate to leave him. We are so close and I get the feeling that once I leave, we will grow apart. What if I never see him again, Orchid?"

"You will, honey."

"Who will cook and clean for him? He doesn't know how to do any of those things for himself. African men leave the cooking and cleaning to the women."

"He can learn to cook or come over here and eat with us. Eno is not alive to do it anymore. You have the younger children to worry about."

"Yes I do. I think my aunt is going to be okay. She plays with the children and talks to me. But I want to come back to visit. This is my home. It's where Papa and Mama are buried."

"One day you will. I promise you, Chiku. No matter where you are, we will meet again."

"But what if you remember who you are and leave the ranch?" she asked.

"That won't stop me from seeing you again. Even if I live far away, I'll see you again. And I'll write to give you my new address. We can write all the time."

The next week was all tears for Orchid. The day Chiku and the children left, Dume didn't come home to say good-bye and Chiku cried. Saying good-bye was heartbreaking for everyone on the ranch.

Orchid stayed to herself that day. She couldn't eat or sleep that night. Ahmed tried talking to her, but she was just so dispirited that nothing he said made any difference. Eno and Din were dead, the children were gone, Chiku was unhappy, and nothing Ahmed could say would change anything.

As the weeks passed, Orchid grew more depressed. It was time to tell Ahmed the truth. But she just couldn't bring herself to do it and when he made love to her, she cried every time he left her room.

One evening Orchid was walking around the ranch as she watched the sun drop toward the peak of the mountain as though it had vanished in the air. She saw Dume walking toward her with a young woman.

"Orchid, this is my sister by my mother. I wrote her a letter to give her news of my father's death. She's gonna stay with me for two or three weeks. Mika, this is Orchid."

Orchid looked at her face, she looked to be about twenty-five, shy with a warm smile. Her dark eyes were slanted deeply into a thin pear-shaped face. She was soft-spoken and shy. Her hair was pinned on top of her head and her blue dress was long and baggy. Orchid shook her hand and they said hello. She wasn't a pretty woman but she had a look of innocence and a glow to her brown, coffee-colored skin.

"I wish I had arrived before the children left. I would have loved to meet Chiku again. Every time Dume writes, he speaks so well of her."

"She is a good girl, smart, too." Orchid still couldn't speak of Chiku without getting all choked up, remembering the horrible day that changed Chiku's life.

Mika sensed it and changed the conversation. Too much sorrow had been around the ranch for anyone to speak of that day so soon.

"When Dume introduced Mika to Busara, she invited them to dinner. They accepted her invitation.

That night at dinner, it was obvious to everyone that Coffie was quite taken with the young woman. First, he looked at her with his mouth open, unable to speak. They talked, and watched each other from the corners of their eyes. Coffie hadn't smiled so much since his breakup with Nordia.

Later in the week, Dume and Mika were over again for dinner, and again, Coffie enjoyed her company enormously. His genial disposition had returned and the pain that was inflected upon him by Nordia seemed to have been forgotten.

Coffie loved watching Mika. During their conversation at dinner, she said that she wanted two children, and of course, she wanted the first to be a son so he could work by his father's side and pass his name down to her great grandchildren. Coffie couldn't keep his eyes off Mika.

After two weeks had passed, Mika decided to stay at the ranch longer. By then, it was obvious that they were in love. Everyone liked Mika. She helped around the ranch and visited with Orchid and Busara every day.

"Mika is just what Dume needed. Now he won't be alone in the house with so many memories around him and no one to talk to. And we all know she's good for Coffie," Orchid said, as she sat in the kitchen watching Busara mixing more herbs. "And maybe onc day soon, Coffie will build his house."

Orchid got up and went to the window. She spotted Coffie and Mika talking. As they talked Mika blushed and lightly touched Coffie's hand. They were a lovely couple.

"You know, I think you're right, Orchid. It's frightening that we think so much alike. I mean, look how we got rid of Nordia." Busara smiled as she looked out the window, too. "They are seeing a lot of each other these days. That boy comes in every evening, eats dinner, bathes and off he goes to Dume's house. She's the right girl for my Coffie, you know." And Busara knew that Orchid was the right woman for Ahmed, too. She knew it when she was visiting her in the hospital. Which was why she brought her to the ranch. What good-looking children they could make.

"I agree, Miss Busara. Mika is the right woman for Coffie. She's never been married and has no children. They can grow together, have a family of their own."

"So, what are we going to do about it?" Busara asked and winked her eye.

"I don't think we have to do anything but wait. It's just a matter of time now."

That night, Coffie joined Ahmed in the library to go over invoices and contracts he would be taking to Nairobi with him. "I'm leaving tomorrow morning now that the children have left and you have someone to keep you company. Also, I think that William may have some news about Orchid. He sure took his time about it."

"Really? Can he tell you who she is?" Coffie asked.

"I hope so. But he wouldn't over the phone. He wants to see me in person. I'm convinced that she's not from around here or from any other tribe. It's been months. We have to know who she is."

"You're in love with her, Ahmed?"

Ahmed frowned and started to answer when Coffie waved his hand to stop him.

"I've known for some time now. I hope everything works out, man. I want her as a sister-in-law. She has grown so strong and everyone on the ranch likes her. Auntie Busara loves her. Orchid belongs here, Ahmed."

"I don't know, Coffie. I want her here but she doesn't belong to me, yet."

"She will, man," Coffie said and smiled at his brother. It seems both of them have found the right women in their lives.

"What about Mika?" Ahmed asked.

Coffie's smiled widened. "I love her, too. She's nothing like Nordia."

"I know, Coffie. Don't get married before I get back, ha?"

"I guess I can wait. But, don't take too long. Anyway, she's waiting for me outside."

Ahmed gave him a playful punch on his arm and chuckled as Coffie rushed off.

Coffie went back to the garden where he had left Mika and Orchid.

"Here he is," Orchid said, looking at Coffie as he stepped outside. He was dressed in a pair of jeans and sleeveless white T-shirt. His eyes smiled as he looked at Mika waiting diligently for his return.

"I think I'm going to call it a night. It's been a long day, Orchid said."

"Amen to that," Coffie answered. "I was up early this morning. Started work at six."

"Why so early, Coffie?" Mika asked.

"So I could spend more time with you this evening."
His eyes were warm as he looked at her.

Orchid smiled and went inside. She looked
around for Busara but she had already gone to her
room. She had been up late ever since Din and Eno's
death. Orchid went into the library where Ahmed
was sitting behind his desk.

"I'm leaving tomorrow for Nairobi again," he said,
looking up and noticing how her hair had grown. It
was soft as feathers, falling into curls almost past her
shoulders. Her face glowed under the light; all the
scars had almost diminished into her natural color.
The disappointment in her face didn't go unnoticed
when Ahmed announced that he would be leaving.
He wanted to grab her and kiss her until her legs
weakened.

"I'll miss you," she said, her hands folded in front
of her. She sat in the chair in front of his desk. "How
long will you be away this time?"

"Only two days. Maybe one day I can take you with
me, Orchid. You haven't been off this ranch since
you got here, except to Sada's house with Coffie.
Would you like that, Orchid? To be alone with me for
two or three days?"

Unable to answer, Orchid could only nod. She felt
the hairs stand up on her arms. She couldn't imagine anything so wonderful, but she knew it could
never happen. As soon as he got back she had to
leave. Her mind was made up. She knew what she
had to do. In her heart, she knew that she had already waited too long, but so much had happened
that it was just never the right time, or they were
never in the right place.

"When I get up tomorrow morning, you'll be

gone?" She heard her own voice crack and tried to smile to hide it.

"Yes, but you'll be up all night, love," he answered ever so softly, so sexy.

She closed her eyes for a few seconds and as she opened them he was watching her.

"I'm going to bed, Ahmed," she said in a suggestive manner. Her lips curved up in the corner of her mouth into a warm smile. Touching his hand as she got up, she bent over and kissed him on one cheek.

It wasn't long before Ahmed was lying near her naked body, kissing her. His hands touched her passionately and a moment later their bodies were enmeshed, just as their mouths had been.

Tonight was special to Orchid and she wanted it to last forever. She wanted to feel his lips hot against hers, feel the weight of his muscular body on top hers. God, she wanted this man forever and ever. And it was a night that they couldn't seem to get enough of each other. Orchid held on to him feeling his body harden as he responded to her every need. And she responded to his.

Ahmed closed his eyes as he felt the passionate intensity of her need, her silky sweetness and the soft flesh against him. He couldn't let go of her.

It was very late when Ahmed went to his room to rest for two hours before it was time to get up again.

When Orchid got up the next morning, Ahmed had already left. All she had left were the memories of what they had the night before.

Chapter 20

Los Angeles, June 2001

"Hey, let's go out, get a bite to eat and pick out our rings."

Marie's eyes sparkled and she quickly turned around to face Steven. "What? Do you really mean it, Steven?"

"Hell, yes. We can't get married without rings can we?"

They were in Steven's apartment sitting at the kitchen counter. Marie jumped off the barstool and threw her arms around his neck. "Now, when are we going apartment hunting?" she asked, and kissed him again, and again.

"I still have some time here. Let's do one thing at a time, baby."

"Okay. Okay. I'll settle for the ring, and you." She was so happy.

Her life and dreams had finally become real. Pretty soon, he would be out of Wanda's house and into one they would select together.

Steven was quiet as he drove to the jewelry store in Sherman Oaks Mall.

After picking out their rings, Steven drove to Los Angeles and exited off Crenshaw Boulevard, making a left on Jefferson Boulevard.

Marie looked out the window. "Where are we going, Steven?"

"To Harold's and Bell's. I feel like having a nice dinner with my wife-to-be." He grabbed her hand as he looked at the joy in Marie's face. "It's a beautiful night, now let's enjoy it."

The restaurant was busy as usual on a Friday evening, but the wait wasn't very long. They both ordered catfish, red beans, rice, and salads. They talked about their plans to be married and decided to find another apartment in the valley.

After dinner they went back to Steven's apartment. Marie's spirits were high as she sauntered into the bedroom where she kept her bathrobe. She looked around the room, seeing no sign of Wanda ever living there.

Steven was in the living room waiting for her. He sat down on the sofa, his head laid back, eyes closed, as he thought of Wanda. When they had planned their marriage, the magic and excitement was there. He didn't feel it with Marie, but he could live with that. Life just wasn't perfect. How did that song go? *"If you don't have the one you love, love the one you're with."* Well, he wondered about that, too.

Chapter 21

Thika, East Africa

There was a flash of anger in his brown eyes. He balled the papers in his hand and flung them to the floor. He paced, and kicked the papers in the air. He was a fool for falling in love with a woman he hardly knew. But he didn't expect the report to tear him apart and take away the woman he loved.

"Married! Married, to whom? Why isn't he here searching for her, placing ads in the papers, passing out posters of his missing wife? Doing something to find his wife?" he shouted across the room. "God-damn, William, why couldn't you have found this out sooner?" he asked, his voice coated with harshness. "It took you months to find this out."

William sat back in his chair behind his desk and waited for Ahmed to calm down. His stomach was flipping over and over and his insides felt sick.

"My man who does that kind of work for me was laid low with his diabetes. I'm sorry, man, but I did the best I could. It was hard to trace, Ahmed. She wasn't found close to the plane crash. I still don't know how she got to your ranch. If you wouldn't have gotten a picture of her to compare with the missing people that weren't found, I would still be searching. William hadn't gotten very much sleep since Busara sent the letter and he had to sound as convincing as possible. Ahmed was no fool, William thought as he looked into Ahmed's angry eyes. He shivered from the thought of Ahmed finding out that he had lied to him. But he was at Busara's mercy. There was nothing he could do.

"What am I going to do, and how will I tell her?" he said, this time getting up to kick the wastepaper basket across the room as papers spilled over the floor.

William had worked for Ahmed since he returned from college to take over his father's ranch. They had become close friends. Ahmed could trust William with all his legal affairs. William was a short, pudgy, dark-skinned African, with small round eyes that were always red as though he hadn't gotten enough sleep the night before, and wire frame glasses rested on the end of his nose. William knew Ahmed as well as he did his own brother, and knew to let him release his anger before he'd listen and make sense out of the mess he had gotten himself into, with the help of his aunt. But Ahmed would never know that. And what good has it done? The woman was married to someone else anyway.

"What do you mean, you still don't know how she got to the ranch?"

"Well, the plane was low when it crashed, which explains how she lived through the crash. The plane broke in pieces that went flying all over the place, and so did the bodies. Pieces of the plane and the bodies weren't in one place. And I never understood why the search was discontinued so quickly. But of course, there was no one on the plane that was important enough to continue it longer. At least in the eyes of the law, and it was a small plane. The plane even took a different route from what was scheduled and left a half hour later. It was like God was against it all the way. You just have to tell her, man," he suggested.

"I know that, man. Don't you think I know what I have to do?" But for a moment he wondered if she really had to know, if he really had to lose her to another? But first and foremost, he was a man of honor. He had to tell her.

"How long have you been sleeping with this woman, man? Under the circumstances that was a dangerously stupid thing to do. Now you're in love with her and she belongs to another." He stopped, sensing he had said enough.

"Don't you think I know that? Damn, I feel like going out tonight and busting some heads, man," he grumbled.

"Then I'll have to get you out of jail. That won't help anything. It would just make matters worse." William got up and poured two glasses of brandy. "Here, you need this, and so do I."

Ahmed drank it down and refilled his glass again and again. He was still pacing the floor, trying to put the puzzle together, but the more he talked about it, the angrier he got. He sank back down in the chair and faced William. "For the first time I have a problem that I can't fix, not with money or my fist. Sure, I know that I have to tell her, but that means I will lose her." He shook his head in disgust. "Damn," he snorted. Ahmed had never faced so agonizing a decision.

"If I don't tell her and she remembers, I still lose

her." He sat straight up in his chair. "There's no winning in this situation and she loves me, too, William. She loves me, not him."

William was tapping his pen against his desk until Ahmed looked at him as though he was going to rip it out of his hand. William placed the pen in the desk drawer. He knew how dangerous and destructive Ahmed could be if he got too angry, and he hadn't been this angry since the time he caught two men climbing inside the kitchen window of his house. One man was nearly beaten to death with his bare hands. The other one pulled a gun, but Ahmed was faster and shot him straight between his eyes.

"When are you returning to the ranch?"

"Tomorrow, maybe the day after. I have to conclude my other business tomorrow morning." He refilled his glass again. "What's the rush?"

"No rush." William was getting nervous. This was going to be a long, dragged out night. If they went to a bar, Ahmed might start a fight, if they stayed in his office, he may destroy it.

William got up and picked the papers up off the floor and placed them into the trash can. He started to set it beside his desk, but changed his mind, set it in the corner out of Ahmed's reach.

"You said she has a mother and sister?"

"Yes. I can imagine what they've gone through," William answered, and took off the navy jacket to his suit and hung it on the coat hanger. The brandy was making him uncomfortably warm.

"I can imagine, too. Man, what am I to do?"

"You already know the answer to that, Ahmed. You have to tell her. Maybe she doesn't even love her husband any longer. She may want to stay with you. Have you even considered that?"

"Yes, I have. But she still has to go back. And once she gets there, she may not ever return. Besides, she may not like Africa enough to make it her home. Have you thought of that?"

"No," William shook his head in answer.

"It's stuffy in here, William. Let's go out and have a few drinks."

"Okay man, but only a couple. After we drink, you go to the hotel or my house and sleep it off. And remember, no breaking heads," William warned.

Early the next morning, Ahmed phoned Coffie to tell him he was going to stay a day longer. But Orchid only heard the news through the conversation between Coffie and Ahmed while they were on the phone.

Orchid had been practicing a speech for Ahmed. She was trying to find a way to tell him that she had to leave. Now, she had to wait a day longer, which would feel like a lifetime and another night of losing sleep.

The next morning she was up early. Orchid needed to take a walk outside and try to clear her head.

She stood on a hill and looked over the Kikuyu ridges to Mount Kenya, which could be seen only in the early mornings, and in the evenings, at certain times of the year. This was a spot that Chiku had showed her and she often went to be alone. Chiku, she really missed her, and wondered if she was getting adjusted to her new home, although she probably would never consider it as her home since she grew up on the ranch. Orchid had been here for only a few months but she knew that leaving the ranch would leave a part of herself behind. Africa was where her heart would stay.

Orchid started back home, and suddenly she stopped in her tracks, remembering something that she had forgotten. She closed her eyes and a face appeared in front of her, the face of a white man. It was the face of the white man who had come to the house about a month ago. And now that she remembered, the man had looked at her strangely. She wondered why she felt as though she had seen him before. The puzzle was falling into place. He wasn't looking for Ahmed. He was looking for her. One of the men that had dropped her off near the ranch so she could be found. There were two of them, but she didn't see their faces very clearly. But she remembered his voice, hearing it in her head all over again. He sound as though he had a cold.

Hurt and half conscious, Orchid had been found lying in some tall, wet bushes. The two men argued and yelled at each other. One man wanted to leave her to die, but the other had disagreed. Orchid remembered hearing him say it would cause trouble. "Those ignorant Africans will say we beat her and may even accuse us of raping her. People will be killed over some woman we know nothing about. I say if you're stupid enough to do it, then drop her in the middle of the road and let her people find her. We've been riding around in circles long enough." But the other voice disagreed. He was concerned about the rainy, cold weather.

"She could die in this weather. Even if we don't know her, we can't let a human die this way. I can't just leave a woman here to die."

Orchid didn't hear any words for a while. She must have lost consciousness again. Then she felt as though her body was moving, floating. She was sure that she had been dreaming, but they were on the road because the ride got bumpy.

"I hope you know what you're doing, you moron."

"I'm going to drop her off at the Bakari Ranch, but far enough away so they can't see us. If she dies, at least we tried. Maybe one of the ranch hands will see her and take her to the house."

"How far is this damn ranch?" he asked. His voice had an angry edge to it.

"We should be there in about fifteen minutes. Make sure she's covered so no one passing on the road can see her."

Again she lost consciousness. She didn't remember when they dumped her or when she was found and taken to the house. The next morning she was being dressed by Busara and taken to the hospital. The man must have been curious enough to see if she was alive, or if she remembered his face. He looked straight into her eyes, but at the time she didn't recognize him. Yet now she remembered his voice, his glassy cold blue eyes, one shining and larger than the other. His face wasn't clear, but she knew the quirky voice. *And now, finally, she remembered how she got to the ranch.*

Orchid walked back to the house and met Busara at the door following her into the kitchen. She had placed fresh flowers in the middle of the table and a small bag of potatoes were on the sink.

"My, we're up and out early this morning. Where have you been?" Busara asked.

"I wanted to go for a walk. I couldn't sleep. I needed to get out."

"Sit down, Orchid," she said, and folded the dishcloth on the table in front of her. "It looks like it's going to rain today. Ahmed is staying in Nairobi an extra day, but I don't know with this weather. And the rain just makes it hotter." Busara got up and adjusted the curtain at the window and sat back down at the table again. "It's time for me to make new curtains. I think I will make some with bright flowers to lighten it up in here."

"Did you make those?"

"Yes, I did. With these old hands," Busara said holding her hands in front of her face.

"Is there anything you can't do, Miss Busara? You do so much around here and you're so natural at it."

"When I was a child, my mother made everything. Unfortunately, she didn't have life as easy as I do here. But she taught me everything I know."

"I worry about Chiku all the time, Miss Busara, I can't get the family out of my head. And Din, I can't seem to forget the gunshot, the screaming, I hear it all the time." She held her head down for a few seconds to compose herself. It was still so fresh in her mind. "It's so hard. Lately Dume is so quiet and withdrawn from everyone. I know he's hurting and missing his family. I'm glad Mika is here with him." Orchid shook her head. An entire family wiped out in a matter of minutes. It seemed so inconceivable to her.

"Of course Dume is hurting. I just wish that he would find himself a nice girl and have a family of his own. That'll make it easier for him, but he will always miss his family, Orchid. Din and Dume were so close. They worked side by side every day. But dead is dead, no one can change it, and Dume is alive."

Orchid nodded in agreement. "Dume and Chiku were close, too. I'm sure he worries about her," Orchid said.

"And I'm worried about you, Orchid. If you don't get ahold of yourself, you're going to make yourself sick. Life isn't easy here. You'll have to learn that." Busara reached over and touched her hand.

"Child, you've grown strong while you've been here, but not strong enough, and you haven't seen everything. This is a wild country and it can work on you. But I know that you can grow stronger and love it just as we do." Busara was convinced of that. "You have to take life as it is here. Like I said, dead is dead. Living is living. That's just the way life is here."

"I know, Miss Busara. I just have so much on my mind."

"I know. You want to remember who you are, where you're from, and who is your family. Stop trying to force something you can't control until it happens to you, child."

Orchid sipped her tea and frowned, not expecting it to be so strong. Busara had made it with one of her herbs. Her eyes watered, her throat tightened.

"More water?" Busara asked when she saw Orchid's cheeks burn.

"Yes, just a little."

If only Miss Busara knew what was really bothering her, she thought. Sometimes she wondered if Busara sensed that she remembered. She wanted to tell her, to cry on her shoulder and ask her would everything turn out as she dreamed so many times. Sure, life wasn't so easy here. You saw newborns and you saw death. But the truth was, she wanted to stay. This is where she belongs, where her heart is. And she wanted to marry Ahmed. Orchid sighed. She had to tell her. She looked at Busara and opened her mouth, "Miss Busara . . ."

"Busara," Ifama stuck her head in the back door

yelling Busara's name as she stepped inside the kitchen. "I knocked at the front door but no one heard me. That tea smells good, oh yes it does. I could sure use a cup."

"Here, I'll get you a cup," Busara replied. "You're up and about early today, Ifama."

"Couldn't sleep last night. Lay awake till after midnight before I slept. Yes I sure did, so I got out of bed and got dressed. And how are you today, Orchid? You don't look well, girl." Ifama said, "No you don't. What ails you, child? A young pretty girl like you should be happy. Get yourself a man, girl. Now, that's what you need." Ifama shook her head.

"It's just a headache. This tea should help," Orchid answered.

"I have something for that, too. I made up a herb mixture for young women's headaches," Busara answered.

Ifama laughed out loud. "I thought the only thing that could cure a young woman's headache was a young man. Good for the mind, too. I remember what it was like to have a healthy buck around my house. Yes I do." She laughed out loud and sipped her tea. Her salt-and-pepper colored French braids were all over her head, and the white, wiry strands were sticking out as wild as the winds. Her large ears perked like those of a young puppy ready to be fed.

Orchid laughed, suddenly amused at the absurdity of her situation. It was men that had caused her headache.

Orchid excused herself and walked out of the kitchen. On her way to her room, she stopped in the library and sat behind Ahmed's desk. Reaching for the phone, her hands felt frozen, trembling as she dialed the number and heard the phone rang.

"Hello. Hello."

She heard Steven's voice on the other end, but words were stuck in her throat as she tried to force them out.

"Hello, hello," he said softly. "Who is this?"

She held the receiver until Steven hung up on the other end. Orchid couldn't say anything and ran to her room.

Chapter 22

"Who was that?" Marie asked and stood beside Steven. She walked in from the bathroom and found him standing in the kitchen with the phone in his hand, his mouth open. He looked as though he'd been spooked by a ghost.

"So, who was on the phone, Steven? Are you okay?"

"I don't know. I kept saying hello but no one answered."

"Then why are you so concerned if no one answered?"

"Hell, Marie. It was just so weird. I could feel the presence of someone there and they were listening to me. I know they were listening. Didn't say a word, just held the phone."

She sat next to him. "I stopped and looked at a lovely apartment today. It's not far from here. Time is running out. We only have a few weeks before we're married. I've been making plans all week," she said, waiting for his response. But he said nothing. "The place is ready, so we can move right in." She stopped talking and looked at him. It was as though he hadn't heard a word she had said.

He picked up the newspaper that he was reading before the phone rang and placed it back on the table again.

She looked at him as though he had lost his mind. People call wrong numbers every day. Why would he be so disconcerted over something as simple as a wrong number? She wondered. Unless, of course, he thought it was Kim? Was she back, Marie thought giving a frustrated sigh? Was it possible that Kim wanted him back?

"Are you sure you don't know who was on the phone?" she asked with concern.

"Yeah, I'm sure. Now why are you so bothered about a wrong number?" As though he had forgotten, he picked up the newspaper again, folded it and pushed it away from him.

"Is there someone else in your life, Steven?"

He turned around and looked at her. "What, what does that have to do with anything? What is wrong with you, Marie?"

"Nothing, I guess." She sat back and lay her head against the sofa. Everything had been going so well for them lately. She didn't want to ruin it.

"Steven? This is too crazy. It's only a phone call with a wrong number!" She circled her arms around his neck.

"I'm just a little tired tonight. I'm so sorry, baby. Let's just forget about this and go to bed." She got up, ambled to the bedroom door and turned around and motioned for him to follow.

"Okay, Wanda."

"Shocked, she swiveled on her heels and took a

step forward, feeling her heart lurch. It was such a blow, she couldn't say anything.

"Look, I'm sorry," was all he could say. "I'm really sorry, Marie." He watched as her smile slowly disappeared, replaced by overwhelming hurt and sadness. And he had put it there. He was truly sorry.

Was it Wanda he wanted to be on the other end of the phone? thought Marie. Lord, am I in competition with a dead woman? Wanda was always the perfect one and it made her sick to her stomach. But she loved him. Once they were married she could make him happy, make him forget Wanda. All she needed to do was marry him, soon.

Late that night, Steven turned over in bed and looked at Marie; she was asleep. He lay there with his eyes closed, but couldn't sleep. The phone call had bothered him and he didn't know why, but it had. He could hear someone breathing, listening, waiting. Someone was there, it was no wrong number, he was sure of it. Had Kim changed her mind, was it really her after all this time, he wondered? Couldn't be. She had made it clear that she wanted nothing to do with him. He thought of Wanda. Could she . . .? No. No, she was dead. He turned his back to Marie and closed his eyes again, but to no avail, he couldn't sleep.

Chapter 23

Thika, East Africa

The nights were the longest when Ahmed was away, and the rain only made the night longer. He still had not returned home, and Orchid was up late, waiting, hoping for his return.

The hardwood floor was cold under her bare feet. Orchid went into the library and selected a book to take back to her room. After reading a sentence and forgetting it right after she had read it, she closed the book and placed it on the table beside her bed.

Just as she was falling into a deep sleep, she was awakened by voices in the library next to her room. Half asleep, she finally realized it was Ahmed's and Coffie's voices. Tomorrow she had to tell him that she remembers a life before him, and she had to call Steven. Once she got home, she would call her mother and sister and decide what to do with her life.

Orchid sighed and wondered what the weather was like in LA. Unable to fall back to sleep, she waited and wondered if Ahmed would come to her room. After she waited for an hour she knew he

would not come to her. She lay there for hours waiting for tomorrow to come. Looking at the small
window, Orchid saw the sun forcing its way through
the clouds giving more light inside her bedroom.

"When will you tell her?" Coffie asked. He looked
into his brother's face. He hadn't shaved in days. His
eyes were puffy, red from lack of sleep and too much
drinking.

"Today, it's time she knows who she is. It blew me
away when William told me that she has a husband,"
he said with a flash of anger dancing dangerously in
his eyes. Ahmed saw red every time he thought of
Orchid having a husband.

"I'm sorry, Ahmed. This is bad news for all of us,
especially you."

Ahmed looked at him, murmured something and
cleared his throat. "Yeah, especially me. I bought her
plane ticket already. She needs to leave tomorrow, as
soon as possible."

Coffie stood up in front of the desk. "So soon,
man? What if she wants to stay a few more days?
Aren't you being hasty about this?"

"Hasty? What do you mean hasty? I've been sleeping with a married woman, which goes against
everything I believe in. It's been too long already.
There's no need for her to stay a day longer, Coffie.
I can't look at her any longer and let her leave." He
pushed the stack of papers that were in front of him
to the side of the desk.

"She loves you, Ahmed."

"I know. I love her, too." He had never admitted it
to anyone before.

"Does Auntie Busara know yet? She's going to be shocked and disappointed."

"Don't let that old woman fool you, Coffie. She's probably been wondering all along if Orchid was married. But, no, I haven't told her yet."

Coffie sat down again and placed both hands over his face. "Man, this is too crazy."

"Now, what's going on in your life, Coffie?"

Coffie stuck his chest out. "I think it's time I build that house."

Ahmed got up and slapped him on his back. "I think you're making a good decision and a terrific choice in a woman, too."

"Thanks man, I wish we were doing this together." Coffie knew that Ahmed had a lot on his mind so he walked out to leave him alone. As he walked down the hall, he started to turn around and knock on Orchid's door, but changed his mind. What could he say to her?

The next morning it was quiet at breakfast. No one ate very much except Busara. She looked from Ahmed to Orchid and when she looked at Coffie he looked just as unhappy as the other two. And Coffie had no reason to be unhappy. Was it her cooking, was there something they were keeping from her? No. She knew that William must have told Ahmed. He looked too miserable.

Ahmed looked like he hadn't slept the entire time he was away. Orchid had been walking around like a ghost, and Coffie had been happy, but not this morning. She would wait until someone tells her. Busara tried to make idle conversation but no one seemed very interested and said very little to her.

Orchid got up first. She couldn't stand to sit there any longer and went to her room. Standing in front of her closet, she was trying to decide what clothing to pack. Should she leave everything except the clothes on her back? After all, Ahmed had bought everything she wore except the red and green dress and the pink nightgown that Busara had given her.

Orchid heard a light knock at her bedroom door and answered it.

"Orchid, it's nice out today. Why don't we go for a walk?" Ahmed asked.

Her heart raced as he looked at her. She noticed again, that he looked at her differently this morning. She had noticed it at breakfast but couldn't figure out why. Now, he had the same look as if he was looking at her for the first time, or the last.

"Sure. Just let me get my sweater," she answered in a soft, passive voice.

"I'll wait outside." He stepped out leaving her staring at the closed door.

This was going to be worse than she had anticipated. Ahmed knew something, something had changed between them, she knew. God, she thought. Could it get any worse? Orchid leaned against the closet door and closed her eyes, willing the tears to stay in check and trying to keep herself from falling apart.

She stepped outside and Ahmed was waiting for her. He looked tired from his trip. But he was staring at her.

"Are you feeling well today?" he asked with concern.

"Yes, no, I mean, okay. I just have a headache this morning." And she was scared. God, she was scared. She walked beside him wondering where was he taking her. Would he want to make love to her?

"There's a small lake not far from here. I don't

think you've seen it yet," he gestured, showing her the direction. But he didn't say anything until they were there.

"Here. Isn't it nice and quiet? I come here when I have some thinking to do. It's quiet and the water is so calm and blue."

Orchid smiled at him for the first time that morning. "Yes, it is beautiful here." She sat against a tree and he sat beside her.

"How was your trip, Ahmed? I missed you. The ranch is never the same when you are away." Why does he keep looking away when I look at him, she wondered?

"My trip was profitable. And I found some information that I needed."

"Good, as long as it turned out the way you wanted it to."

"When Coffie and I were children we used to play up and down the hill over there," he said, looking up at a flock of birds flying overhead. "My father was the only one that knew we'd come here. But I guess everyone has their favorite spot."

"Yes, I guess every one does. When I was home I had mine, too. I used to go for long walks by the pier in . . ." Her mouth fell open and she looked at his face. His jaws had tightened and his eyes were wide with questions.

"You used to go where? How long have you remembered, Orchid? How long?" he shouted at her.

Oh God, what have I done? "I was going to tell you today. I wanted to tell you before but so much had happened and so fast, Ahmed. It was always one thing after another."

"Damn you. How long, I ask you?" He stood up and grabbed her up by her arm.

"You are hurting me," she cried out.

"When did you first remember, I asked you?" He was getting out of control with rage and anger.

"The day, the day in the cave. After the shots, the snake was so large and the shots were so loud, my ears rang and my head was hurting so badly, I remembered, I remembered," she screamed out a loud cry, falling to the ground. "And I wanted to die right then and there. Oh God, it all came back. Why did it come back to me, why now?"

He stood there, looking down at her. How could she not tell him? He had fallen in love with her, trusted her, and wanted her more than any other woman.

"How could you not tell me? You had so many chances. We were together so many times after that day in the cave. You could crawl under me, but you couldn't tell me?"

She got up and grabbed his arm, but he pushed her away. "Don't touch me ever again. I found out who you are when I was in Nairobi, but unlike you, I didn't keep it a secret. You know why? Because I love you." He threw both hands up in the air and turned his back to her. "You're out of here tomorrow morning."

"Ahmed, please don't send me away like this. Please don't, please listen to me, please," she pleaded and cried, struggling to make him understand. "I'll do anything, Ahmed. It's not what you think."

"Oh yes it is. You are a liar woman, and you took advantage of the way I felt about you. I can't trust you, Orchid. I don't know you." His face was filled with accusation, and he was insensitive with his words, callous, his voice harsh. He looked at her as though she were no more than a stranger to him.

She was angry and hurt at his allegation, but she had to make him understand what she had been going through and how she felt about him.

"Just listen to me. I've been going through hell since I regained my memory. I was going to tell you today, I swear," she was saying. "I haven't slept one good night since I remembered."

Impatient and unsympathetic, Ahmed yelled at her again. "You were going to tell me today? Do I look like a fool to you? You think you can tell me anything. Well, I don't know what kind of husband you have, or what kind of person you are, but spare me from your lies and excuses." Ahmed reached for her again, his fingernails dug into her arm. "You're leaving this ranch tomorrow."

"Please, just try and understand for a minute."

"Understand what? That you've been sleeping with me and telling me how much you love me? Was it all a lie, too, Orchid?"

Shaking her head she looked up at him, the sun and tears together were blinding her. "I love you more than life, Ahmed. Couldn't you tell when we were together? I want you so much," she cried.

"What is it you want so much from me?" He grabbed her with one hand and tore the top of her dress with his free hand. Is this what you want?" He slipped his hand under her dress feeling her flesh. "Is this what you want, Orchid, or Wanda, or what ever the hell your name is? Is it?" His eyes were hot with rage as he looked into hers.

Orchid slapped his face with all her might. "Don't you ever touch me that way." Pulling away from him, she fell to the ground.

Ahmed looked as though someone had thrown cold water in his face, as though he had come out of a deep sleep or a bad dream. He walked away, leaving behind a rush of cold air and a trembling in her stomach.

He was too angry to think clearly and this behavior wasn't at all like him. Without looking back at her, he headed to the stable and rode out fast on his horse.

She yelled after him, calling his name, but it was as though he didn't hear her. She placed her hands over her face and slid down to the ground where she cried for two hours before she walked back to the ranch.

Ahmed never came back to check on her.

"I've told you everything, Miss Busara. All I can say now is that I'm so sorry for everything," Orchid was saying. She had told Busara everything about her past.

"I'll never forget all you've done for me. With a deflating sigh, she had to close her eyes and turn her face away to try and calm herself. "May I write you from time to time? I would love to keep in touch with you."

"Of course you may write to me, Orchid." Busara sat on the bed next to her. She would miss seeing Orchid in this room when she leaves.

"Ahmed hates my guts. I know that I should have told him. I tried so many times, but not hard enough. I realize that now."

Busara gave her a tissue and she wiped her eyes and blew her nose.

"I should have known that something was very wrong. You've been so despondent lately. And that horrible plane crash. God was on your side. Thank

Him everyday that you are alive, Orchid. He gave you a second chance. Take it girl, be happy."

How could she be happy, Orchid thought? She felt like her life had just ended.

Trying to force her hands to stop quivering, Orchid folded them, placing them in her pockets, her lap. She looked around Busara's room remembering the first time she was in there.

"I really don't want to go back, Miss Busara. I'm no longer in love with my husband," she admitted. "Who knows, he may not love me either."

Busara felt a glimmer of hope and wondered if she would ever come back, or could she and Ahmed see their way through this if she did come back. After all, anything is possible. And Busara was certain that one day Orchid would come back. But it would take time for her to put her life in order at home before she does come back. But she would. Busara always knew.

"Even if my husband doesn't want me, it doesn't mean that Ahmed would ever let me come back."

"There's nothing simple in this life, Orchid. I'm just glad the two men brought you to our ranch. And Ahmed won't hurt forever. He'll go around cursing and grumbling for a while, and of course he'll be lonely and miss you. But one day he'll be happy again. And I hope you are, too."

"Yes Ahmed would be happy again, but with someone else," she said, feeling as though she was going to throw up like she had earlier today. Just the thought of Ahmed loving someone else made her feel ill. Ever since he had left her alone, she had been sick to her stomach.

That evening at dinner, Orchid stayed in her room. Ahmed ate very little and left the house again. Coffie finished and went to Dume's house to visit

Mika. Busara sat alone in the living room. The house was so quiet. It was as if a dark curse was lingering over it. One could hear a pin hit the floor.

Orchid went inside the library and sat behind the desk. She dialed the number, but when Steven answered, she didn't hang up this time. She held the receiver to her ear, not saying a word, just listening to his voice, trying to will herself to speak.

"It's me, Steven. It's Orchid, no, I mean, Wanda."

Feeling incredulous, Steven held the phone so tightly he could feel his knuckles beginning to ache. He sat down slowly, hearing his own heart beating wildly in his chest. "Who is this? Why are you playing this sick game," he yelled into the phone. "Who in the hell are you?" But for some preposterous reason he couldn't hang up. And the voice on the other end sounded so much like Wanda's voice. No, was he losing his mind? How could it be?

Steven placed the glass to his mouth, taking long swallows of the wine then choked and coughed as it went burning down his throat.

He repeated again. "Who are you?" he yelled louder this time. But, still, he couldn't bring himself to hang up as he thought of the phone call the previous evening.

"Steven, listen to me. I'm alive and well in Thika, which is in Kenya. I survived the plane crash."

"No, no. I said who are you?" He was sure that his dinner would come up.

This time he hung up. If only he could find out who was playing with his mind. He rubbed his hands hard over his face and looked at the brandy sitting on the bar. He needed a stronger drink, and fast. The wine wasn't strong enough to dull his brain. He needed to forget this phone call. As he gulped down a half glass of brandy, the phone rang again. He stood and listened to it ring five times before he answered. When Steven picked up the receiver, he didn't speak. He just held the phone; afraid the voice would reappear.

"Steven, please don't hang up this time. There were five bodies that weren't accounted for and I'm one of them. I couldn't keep our date we set for three weeks, but I'm here now. I'm alive, Steven," she said softly.

Steven dropped the glass on his foot. "Goddamn," he yelled, carried the phone to the living room and flopped down on the sofa. His knees were too weak to stand and now his foot ached. No one else knew about their date. He hadn't even mentioned their last words to her family or to Marie. It was something said privately between the two of them every time she traveled. And he had thought of it so often. Steven felt cramps in the pit of his stomach. Was he dreaming, was it really Wanda?

"Oh God, Wanda. Is it really you?" He wiped his forehead with the back of his hand. "Where have you been all this time?"

"I've been living with an African family that was kind enough to take me in when I was released from the hospital."

"I don't know what to say. I'm so happy that you are alive, when are you coming home? Should I come to get you?" He went on and on, rambling, talking so fast that he wasn't making any sense. He reached for the glass of brandy but forgot it had spilled on his foot.

"Did they treat you well? No one hurt you, did they?" He squirmed, resting the phone on his shoulder as he refilled his glass again. Oh shit, what about

Marie, he thought? So much had happened to him in just six months, Kim, Marie. The last six months had been like a lifetime. What else could happen?

Steven listened as Wanda explained to him what had happened to her and how she had been living since the accident. But from time to time he noticed her voice would drift off and she would become quiet, choked up, and couldn't speak. He could only wonder what had she been through.

"Steven, please don't call my family or Marie until I get there. I want to do it. And you know how emotional Marie gets. I can't imagine how hurt she must have been and how happy she'll be when we see each other again. I've thought of her so much lately."

"Yes, baby. I know how emotional Marie will be when you get home. Believe me I do," he said and shook his head, disgusted at the thought of even telling Marie.

"I'll see you in two days, Steven." She gave him the time of her arrival, the flight number and hung up.

Chapter 24

Los Angeles, August 2001

Steven hung the phone up, but so much was going through his mind that he wouldn't ask Wanda over the phone. Does she still have both arms, both legs? Was she still beautiful, or does she have permanent scars on her face? He wondered if she might have burns all over her body. How could he live with her if she were missing one of her limbs, he thought with fear. And he had forgotten to ask her if she was afraid to fly back. Maybe he should have offered to fly there and bring her back.

Only having two days to replace all of Wanda's things, Steven ran through the house pulling boxes from the closets, placing pictures on tables until he heard the doorbell ring. "Marie," he whispered. God, he had to tell her. He stopped and rushed back to the living room to answer the door.

Marie walked in and gave him a quick kiss on his cheek. She started to walk past him but stopped, looking at him with concern. He looked as though he hadn't even seen her. "What is it, Steven? Are you ill?"

"I just spoke with Wanda. She'll be home in two days." Steven watched Marie, but she looked at him as if he was insane.

"Steven, how can you be so stupid?" Marie asked with a smirk in the corner of her mouth.

He walked to the kitchen and came back, and pushed a Coke in her hand, then pointed his finger in her face. "Don't call me stupid, ever. I know my wife's voice."

"Okay. Okay. Don't get angry. Just chill a little. I just don't know how you could let someone play with your head like that." She sat on the sofa and looked at the solemn expression on his face.

"Listen to me, Marie. And don't talk to me as though I'm stupid. I had a long conversation with my wife. I think I know my own wife. Now, don't you be stupid. Clear your head. She'll be home in two days." He sat on the sofa next to her and placed both hands behind his head, resting his head back on the sofa.

"But if it was Wanda, she would have called me, too." Marie was facing him with disbelief written all over her face.

"No. She doesn't want to give you or her family the news over the telephone."

"And she told you that?" she asked, looking at the boxes he had pulled out.

"Yes. She told me that." He took a long swallow of his drink and sat the glass in front of him. He'd had enough to drink for one night. Besides, he needed to stay sober and keep a clear head. And as he thought of it, there were things of Marie's in the apartment that he had to get rid of. He had a lot to do in only two days.

"This is just too absolutely, fucking crazy to believe. Did you tell her anything at all about us?"

He looked straight into her eyes. "Think about it, Marie. Why would I tell her a thing like that over the telephone? Have you lost your mind?" Feeling a headache coming on, Steven went into the kitchen and took a couple of aspirins.

When he returned to the living room, Marie was sitting on the sofa crying, with both elbows on her knees and her hands covering her face. "We were so close and this happens. It's like a nightmare, Steven. You'll have to tell her sooner or later."

He just looked at her, not understanding what she was asking him to do. He was already a married man. "Tell her what, Marie?"

"What do you mean, tell her what, Steven? Tell her about us, of course. We were planning to get married, or did you forget? Three weeks, that's all we needed. We would be getting married," she snapped, her feelings hurt that he would have to ask.

"One would have to get a divorce before marrying another," he replied. And he had no intentions of divorcing Wanda for Marie.

"What about the apartment we put the deposit on?" she asked.

"Cancel it, what else can I say. We certainly can't move in it now, can we?"

Marie wiped her eyes and looked around the room again. "I see you couldn't wait before you started to pull her things out again." It had taken too long for him to put Wanda's things away, now, they'll be right back again, Marie thought bitterly. She looked around the living room, and everything was neatly put back in place. Their wedding picture, the painting that Wanda and Steven had selected together was

hanging back on the wall. How many times had
Wanda told her the story behind that damn, ugly
painting?

   She had to be sleeping because this could only be
a bad nightmare. A movie, or even something you
read in a novel. Something like this just doesn't
happen in real life, to real people. Lord, how would
she live through this, and they had gotten so close.
All they needed was three weeks, three weeks, she
kept repeating to herself, and now this. Her dreams
were finally so close to coming alive for her. And now
she loved Steven more than ever, wearing his ring,
making plans for their wedding day was real, not this.

   "Marie?"

   "I'm sorry. What were you saying?"

   "I said it's amazing that Wanda lived through the
plane crash."

   "Yeah, amazing." She could hardly speak. Her
mind was racing beyond Wanda's first day home. She
was worried about Steven and Wanda's sleeping
arrangements. Will they make love? Does Wanda still
love Steven? Sure she does. She knew without asking.
How many times had Wanda told her that she was
in love with her husband?

   "You want to help me put some of her things back
in place tonight?"

   Her heart sunk. She couldn't believe he was asking
her to help place his wife back into his life. They were
going to be married, she loved him. How he could
be so cold and callous was beyond her.

   "No. I can't help you. All of a sudden I feel sick."
Looking at Wanda's pictures on the wall, the photo
of her and Steven, the thought of Wanda coming
back, she had to leave. Marie got up and grabbed her
purse. "I've got to get out of here."

"Marie, wait." He held her close to him. "I know how you must feel." He held her face in his hands and looked into her eyes. "I know, baby. But right now it's out of my control."

"Well, who's gonna control it, Steven? Wanda?" She pulled away and ran out the door.

Once Marie was home, she threw herself across her bed and cried. Why God, why? Haven't I've suffered enough, waited long enough? How could I get so close only to be pushed aside again? She stood up and threw a glass that broke in pieces against the wall. She hadn't been drinking, but tonight, she needed some bourbon, straight on the rocks. She needed to strike out, scream. She had never been in such pain and felt so helpless. But she wasn't helpless yet, and she wasn't beaten either. First, she had to see Wanda and Steven together. And once Wanda gets home, they had to talk so that she could find out how she feels about Steven. No, she wasn't helpless yet. And Wanda wasn't going to take what belonged to her, again. Not this time.

Chapter 25

Orchid was relieved and disappointed when she walked into the kitchen and Ahmed wasn't there. She knew he was deliberately avoiding her. Although she didn't blame him, she was sorry that she couldn't apologize and say good-bye to him in person. Most of all, she was sorry that she couldn't fall into his arms and ask him to marry her. She would happily give up everything for his love again.

Coffie and Busara were having breakfast when she walked into the kitchen.

"Would you like some breakfast, Orchid?" Busara asked.

"No thanks, Miss Busara. I just wanted to say that I'm ready to go. I'm leaving everything that Ahmed bought me, but I am taking the red dress you gave me. I'll think of you every time I wear it." Her eyes were burning with tears, but she already knew it would be painful to say good-bye. She just never knew that it would be on such bitter terms with Ahmed. Why couldn't he believe her? Why couldn't he just ask her to stay? But she knew him better. He was a man of honor, and she was married.

"I want you to leave everything, dear. You may return one day," Busara said.

"Yeah," Coffie said. "You belong here, Orchid." He sipped his coffee, stood up and held his arms out to her. "You are the sister that I've never had and always wanted."

Once she fell into his arms, she whimpered like a wounded child.

"Don't cry, Orchid. This is a sad day for all of us," Coffie was saying. "Come into the library with me."

She nodded as he held her hand and led her into the library. "Here, sit here next to me." He guided her to the sofa. "Are you in love with your husband?"

Orchid was staring at the multi-colored rug in the center of the floor. Coffie held her chin up so he could see her face.

"No. I'm no longer in love with my husband. But I have to go back, Coffie. It's the right thing to do. And I have family in Chicago, too. Besides, what difference does it make at this point? Ahmed would never let me stay here. I've been so wrong, Coffie. But it was so hard to tell him and so much was always going on. I just waited too long. He'll never trust me again, I know. But I can't blame him."

"If you love him as much as you say you do, then, take care of your business at home and try to come back. At least try, Orchid," he said, trying to convince her.

"I love Ahmed. I love Africa and everyone on this ranch, but I have no place here, Coffie. It's too late. I saw his face and looked into his eyes. He doesn't want me anymore. If I have to live unhappy for the rest of my life, it's my fault. I do want Ahmed to love again and be happy even though it won't be with me." She kissed Coffie on the cheek. "It's time I leave, my friend."

"Dume is driving you to the airport." Coffie kissed her on the cheek and turned to walk out.

"Coffie, kiss Mika for me and be happy."

"I will. Take care of yourself, Orchid, my friend."

Just as she pulled her sweater out of the closet, Busara walked into her room.

"How did you sleep last night, Orchid?"

"I'm so nervous about flying again that I didn't sleep at all last night. And I was afraid to eat anything for fear it might come up."

"I thought so." Busara pulled a small bottle from her apron pocket. "Take this herb with you. Take one pill before you leave, and another before you get on your connecting flight. It's powerful and you'll sleep all the way."

Orchid pushed the small bottle into her dress pocket and the two women hugged. She couldn't say any more and ran out, jumped in the jeep that was waiting for her and waved again as she saw Busara peeking out the window.

Busara went back to Orchid's bedroom and stood in the middle of the floor. She would miss her, but she would see Orchid again, Busara was certain of that.

Dume placed Orchid's bag inside the car. As he drove around the ranch, Orchid looked at some of the places that she and Chiku used to go for long walks and talked as though they were sisters, rather than friends. She passed the tree where she and Ahmed had stopped one evening and made love.

She had never felt such a beautiful experience in lovemaking before.

"I have Chiku's phone number. When you speak to her, would you tell her that I love her and after I'm settled, I'll call her? Will you do that for me, Dume?"

"Yes, I'll tell her. On my next vacation, I'm going to see my brothers and sister. I miss my family."

"I know you do, Dume. That would please Chiku. She hated to leave you alone but because of the younger children, she had to."

He stopped the car in front of the airport. "I hope you have a good and safe trip, Orchid. We'll miss you."

Almost in tears, she couldn't answer. Orchid nodded her head and got out of the car as fast as she could. She started to walk when she heard Dume yell "Kwaheri" (good-bye).

Chapter 26

Los Angeles, August 2001

As the plane was descending to LAX, Wanda looked out the window. She was home. She could still feel the effect from the herb—she was still sleepy. With any luck at all, it would help stave off the anxiety she was feeling. She pulled the small package out of her pocket and opened the top. Two left, she thought. One to help her through the night. One left, and what would she do after that? How could she get through a life that she doesn't want, and with a man she doesn't love? But Steven was her husband and she had to try.

At British Airways, Steven went to the men's restroom, the gift shop, and then the flower shop to buy a dozen roses, and back to the gate where Wanda's flight should be arriving in ten minutes. He looked at his watch, and waited nervously. He heard someone call his name and it was Chuck and Brenda. "We called you at home but you had left, man," Chuck said.

"Thanks for coming." Steven kissed Brenda on the

cheek but her attitude toward him had become distinct and dry and Steven couldn't figure out why.

Brenda stood close to her husband and waited for Wanda. Otherwise, she would not be caught in Steven's company after he and Marie were seen caressing each other on the patio at Chuck's last birthday party.

The flight ended up being twenty minutes late. As the passengers began to come out, Steven looked at their tired faces and stiff movements caused by the long flight. He paced the floor, waiting for her, looking at his watch, sniffing the roses in his hand.

"There she is," Steven said to Brenda and Chuck.

Finally, Wanda came out as the last passenger on board. She saw Steven with roses in his hand. And then she saw Brenda and Chuck and hesitated. She didn't want any of their friends there to meet her except Marie, and she had told Steven not to tell her until she got home. But as she walked, it seemed as though she still had miles to go before she got close to him. And with every step she took, every breath she took, she thought she would die before she reached him.

Steven looked in Wanda's face for scars, but there weren't any. She still had all her limbs. As she came closer, the only thing that he noticed different about her was her eyes. They were sad, bleary and red. Tears glistened in her eyes as they looked at each other. Her hair had grown longer and she wore no makeup. She had gotten thinner, too, and as she got close to him, he saw the scars on the right side of her face that looked as though they were fading away. He wondered what her face looked like right after the plane crash.

"Hello Steven," she said and reached for her roses. "You didn't forget. Roses just like always."

"I knew you would appreciate them," he said, and gathered her into his arms. Steven felt her small frame tremble and held her tighter. "It's all right, baby. Everything is going to be all right now. You're home at last. And you're safe, baby."

She pulled away. "I know. I know, Steven," she whispered.

Wanda and Brenda hugged each other and cried as they looked at each other and hugged again.

"Now, it's my turn," Chuck said. "You look wonderful, Wanda. God bless you. You are one lucky woman," he said, as tears formed in his eyes."

"What about your luggage?" Steven asked.

"Luggage? It was lost in the crash. What you see is all I have." Luggage, how could he think that I would have luggage, she thought to herself.

It was August and as they walked to the car, Wanda felt the warm sun against her face. She noticed Steven constantly staring at her from the corner of his eye. She breathed hard, this was indeed a hideous and most dreadful moment in her life. Her legs were weak and she was going into a home where she no longer felt she belonged, or wanted to be, with a man she no longer loved.

"We will come to see you tomorrow, Wanda. We had to welcome you home," Brenda said, and began crying again.

Wanda held Brenda in her arms. "I'll be looking forward to seeing you tomorrow." She kissed Chuck again on his cheek and they said good-bye.

She was quiet during the ride home as Steven made small talk about his life without her. Once she was home, she walked slowly through the apartment.

Nothing had changed. Wanda showered and changed into her long, green bathrobe. She stood in front of her closet and her clothes were still there. She walked away and looked at their wedding picture on the dresser. It was so strange that everything looked the same to her, but it seemed so long ago since she had seen it all. She had been away for six months, but it felt more like years had passed between her and Steven and the apartment.

"I'm surprised you kept so many of my clothes," she said, as she looked inside her closet. She and Steven had separate closets.

Steven was standing in back of her. "Karen took some home with her. I had packed the rest in boxes, promising to send them to Chicago, too. But baby, I just couldn't do it. It would have been like saying good-bye all over again."

Steven sat on the edge of the bed, watching her every move as though he was afraid to let her out of his sight. He felt a distance between them. She had undressed and completely dried her body off before she came back into their bedroom where he waited for her. It was different—they used to shower together and he always dried Wanda's back for her. They were so romantically involved. But he knew that she had been through a terrible trauma, and they had been apart.

"Sit here, next to me, Wanda. I want to know everything you did in Africa. And I've never heard of Thika."

"Thika is very small. It's in Kenya, Steven," she explained.

"What about the family you lived with, were there many men, was it a small village?"

First, she explained as best she could how she ar-

rived at the ranch and he cringed with every word
he'd heard. She went on to tell him about the people
that lived there.

"There was Busara, the aunt, Coffie and Ahmed,
the two brothers who owned the ranch. It was big
and beautiful and stretched for miles. The ranch was
handed down from their grandfather. They raised
cattle and Ahmed was a smart man. He made a lot of
good investments and does well." She stopped, pre-
tending to adjust the belt around her robe. Talking
about Ahmed hurt her deeply. The phone rang and
she waited while Steven answered.

"What newspaper are you with again?" He looked
at Wanda as she waved her hand to let him know that
she didn't want to speak with anyone.

"Mr. Gray. If only your wife would give me twenty
minutes of her time."

"No. I'm sorry. My wife is very tired. She just got
home less than an hour ago." He hung up.

Wanda sat on the bed and shook her head in disgust. "This is just what I didn't want. I don't want
reporters ringing the doorbell."

Steven rushed to her side. "You being alive is so in-
credible that people want to see for themselves,
Wanda." He got up and opened the blinds, walked
out and returned with two glasses of orange juice and
gave one to her.

"Now where were we," he asked.

"Anyway, I had my own room. So much went on,
the rain storms, wind storms, the dry heat. And there
was this beautiful garden with all types of flowers. Oh
and there were animals and tall flame trees, mountains. It was always so dark at night, looking up at the
sky, the stars seem so near and the sky was so blue.
You could hear animals from far away.

He looked at her without interrupting as she talked.

"They called me Orchid, Steven," she said with a smile. "It was exciting, so much drama. Children laughing and playing games that I had never heard of before. And there were people you got close to and then lost them. There was always so much going on." As she talked about the ranch, her eyes had gone from sad to happy, dancing as she spoke, her set features were beginning to relax, a smile playing delicately in the corners of her mouth. And when she stopped, she became quiet and remote again.

For the first time in their marriage, Steven felt left out of her life. What had happened to his wife in Africa?

It was late and Wanda was tired. The phone had been ringing continuously from friends and two different magazines.

She was humming a song that Busara used to sing when she stepped in front of her bedroom and saw that Steven had pulled the comforter and blanket back on their bed. He was standing with his back to her fluffing their pillows. Wanda stood motionless, her heart thumped hard inside her chest. She couldn't sleep in the same bed with him. Not tonight. Not so soon. She went back downstairs and made herself a cup of tea.

"Ready for bed, honey?"

Wanda jumped, almost spilling her tea. "Steven, I'm sorry. I need to sleep in the guest room for a while." She placed her cup on the table and looked at the disappointment written over his face.

"I just need more time, Steven. I'm tired, I don't

feel very well and the flight was stressful and gave me a headache." She held her hands to her temple and sighed. "It's just for a while."

He held his hands up to stop her from talking. "I understand, baby. You were brave to fly back alone. I think you handled it well. Hey, when are you going to call your family and Marie?" He sat at the table opposite her.

"Tomorrow morning. I can't bring myself to call them tonight."

"I know. And it's late. Why don't you go to bed? Tomorrow I'll cook you a good breakfast just the way I used to."

Funny. The time she spent on the ranch, she never really thought of the things that she and Steven used to do together. Not even the small things like cooking her breakfast, or the times they jogged together early in the mornings before leaving for work, or met for lunch sometimes. When she regained her memory, she never thought of any of those things. They used to be so special to her.

She poured half the herbs in her tea. And now she was beginning to feel sleepy and relaxed again. Wanda smiled to herself. Busara sure knows what she's doing when mixing her herbs. She should have asked for more.

Wanda got in bed feeling the effects from the herbs and soon was fast asleep.

Steven was in the living room watching a movie when the phone rang. He sighed and answered on the first ring. It was Marie on the other end.

"Why in hell are you calling me? You're not suppose to know she's home until she calls you tomorrow," he whispered.

"I couldn't wait to hear your voice, Steven. You hadn't called me all day."

"This is bullshit, Marie. You know I can't call any time you want me to. Besides, this is her first day home, right?" he snapped in an angry and impatient voice. "Give me a break, will you?"

"Yes, but I waited all day."

"Yes, but nothing," Steven interfered. Don't call here for me anymore, just as you didn't before Wanda was missing. When she calls you tomorrow, you better be surprised, too." He hung up before she could answer him.

Marie took another sleeping pill along with a glass of vodka. She hadn't slept since she got the news that Wanda was alive. She felt lonely and sat on the sofa and cried. "They're sleeping together again," she cried out loud. She could feel it and hear it in Steven's voice. Closing her eyes, she had a vivid picture in her head of Steven and Wanda making love; she telling him how happy she is to have him back. Wanda had done it to her again. Refilling her glass, she tried to shake the image out of her head. But when she closed her eyes, they were there again kissing, holding on to each other. "No. No. No," she yelled. This couldn't be happening.

Before she could finish her second glass of vodka, she was out cold on the sofa.

"Marie, calm down. It's really me. I'm alive. I know it's shocking," Wanda was saying and smiled at Steven as she talked. He was sitting at the dining room table with her.

"We just finished eating breakfast. Steven cooked like he always had when we were home together on the weekends. Isn't he sweet?"

"Steven cooked breakfast?" Marie flopped down in a chair choking with envy. "How nice of Steven. Have you called your folks yet?"

"No. I will as soon as I hang up. Why don't you come over for lunch today?"

"Wanda," Steve interrupted. "Baby, maybe you should rest today. You've been through so much with the long flight and all. I want you a hundred percent," he said, trying to convince her.

But Marie heard him. "Sure, I would love to come over for lunch. I have to see you in person so I will know for sure that I'm not dreaming."

"I know what you mean, girl. I had a difficult time trying to convince Steven that it was me on the phone. Now, get dressed and hurry over. When you park, call me from your car. I don't want to open the door for some reporter."

"You mean reporters have been coming around?" Marie said and smiled. She had made the phone call to the LA *Sentinal*. She intend to do anything she could think of to make Wanda and Steven as uncomfortable as possible.

"Marie says that she wants to come over. And later Chuck and Brenda want to come over, too."

"You can always call them back and say you're too tired, Wanda. They can come over tomorrow."

"It's okay, Steven. They're our friends and I want to see Marie." She smiled at him. He was trying so hard to be protective toward her. She was beginning to feel guilty.

"Okay. So what do you want for lunch?" he asked, standing up in front of her.

She closed her eyes trying to decide. "Pizza," she answered.

"Pizza?" he frowned.

"Yes. I haven't had a good slice of pizza since I left."

"Pizza it is. Anything for you, baby. What about a salad to go with it?"

"Salad sounds great, Steven."

Wanda was dressed in a pair of jeans and red sweater by the time Steven got back with the pizza and salad.

He stood back and looked at her. "You look great, baby. Little on the thin side, but great. I always did like my women thin."

Wanda smiled. "Thank you, Steven." The long gaze he gave her made her turn her head and she refilled her glass with water. She felt so nervous that she spilled the water as she sat the glass back on the table.

He stepped closer to her. "Are you all right, Wanda?" he asked with concern. "You used to call me honey most of the time," he said, touching her hair.

"Is that the doorbell?" she asked, still standing stiff from his touch.

"Yes. I'll get it."

Wanda wasn't ready to encounter any intimate moments with Steven. And she wondered how long they could sleep in separate rooms before he starts to complain. She looked at the clock again, it was almost two. She would have to wait another hour before she could call Chicago and contact her sister. It would be better to call her first before she calls her mother. Betty gets too excited to handle such shock alone. And she had to leave on the first flight out to Chicago before some newspaper there gets word that she's back and alive.

Marie walked right past Steven without acknowledging him. He stood at the door watching her as she strolled into the kitchen with Wanda.

"It's really you, girl," Marie said, holding her arms out to Wanda. As they held each other, Wanda's back was turned to Steven and Marie faced him. She rolled her eyes up at the ceiling. It was easy to see that she was uncomfortable and extremely revolted with their circumstances.

"Sit down. Steven bought pizza for lunch and set the table for us."

"Oh. Steven seems to be a good little housekeeper these days, aren't you, Steven?" Marie snorted.

"Just doing the best I can. I've always waited on my wife when she wasn't feeling well," he said. His eyes narrowed fractionally as they studied her face. She had better not make trouble for him, he thought, looking at her, giving a hint of warning.

Again, Wanda had to explain what happened in Africa and Marie listened with interest. She would have to explain in detail all over again when Brenda and Chuck comes over and when she sees her mother and sister. The explaining was too much, too overwhelming as she spoke of Ahmed.

"And there were no handsome, naked men running around that ranch?" Marie asked.

Wanda laughed out loud. "If there were I didn't see any." She bit into the pizza. "This is so good. I haven't had pizza since the last time we met for lunch, Steven."

He sat two tall glasses of 7-UP on the table.

"Aren't you going to join us, Steven? After all, you rushed out to get lunch for us?" Marie asked.

"Yes, and I was glad to do it, but I'm not hungry. I'm going to watch TV and you ladies can be alone for a while." He squeezed Wanda's hand and walked out.

Marie was so furious she thought she would burst. He was being the loving husband. So where did that leave her, she wondered?

Wanda excused herself and headed for the bathroom. Once she was there, she washed her face in cold water and looked into the mirror. Quickly, she placed the top down on the toilet and sat down. What was wrong with her? For a moment she thought that she would vomit, but it passed. It was between the pizza and her nerves. She knew it had to be nerves. The strain of being there with Steven day and night, and she couldn't go one minute without thinking of Ahmed. And every time she did, she could feel herself slowly dying inside. She was trapped into two worlds that were so far apart.

"Are you all right?" Marie asked.

Wanda sat back down again. "Yes. Just an upset stomach, that's all. I ate some very different foods while I was in Africa. I even learned to cook some."

"You?" Marie laughed. "You can't cook that well, Wanda."

"I had to learn. I learned a lot while I was there, Marie. And I learned to appreciate life more and living, just waking up and being alive and well. That's what Africa does to you. It's so different."

"You look so sad when you speak of it, Wanda. Are you keeping anything from me?" Marie asked suspiciously.

Wanda looked at her long and hard. She was drinking again. It had been a long time since she looked this way. Her eyes were red and she looked tired. Wanda could smell the alcohol on her breath when she hugged her. She wondered what had started her to drinking again. She did it when her husband had left her, but she got better and was only drinking an occasional glass of wine. Later, she even stopped drinking the wine. Wanda was sure that she was on the hard stuff again.

"Are you sure that you don't want to tell me anything more about Africa, Wanda?"

"No. Nothing. It was just hard that's all. Not remembering who you are or where you came from, not knowing if you had a family or not." She looked away so Marie wouldn't push her any further. And she didn't want to tell anyone that she waited a month before Ahmed found out. Besides, she didn't trust Marie when she was consuming too much alcohol.

"Now, is there anything you would like to tell me, Marie? You know that anything you tell me would never go any farther than you and me."

"Yes, as a matter a fact."

"Do you ladies have everything you need?" Steven asked.

Marie cleared her throat and stood up to leave the kitchen. "The lunch was good, girl. I just had to see for myself that you were back with us."

"Are you leaving so soon?" Wanda asked with surprise. "You just got here, Marie."

"I know. I forgot to take a report to my office and they were expecting it early this morning." She grabbed her purse and headed for the door.

Wanda walked behind her. She grabbed Marie by her arm and hugged her tightly. "I'll let you know when I'm leaving for Chicago. But I do intend to see you before I leave. Maybe we can go to lunch or a movie."

"You're leaving again? You didn't say anything about going to Chicago, Wanda. You've just got home," Steven protested.

"We'll discuss it later, Steven."

"I'll call you tomorrow, Wanda." Marie walked out without saying anything to Steven.

When she stepped outside, she wondered what he was doing. He acts just the way he did before Wanda left. She had to talk with him and remind him that they had planned to get married. Marie was so upset, she could hardly unlock the car door. Once she was inside, she sat for a while before she was calm enough to drive home.

Wanda went into the living room where Steven was watching TV. She sat beside him. "I'm worried about Marie, Steven. She's drinking again and she doesn't look good. I think she was about to tell me why when you walked into the kitchen."

Steven turned to face her. "Wanda, you know Marie. She gets moody sometimes. I don't think it's anything to worry about," he said, looking back at the television.

"No. It's more than that. She's hurting and drinking. And you know what bothers me the most?"

Steven's head jerked around. "What's bothering you?"

"She hugged me and said that she missed me, but I didn't feel that bond between us like we used to have. I wonder what has happened to her. Have you seen much of her since I've been away? She didn't mention that she was dating anyone. Or maybe she is and they're not getting along well."

Steven turned in his seat as though he had gotten uncomfortable. "I saw her a couple of times, but we didn't talk long enough for me to sense there was anything wrong. Now stop worrying about her. You're home and you have a lot to think about. Are you planning to go back to your job anytime soon?"

"Yes. But I haven't thought too much about it. I need time to visit my family and decide what I'm going to do."

"About what?"

"I don't know yet. I just need the time, that's all." She looked as though he was pressuring her.

"Take all the time you need, baby. Now what's this about you're going to Chicago? You just got home, Wanda."

Wanda, she thought. The name sounded like hers, but it also sounded so strange to her.

"My mother is getting too old to take surprises over the phone. Look how hard it was to convince you that it was me on the phone. Besides, I have some business to take care of. After all, I'm not dead any more. I still have money there that my Dad left me. I may come back and buy a house."

"What about this place?" he asked in surprise. "You always loved it so."

"Nothing is wrong with it. This place is nice. I just thought it would be a change to live in a house with a large backyard and a garden with beautiful flowers blooming in the spring. While I was away, I found out that I like working in a garden."

Steven sighed. "Well, it's still early and I need to go into the office for a couple of hours. You don't mind do you?"

"No, of course not." The phone rang. "Why don't you answer it, Steven. It may be that lady from that magazine again." She got up and went back into the kitchen.

After a few minutes, Steven went into the kitchen and Wanda had started to place the dishes into the dishwasher.

"It was Chuck. He says Brenda's mother is very ill and she had to go over to her house."

"Good. I don't really want to see anyone else today anyway," she answered.

He went into the bedroom to change his shirt. When he came out, he kissed her on the cheek and left.

"Karen, I have to come."

"Why don't you bring Steven with you instead of flying alone, besides, you just got home? And where is he anyway?"

"He went to the office for a couple of hours," Wanda answered, as she was looking at a picture on the table of herself and her sister when they were children.

"Would it be easier if Mama and I came out there? Your nephew is in Dallas with his father."

"No. I'm paying for my ticket first thing tomorrow morning and I leave the day after. I've already made reservations."

"You are either brave or crazy. If I were you I don't think that I could hop on a plane so soon. But in any case, call me when you get the flight number. I'll be at the airport waiting." Karen got all choked up again.

"Karen don't cry. See, you have me crying again," Wanda said, and cried out loudly.

"I'm just so, so happy to hear your voice again. I've been so sad, so hurt, Wanda. Mama got ill after the search was over. It's been so hard on us. And you are my only sister."

"I know, Karen." She was crying so it took a few minutes before she could speak again.

* * *

Marie flung the door wide open, standing there with her arms folded across her chest. Steven just stood and watched her so she took a seat on the sofa and looked the other way.

"I didn't like your attitude today, Marie. At a time like this, one would think that you could think of someone other than yourself for a change," he said, and got up to open the can of Pepsi that was on the table next to the quart of vodka on the table.

"Someone besides myself?" she bellowed. "I can't believe that came out of your mouth. Who in the hell thinks of me? I was going to be married in three weeks, and look what happened. So, I ask you, Steven, who thinks about me?" She stood up and threw the pillow off the sofa and started to adjust the belt around her bathrobe to close it tighter.

"Leave it open so I can look at you." Steven sat on the sofa and she stood in front of him.

She dropped the belt to the floor and wiped the tears from her eyes.

Steven got up and motioned for her to lay on the sofa. "I didn't come over here to fight with you." As though he couldn't wait, he opened her legs and entered her, hard and fast and deep.

Marie moaned as his body completely covered her. And when she wrapped her legs around his waist, giving him everything that he needed, he went even deeper inside of her until his breathing became shallow, and his body stiffened. He lifted his body but stayed on top of her. Seconds passed, and he entered her again, and again she welcomed him. All the tension was released and replaced with the pleasure they had shared so many times together.

"This is crazy, Steven. Everything is out of control. My life won't be shot to hell because she's back."

Abruptly, he got up and looked down at her. "I know, but what can I do, Marie? She's going to Chicago in two days. We can talk about this when she leaves." He tucked his shirt into his trousers, and zipped them up.

She sat up, pulled her robe close around her. "You tell me when she gets back. I can't do this anymore, Steven, and I won't go to her house and pretend that I'm glad to see her when I'm not."

Steven stopped in mid-motion. "What are you talking about?"

"I'm saying that I can't continue to put on a masquerade like I did today just to protect Wanda. I'm human, too, Steven."

He slipped into his shoes. "Can't we finish this conversation after she leaves? I've got to go now."

"Sure, but we have to decide how to settle this once and for all."

He grabbed her arm and pulled her close to him. "You know, Marie. When I asked you to marry me I thought my wife was dead. But she isn't. So don't do anything you will regret."

He looked so serious and so sedate that he almost frightened her.

"I'm not kidding. We'll finish this conversation when Wanda leaves." He pushed her away and walked out the door.

Marie just stared at the door for moments before she sat down again. She had no idea what direction her life was going. Or where it would end.

Wanda drove down all the streets that she was familiar with, but the only difference was, she didn't belong on any of them, not even the one she lived on.

Wanda had purchased her plane ticket. She needed to get out and try to clear her head. She had persuaded Steven to go back to work a day early and she had the day to herself.

While she was driving, the city streets were busy and the air was warm. She would be so happy if only she was in Thika, walking outside and seeing the children playing games, the women washing their family clothes, men planting crops, and when she walked around the garden, the smell of honeysuckle lingering in the air. She wiped tears from her eyes. Wanda had never felt such misery.

First, she had to go to Chicago and do some soul-searching. Make plans for her future. Was she going to stay with Steven, go back to her job, or maybe even move back to Chicago? But one thing she was sure of, she no longer loved Steven.

She felt a cramp in her stomach. Steven had mention that the flu was in the air. And that was exactly the way she felt. Maybe she should go to see the doctor before she goes to Chicago but she was so close to home and hadn't made an appointment. She exited Havenhurst Boulevard off the 101 Freeway and drove home.

Once Wanda was home, she went upstairs and pulled out the extra suitcase and started to pack some of her clothes. This time she would pack only a few kick-around clothes just to visit her mother and sister. She walked into their bedroom, and Steven had left everything the same as it was six months ago. The picture on the dresser that they had taken together on their last vacation, the white twin bathrobes he had bought when she was angry with him. All of a sudden she needed to get away from their apartment. God, she wondered what had happened to her? This was her home, Steven was her husband, what had happened to all of it? *Ahmed.*

As Wanda was driving into the garage she saw a black Infiniti parked in front of her building. It was the manager of the LA *Tribute.* She parked and went back to the front where the car was parked. Nick stepped out of the car. He was tall with blue eyes and blond hair. His wire-framed glasses rested on his nose. He smiled and took Wanda into his arms.

"We missed you, dear. Everyone at the *Tribute* says to give you their love. He stepped back and looked at her. "You look just like your old self, Wanda."

Wanda smiled with tears in her eyes. "Come on inside so we can talk. I've got a lot to tell you." She held his hand as they walked.

Once they got inside Wanda told him to have a seat on the sofa and she sat next to him. "I wondered what was keeping you so long, Nick," she said, looking at the pen and pad in his hand.

"You know me too well, Wanda."

"You hired me, taught me everything I know. Want something cold to drink?"

"No. I just want the story so we can get it over with. I'm sure it's not an easy subject for you to talk about."

"No. It's not easy but I'll do it for you." She began with the plane crash and Nick listened closely, asking questions to make sure he didn't miss anything. It took an hour but Wanda felt at ease with him. Since the both of them were journalists it made it easier and she knew what questions he would ask her.

"Well, I think I have enough information to write the story. Have you talked to anyone else?"

"No, and don't plan to. They got up and she walked him to the door.

"When you're ready to work just call me. The job is still yours." He kissed her on her forehead and walked out.

That night Steven and Wanda talked about their friends, but she wasn't ready to scc any of them. She told him that Nick had been over and that she gave him her story.

"Was it very hard to talk about again? I know he must have gotten as much as he could out of you."

"He did but it wasn't so bad." She sighed, wishing she was already in Chicago.

"The dinner was delicious, Wanda. I really didn't expect you to cook."

"I didn't go to work today. You know that I cook when I'm home," she replied.

"I know. But you had a bad time and a long trip home. I want you to get yourself back in shape first."

"Steven, I'm fine, really. Why don't you go and watch TV while I put the dishes in the dishwasher." She was clearing the table and reached over him to get his plate. The top buttons on her blouse had opened and she wasn't wearing a bra.

Steven saw the top of her brown breast, smooth satin and beautiful. Her curly hair fell to one side of her shoulder and her scent was intoxicating. If things were different between them, he would take her to bed and make her forget the dishes. How many times had they stopped in the middle of something to make love? The thought brought a smile to his face.

Wanda was up early the next morning rushing around the house nervously. Today she would see her mother and sister. "Steven, I'm ready," she yelled, standing impatiently at the bottom of the stairs.

"Coming."

She had gotten her jacket and suitcase and waited at the door for him.

"Nervous, ha?"

"Yes. I can't wait to see my mother's face. She gets so emotional, you know. And this time she has a right to."

"Are you sure you'll be all right on the plane, Wanda? I could take off another week to fly with you."

"Don't worry, Steven. I have to get used to it sooner or later. But yes, I will be nervous. As soon as I get on the plane, I'm going to buy myself another drink to help me relax. But at least the flight is shorter than it was flying from Africa.

Wanda arrived in Chicago on time and Karen was waiting for her. As soon as the two sisters saw each other, they hugged and cried. People watched and smiled. But they only saw each other.

"Wanda, you just don't know how much I've missed you. Mama will be so pleased." The two sisters stood apart to get a good look at each other.

"You're thin, girl, but Mama will take care of that. She was cooking when I left. Now she'll cook every day you're here." Karen started to cry again and Wanda held her in her arms.

"I know. It's all right now, Karen. Stop crying."

"I will. It's been so hard." Karen blew her nose. "I was so hurt and shocked looking at the news on TV about the plane crash. You have no idea what it was like. Mama wouldn't move from the TV, she couldn't

eat or sleep. She just sat in that one spot on the sofa."
Karen shook her head and blew her nose. "But you
are alive and home. Now I can sleep through the
night again."

"I was so blessed to have a family take me in when
I left the hospital." They hugged and cried some
more.

After Wanda got her suitcase, they went straight
to their mother's house.

"Let me go in first so I can try and prepare her.
Then I'll come out and get you," Karen said as they
stood in front of their mother's door.

Wanda looked up and down the street. She remembered the way she and Karen used to ride their
bikes with the other kids that lived only five houses
down the block. The memories made her smile. She
looked at her mother's home, the home she and
Karen were raised in. It was white with brown trim.
The tall tree was still there with leaves falling to the
ground, making their way to the sidewalk. How many
times had she or Karen raked the leaves up while
their father trimmed the grass?

"Is that you, Karen?" Betty yelled from the kitchen.

"Yeah, Mama, it's me."

"Good." She walked out drying her hand on a dish-
towel. "I just put the corn bread in the oven. Honey,
I made some chili," she said, looking at the picture
over her fireplace, the same picture that Karen and
Wanda had in their homes.

Karen followed her mother's eyes. She was sure
that she was thinking of Wanda and their father. Her
mother had aged and was still grieving over their
deaths.

"Mama, what were you thinking?'

"The same thing as I do every day. I ask God why

did he take my husband and child away from me? But I thank him for you and Jeffrey. You're all I have now. Losing a husband is bad enough, but a child. I cry every time I hear a child's death on TV because I know what their parents have to go through." She wiped her eyes with the white apron that she was wearing.

"Come here, Mama, and sit down." Karen held her arm and guided her to the sofa. Betty wasn't an old woman but the agony that tore into her heart day by day had told a story in her face and eyes.

"What is it, Karen?" she looked worried. "Is it something bad? Lord," she said out loud. "How much more can I take?"

"Mama. For a month you didn't believe that Wanda was dead. Have you finally accepted it?"

"What is this all about, Karen? I don't want to discuss it," she snapped. "I can't stand wondering if my child was in any pain when the plane went down. Or if she knew that she was going to die."

"Just answer me, Mama."

"I don't know what to believe anymore. Yes, the truth is I have accepted it. If she was alive, she would be home, wouldn't she?"

"What if she didn't remember her way home?"

Betty looked strangely at her daughter. "Look, Karen. I don't want to hear any more of this nonsense. She's dead. My child is dead," she said, her face frowned with pain, and she began to cry.

"Wait here, Mama." Karen got up and went outside. Betty held her hands to her face, crying, shaking her head.

"Mama! Mama!" the familiar voice called her, "Mama."

Betty took her hands from her face and cringed in-

wardly. Had she lost her mind, had she, she wondered? She screamed Wanda's name and cried and
held her baby. The Lord had answered her prayer.
All three cried and talked at the same time, and cried
again.

Betty pushed ringlets of curls from Wanda's face
and held her in her arms.

"I lost my memory, Mom. When I did remember, I
couldn't give you this kind of news over the phone."

All three went into the kitchen and sat at the table.
"Mom, you just don't know how many times I've
thought about us sitting around this table again. I
think I was six years old when you and Daddy went
out and bought it."

"That's about right," Karen answered, placing
three bowls on the table. They ate chili, rice, and
corn bread for dinner. At nine they went over to
Karen's house and stayed up almost all night talking.

Finally, at three in the morning, Betty went to bed.
Karen and Wanda stayed up talking about Africa.

"Okay, what's going on in your head, Wanda? Why
are you so unhappy?"

"What do you mean?" Wanda answered.

"Girl, you know what I mean. I know when you're
happy or unhappy."

"That's why I wanted to come home and not have
you and Mom go to Los Angeles. I need to talk,
Karen," she said, hanging her head down.

They were in Jeffrey's room and Wanda was lying
across one of the twin beds.

Karen sat beside her. "Tell me. What's wrong, girl?"

"I couldn't remember who I was until a month
ago. I didn't call because I wanted to do that from
Los Angeles. During that time, I fell in love with
Ahmed. Karen, I don't love Steven anymore. I don't

like LA or Chicago. I want to go back to Africa and live there."

Karen put up both hands in front of her. "Wait. You're going too fast, girl. How did all this happen?"

"It happened. I fell in love. I fell madly in love. I never knew what it was to fall deeply in love until I met Ahmed."

"With the African, you fell in love with an African, with him?"

"That's what I've been trying to tell you."

"That's deep, Wanda. Lord have mercy," Karen said, shaking her head, as though it was all so unimaginable. "What in hell are you going to do? You're already married. Maybe in time, you will feel the same about Steven again. After all, you did love him once, Wanda."

"That's right. I did love him once. But when I really think of it, I wasn't that much in love with him. I'm in love with Ahmed." She sighed, and got up to look at the picture of her nephew dressed in his football uniform. "He's a handsome kid, Karen. You've done a good job raising him alone."

"Thanks. Now girl, I don't know what to tell you. This is something you have to work out on your own, Wanda." Karen ran her fingers through her short black hair. It shone like silk. She ran her tongue over her white teeth and rested her head against the pillow.

"I can't stay with Steven and I can't go back to Ahmed."

"You what? This is getting worse. Why can't you go back?" Karen got up and went to the other twin bed and sat next to Wanda.

"Ahmed hates me." Wanda told her what happened and cried in her sister's arms.

"Girl, now you got me crying, too. The only thing that you can do now is forget that African. Maybe this is the first time you really fell in love. But you will again. If not with Steven, then you will with someone else." Karen watched Wanda wipe tears from her eyes. She grabbed a tissue from the box and wiped tears from her eyes, too.

"You better get some sleep so you can go to the office tomorrow," Wanda finally said.

"I put in for the rest of the week. As long as you're home, I'm staying home, too. We have to deed the townhouse back to you."

"No we don't. If I stay in LA, I'm buying a house. The townhouse is my nephew's."

"You really don't know what you're going to do yet?"

"I keep saying I don't. I also keep saying that I should give my marriage another shot. Steven was a good husband. He's being so patient with me. Maybe when I get home, I'll feel differently about him. I just have to try harder, at least give him that. But I'm not sure I can," she said sadly, and held her hand against her chest. "I just don't feel it here anymore."

"He's your husband, honey. Give your marriage more time. You know, maybe if you slept with him, it may help."

Wanda nodded. "Maybe. I know you're right. Now, I'm tired." She kissed Karen on the cheek, and crawled between the sheets.

The next morning, the smell of bacon, eggs, and coffee awoke Wanda. She got up and washed her face, brushed her teeth. Still in her gown, as she walked into the kitchen, she could hear Betty rattling pots and pans.

"Smells good, Mom," she said, pouring herself a

cup of coffee. "You know, I still miss this house." She sat at the table and grabbed a plate.

"Is Karen still asleep?" Betty asked.

"No. I heard her on the phone. Probably giving instructions to her staff. You know she can't take a couple of days off without calling that county office. She mentioned something about a new social worker that needs training."

Karen walked in and sat at the table. Betty said, "It sure is good to see my two daughters here with me. I got on my knees last night and thanked God." Betty started to cry again and Wanda got up and gathered her in her arms.

"Are you going to cry every time you see me, Mom?"

"Yes. For a while anyway."

That night Wanda packed the few things she had brought with her. Betty was quiet and Karen was trying to keep her mother in good spirits.

"How is Marie, Wanda? I saw her aunt a week ago. She says that girl never calls home like she should," Betty said.

"I hate to say it, but she's drinking again. I'm going to have a long talk with her when I get back. You know, Karen, she was so remote, empty. It's hard to explain. I know she's glad that I'm back but something was missing between us."

"What do you mean?" Betty asked, and took a seat next to Wanda.

"Well. I just couldn't seem to get close to her. She kept snapping at poor Steven and he was trying to be so nice to her. And I could smell the alcohol on her breath. I'll give it a couple of days and go talk to her. Maybe we can go to a movie, or dinner. She probably wants to talk as much as I do. We'll have to get together when Steven isn't around."

"What time will you get home tomorrow, Wanda?" Betty asked.

"By noon tomorrow, Mom. Stop worrying about me. I'll call you as soon as I get home."

Betty had aged a bit, just as Karen said. Her short-cut hairstyle helped, but Wanda could see that her skin had darkened and the lines around her eyes were more visible than before.

"Hey, why don't I make some hot chocolate. It's chilly in here, don't you think Wanda?" Karen asked, pulling her black velvet bathrobe closer to her body.

"Good idea," Betty agreed.

Chapter 27

Marie hung the phone up and rushed around the apartment, trying to put everything back in place. She hadn't made her bed or washed the dirty dishes that were left in the sink the night before.

About the time she finished and changed into her short pink dress, the doorbell rang. She stood in front of the mirror one last time and brushed her hair back. It was so good to see Steven. She had been so angry the last time he came over. Maybe tonight she could convince him to tell Wanda the truth about them.

Steven walked in and noticed the bottle of wine that she had left on the coffee table.

"You want a drink?" she asked.

"No, Marie, and it looks like you've had enough, too," Steven answered.

She went into the kitchen and dropped the glass in the sink, watching it shatter in pieces. "Okay. So you don't want a drink," she said, strolling slowly away from the sink and took a seat on the sofa. "Are you going to spend the night with me, Steven?"

"No. I can't stay." Steven sat on the sofa next to her,

looking at her as she placed her legs over the arm of the sofa.

Marie felt her body stiffen and turned around to face Steven. "She's in Chicago. Why can't you stay with me tonight?"

"Because of the way you've been acting lately. Wanda thinks you are drinking again, which you are, and too much, I might add. She's curious to know what's bothering you; are you hurting over something or someone, or what's the problem?"

Marie threw her head back and laughed out loud. "Did you tell her what's bothering me, Steven?"

"No, but I did come to tell you that we're finished. It's over between us."

He was cold and calculating with his words, talking slowly so she could understand each word clearly. "I would have married you if my wife was dead, but she's not. And you've shown me a vindictive side of you that I can't tolerate. Marrying you, I would be a glutton for punishment. Besides, a person that abuses alcohol can't be depended on or trusted."

Marie felt an excruciating pain in her right temple. She stared at him. Her eyes were full of hostility as she opened them widely. "You can't mean that, Steven. I've been here for you. I stood by you even before she was missing."

She was getting loud and hysterical, waving her arms, crying. "I was always here waiting, waiting for a phone call, anything, but I stood by you, you low-life jerk," she screamed. "How can you sit here, look me in the eyes and be so cruel?"

He almost pitied her as she pleaded for him to stay.

"She'll never know, Steven. Stay here tonight. Tomorrow when she gets home complaining about her headache, how tired she is from her trip, you'll feel differently. Come on, Steven, you know you want me." She stood up, unzipped her dress and let it fall to the floor. "You know you want me, Steven. You always do."

She took a step closer to him, but he got up and stepped out of reaching distance.

"It's too late, Marie. The truth is that I've never been in love with you. I think you knew that. My wife is home. I won't leave her for anyone. Tell you what, I'll pay for the rings and you can keep them."

"You'll pay for the rings, the fucking rings? That's insulting. You're just full of insults today, Steven," she yelled louder, pulling up her dress back on her shoulders.

He opened the door and she ran after him. "You bastard, you dirty bastard. You're no man, you know that?" she snorted, crying and yelling like a wild woman. "You'll be sorry, you'll be sorry for this, Steven. You just wait and see. So go on, go, but your day will be much sooner than you think. Much sooner," she said loudly.

He stopped to talk to her, but changed his mind. She was drunk and didn't know what she was saying, besides, tomorrow; she wouldn't remember half of what she said tonight.

"Good-bye, Marie." He looked at her one last time with disgust written all over his face, and walked to his car.

Once outside, he felt the fresh air, the sky was resplendent with stars. Steven got inside his car and drove off.

"I'm glad you're home, Wanda. I missed you," Steven commented and sat the suitcase on the floor at the bottom of the stairway.

Wanda stood near him. "What smells so good?" She held her head up and sniffed.

"I baked a chicken and made a salad for dinner. Are you hungry, honey?"

"Yes, but just a little." She gave him a warm smile. He was trying so hard, and without warning, he circled his arms around her waist and kissed her.

"There. Why don't you get comfortable and I'll mix the salad. Change clothes and put your feet up and rest."

Lifting her eyebrows, she tried to freeze her features into a casually indifferent look. He was taking her too fast.

Wanda picked up her suitcase and went upstairs to the guest bedroom hoping that Steven wasn't anticipating that they would share their bedroom and bed.

Dinner was quiet, and all Wanda could think of was getting through it without getting any sicker than she already felt. She was tired, flying was still stressful and she didn't have any more of Busara's herbs to relax her and help her sleep. She changed into her long bathrobe and went back into the kitchen.

"Did you unpack already, baby?" He placed his fork on his plate and refilled his glass with water.

"No. It can wait until tomorrow. I've laid my pajamas out on my bed. I am jumping into them early and turning in."

"Too many flights can be tiring. I still think it's too soon for you to fly alone, Wanda."

"Yes. Maybe it is. I hope I sleep well tonight. You know, Steven, the bed in the guest bedroom is really comfortable. I should sleep like a baby tonight."

He nodded solemnly. "I see."

He looked disappointed, but what could she say? Before she went to sleep her mother called and cried again.

Chapter 28

At eight the next morning Wanda was in the kitchen making a cup of coffee. Steven had left before she got up. Wanda knew he was gone because he probably was still angry from the night before. After she had chatted with Steven for a while she went to her room.

Steven tried to conceal his frustration and impatience. He stayed downstairs and watched television, trying to figure out what he could do to get his wife back. Was she still in love with him? What had happened to Wanda while she was away and why couldn't they pick their lives up where they had left off?

He got dressed the next morning and looked in on her, but she was still asleep, and he was still pissed. He looked at his watched and rushed out, slamming the door behind him.

The phone rang, but instead of answering it, Wanda ran into the bathroom and dropped to her knees in front of the toilet. After she finished vomiting, she splashed cold water against her face. As she got half way to the living room, the waves of nausea were so relentless, she was sure that she wouldn't make it back into the bathroom in time. She reached the bathroom door, and grabbed the wastepaper basket and started again until her stomach was empty. Now she was totally convinced that she had that terrible flu that Steven had mentioned. She had heard about it on the news last night when they were watching the TV. And she hadn't taken the flu shot this year.

Wanda walked into the living room and lay on the sofa with a cold towel placed on her forehead. The phone rang again but she was too ill to get up and answer.

Steven was concerned. He had called twice and both times Wanda didn't answer. He sat behind his desk feeling guilty. She was ill last night and he had left without saying good-bye. Maybe he would surprise her by bringing her lunch home today. Yes, she would like that. She was always so pleased when he did little things like that for her, he thought, and decided to accomplish as much work as he could before noon. She may be so pleased, who knows, he may get lucky today.

After keeping a slice of toast down, Wanda called her doctor's office and the nurse said that he could see her within the hour. She showered, dressed and rushed out of the apartment.

"The nurse hugged her. "We haven't seen you in awhile, Wanda." She didn't know that Wanda had been in the plane crash. "We have so many patients coming in with the flu. It's pretty bad."

Wanda followed the nurse into the examining

room and removed all her clothing as she was instructed.

Waiting for the doctor to come in and examine her, she lay on the table and closed her eyes.

The doctor came in and examined her. Just as he finished, there was a knock on the door. The nurse stuck her head in. "Dr. Reed, your wife is on the phone," she whispered.

"Excuse me, dear. This should only take a few minutes. In the meantime, you just lay here and relax. I have some questions to ask you when I get back."

This was the first time that Wanda had noticed his blond hair was thinning.

Wanda heard the soft knock on the door and Dr. Reed walked in with her file and a pen in his hand. He touched her shoulder and stood in front of her.

"How long have you been feeling ill, Wanda?"

Oh, two, maybe three weeks. But it's getting progressively worse. I've been under so much pressure, so stressed out lately. Dr. Reed, do you think that I'm going into some kind of deep depression?" she asked. "And I get ill every time I eat."

He felt her stomach again, pulled on a pair of rubber gloves, placed her feet apart, and examined her. "When was your last menstrual period?"

"Last month."

"Are you sure of that?"

"Yes, I had it . . . Oh, my God. It was the beginning of last month." She shook her head and placed her hand over her month. Suddenly a thought struck her. "God," she whispered. "Yes, it was the beginning of last month, but it actually started on the twenty-eighth of the month before."

"So that means you didn't have a period last month and this month is almost over."

Dr. Reed stretched his head. "You are pregnant, dear. Congratulations."

Wanda couldn't say anything. She wrung her hands and laughed, suddenly amused at the absurdity of her situation. She doesn't want Steven and Ahmed doesn't want her, and now she's pregnant with Ahmed's baby. Without realizing it, she placed one hand against her stomach.

"Are you all right, Wanda?" Dr. Reed asked, and held her hand in his.

"Yes, sure. I better go home now, Dr. Reed. Thanks for getting me in today. I have to leave."

"Don't forget to make an appointment," he said when she got up to get dressed.

After she finished dressing, Wanda hurried out the door.

"Don't forget to make your appointment," the doctor yelled after her. But she kept walking as though she didn't hear him.

Just when she thought nothing else could go wrong in her life, she heard a strange noise coming from under the hood of her car. Thank God she was only five blocks from her apartment.

Pulling up in the service station, she saw a brown jeep and thought of Coffie. How many times had Busara told him about driving it so fast? She smiled at the thought and went inside.

"I heard a strange noise when driving my car. Who can take a look at it?"

A nice looking man overheard Wanda and came out from the back. "We have two cars ahead of you, Miss."

"Fine," Wanda said. "I'll leave it. Please call me at

home and get my approval before any of the work is started."

"Sure. Fill out this invoice and leave the keys with the young lady here. We'll call you later today."

"Thank you." She left the keys and decided to walk home. Besides, it wasn't far. Maybe walking would relieve some of the stress. Stress, she thought. That's putting it mildly.

She had gotten herself into a mess and didn't know what to do about it. "Pregnant?" she whispered to herself. Lord, what was she going to do? And as she thought of it her heart was racing, she was so scared, her knees felt weak. She began to walk fast.

It was almost noon when she got home and went straight to the refrigerator to get a glass of cold water. The weather was warm outside and she needed something cold to drink. Wanda took long swallows letting the cold water cool her throat.

Wanda sat at the table, nervously tapping a pencil against the phone book that was in front of her, and trying to make sense of what had happened to her the last six months of her life. There had to be a reason why her life was spared in the plane crash, but the rest of it was questionable, and she couldn't figure it out.

She got up and walked through the house from room to room. Picked up the phone to call Marie, changed her mind and hung up. She wasn't ready to talk to anyone. She turned on the answering machine and listened to Brenda's message. Again, she wanted to come over but she was in no condition for company.

Feeling a surge of restlessness, Wanda decided to go out and sit by the pool. It was warm enough outside, and she couldn't sit in one place. She had to keep moving, thinking.

She walked outside of the glass patio door from the dining room and around to the back, inside the locked gate to the pool area.

She sat on one of the patio chairs, lay her head back and closed her eyes. Like earlier today, she placed one hand on her stomach, wondering what it would feel like when the baby starts to grow. Was it a girl or boy?

Steven came home with a bag of Chinese food. He didn't see Wanda's car, but as he placed the bag on the table, he noticed her phonebook was open to the page where her doctor's phone number was listed. Good, he thought, and decided to stay home until she got back.

Steven called the accounting firm and told them that he wouldn't be back until tomorrow morning. They understood, knowing that Wanda was home again.

He went back to the kitchen and started to set the table when he heard her walk inside the apartment.

"I'm in the kitchen, baby. I got a surprise for you. Like I said, I want you a hundred percent before you start doing too much around here. I miss the way it used to be between us, don't you?"

Steven jumped. "How did you get in here, and Wanda isn't home."

Marie stood in front of the table. "So, you miss the way it used to be, ha, Steven? We'll just see about that. I'll have to wait for Wanda."

"I thought for sure I had locked the door." He

stopped and looked at her again. "I was sure the lock was on," he said.

She took a step closer to him. "It was locked." She held her hand up. "I got a key of my own. Before you came along Wanda and I used to be close friends and had keys to each other's apartments. You know, in case one of us got ill, needed a place to stay, or whatever. Then you came along and ruined our friendship."

He looked at her knowing that she had been drinking and had to get her out of there before Wanda got home.

"Then, Wanda disappeared and came back and ruined our relationship, we were going to be married. Three weeks were all we needed. Just three damn weeks. We had picked out an apartment, the rings." She laughed out loud. "Now isn't that something, Steven?"

"Look, Marie. Wanda will be home soon. This is not a good day for visitors." He placed two glasses on the table and pulled the napkins from the cabinet. Then, without a warning, he reached for her arm but she shook him off.

"I'm waiting for Wanda, and I'm not going until she gets here. It's time to tell her, Steven."

He had to do something fast. Steven's hands were balled into fists. "You fool, get out of here," he insisted nervously, and pointed to the door.

Wanda had fallen asleep and awakened with a start. Squinting, the sun was in her eyes as she opened them slowly. She looked at her watch. An hour had passed. It seems as though she couldn't stay awake lately. She closed her eyes again, but the sun was getting too warm. Maybe if she went back inside, she would fall back to sleep.

The patio door was cracked open and Wanda heard voices. Recognizing her husband's voice, she rushed inside.

They were in the dining room, yelling when Wanda stepped inside. She looked from Steven and back at Marie. "What is going on in here? I sat by the pool for an hour and here my husband and best friend are yelling at each other."

"Where's your car?" Steven asked. It wasn't in the garage.

"Repairs. I heard a noise when I was driving from the doctor's office. Now, what's going on here?" Wanda took a seat at the table. Steven and Marie were standing as though they were about to go into battle.

"Steven and I have something to tell you, Wanda."

Wanda motioned for them to speak. "Well, I'm listening."

"Marie is drunk. She was just leaving, baby." He walked over to Marie, but she moved aside and surprised them.

Wanda was so confused by their behavior, and what she didn't expect was for Marie to pull out a gun from her purse and point it at her.

"Now, we're all going to sit down and have a nice little chat. Just the three of us. And you know what, Wanda, you should have died when you had the chance to. That way you wouldn't have to experience death twice in one lifetime."

They walked into the living room and Wanda sat down slowly on the sofa.

"Look, Marie," Steven said. "What are you trying to prove?"

"Sit, Steven, or Wanda will get it right now," she said bitterly, her face twisted with an ugly frown.

"Marie, where did you get a gun from?" Wanda asked.

"It was meant for safety. My cousin gave it to me because I'm a single woman living alone. The smartest thing he ever did, the son-of-a-bitch. Now, where do we start?"

"I need to know what is going on here? We've been like sisters, what is this? Do you know, Steven?" Wanda fretted. "Please tell me what have I done?" She looked at Steven who was obviously as surprised as she was.

"Maybe Steven can tell you, Wanda."

Steven looked as though he was in shock. His month was open; he stared straight at Marie. If only he could place his hands around her neck, he thought.

Marie raised her hand and pointed the gun at Wanda again.

Wanda's stomach must have turned a flip; she grabbed the arm of the sofa for support.

"Start talking, Steven," Marie snapped.

"Okay! Okay! But lower that thing. If you want to point it at someone, point it at me." He looked at Wanda as if he wanted to cry. He never meant for it to happen this way.

"Wanda, this is all my fault. Marie and I were having an affair a year before the plane crash."

"You what? Tell me you're lying, Steven. Please tell me it's not true. Marie was my best friend. My very best friend," she repeated. She shook her head in disbelief. Was this a nightmare? Was she still asleep? What else could happen to her today?

"I'm so sorry, Wanda, but it's true. I need to explain."

"Okay, explain, Steven, tell her the rest." Marie pointed the gun nervously and clumsily as though it was too heavy.

"Will you sit down with that damn thing?" he yelled at her.

"Steven, please, don't piss her off any more than she already is," Wanda cried out.

Marie sat back easily in the chair. "Tell her, Steven."

"After the plane crash, I broke it off with Marie, but I was so despondent, and I had gotten into another relationship that didn't work out. I just couldn't stand being alone, Wanda. You know how I am. I can't stand living alone. Please understand," he said, touching her hand. "You know I can't be alone."

Wanda pushed him away. "You miserable, dirty, two-timing screwed up jerk. Don't you touch me. Don't you dare touch me. I'm about to lose my life over your pathetic shit. You're never going to touch me again. And with my best friend? How could you, Steven? Why couldn't you be with someone I didn't know?"

He held his head down feeling sick, but he had to continue. He had to make Wanda understand. "I went back to Marie and asked her to marry me," he said, not able to look at Wanda's face. And for the first time, he did feel dirty and ashamed. If only he could get Wanda out of this mess, alive.

"So you see, Wanda. You did it again. You came between Steven and me."

"What do you mean 'again'?"

"Remember the first time we met Steven? He walked to our table, I wanted him, but he chose you."

Wanda frowned and closed her eyes. She remembered that night so clearly. "Why do you blame me for that? I didn't force him to come to me. If you would have told me that night, you could have had him. That's how much I cared for you, Marie. I would not have let any man come between our friendship," she said, and held her hands to her face as though she was crying. "I was your friend remember, Marie? Do you remember?"

"That was a long time ago, honey," Marie said with a lazy look. "Things changed."

Wanda knew she had been drinking, but how much? She was beginning to look tired, sleepy. If only she could keep her talking a little longer. Then maybe she could grab the gun from her hand.

"Do you remember the times when it was only the two of us? Remember your last divorce? I was there for you, Marie. He took your car, and I gave you money for a down payment on a new one. Don't you remember?" She kept her own tone carefully neutral. She didn't want to appear angry or frightened with her. But her stomach clenched with apprehension and dread. *What would Marie do next?*

"Sorry, Wanda. But, it's too late now. You took away the one thing I really wanted, your husband." As she talked, her expression remained impassive. She was so tired, so very tired and needed to get it over and done with so she could sleep. Marie had stayed awake all night planning for this moment. She intended to end all their lives because she couldn't live without Steven, and she wasn't going to let Wanda take him away.

"Look, you stupid . . ."

She sat up straight, her eyes wide open with rage. She was hurt. He had hurt her repeatedly, even now, he still insisted on insulting her.

"You call me stupid and I have the gun? Your life is in my hands, Stupid. For the first time in our relationship, I'm in control here, not you."

"Please, Steven," Wanda said. "You've done enough already," she shouted at him, livid with rage.

Now, close the blinds, Steven." Marie said, pointing at the large window.

"Why? What are you going to do?" he asked. "We can talk this over, Marie. I'll do whatever you want. Trust me, baby. I'm here for you, just let Wanda go, please."

"It's too late, you hear me? It's too late. She'll go to the police and have me arrested."

"No I won't, Marie. But I want all of us to get out of this alive," Wanda explained.

"I said close the damn blinds. Now, Steven." She began waving the gun in Wanda's direction.

Steven stood up and went to the window. He tried to see if there was anyone outside, but there wasn't.

"Hurry it up," she yelled.

With shocking clarity, Wanda thought of her baby, she thought of Ahmed. She had to live for her child, and for the first time today, she wanted the baby more than anything she ever wanted before.

She looked at Marie again, trying to think of a way to convince her to stop this madness. Would Marie shoot her if she screamed so her neighbors could hear her, should she just run for the door? So many thoughts were going through her mind. Her eyes flickered with indecision, how could she handle this? God, what could she do?

Steven closed the blinds and took his seat next to Wanda. "Marie, tell me what you want me to do? Do you want me to go with you now? Just tell me what to do?" he pleaded.

"It's too late, Steven. You treated me like dirt. It's too late for all of us." Then she murmured something to herself.

Steven couldn't understand what she was saying. The alcohol was affecting her thinking. But she held on to the gun, pointing it from Steven to Wanda.

Wanda was frantic. God, don't let me lose my baby. It's all I have left, she prayed. But the sitting and waiting was too much, and the anxiety was making Wanda sick. She was unable to control the shivering, feeling a deep tremor course through her. She had to do something, quick.

Abruptly, Wanda got up, but Steven grabbed her arm. At that moment, Marie pointed the gun and aimed at Wanda, but Steven jumped in front of her. The gun went off. Wanda heard a loud scream. She was sure that she was hit. Everything moved as though they were floating.

Steven held Wanda, his weight dragging her down to the floor with him. He heard Marie screaming, yelling his name.

Wanda was blinded by fear. Was she going to die, was she shot? Blood had covered the front of her white blouse, warm, sticking to her skin. She fell as Steven pulled her down with him.

"Wanda," he whispered. His eyes closed, his hands released her arm, he fell limply to the floor.

Wanda realized that Steven had been shot, not her. He had crumpled to the floor and she was by his side.

Marie screamed, raised her hand and pointed the gun at Wanda. For a few seconds, which seem like hours, the two women's eyes were locked on each other. Wanda froze in her tracks and Marie opened her mouth to speak, but said nothing, instead, she ran out the door.

Wanda ran to the phone and called the police. But as she was talking, she heard Steven groan. Luckily, he was only shot in his shoulder and not his chest.

Wanda was sick as the paramedics took Steven's body away. The police officers finished taking the report. Once they left, Wanda left to be with Steven at the hospital.

Later, one of the officers called her at the hospital to inform her that Marie was in custody. She had waited in her apartment until they came. The officer said the gun was on the table in front of her. She was prepared to be arrested. "Now, it's over, Mrs. Gray."

The next morning, Wanda asked Steven why he cheated on her. Had he stopped loving her, was she not enough? She sat in the chair next to his bed. His shoulder was bandaged all the way down his arm.

"I tried to do everything to please you, Steven. I just want to know why, and why my best friend?"

He could barely move his body, but he owed her an explanation. "It was never you, Wanda. And for what it's worth, I've always loved you. I never stopped. It's just that Marie was always there. Most of the times that we were together, it was she who called me. Not that I'm making any excuses. I know that I did wrong and you didn't deserve it. You were always too good for me. But I swore, if you give me one more chance, I promise, baby, I will be the kind of husband you deserve." He frowned as he moved his arm.

"That can never happen, Steven. I'll be filing for a divorce today. In the meantime, I'm packing your clothes. I'll put them in your car and drive the car to

Chuck's house. I don't want you coming around for anything. Do you hear me?"

He nodded. "I'm so sorry, Wanda."

"So am I. Well, since you're going to live, I guess this is good-bye. There's no more to say," she said, almost feeling relieved.

The next stop Wanda made was to the police station to see if they would let her see Marie. But they said it was too soon. The second stop was to see a lawyer that a friend of hers had gone to for her divorce. Wanda started her divorce procedures and then drove home.

Standing in the spot where Steven was shot, she got a bucket of water, soap, and a brush and scrubbed the blood off the floor. After she finished, she threw a rug on top of the wet spot so she wouldn't see it as she walked through the house.

Wanda went to the kitchen and cleaned off the table. She emptied the Chinese food down the garbage disposal and threw the empty cartons in the trash. When she looked at the clock, it was almost noon. She sighed, went to the bathroom and washed her face and brushed her teeth. She came back downstairs and made a cup of tea, two slices of toast and scrambled eggs and bacon. She ate and placed one hand on her stomach. Although she wasn't hungry, she had to eat something for her baby's sake.

That night, Wanda realized that she had no husband, no one but her baby. Ahmed had a right to know he was going to be a father. If he didn't talk to her, she would move to Chicago and raise her baby herself. She could always go back to her old job and stay with her mother until she got a place of her own.

After holding the phone in her hand for thirty minutes, she dialed his number, but as soon as she heard his voice, she cried, and cried, and could hardly speak. She tried to, but the only sound that emerged was another eruption of tears.

"Orchid! Is it you? Listen to me, Orchid. Talk to me," he kept saying. He wanted to talk to her. She couldn't believe that he actually wanted to talk to her. "Ahmed, Ahmed, my husband was shot, but he's not dead." Wanda heard Ahmed gasp on the other end of the line.

"Orchid, did you shoot your husband? Did he hurt you, my love?" He was talking so fast and sounded so worried about her.

"No, it wasn't me. Someone else, but he will be all right. I filed for a divorce today and he won't be back ever again. I'm alone. My baby and I are all alone. Your baby, Ahmed, the baby belongs to you. I thought you should know that I'm pregnant with your child . . ." She began sobbing, unable to continue talking.

"You what? Oh Orchid, we're going to have a baby? A baby, it's mine?"

"Yes. I found out today. And I'm happy about it. I want your baby, Ahmed." She sniffed and blew her nose.

"I should have never let you go alone, Orchid. I was so angry and so hurt, but I should have never let you go alone. I'm coming out there to bring you back home where you belong. We'll be married. I love you, Orchid. I love you so much."

She sat on the sofa. Hearing his voice was music to her ears. "Oh God, Ahmed. I love you so much. I've been so miserable without you. When are you coming?"

"I'm getting the next flight out." He hung up. And she cried.

She was so tired, drained and so happy. Wanda went upstairs and changed into a gown and crawled in bed. She was falling asleep when she remembered. Damn, she hadn't returned the call at the repair shop for her car.

Chapter 29

September 1, 2001

Wanda ran around the apartment, getting everything ready for Ahmed's arrival. In the guest bedroom,
she changed the sheets on the bed, dusted the furniture and placed fresh towels in all three bedrooms. She
stood in front of the mirror, and had changed clothes
three times. When she looked in the closet to get a pair
of shoes, it looked as though Steven had never lived
there. Everything that belonged to him was at Chuck's
house in his car. And to think he had nerve enough to
ask her to take him back. The man had balls, she
thought.

Two days, and Ahmed would be arriving. She
wanted everything to be perfect. She even placed two
champagne glasses on the table so they could drink
to their new life and new baby, but since she was
pregnant, she would have 7-UP.

As she stood in the bathroom combing her hair,
she tried to remember if she had forgotten anything.
Wanda grabbed her purse, and when she got to the

door, she looked around once more and walked out. *She was going to get Ahmed.*

It was a warm day in September. Wanda got out of her car in the parking lot of British Airways at LAX and dashed across the streets along with the crowd.

She waited at the gate for Ahmed to come out. Finally, she saw him, tall and good-looking. He walked with such authority, one would think he owned the world. And seeing him was all she had dreamed of. Finally, she felt safe again.

She ran into his arms, and he picked her up as she circled her legs around his waist, and her arms around his neck.

He kissed her over and over again. "I've been so unhappy without you, Orchid. I hope we have twins," he whispered in her ear.

A middle-aged couple walked by and smiled as they saw the couple kissing and holding hands.

They walked hand in hand. She was so happy that she could burst, and when he looked at her full soft mouth, he stopped and kissed her again.

"How is Coffie and Miss Busara?"

"Good. They are happy that you are coming back. Busara said she always knew you would be back. That woman, she knows everything."

"And Dume?" she asked.

"He's better. He's leaving tomorrow to go and see Chiku and the children. And Chiku likes her new home and gets along well with her aunt."

"I think of her all the time. Luggage pick-up is over here. I want to hurry and get you home," she said with a wicked smile. My mother and sister will be here next week to lease the townhouse, but we will be gone before they get here."

"Are they coming to Africa for our wedding?" he asked.

"Yes, of course. My mom will love it there."

They picked up the luggage and headed for the car. Ahmed looked around and grabbed her hand as she led him across the street to the garage.

"Will you ever call me Wanda?" she asked looking up at him.

"No. You are my Orchid, sweet as a flower. Orchid will always be your name to my family."

Wanda's voice took on a pensive tone, as she looked him directly in the eye. "Africans have names with meanings. You've never told me yours."

"Ahmed means, 'one who is praiseworthy.' Do you like that?"

"Yes. I like that very much," she said, and drove off.

In three days she would be returning home to Africa, go to Busara's flower garden, which was Orchid's favorite place. She would smell the honey-suckle, the fragrance of the African marigold plants, the deep purple violets, and Busara's beautiful or-chids, and live the rest of her life where the flowers bloom in Thika.